HOT TODDY

a novel

by

T.C. Collins

Prologue

Her name was Sidney, and she looked amazing in a fifty-thousand-dollar Fendi fur. As did I, I must admit. We were both booked on a modeling job at the Fendi store in South Coast Plaza, complemented by a diamond show, and getting paid eight hundred dollars to walk the runway cloaked in luxurious fur and Cartier's finest jewels. Not a bad way to spend a Thursday evening—plus, we got to drink all the Veuve Clicquot champagne we could handle.

I'd walked a few shows before, but I wouldn't necessarily consider myself a model. It was more of a fun way to pass the time and make some extra cash when I wasn't helping manage a clothing store, laying down the law for sales girls not much younger than me. It was easy to get bored sitting in the store all day long, mall music keeping shoppers artificially happy. Much more exciting to sip champagne and wear extremely expensive clothes, even if I had to give them back at the end of the night.

The girls I usually modeled with were beautiful and boring. They don't drink too much of anything but pressed green juice, and they flip their noses in the air when you speak to them. But meeting Sidney that night was like meeting the kindred spirit I'd been desperately seeking all my life. We hit it off instantly, between realizing we had so much in common, from the same model car to the shocking revelation that we both had brain tumors, removed, of course—not our brains, the tumors. What are the odds of that? After chatting and laughing hysterically, we took turns claiming the spotlight on the glittering runway in front of Orange County's elite. We were dripping with confidence, soaking in every drop of our audience's attention in the warm gold lighting.

A few glasses of champagne each and suddenly we were daring each other to walk down the runway buck naked under our full-length mink coats. Grinning, we stripped down with gusto and walked immediately, the fur lusciously soft as satin against our bare skin. We were instantly fearless together, and I knew that when we said good-bye at the end of that night, it wouldn't be the last time I'd see Sidney Steele.

CHAPTER ONE

It doesn't take long to drive home to Long Beach, the warm air whipping my hair across my face through the open window in my Jeep. As nice as it was to be in such a glamorous place, it's always a relief to come home to my real life. It's late by the time I pull onto Obispo Avenue and park in the tiny lot behind our two-bedroom apartment, my old Jeep turning off with a sigh. I know the right thing to do is to be as quiet as possible; Brody has to get up early in the morning to work at his buddy's car-detail shop, but part of me wants him awake right now. It's been such a long, fun night, and I'm excited to tell him all about it. I pull my shoes off and let them thump on the ground, and before I know it, he's up and shuffling through the living room on his way to the bathroom, almost hitting the wall with the entire right half of his body because he's so tired.

"Hey, babe," he mumbles. "Did you have fun?"

"Yeah, I had a great time! Sorry I woke you," I answer.

"It's okay, hon. Come to bed."

"I will, after—"

"After you wash your face, I know, I know," he says, finishing my sentence.

Brody and I have lived together almost four years now, and we're still as in love as the day we met, back when we were both only eighteen. In many ways, we grew up together, going to tons of concerts, and learning how to navigate early adulthood by leaning on each other for support. I know I wouldn't be half the person I am today without him. Sometimes I'm comforted by that fact. Sometimes it scares me that I feel I owe him so much for showing me the ropes of living on my own so far from home.

I crawl into bed, and he rolls over to spoon me, just the way he always has.

"Hey, stop that. I need to get some sleep. I have to be up early to open the store tomorrow," I say as he tries to maneuver an extralarge surprise between my legs. He holds my waist tighter, and I can't help but feel his perfectly hard surfer's body against my back. Who am I kidding? I flip over and have the ride of my life.

*

The alarm goes off at 6:30 a.m., and I'm jolted awake, grumpy already. The bed is empty and cold beside me; Brody is already at work by now, doing custom detail work on all the Porsches, Ferraris, and other elaborate and rare cars for the superwealthy residents of Belmont Shore and Naples Island. They all come in for a two- or three-hundred-dollar detail at least once a week. After all, they can't have crumbs on their mink floor mats, as Brody always says to me.

I'm up and in the shower, and before I know it, I'm driving down Pacific Coast Highway, taking the long way down to work so that I can watch the first rays of sun hit the ocean. The traffic may be terrible, but I've been doing this drive practically every day for a year now, and the view makes it all worth it.

I'm replaying last night's events in my head, remembering all the diamonds and fur, and the exhilaration of the powerful people who are there to look at *you*, when suddenly my phone rings, Sidney's name popping up on my screen.

"How funny, I was just thinking about last night too!" I answer.

She laughs a tinkling, musical laugh. It sounds like the way you imagine a fairy godmother might laugh before she makes all your wishes come true.

"Okay, well I just wanted to let you know about this amazing party tomorrow at this mansion in Malibu. You *have* to come with me," she says.

"Sounds great. Brody surfs on Saturdays, and maybe I could spend the night up there. I'm off Sunday too. If that's okay with you, I mean."

"Of course it is! I can't wait! We'll get into all sorts of trouble. You're never going to want to go home to that cute little surfer boy of yours!"

Now it's my turn to laugh. "Okay, okay, Sid. Very funny. I'll give you a call when I'm heading up to you tomorrow."

"Great! Ciao, baby!" she trills and then hangs up. Cool, plans for Saturday. That would certainly make this boring day go by faster.

Finally, I'm on the outdoor escalator that carries me to my job comanaging the Forever 21 store. It's weird that they'd hire a twenty-one-year-old to manage a whole store, but I guess they had no other choice since my boss ran off with her Camaro-driving hillbilly boyfriend from Bakersfield a month ago. I think they went to Las Vegas to make their fortune or something, so Chloe and I got promoted from sales girls to comanagers. I guess we were the oldest ones, and the only ones dumb enough to take such a crappy job managing teenagers.

"Morning, Chloe!" I yell to the back as I walk in. She's always here first. Really, I should be here earlier too, but I can't stomach getting here any sooner than I have to. Two more girls straggle in behind me for the morning shift. They look like hell, like they've been drinking all night, and they glance at me sideways like they're scared I'm going to yell at them for being late. They hurry to sweep and straighten up the store so that I won't, and I can't help but laugh. Never in a million years would I think of myself as a boss, much less a boss who yells at teenage girls for staying out all night, partying like I do myself.

The day goes by without a hitch, except for one of the girls making an emergency trip to the bathroom in the middle of the afternoon rush to throw up. On the way out to my Jeep, I feel a wave of excitement about the Malibu party and my life in general. Now that I'm no longer working double shifts at the Yard House, waitressing and hostessing, and working my retail job too, I have so much more free time. The money was better then, but I never had any time for myself. Now, I have time for lunch with friends and superfun parties and concerts, even if it means Brody and I have to eat ramen noodles most nights. I don't mind so much. I never care what we're eating because we have so much fun together. Laughing with him doesn't leave me hungry for much else, and it's been that way since the moment we met.

I remember it was the perfect California sunset that evening: pinks and oranges and yellows splashing down into a sparkling ocean, matching the bonfire on the beach we gathered around. My college roommate, Kate, and I didn't know many people there, but when you're invited to a party in the backyard of a twelve-million-dollar beach house in Laguna Beach, you just don't say no. When we arrived, there were about fifty people there already, milling about on the beach, but I spotted Brody immediately through the flames of the bonfire. His white T-shirt was off and tucked into his army-green cargo shorts like a rag. He was talking animatedly to a friend, his sparkling smile so happy and sexy that you knew it had to be real. Just after I finished undressing him with my eyes, he looked over and caught me staring, his blondish-brown dreadlocks sweeping over his shoulders as he met my gaze with his piercing blue eyes.

I blushed and tried to look away, but he held my stare for a second too long and then smiled and pointed to his beer as if to ask if I wanted one. I smiled and nodded slowly. He disappeared through the crowd, and Kate slapped my arm and asked me why I was drooling. Before I could gather myself enough to tell her, he'd already returned with my beer, and I just knew that I was a goner. We sat on the cool sand and talked all night, his friend Lew playing guitar in the background. At three in the morning, we looked around and realized that everyone had already gone home, except for Kate and a few guys left inside.

We moved up to the deck and cuddled on the sofa, and when he asked if he could kiss me, I couldn't say "yes" fast enough. He was electric, and nothing could stop us as we made out on the couch with the waves crashing below us, not even our friends, who shouted out the window to taunt us every now and then. When Lew walked up and asked Brody what the deal was, Brody simply replied, "This is my new girlfriend, bro. LJ." And we'd been together ever since.

*

At home, I make a pack of noodles and then wander over to the closet to attempt to do my laundry. Brody isn't coming home until later; he's out surfing with the boys, so I might as well be productive. The laundry pile is a bit scary, so I light up a pinner joint I find in a smooshed-up Camel pack on the couch and then put a load in. I settle in to watch *Amy*, the Amy

Winehouse documentary, for the second time, and before she can flash her authentically brilliant smile once more, Brody and his buddies come through the door with their surfboards, smelling like the ocean. Their boards are always getting thrown all over the house, leaving the Sex Wax they use on them ground into the carpet along with tons of sand. The boys plop down all around me in the living room, Lew asking if Brody will break out a fatty, and Brody replying he will only if Lew plays guitar for us. Lew has come a long way since our college days at Cal State, Long Beach; his voice is so amazing and clear now that you would think you had the radio on. I get up to finish the laundry and relinquish the remote to the boys; now that they're home, I no longer have living room control.

As I squeeze past the boys on the couch, I playfully bop Brody's little brother on the head. Brooklyn is young, but at six foot three, he's the hottest kid you've ever seen. I'm always trying to take him to open calls for modeling, but he always protests, saying, "I just want to surf, dude." He's crazy not to go. He'd make millions.

Brody's older brother, Braden, sits on the other end of the couch, and I give him a smile as I walk into the next room. He's a big teddy bear of a guy; I can totally see him as a kid, steering his two younger brothers away from harm. Trying to at least. Long Beach has always been their stomping ground. They know everyone. And Brody's good friend, Brad, playing sublime acoustic guitar and singing with his band at huge, wild backyard garage keggers was always an awesome highlight to our endless summers. Especially when no one got into fistfights or got arrested.

We kick everyone out at midnight, and I head down to the bathroom for a late-night shower. It's been a long day, and I'm eager to let the hot water wash it all away. I've just tipped my head back into the shower stream when Brody comes banging at the door.

"Hurry up! I have to drop the kids off at the pool!" he says, laughing hysterically.

I cringe and try to ignore him.

"C'mon!" he insists. "My shit's been doing push-ups on my *cojones* for twenty minutes...I'm coming in!"

"Oh my god, gross. No! Give me one minute!" I turn off the shower and open the door. "It's all yours, my darling," I say with a sarcastic smile and a dripping towel. He gives me a big, stupid grin and a hard kiss on the cheek.

"Thank you, babe!" he calls out, slamming the door behind him.

The next morning, before he leaves for work, he pops back in the bedroom to kiss me. He never leaves without kissing me good-bye. I sleep for another few hours before I'm in the kitchen, looking for Earl Grey tea to start the day. I can't find the honey though; things always seem to be disappearing from the house since we always have so many people over. It's great having a full house, like a giant family, but with so many guys over all the time, it's like I have to play mom. The honey will disappear, or the ranch dressing. Who steals ranch dressing? And then it's up to me to replace it, or no one else will. It's okay though. I wouldn't trade my life for anything.

Okay, now what am I going to wear? Tonight's the big night. The party starts around sunset, so I need to boogie if I'm going to make it to Sidney's soon. I'm used to having to leave early to make it to places on time; between LA traffic and living near the beach, it's a wonder I get anywhere at all. I decide on a drop-waist sleeveless short black dress with pleats at the bottom and the black heels with the thin strap around the ankle that I always wear. At some point, I'll need to update my wardrobe if fancy parties are going to become a regular thing.

I shower, straighten my hair, throw my clothes and makeup into a bag, and am on my way to Sidney's by four. It'll be interesting to see her house. I know she lives with four guys, which has got to be gross, but at least it's nothing like the drama of living with girls!

I ring the doorbell, and the door bursts open in a puff of smoke.

"Get in here, bitch!" she squeals. I follow her up the stairs to her room where all her roommates are sprawled out on her futon and on her bed, sharing a spliff.

"Guys, this is my new best friend, LJ. Be nice to her. She's sweet," she tells the guys, and they nod in my direction. She turns to me. "What did you bring to wear tonight?"

"Just a black dress," I say, watching her sort through her closet. She has incredible clothes, the kind of designer clothes I could only imagine owning. Leather skirts and ornate lace dresses float down around her feet, and she kicks them aside to make room for even more to try on. "I'll wear a black dress too; that way we can show off our rims and wheels together, hashtag slay," she says with a wink. One of the guys hands me the spliff, and I melt into the futon with them. Thudding comes from around the corner, and a giant black dog enters the smoky room, the randomness of which makes me start giggling uncontrollably. He bounds up to me and starts licking my face; he's so enormous that he doesn't even have to stand on his hind legs to reach me. One of the guys reaches forward to pet him and introduces him as Smalls.

"Smalls?!" I gasp. "Why isn't he named Biggie? He's huge!"

"It is! It's Biggie Smalls," one of the guys, whose name I learn is Jona, says to me.

"Ha! Cool. Love it," I add.

The guys start to filter out of the room as soon as Sidney starts spraying her perfume. Clearly it's girl time, and they don't want to be anywhere near the line of fire. We put on some Bob Marley, and Sidney starts changing and dancing around the room naked. She clearly has no problem being naked in front of people; I admire that boldness in her. I can feel my high kicking in, a sort of hold-on-for-the-ride paranoid moment that I try not to acknowledge in front of Sidney.

"How does this look?" She stands in the doorway to her bathroom, one hip jutted out to throw the already-tight black dress even higher, her blond hair falling comically over one eye. She looks incredible, and I tell her so.

"We're going to get in so much trouble together," she says, rushing over to hug me. "C'mon, let's do some makeup and get you changed. There's a beautiful sunset on the drive up the coast. I don't want to miss it!"

By the second joint, I'm feeling very comfortable. We're both half naked in the bathroom, doing makeup so that it doesn't get on our dresses, and I'm feeling bolder by the minute. After two hours, we certainly deserve to be bold; she looks like a sleek blond bombshell, and I look pretty good too. Actually, I'm shocked by my reflection—Sidney did my eyes, and they look feline and mysterious, like I hold all the secrets in the world and I'd have to kill you if I told you any. She throws her arm around me and laughs when she sees me staring at myself. "I'd do you!" she says. "All right, babe, let's rock this town."

*

I can see the stars reflected in the pool below from my vantage point on the second-floor balcony. The white cabanas surrounding the pool are filled with guests, some of the drapes discreetly closed against the extravagant party. Sidney's been gone for some time; she left me here at the bar to get another drink, but that must've been an hour ago. I don't mind much. Just being here is enough. Besides, it's nice to be on my own for a moment, occasionally chatting with guests and enjoying the amazing scenery.

I drift along the balcony, which extends around the length of the house, peeking in on each of the rooms that open up to the night. When I see inside the last room, I suddenly try to stumble back out, but it's too late.

"Bump for the road, cutie?"

A group of people surrounds a glass coffee table with the largest mountain of blow I've ever seen. I look around at the group; I don't know any of these people from the few I've met, but they seem kind enough. A man in the center of the group, with a girl on his lap, smiles at me. He must be the one who invited me in. He probably doesn't know that he's got white powder all over his nose.

"Um, sure…" I say, stepping gingerly into the room. I've only ever done cocaine with people I know, usually with girlfriends on our way to the club. Even then, it's only been a handful of times. I tug my short dress down a bit and kneel next to the coffee table, and someone hands me a hundred-dollar bill. When in Rome, right? Bending over, I snort the biggest line of blow I've ever done.

Holy shit. I feel like my heart's going to beat out of my chest. I try to act normal but struggle to focus and stand back up.

"Good, eh?"

"Ah, yeah. That's real good," I reply. I've got to get out of this room. I need to get outside. I need air.

"Thanks, guys. I'll see you downstairs," I say to the group. When I turn around, the guy reaches forward and pats my ass good-bye.

I smile and keep moving outside and then through another empty room to the big glass staircase. I need Sidney. Where is she? There are people everywhere, crowding the top of the staircase. I almost call out for her, but I don't want to make a scene. I shuffle through the crowd to get to the stairs, but once I start descending, things start changing. With each step, everything gets clearer and vibrant. I pause. The stairs are sparkling; the people are smiling brightly; everything is beautiful. There's something empowering about watching the party from here, separate from the madness and the crush of people high atop a sparkling glass staircase. I can't stop smiling, and after a few minutes, it all becomes too much; I have to join them on the dance floor. I rush down the stairs and thrust myself in the middle of the crowd, immediately swaying with them, hands in the air and hips swishing from side to side to the thumping badass beats from the DJ. A pair of hands appears on my hips from behind, and they feel warm and safe, guiding my movements and feeling my curves. When they slip under my dress, I don't object, releasing my basic instinct of morality, and provocatively leaning back into some soft blond hair falling over my face. I've never felt more happy, or more alive, than right now, fading into this moment with her.

CHAPTER TWO

The next morning, it's a beautiful day in LA, sunlight filtering through the trees that attempt to shield diners from the paparazzi camped across the street. A burst of clicking and yelling, and I see Kim K. leave the restaurant. Honestly, I couldn't imagine being hunted like that. I'd hate it. I need my anonymity so I can be hungover in peace.

My spinach salad with egg whites and lemon dressing arrives, and I instantly regret not getting something greasy to soak up all of this alcohol. I'm dying for one of the loaded bacon, egg, and gooey cheese croissant things from the café around the corner from my house, but this will have to do. I can't very well be at Fred Segal eating something so bad for me, surrounded by some of the most gorgeous people in the world.

Sidney sits across from me, checking her Instagram and picking at her salad from behind blue reflective aviator sunglasses. The effect is disconcerting. I can't see her eyes. I can only see my own reflection. And I look like shit. I don't know how she does it; she's positively glowing, and I know she partied harder than I did. She looks like she just had a full eight hours of sleep and then went to the spa before brunch. Her tan is set off by a crisp tight white tank top and tiny white shorts and a black skinny belt with a gold buckle. When she brings her fork to her mouth, a shining gold charm love bracelet slides up her slender forearm.

"Okay, so I'm thinking after this let's go to my friend Stephanie's house. I need to stop by to talk to her, and she'll positively *love, love, love* you!"

"Sure, that's fine," I say. I don't need to be back in Long Beach until the evening anyway.

"Okay, great!" she says, white teeth gleaming in the sunlight. "She's got this crazy condo; you're going to just love it. She lived in the Playboy Mansion for a while. She was Hef's number-one girl. Back in the day. But now she lives on her own with her pet monkey. She's in this round glass building overlooking Hollywood. It's totally old school glamorous. You'll love it! Are you finished, LJ? Let's go!"

*

"Hey, bitches, over here!"

A woman with the most platinum blond hair I've ever seen in my life poses at the end of her outdoor hallway, wearing a hot pink velour jumpsuit and positively busting out of it. A monkey jumps from one shoulder to the other.

"Stephanie, oh my god! You look absolutely fabulous!" Sidney exclaims, walking up to her and kissing her cheeks. "Sweetheart, I want you to meet my best friend."

I step forward, unsure if I can shake her hand without the monkey jumping on me. "Hi, Stephanie, thanks for having me. I'm LJ," I say.

"Yeah, this is my bestie, LJ. She's amazing, and so are you, and I just know you two are going to love each other!" Sidney links her arm through Stephanie's, and they walk into the condo together. I follow behind.

Sidney wasn't lying when she said that this place was spectacular. The view of Hollywood over Sunset Boulevard fills the floor-to-ceiling windows like artwork, permeating the condo with sunlight. It's breathtaking. Her place has such an old-Hollywood vibe. I can almost see the one-and-only Marilyn Monroe floating through the living room, magically captivating whoever was there.

"LJ, sweetie, come over, and have some vino," Sidney says, perched on the couch with Stephanie. She offers me a glass of chilled white wine, the monkey watching with wide-eyed interest.

"Your monkey is so cute; how old is she?" I ask Stephanie.

"Is that what you're supposed to ask someone with a lady monkey? Don't you know not to ask a woman's age?" This is definitely a first for me.

Stephanie gives me a withering look as she scratches the monkey between the ears. "*She's* just a little monkey. I've had her for a year." She starts cooing and kissing the monkey. "Yes, you are, aren't you, Chanel? You're *my* wittle baby mookie monkey! My wittle baby monkey forever and ever and ever, my wittle sweetheart baby monkey pie pants! Yes, you are."

I clear my throat. I'm all for loving your pet, but this girl is taking it to another level. And with a monkey. It's sort of strange, I think.

Sidney, on the other hand, is completely oblivious to Stephanie's absurdity. She sips her wine and laughs her sparkling laugh, Cartier bracelet shining in the sunlight.

"So anyway, well, I'm making fifteen hundred to three thousand dollars an hour; it's simply fabulous!" Stephanie says, grinning madly.

I nearly spit out my wine. Excuse me, *how* much is this monkey lady making an hour?

Sidney turns to me with a look and then quickly replaces it with a smile.

"Stephanie is with the La Belle Fleur agency in New York," she says to me and then turns back to Stephanie.

"Oh, French? Is it associated with Elite Model Management? They're our rivals," I say. I've been with LA Models for a year now.

"Umm, no, honey," Stephanie says rolling her eyes. "It's an elite escort agency."

"Oh," I say. I take a big gulp of wine in an attempt to act casual. Okay, so this girl is a prostitute? I guess that's how she can afford this place.

At this point, Chanel, the monkey, takes off running into the next room, and Stephanie goes chasing after her. I quickly turn to Sidney.

"Sid, what's going on here? Why are we even talking about this?"

"Because I can barely pay my bills with just modeling, that's why," Sidney snaps. "Ugh. I knew you'd have a problem with this!"

"A problem with what?" Stephanie says, walking back in with the monkey cradled in her arms. I can see a small red bite mark on her hand that she tries to hide.

Sidney throws a smile back on her face. "Oh, nothing. LJ's just not quite ready to work for them. So what do I need to do to get started?"

"Well, you've got to go there, so Alexandra can meet you in person. She's in NYC, and then you can work in New York City, or here in LA, or anywhere in the world you want to go. I can call her and send her your picture and see if she's interested, if you want."

"That would be great. Thank you so much, girl! I'll give you a modeling pic from my book."

"Great! Hey, LJ, what about you? It's really great money and a ton of fun!" Stephanie glances at me.

"Ah...I have a boyfriend."

"What does that even mean?" Stephanie snipes and rolls her eyes again.

Sidney leans forward and smiles. "Like I said, she's not ready."

"Okay. Well I have things to do," Stephanie says, standing up.

"Sure, we can talk later. Let's do drinks soon!" Sidney says, kissing Stephanie's cheeks. I merely nod at her and thank her for the wine and then follow Sidney out the door.

We aren't more than five steps out of the condo when Sidney turns on me.

"LJ, what in the actual fuck? Are you trying to ruin this for me? Or just trying to make me look stupid?"

"Dude, what are you talking about? I had no idea what we were walking into there; you didn't tell me that she was a prostitute!"

"She's not a prostitute; she's a high-end escort! There's a huge difference, and it's not my fault if you can't see that. I swear to god, if you ruin this for me...I can't even—"

"Chill out. It's all you, sister. Really. You can do whatever you want!"

She walks away from me, little white shorts sashaying toward the elevators, and angrily punches the elevator button. When the elevator arrives, she walks inside and then turns back toward me.

"Well? Are you coming?"

I stand for a moment longer and then follow her into the elevator just before the doors can close on me.

"Hey, I'm sorry, okay?" Sid looks suddenly contrite. "I was just *thinking* about it. I mean, bills are really hard."

I know the feeling. Suddenly, I can't be mad at her.

"Hey, I don't mean to be judgey, okay? I'm just worried about you. You don't have to be like Stephanie to pay your bills you know."

"I know. But, I do. I know you're looking out for me. That's why I love you, doll. I won't do this right now, okay? I don't have to do it now."

The mood lightens suddenly.

"And what the hell is up with that monkey?" I ask her, and she bursts out laughing, all tension gone.

*

Monday morning and it's back to Fashion Island, but the day is anything but normal. As soon as I walk in, I can see that Chloe is already there, and she's in tears.

"LJ!" she wails the second I walk in. "LJ, my boyfriend dumped me. I don't know what to do."

"Wait, slow down. What happened?" I ask.

"He said he needs some 'space.' Seriously, LJ, I don't know what I'm going to do without him. It's been three years."

Just then, the younger girls walk in, and Chloe rushes to wipe her face.

"Hi, boss ladies!" one of the girls exclaims. She's practically glowing, and I already know what's coming next.

"I have big news, y'all!" she says, grinning her big Texas smile from ear to ear. "I'm pregnant! And Mike and I are getting married!"

Chloe and I glance at each other and summon happiness for this poor teenage girl. She and her boyfriend have only been together for six months. We've seen this enough times to know how it'll end.

Later in the back, Chloe takes her anger out on unpacked merchandise. "I hate this job. I hate my life," she says, ripping tape from a box of shirts. "I'm going to have to move out of the apartment, and I'm not going to be able to afford one on my own. I'm probably going to have to move in with my parents. God! I just wish I could make thousands of dollars doing nothing. Don't you, LJ?"

Honestly, I've been doing pretty well with my side modeling gigs, but the money is inconsistent and really just helps pay off some of my credit card debt. It doesn't even touch my student loans, which are growing each month because I can only afford the minimum payment.

"Yeah, I guess so, Chloe. But money never comes for free—you know that. Life is sometimes hard, and that's okay; it will be okay, Chlo. I promise it will be," I tell her.

"No, it's not!" she says. "I work my ass off, give myself fully to the guy I *think* is my soul mate, and then he dumps me! I can't make it on my own. I'm a Sunday school teacher, and all I can do is cut hair. Average at best! Coming to work here with you is the most fun I have, LJ. How am I going to make it out there without him?"

I don't know what to do other than give her a big hug and let her cry on my shoulder. She's kind of right; without a college education, she won't have many options besides the ones she's already taking. I don't know what I'd do if I were her. At least her parents live here. She can move in with them if money really becomes an issue. If I were in her situation, I'd have nowhere to go really either. I'd have to go to St. Louis to live with my dad or San Diego to live with my mom; I definitely couldn't afford an apartment out here without Brody. It's odd how stable your life seems until one piece of it drops out. It's only then that you realize how precarious it all is, how dependent we all are on each card staying in the right place. Without each card, my house would come crashing down too. Stability is a fallacy—the only way we can truly be stable is if there is no house of cards, if we only depend on ourselves. But, that's easier said than done.

I'm still ruminating on these thoughts when I sit down for lunch in the food court with my salad. Usually Chloe joins me, but today I'm on my own since she ended up leaving early to figure out her next move. I pull out my phone to check my Snapchat and Instagram, and I see that I've got a text from Sidney asking me to call her. I haven't heard from her since she dropped me off at my car yesterday. Things were tense after the weirdness at Stephanie's, but clearly she's moved past it. Her text is full of smiley-face emojis and exclamation points. With nothing better to do while I sit here, out of curiosity, I dial her number.

"LJ!" she exclaims the second she picks up. "Doll, do I have fantastic news for you. You better be sitting down. I'm about to change your life."

I laugh. She certainly has a way of putting the past behind her. "Okay, Sid, what's up?"

"Honey, I'm just totally running shit for you over here! I just so happened to give your picture and measurements to a casting director the other day, and he wants you to be a stand-in for Keira Knightley on her new movie! Cancel work tomorrow; the fitting is tomorrow morning."

"Whoa, are you serious? Sid, thank you so much!" I can't believe I was ever angry at her. She really is looking out for me. Working as a stand-in is guaranteed three months of solid work, after which I'll be able to get my third SAG-AFTRA voucher and finally be able to join the Screen Actors Guild. This would open a lot of doors for me in a very big way. This could very well change my life.

"I gave your number to casting, so someone over there should give you a call today to let you know when and where to report for work tomorrow," she says. "Now listen, I had to lie a little and say that you were five-ten like Keira, so you'll just have to stand tall, but you're just about that height, anyway, so it shouldn't be a problem. Now, baby, I've got to go, but you can thank me this weekend when we go out on Saturday. I'm going to want to hear all about it over tequila shots and guacamole—no excuses!" And with a loud kiss, she's off the line.

*

It's six in the morning, and Brody wakes me up with a naked kiss and a hot romp before he leaves for work. I spring out of bed, recharged and excited for the day ahead and very thankful that Chloe was able to cover for me at the store on such short notice. In a way, it feels like this is the first day of the rest of my life, as corny as that sounds. As I make my oatmeal with honey and a few blueberries, I glance at a poem by William Arthur Ward that some guy was handing out at Venice Beach one day. I've had it taped to the refrigerator for as long as I can remember. I call it my *risk paper*!

To laugh is to risk appearing a fool.
To weep is to risk appearing sentimental.
To reach out to another is to risk involvement.
To expose feelings is to risk exposing your true self.
To place your ideas and dreams before a crowd is to risk their loss.
To love is to risk not being loved in return.
To hope is to risk despair.
To try is to risk failure.
But risks must be taken because the greatest hazard in life is to risk nothing.
The person who risks nothing, does nothing, has nothing, is nothing.
He may avoid suffering and sorrow,
But he cannot learn, feel, change, grow, or live.

Chained by his servitude he is a slave who has fortified all freedom.
Only a person who risks is free.

I love that poem. It makes me smile, gives me spirit, and pushes me to test my limits. I'm happiest when I feel that I'm risking something, as I do now. I can't stand the idea that I'm wasting my life, that I'm not taking advantage of every possible moment and experiencing my life to the fullest. My worst fear is being trapped in an uninspired, stagnate routine, not experiencing new things or learning anything new. Life is just too short.

CHAPTER THREE

After breakfast and a cup of tea, I take an extralong hot shower to steam myself. Then it's powder, mascara, gloss, straightened hair, and dark skinny jeans with a white T-shirt. I leave at 10:30 a.m. to give myself plenty of time to get up the 405 freeway; I don't have to be there until noon, but this is a big deal—I can't be late.

When I pull into the main gate, it's hard not to be awestruck by the giant cream arches and intricate scrollwork. The road is lined with palm trees, and I feel like a movie star when I'm whisked through the gates and directed to the wardrobe department. I park and make my way to the green door and into an area crowded with large, full rolling racks of beautiful clothes. As I go through the racks, I can't help but touch a few of the fabrics, silk gowns slipping through my fingers. I start to think that I'd give anything to wear these dresses, and that's when I remember—that's exactly what I'm here to do. I almost start flipping through the racks to find my favorite outfits when a woman comes from around the corner and startles me. She's dressed in all black and has a short black bob to match, and she looks me up and down through red-rimmed glasses before consulting the clipboard in her hand.

"Lillian James Volpicelli, I presume?" she asks in a clipped voice.

I clear my throat. "Yes, that's me. I mean, everyone calls me LJ. But that's fine."

I stop rambling as she scoots me up onto the apple box and begins to measure me, making notations on her clipboard. Another woman walks in and introduces herself as Claire. She seems much nicer and smiles at me apologetically until the woman in black is done measuring me.

"She's not the exact height, but she'll do," the woman in black tells Claire before leaving the room.

Claire turns to me and sighs. "So that's Delilah, she's the head of costume design," she says. "She insists on measuring everyone herself. You'll learn how to work with her."

She pulls out a rack of dresses, pants, and shirts, all with note cards pinned to the hangers.

"Keira has forty-eight costume changes, so we're going to try everything on you first. Have you worked as a stand-in before?" she asks.

"Actually, I haven't," I admit.

"No worries!" Claire says. "It's really not hard. Basically, you're going to do the time-consuming stuff while Keira is off rehearsing, or relaxing, or in makeup. So you'll change into her clothes, go on set first so they can get the lighting right on you for her, and maybe even deliver a few of her lines and do some of her blocking if the director needs you to. Sound good?"

"Absolutely!" I answer. Actually, it all sounds incredible. I'm going to meet the director and loads of other important people, including Keira Knightley! This is huge.

By the end of the day, I'm exhausted, but I'm the happiest I've been in a long time. A day spent in haute couture isn't a bad day at all, and I even got my third voucher, so now I can join the union after I save up the three-thousand-dollar joining fee. With a full movie schedule ahead of me, I should have that money in no time at all.

I pull out of the studio at 5:30 p.m. with a call time to be back on Monday, and I already can't wait to be passing through the gates again. My joy is short lived though; I've been released right into traffic, and I'm at a standstill for so long that my Jeep starts to overheat. I end up needing to drive with the heat on full blast and the windows down the whole way home in eighty-five-degree heat. I won't let traffic and a bit of sweat get in the way of a great day though. Now that I've been picked up by the film, it's time to quit my job at the mall. I call Chloe from the car and let her know that I'll be quitting soon, and though I know she's disappointed to see me go, I know it's the right decision for me. I can't be working at Forever 21 forever. I never even intended to work there as long as I did. I feel like a giant weight is off my shoulders now that I'm almost out of retail, and I drive home with a giant dopey grin on my face the whole way.

As I park in front of the house, I see in my rearview mirror that Brody is pulling in too.

"Hi, babe," I say as he walks over to me for a hug and a kiss.

"How was it?" he asks. "Did you get the voucher so you get paid more?"

"I did!" I say. "When I make enough to join the union, then I'll finally be making decent money, and I can even get insurance! Can you believe it? Insurance!"

"I'm glad you're happy with this, hon. It sounds like it will be a great opportunity for you. Now what are we having for dinner?"

"I can make some angel-hair pasta nests, and we have leftover pesto chicken from last night…" I say, thinking aloud.

"Yum. I'm in, babe; whip it up," he says, squeezing my butt as we walk into the house.

*

After dinner, I make some green tea with honey and a dash of milk, and we break out the bong, a nice two-foot glass that we pack and smoke while watching *Straight Outta Compton* and the news. I'm so relaxed; if only every day could be as wonderful as today, I'd be a very happy girl. Now to make it through tomorrow and I'll be free too. I've got to call the corporate headquarters and give my official resignation, and with all of the recent turnover at the store, I know they're not going to be happy that I'm leaving too. But, I fall asleep with visions of glamorous movie sets and designer clothes in my head.

*

What becomes my last day at Forever 21 is fairly uneventful. After opening the store with Chloe, I call the corporate office and find out that my two weeks isn't needed; they can have someone from their sister company come down to take my place after today. I hang up, a little disturbed that I'm so easily replaced—I have to remind myself that I'm leaving for something better, and I shrug it off. This is what people do—they take jobs and then quit them for better ones. They move up and move on. I can't take it personally that a job I didn't even really like in the first place didn't really like me back.

At the end of the day, I give Chloe a big hug and promise to call her for lunch soon. I hope she likes my replacement. She needs someone good in her life. On the drive home up Pacific Coast Highway, I have to take a few deep breaths. Change is scary but necessary. I remind myself of my risk poem and turn up the radio to start a car dance, drowning out my thoughts. I start to smile—the sun is setting over the ocean, reflecting brilliant colors, and I focus in on the surfers in the water on Huntington Beach and notice two dolphins riding through the waves with them.

I feel like I'm driving toward my future. I know I made the right decision—I just know it. The only way to go from here is up.

*

The sun comes up at six thirty in the morning, and I wake up still being spooned.

"We slept so well," I say to Brody, reaching a hand behind the pillow to touch his head.

He squeezes my waist. "I know. What time is it?" he says. "Want to meet the guys down at Thousand Steps with me?"

"Hell, yeah!" I jump up and throw on a rainbow bikini and sweatpants, Reefs, and a Volcom hoodie. "Come on, babe!" I jump on him in bed to get his lazy bones moving.

Getting out on the beach early in the morning is one of my absolute favorite things. Driving down to Laguna Beach, I have my feet out of the window of Brody's gray VW bus, our boards and towels in the back of the van. There's something about the crisp air and the new sun that makes me feel so free, like I'm doing everything right and everything is in its right place, but at the same time, like I'm doing something that makes me feel so alive.

We pull up to the little shack that someone converted into a tiny restaurant off of Pacific Coast Highway on the Newport Coast. It only serves simple sandwiches with mayo and cheese, some small sides, sodas and shakes, and it all tastes just like Mom made your lunch. We get coffee and two tuna sandwiches and potato salad to go in brown paper bags, my favorite, and head down to park the bus at Seventh Street, so we can run across the PCH and make our way down the thousand steep concrete steps to the best hidden beach in Laguna. I descend slowly so I can take in the neon-pink Bougainvillea and the crisp-white patio furniture on the back porch of a nearby house overlooking the ocean. The water looks almost pink in the early morning light, and Brody, who is now only a speck below, is almost to the bottom of the steps, his wet suit half on.

Once I get down to the bottom, I kick off my Reefs and take a left down the beach to see my dream home high up on the cliff above me. This is my favorite beach in the world; all the homes overlooking the ocean have outdoor elevators down to the sand—it's fantastic. Just ahead is what I call my future home. I could stare at it all day—entirely white with balconies off of every room, tons of huge windows, a pool, and gardens, I think, from what I can see from the beach. The house looks pastel pink in the light from the rising sun. Nestled back on the cliff, it's definitely a naked house; my test for all houses is to see if you could walk around naked at any time during the day without peeping neighbors catching a glimpse. I actually only assume that there's a pool since I can't see it from the beach either, but honestly, who cares if there is one...

I turn around and take a deep breath, exhale, and sit on the sand to admire the ocean. Glassy and perfect. The guys are already cutting up the waves with skill and ease, and it's easy to see their passion for the sport from here. I'll go in for a dip later, but for now, I'm content with my coffee and gossip magazine, and the new book I'm reading, *The Notebooks of Leonardo da Vinci*. When I do go in, I'll swim out past the surfers and just float around today. The last time I was out there, the water was so clear that you could see the bottom even though it's fifty-feet deep. And then some dolphins swam by and scared the hell out of me.

I lie back in the sand and just breathe. It feels like the stars are aligned, and a whole new world is coming to light just for me. A rad start to a great beach day.

*

The next thing I know, my alarm is buzzing, and Brody is shaking me awake in our bed.

"Time to get up!" he tells me. "It's your new job today!"

I get ready quickly as my excitement starts to set in. We're still shooting at the sound stage for now, and next week, we'll be filming on campus at the University of Southern California.

I make it back up to the Melrose Studios, only spilling a little bit of hot tea on myself, which is quite an accomplishment. I'm still fifteen minutes early, and as soon as I'm there, they rush me out right under the lights. Working on set is more exhausting than I expected; everyone rushes around for twelve to fourteen hours each day, and everything's an emergency. Only three more months of this, I tell myself. I still feel grateful though. With my vouchers, all I have to do is save the three grand to join. Simple, right? Ugh.

The weeks pass, and it starts to turn into fall, or at least LA's version of fall. Filming on campus is absolutely gorgeous and reminds me of fall in St. Louis. I used to ride horses on my dad's farm nearly every day, the golds and reds of the trees whipping past me as I rode faster and faster. When it was warm enough, I'd ride my horse, Lightning, in a swimsuit so that I could jump right into the pool when I finished. My dad would always yell at me for doing that since the horsehair that would come off of me would clog the pool filter, but I'd still do it. I guess I've always been too much of a rebel to say no to fun.

Over the weeks, I finally saved enough to join the SAG-AFTRA, so now I'm making around three hundred dollars for eight hours of work. Then overtime after eight hours, then double overtime…it starts to become very lucrative to work twelve- to fourteen-hour days. I'm paying off my student loan debt too, and although it'll take a long time to completely pay it off, it feels incredible to start. Plus, I'm able to buy nicer clothes so that I fit in a little bit better with Sidney's crowd in Hollywood. I never thought that I'd be the kind of person to put much stock in good fabric and well-cut clothes, but hanging with LA's elite has made me conscious of this whole other world I've been missing.

Working so much has made it difficult to go out with Sidney; most nights I just hang out with Brody, either sprawled out in front of the TV or going to his boss's house in Belmont Shore and drinking beer all night. I've been smoking a lot of pot and surfing during the days I'm not on set, so by the time the weekend rolls around, I'm ready to get dressed up for a girls' night. Luckily, Sidney calls with an offer to do a fashion show, eight hundred dollars for the whole night and free drinks and clothes too. It's some guy she's dating's twenty-third birthday, and although it always seems like she is in love with one guy or another, I'd be happy to get in on this party. Wouldn't miss the fun.

It's Friday night, and Brody and I decide to stay in, which I'm perfectly happy with after my long week. Plus I expect Saturday with Sid to be a long, drunken night, so I'm content snuggling with Brody on the couch. We fit together like puzzle pieces and only unravel when our takeout arrives, eggplant parm and minestrone soup from the little Italian place down the street. It always hits the spot.

We sleep in until eleven thirty. When I try to get out of bed, Brody grabs me by the waist and throws me down, laughing. He starts kissing my belly and then starts to head down south, but I have to stop him.

"Babe, I have to go get in the shower," I tell him.

"Ugh." He flips over, shaking his head.

"I'm really sorry. I just have to get going. I have a fitting."

He sighs, sparking a joint. "Okay. Do what you need to do."

*

I speed up to Hollywood and pull up right in front of Jean Paul's, the designer for the show, apartment. His place is packed with naked model bodies and rolling racks, and when I try to apologize for being late to him because of traffic coming up from Long Beach, he purses his lips.

"When are you going to move up here, you skinny bitch? All that driving and you're rocking all of your bookings right now. What the fuck, girlfriend? Okay. Get over here. Let's look."

He snaps his fingers three times in front of my face, and I have to smile. He certainly is sassy, and I love him for it.

"Soon, I promise. I'll move up here soon," I tell him, even though I have no plans of moving anywhere. I like my beach life, flip-flops, and days on the sand with the guys and a fatty Humboldt joint. Perfection. But he's right about one thing—the daily commute to Hollywood absolutely sucks.

I see Sidney flipping through a rack of clothes in a corner, and the second she sees me, she pulls a tank top with cutouts all over it and black-velvet crisscross straps across the back out and holds it out to me.

"Hey, hot stuff! This one would look so insane on you."

It's good to see her; no matter that it's been a few weeks since we've hung out, it still feels like she's got my back, like she really cares about me and wants me to succeed. I trust her.

I try on the tank top, and she's absolutely right. It does looks good. I turn around to show her.

"Holy shit," she says, hand on her hip. "Okay, you're wearing that with these little black-lace shorts and fishnets and heels and these belts and bangles."

Jean Paul comes over and spins me around.

"Fucking fabulous. Okay, you're wearing that for sure, and this one too." He hands me a hot fuchsia cap sleeve minidress with a black zipper halfway down the front that makes it look like a wet suit. A little risqué for my taste but super fun at the same time.

"Same heels? Yes. Finished. Go!" With a slight push, Jean Paul turns to the crowd of models. "Okay, girls, listen up. Hair and makeup is backstage starting at seven thirty this evening, and if we haul ass, then we'll be ready to go on with the show at ten. Or ten thirty. Well, maybe eleven…with all of you bitches, I'm crossing my fucking fingers. All right, whoever's been okayed on their outfits for tonight, please get out of here so I can fucking breathe."

Sidney and I grab our bags and head out the door. I follow her to her house, zipping around the curves on Mulholland Drive. Some days you can see the ocean from up here, sometimes even the curves and coves of California along the coastline too. Not today though—the smog's extremely heavy. It's a gorgeous drive at night, when you can see all of the city lights. And I love the parts of the road where you can see both the valley lights out one side of the car and the lights of Los Angeles out the other. You really feel like you're on top of the world.

*

Back at Sidney's house, we spark a joint and make some green tea. We need rest before the fashion show, so we get comfy in bed and stream *Sex and the City* and then pass out for a light snooze before our long night. When I wake up, it's dark out, and I can hear the shower going. I need to pee, so I knock on the door, and Sidney tells me to come on in.

"Hey, Sid, sorry. I just need to pee."

"Okay, go ahead; just don't flush! I'll be right out."

Seconds later, she steps out of the shower, steaming and covered in water droplets. She twirls a towel around herself and spins past me on her way to the room. A few minutes later, she's dressed and ready to go.

"Wow, you're quick," I say, splashing cold water on my face.

"Yep, let's get you moving now. Come on, LJ, chop-chop!"

*

The club is empty of partiers but bustling with people setting up the runway and adjusting lights. Sidney and I make our way backstage to hair and makeup. The drink of choice is vodka, and although I'm a Jack girl, I make myself a vodka cranberry to get in the mood. The ladies sit me down quickly and start on my hair, which they tease at the crown, spray, slick back my bangs, and then bring to the top of my head in a high ponytail. Voilà, instant glamour. The makeup woman comes in and adds charcoal smoky eyes, false lashes, neon-pink matte lips, bronzer, and some crystal-chandelier earrings that graze my shoulders.

"Hey, Sid, are you finished?" I call through the hustle and bustle.

"Yeah, baby, in a minute," she calls back.

Just then, I glance over and see Justin Bieber talking with and smooching one of the models. Shoot, he may be getting older, but he's still totally hot. I think I remember seeing a picture in some magazine recently with the two of them riding bikes around Venice Beach. The article said she was in her early twenties. They make a very sweet pair. I have nothing better to do, so I make my way over to them to get a better look, hoping he doesn't notice. There are too many people around, and he just keeps kissing his girl. Oh shit, he just saw me staring.

I do an about-face and head to the minibar they have set up for us backstage, pretending like I was always heading there to get drinks for me and Sid. I casually order two vodka cranberries and then walk over to Sidney, forcing myself not to look in their direction again.

"Oh, hey, hot stuff, thanks," Sid says, taking her drink from me. She's still having her makeup done, but she already looks incredible. Very robot meets snow bunny, all silver and white and totally sexy. I sit on the floor with my drink and tell her about my encounter, and she immediately turns quickly and leans out of her seat.

"Sid! Stop staring! He already saw me doing it!"

Sidney turns back to me, laughing. "Oh god, LJ, calm down. You're totally flushed. Don't be embarrassed; he's a pop star. I'm sure he's used to psychos at this point."

I whack her knee, and she laughs again.

It's eleven, and the chaos backstage has now become a steady roar as everyone rushes to get ready. We're already half an hour late, and I don't think everyone will be ready for at least another half hour. I hear yelling and see Jean Paul balancing on a barstool not too far away, looking spectacular in a sheer white shirt and leather pants.

"Okay, girls...*girls*! Everyone! Can I have your attention? I need you all to be ready to go, in line, dressed and ready in twenty minutes. Okay! Good. Everyone looks fucking hot! Carry on. I'm very happy. Thank you, ladies, for getting your tiny asses in gear! My god."

Twenty minutes later and miracle of miracles, everyone is ready. All the models line up, hair and makeup touching us up as we wait to go out. The music comes up, and the lights go down, and my heart starts beating faster. I love this, this energy that pulses through us as we wait to go onstage. This anticipation, the intake of breath, the vibration of the floor from the music, the nervousness, and then the release into the lights. The first girl, a stunning blonde, struts down the runway in time to the music and the crowd starts screaming for her. They've clearly been drinking just like we have backstage, probably even more while they waited for the show to start.

The stage manager pushes the next girl onstage, and I'm startled to see that it's Sidney. I lost her in the mad dash for the line, but there she is now, statuesque on her heels and swiveling her hips. She glows in the spotlight, and I can't take my eyes off of her. Neither can the crowd. Sidney joins the blonde at the end of the runway and takes her face in her hands. They start to kiss, with tongue, and the crowd goes wild! I'm transfixed, as is everyone else, and then suddenly the stage manager pushes me out into the spotlight as well. I almost stumble but regain my composure just in time. I try to focus, imitating Sid by swiveling my hips as I stride down the runway. Sidney and the blonde head back up the runway, and Sid shoots me a huge smile as we pass each other. Now it's my turn at the end, and I pop my hip out and lift my chin and smile as the crowd below cheers for me. I try to keep my eyes straight ahead at the cameras, but I can't help but glance down at the thousands of screaming faces below me. The adrenaline is unreal. The noise and thumping beats are running through my veins as I turn to walk back up the runway. And before I know it, I'm back out again in my second outfit.

All the beauty magazines and big fashion bloggers and vloggers are there. I guess LA is trying to keep up with fashion week in New York City. We aren't there yet, but watch out because here comes the Wild West! We did wear a lot of designer labels for the show. And they let me keep the satin fuchsia Burberry dress, which doesn't usually happen with something that pricey. I just keep it on for going out to dance afterward.

With an outrageous show under our belts, Sidney and I walk out from backstage onto the main floor with everyone. First things first—Sid heads straight to the VIP area to find her birthday boy. He's the definition of the LA players club, and all of his friends are the same. They exude wealth, from their clothes to the way they hold themselves. They're nice enough though, giving us hugs and high fives and compliments on the show. Sid's guy has his arm around her shoulders, and she's positively glowing, a champagne glass already in hand. A tall, dark, and very handsome guy touches my elbow and hands me a champagne flute, leaning in to say, "You guys were so hot up there," in my ear over the pounding club music.

"Thank you!" I scream back. These clubs are always so loud. He holds out his hand to me and introduces himself as Cole.

"And you are?" he asks, eyebrow raised.

"LJ," I answer.

He shakes his head. "I can't hear you." He pulls me in closer, so that our faces are just an inch from each other. I notice the stubble on his chin, his piercing green eyes, and his spicy aftershave. He's totally hot, but of course, I'm taken. I back away reluctantly with a smile and repeat my name.

"LJ," he repeats. "What a beautiful name." He smiles, and his perfect teeth dazzle me. He places the palm of his hand on the small of my back, and my pulse quickens, and I get chills all over my body. "A beautiful name for a beautiful girl."

"My boyfriend seems to think so too," I tell him, hoping that he'll get the hint. He just smiles wider and keeps his hand right where it is. He doesn't flinch. Totally arrogant rich kid. I can see right through him.

The rest of the night passes in a blur of music, dancing, drinks, and flirting. There's no harm in looking after all, and accepting drinks from Cole is harmless enough. By the time 3:00 a.m. rolls around, I'm ready to go home. We've been drinking for hours, and I know that all of this vodka and champagne will not be my friend in the morning.

"Sid...Sidney...how 'bout it? Are you almost ready?"

Sidney twirls toward me and flings her arms around my neck, kissing me on the lips.

"You're the best, you know that, right? You're the absolute best. My faaaavorite," she says, slurring.

I laugh and hug her back. "You're my favorite too, Sid."

She straightens her arms so that she can see me better and looks into my eyes. "Seriously though, LJ, you mean so much to me. I'm so glad we're friends."

"I am too, Sid. You've been so good to me and opened so many doors for me; you're one of the few people who really has my back. You're so awesome!"

Sidney hugs me again and then tugs me toward the door. "C'mon, sexy lady, let's get out of here!"

The guys leave with us too, and while Sid and her guy hail us a cab, Cole grabs my upper arm to bring me closer to him and then bites my ear.

"Call me sometime. So we can fuck."

I start to question him, but he presses his finger to my lips to stop me from speaking. His other hand presses his business card into my hand, and then he's gone.

I can't even begin to think about all of that. I toss his card on the sidewalk and get into the cab with Sidney to head back to her house, and we jam out to BPM the whole way back.

*

The next morning I wake up, and I can't even remember walking in the door from the party. I groan, and Sidney, in bed ɔ me, responds with a likewise groan.

"Giiiiirl, last night was so much fun, but I can't even talk with this headache right now," she says.

"Yeah, you're telling me," I say. I look under the covers. "Dude, I'm still wearing my dress."

She laughs and hits me with her pillow. "I think Cole really likes you!"

"Oh, stop it."

"I'm serious! I've never seen him so smitten!" She starts poking me in the ribs, and I bat her hands away as best as I can. It's hard to see with my eye makeup from the show smeared and crusty all over my eyelids.

"I doubt he really likes me. He doesn't even know me," I tell her. "He just likes me because I'm unavailable."

"Nope, he likes you cause you're a smokin'-hot, delicious smoke show!" she says. "You should fuck him!"

"Sid! Really?!" I get out of bed and head to the bathroom to wash my face. I know that she hasn't met Brody yet, but it's getting annoying that she treats my relationship like it doesn't matter. It's everything to me, and I wouldn't just throw that away for a night with some guy named Cole, no matter how many times his face flashes before my eyes while I scrub my face.

I walk back into the bedroom and see Sidney on her side, facing away from me. I climb into bed next to her and softly ask if she's mad at me. I didn't mean to upset her; I just want her to understand what I'm going through.

"Are you mad?"

"No, gorgeous, I'm just sleeping over here. Can you let me sleep for a few minutes, and then we'll go get some coffee. How's that?"

"That's fine, Sid. Sleep sounds good."

And we pass out for hours, happy to let our exhausted bodies rest in the downy cocoon of her warm bed, with the knowledge that our best friend is safe and sound beside us.

*

The high-pitched dance tune of Sidney's phone yanks us from our slumber, and with a jolt, we realize that it's one in the afternoon. I'm eager to get home to Brody after last night's events, so I jump out of bed and start packing my bags. Sid and I drive separately to Starbucks and don't speak much in line while we check our phones. A text I send to Brody goes unanswered, and when I try to call him, the phone goes right to voice mail. Strange. He probably let his battery die or lost it or something.

After we get our coffee, Sid and I hug good-bye at the door and part ways. I get to my house less than an hour later, and though Brody's car is in the driveway, he's not home. I shower and get comfy on the sofa, flipping on the Food Network with a bag of mustard pretzels in hand. I love trying out the show's recipes when I can.

Just then, the door opens, and Brody walks straight into the living room, standing in front of the TV and blocking my show.

"LJ, I need to talk to you."

My stomach immediately ties up in knots. Brody is never this serious. I hold my position on the couch, afraid to move. If I move in this moment, it makes it all that more real.

He starts talking, letting his eyes dart around the room. His face is flushed, and he can't keep his hands still. I'm terrified to hear what he's about to say.

"Well, you know how I went to that party last night?" he starts. "Well—"

"What, Brody? Spill it! What happened?" I turn off the TV and tuck my knees up to my chin. The sinking feeling keeps going deeper and deeper, my stomach a bottomless pit that is swallowing me whole.

He starts crying. "There was this…this girl. She had these big fake boobs." He shakes his head. "We kissed, and I felt her up. I'm so, so sorry, and I didn't mean it, and it was just because I was drunk, and I know that's not an excuse but, I love you so much…"

I take a breath and process this info. It hurts like a knife.

"Babe, please say something. Please! Can we work through this? I can't lose you."

"So…you only kissed this person?" I say, searching his face for sincerity.

"Yeah. I might've felt her up a little bit, but that's it. I promise."

"Brody, I can't believe this! Why would you even do something that stupid?" I'm crying now, and he is too. I can't imagine not being with him though. I'd be lost. I'd been planning our family in my head for years. And even though he's causing me pain, all I want to do is have him hold me and make it better. I look up at him, and he rushes forward, wrapping his arms around me. My tears soak his shirt.

"Who was she even?" I ask.

"Nobody. She doesn't even live here; she was here from out of town. Monterey, I think."

"Oh my god. Shit, Brody, did anyone see you?" I think of all of our friends at the party, watching the love of my life kissing some fucking bimbo with fake boobs, and I start to lose my mind.

"No, no one saw me! We were in the bathroom."

I space out and imagine them there, her ass pressed against the sink, her tits pressed up against his chest as he groped her mouth with his tongue. The thought makes me sick. I instantly want to know more. Was she blond? Brunette? Did she look like me?

I shake the thoughts from my head. I do want to work through this with Brody, and details don't matter. What matters is us and getting over this speed bump in our otherwise perfect relationship.

"Brody, we can work through this, I think. It just can't happen again. Okay?"

He nods and then leans his forehead against my chest, taking refuge in me. I rest my chin on his head and hold him close. What frightens me more than the fact that he kissed someone else is the thought of being alone, I realize. It's more than the fact that he can't lose me. I can't lose him.

We spend the rest of the day on the couch and order a pizza, but instead of cuddling like we usually do, we sit on opposite ends of the sofa. He gives me full control of the remote, and whenever we make eye contact, the air between us is thick with the tension of questions that no one wants to ask. I can tell he feels really bad. He looks like a little lost puppy over on his side of the couch. It makes me smile a bit, even though I don't let him see that. It's kind of nice to see that he needs me as much as I need him. Besides, it was really only just a kiss.

I go to bed early, and Brody gives me space, spending the night watching TV on the couch. When I wake up, he's there next to me, sleeping and peaceful. I feel lost. I reach out to touch his side, and he sighs in his sleep when I do, relaxing into my touch.

I'm on set all week at the USC campus. It's a long week, and all I do is work and hibernate at home, not talking to anyone. Brody tries to make everything as cozy as possible, buying all of my favorite foods and staying out of my way. Finally, Friday rolls around. I make plans with our mutual friend, Sunny, to get drinks in Belmont Shore. I could use some girl time after this stressful week. The evening is balmy, so Sunny and I sit at a corner table on the patio and order double Cadillac margaritas with salted rims, and for the first time in the past week, I feel like life could get back to normal.

Sunny and I talk about work while we drink our margaritas and share a bowl of guacamole and chips. I tell her about what it's like to work on the set, how many hours it is, and how hard everyone works, and she tells me about what tattoos are the most popular right now and how well her tattoo parlor is doing. She's been working as a tattoo artist for years, and her arms are covered with ink. She tells me how she's debating starting an eagle on her chest with its wing spanning up around her neck.

Sunny is very different from my glitzy Hollywood girl-friends, but I love different life perspectives. And I've always had an eclectic group of buddies around me. Lovely people come in all colors and sizes.

Sunny takes a sip of her margarita and cocks her head to the side and scrunches her brows.

"You know, it's so cool of you…how you're so cool with everything."

"With everything. What?" I ask.

"You know. With what happened with Crystal."

"Who's Crystal?"

"That girl Brody screwed in the bathroom at Stark's party last weekend."

CHAPTER FOUR

The falling-pit feeling in my stomach is back again, and I have to grab the table to steady myself so I don't pass out.

"Oh my god, LJ," Sunny says. "I'm so sorry. I thought you knew. Shit, he told me he told you."

"He told me he just grabbed her boobs, and they kissed a few times!"

I feel like I'm going to pass out again. I don't know what to do, if I should stay there or if I should leave. What I want to do is to march across Long Beach, find Brody, and beat the shit out of him until he's bleeding and dead. He lied to me. He straight up lied to my face. He lied to me all week. He slept with another girl, after four years of being with me. I hate him. I hate him so much!

Sunny looks nearly as angry as I am. "I'm going to kick his ass, LJ. I can't believe he lied to you like that! And lied to me too. That motherfucker."

"You know this girl?" I ask.

"Yeah, I do. She lives up north in Monterey. I gave her a tramp stamp once too. A butterfly on her lower back. Typical. And we've hung out a few times at some other parties too."

"Get her on the phone," I tell her. Sunny starts to shake her head, but then I insist. "Just do it, please. Just put the phone up to my ear when she tells you..." I can't even say the words. "When she tells you. I won't say anything. I just want to hear her say it. Can you do that for me, please? Just do it for me. I need to hear it from her."

Sunny dials her number, still shaking her head, and they talk for a minute, then she gets down to business. She asks about Brody and then puts the phone on speaker. I hear a chipper voice on the other end, and I can't help but hear her boobs bounce as she recounts sleeping with my boyfriend.

"Oh yeah, girl, we fucked a few times, in the bathroom and then behind the house in the alley. He's huge! It was so fucking raw. Hey, isn't his girlfriend one of your good friends?"

Sunny yanks the phone back before I grab it. "Yeah, and she's a total sweetheart. You shouldn't have done that. Gotta go."

Sunny's my good friend. She busies herself putting her phone away as tears stream down my face, polite enough to look away and give me a moment. I can't hear anything anymore; the sounds of the bar and the street have gone silent. Or maybe I've gone deaf.

Sunny stands up and throws money on the table. She holds her hand out to me, and I take it. "Let's get outta here, sister."

"Okay," I whisper. She walks me to my car, and I tell her that I'm fine. I just want to be left alone.

"Do me a favor, Sunny? Don't tell him that I know. Will you do that for me? I want to make him tell me himself."

"Okay, sweetheart. Whatever you want. Call me later. Love you." With a kiss on the cheek and a wink, she's gone. I open my car door, sit down in the seat, close the door, and lock it.

And I sit there. And sit there. For two hours. Not blinking. Just frozen.

I finally muster the strength to start the car and drive the few blocks home, but I'm still in a daze. I spent the past two hours getting more and more pissed off, and I know exactly how I'm going to get him to tell me himself.

*

Brody walks into the living room and flips on the lights. He nearly jumps out of his skin.

"What the fuck, babe? You scared the hell out of me!"

I sit on the couch, stoic and unmoving. He's visibly unnerved. Good, he deserves it.

I turn to look at him, and he waits for me. "How are you doing?" he asks.

"I just had drinks with Sunny down on Second Street."

"Oh good, did you guys have fun?"

"Oh yeah. We had a blast. And you know what? She brought a friend with her. Crystal. Crystal went on to say how you had sex with her last weekend at Stark's party."

He just stood there, right in front of the TV. Just like last time, right in the same spot, rocking slightly back and forth. Then he just shrugged. "Yeah."

I burst into tears. That's it for me. Over. Done. Finished. I'm so hurt, and I don't know what to do with myself. I'm fucking livid. There's nowhere else to go. Where do I go? I feel so alone.

He moves toward me, and instinctively I put my hand up to block him. I don't want him anywhere near me; the very thought of him touching me is repulsive.

"I'm done. I'm fucking done! I'll find somewhere to go. Just leave me alone. There is nothing you can *ever* do or say to fix this!"

He hangs his head down and walks out of the living room. He opens the front door and then turns back and mutters an apology. I don't want his apologies. I want him not to have cheated on me.

I hear the front screen door close, and I know that's it. He doesn't come home all weekend. I curl up in sheets and pillows on the living room floor and sob. I thought everything was perfect. We were so in love and lucky that no one else had the same magic we had. Everyone was jealous of our perfect relationship.

Monday comes around, and I pull myself together enough to go to work. Luckily, I don't have to do anything other than let them tell me where to stand on set.

On the drive home, I have the overwhelming urge to talk to someone who loves me, to let them comfort me. I wish I could call my mother, but she and I have never really been that close. Ever since I was young, she never made me feel like I mattered. In fact, when she got angry, she'd tell me that I was a burden, and she regretted having me and that I ruined her life. Granted, she was twenty-five years old with four kids when she got a divorce, but I never forgot the things she said. I've spent too much time thinking about them, letting them permeate my psyche. No, I can't call my mother now. Instead I call Sidney. She's always so happy and full of life, exactly what I need.

"Hey, sexy lady!" she trills on the other end, and I have to smile at that.

"Sid, I'm not good right now." I tell her what happened, and she listens quietly.

"Doll, I know this is super hard for you right now," she says. "But we're going to fix this. We're going to put you back together, okay? It's all going to be okay. I promise you. Don't worry about anything. You're going to be better than ever in no time! I promise."

Hearing her voice is like a balm for my open sores. I start to cry silent tears, but they're not tears of sadness—they're tears of relief. I'm not all alone in this after all.

"Listen, baby, I've got a plan. First we've got to get you out of that house, and I've got the perfect thing. You know Tristan, my roommate who lives downstairs? He's moving out in two weeks, and then we get you to move in his room. We're going to live together! We'll have the best time! We'll just hang out and go party all the time! What sounds better than that? It's going to be soo good! You wait and see. That surfer dude never deserved you for as long as he had you."

Living with my best friend sounds amazing. Thank goodness I have someone to make decisions for me right now. I'm definitely in no place to make them for myself. I agree to Sidney's plan, and we get off the phone. When I get home, the house is filled with stargazer lilies, and incredible long-stem red roses, my favorite. I hear movement in the bedroom; Brody must be here. He knows I love fresh flowers, but the sweet scent and all of the beauty isn't having the same effect on me as it usually does. It's making my stomach flip instead. I cringe.

I find Brody in the bedroom and tell him that I'll be moving out in two weeks. He's brokenhearted, but I have no sympathy. He's the one who broke mine first.

CHAPTER FIVE

The day finally comes to move out. I rent a U-Haul, and Brody and his brothers are very nice and come help load it up for me. We're all tense and barely talking to each other. The mood is somber. His brothers are mad at him and ask me to stay, saying that they'd make sure he stays in line, but it's too late for me. At least they make me crack my first smile in weeks.

Brody drives the U-Haul up to Burbank, and I follow in my Jeep, and by the afternoon, I'm all moved into Sidney's. When I arrive, the house is empty since Sidney is away visiting her mother in Texas, and the other guys must not be home. Brody's brothers help unload the truck and then leave, but Brody stays behind, helping me unpack and spending one last night with me. It's over, but we owe it to ourselves, to what we had, to spend one last time being close. I know it's wrong to sleep with him, but I do it anyway. We were together for almost four and a half years. It's hard to say good-bye to that right away.

The next morning, we hug and say good-bye. Neither one of us cries. We're too emotionally spent. He takes my face in his hands and says, "I could never take care of you the way you deserve to be taken care of." And with that he kisses me once on the forehead. Then he turns and walks down the driveway with one last wave.

The house feels empty and unfamiliar without anyone in it, but it's time to get started on my new life, I tell myself. I sit on the bed, tucking my legs under the rumpled sheets, and pull out my phone. I have several voice mails and Snapchats that I haven't had the time or the wherewithal to check, but there aren't any excuses left. I listen to the first voice mail and get the first bit of good news I've had in quite a while. *Glamour* magazine wants to shoot with me, but the shoot's tomorrow at the Viceroy Hotel in Santa Monica. I call the woman back, hoping I'm not too late, and it turns out that my replacement had to cancel, so I can do it after all. It's a 5:00-a.m. call time on a Sunday, which sucks. This is going to be another long week of work, but it's good to keep busy right now. Plus, Sidney gets home on Friday, and I know she's going to want to celebrate my moving in. Oh boy, what have I gotten myself into with her? But oddly enough, I am excited for whatever happens next.

I wander around the house, popping my head in the guys' rooms to see what they're like. Elliott's room is next to mine. I've only seen him smoke pot, play on his computer, and strum his guitar, a loner, for the most part. Jona's down the hall with his big dog, Smalls. They're both so sweet. He mostly plays video games when he's not at work or night school. Then Collin lives upstairs, across the hall from Sidney, and they share a bathroom. He's always yelling at her to put some clothes on. I'm sure he liked the shock of it at first, but after three years of living together, they're more like brother and sister. He's the oldest in the house at thirty years old. He's a software engineer and a little nerdy but cute and sweet. It's a good mix of people in the house.

I pack everything I need for the shoot tomorrow and take a shower in my bathroom for the first time. It's strange being here as a roommate rather than Sidney's guest, and I have to keep reminding myself that this is my house now too. I catch a glimpse of myself in the mirror and am shocked by my appearance. I've lost ten pounds through the breakup, and it's worked wonders on me. My stomach is completely flat, and my collarbones are more pronounced, casting shadows where there used to be only a little definition. I guess, on the bright side of a broken heart, this is all working out for my modeling career. Or I'm just concentrating too hard on trying to disappear.

*

I wake up the next morning feeling refreshed for the first time in weeks. Being out of the house I shared with Brody just feels better. The walls of my new bedroom aren't weighed down by our old memories. The windowsill is just a windowsill, not a place where my hands pressed while he made love to me. The wall behind the door is just a wall, not a place where Brody would let the door bump, leaving a doorknob dent. Everything (not counting last night) is fresh and clean, a new start.

It's still dark outside while I get ready, but I like that I'm ahead of the day. It makes me feel more productive, like I've got my life under control. By the time I pull up to the Viceroy Hotel, I'm on an all-time ego high. Fuck people who don't appreciate me. I'm a model shooting at a fabulous hotel. All he did was detail people's cars. I stride into the hotel lobby mad as hell but instantly feel calmly at home among its modern glamour. The lobby is amazing! I've always admired interior designer Kelly Wearstler's work. Her unexpected designs constantly push the envelope. They're the opposite of boring, which is exactly how I want to live my life from now on. For too long, my life was about relaxing on the beach and coasting by with my job in retail. No more! From now on, I'll always push the envelope and do the unexpected. Life is too short to drift through on autopilot.

The front-desk attendant directs me to the penthouse, and when I enter, I'm swallowed by the bustle of people scrambling to set up the shoot. A gorgeous African American girl walks up to me with a giant smile.

"Hi there! You must be the other model," she says, her high-pitch voice like a cartoon mouse. "I'm Naomi."

I'm instantly made happier by her presence. She links her arm through mine and brings me over to hair and makeup, and she chats with me while the talented glam squad does their thing. She's by far the nicest model I've worked with, and one of the most beautiful too, like a lighter-skinned Naomi Campbell, but, of course, with less anger. She hasn't thrown anything at me yet.

The shoot is for a story about sleepovers, which means we get to wear a ton of nighties and lingerie. The rolling racks are full of La Perla and Victoria's Secret, and I spot a few French designers as well. When the sun rises, the light streams through the double doors leading out to a balcony, and the room fills with a warm, lemony glow. Naomi and I spend the day giggling while jumping on the bed and tossing pillows around. We have an absolute blast. After eight hours, we all move downstairs to shoot next to the pool. I change into a cute red-and-white tank top with hearts and little shorts with stars and lace and drape myself over a hot blond model boy on the pool chairs. We laugh and flirt playfully and have so much fun that I forget that we're working. By the time the sun sets, the photographer calls it a wrap, and Naomi and I go back upstairs to get changed, and we exchange numbers so that we can hang out later. Another instant best friend, I just knew it.

We walk to the elevators together, and before we part, Naomi turns to me.

"I'll call you soon. I know lots of great photographers, and I have tons of good friends who are all repeat clients of my agency. They all do big jobs. I'll introduce you!"

"Thanks, Naomi. You're the best!"

"Most of the people I work with know me as Nicole; that's my middle name. But you should call me Naomi."

"Okay. I totally get that. Everyone calls me LJ, short for Lillian James."

"What do you want me to call you?"

I consider that for a moment.

"I'm not sure. Which one do you like better?"

She pauses and appraises me. "I like LJ! I think it fits you better; it's fun and carefree."

I have to smile at that. She reminds me of some of my supercool friends back home in St. Louis, so calling me LJ fits.

*

After that, the rest of the week passes quickly. I get a call from Sidney while she's on the road with a girlfriend—her mother bought her a new little white Jetta convertible, so they decided to road trip it back to LA, blasting music and eating junk food the whole way. I tell them to bring me some ranch corn nuts home. They laugh hysterically the whole time I talk to them, and I'm sure they're stoned out of their minds. They'll be home Saturday afternoon, so I just have to get through this week on set in one piece so that I can party with them on Saturday night. It's funny how just a few months ago, being on set was the highlight of my life, and now it's something I have to get through so that I can get to my weekend. I guess you can make anything become normal once you get used to it.

The week's coming to an end when I hear from Naomi; true to her word, she sent my picture to some of her clients, and they want me to join her on Sunday to shoot an ad for a new jean company. I'm really starting to rack up some jobs now—my career is really taking off. I should be happier than I am, but it's hard missing Brody and all. My roommates tend to stay locked up in their rooms all the time, if they're even home. I have this big house all to myself, and while I'm feeling more and more at home, I still miss Brody. A lot. We haven't talked at all, and I feel far from my old life, even though it's only been a week. I have to keep reminding myself that I need to keep moving forward, not backward.

I'm thinking about this while I stand in the kitchen on Saturday morning in a T-shirt and Brody's old rolled-down boxers, waiting for the kettle to boil for my tea. Jona walks in and nods a groggy hello to me, Smalls following close behind. I bend down to pet Smalls on his chest and suddenly stand up with an idea.

"Hey, Jona, what would you think if I painted the walls in my room? That wallpaper isn't quite doing it for me."

"Sure, yeah, do whatever you want. It's your room now," he says.

I hightail it down to the Do-it hardware center down the road, not even changing out of my shirt and boxers, and buy a ton of red paint. I can't wait to cover the hideous flowered wallpaper that's straight from the '80s. I can't believe a guy lived there before. When I get home, I lay down newspaper on the wood floor and get to work, painting a few coats on and leaving the trim and closet doors white. Seven hours later and I've got a completely new, sophisticated room. Just in time too—Sidney and her friend walk in right as I finish cleaning up the newspaper from the wood floor.

"Hey, hot stuff!" I hear from the kitchen. "Get your sexy ass out here!"

I walk into the kitchen and see Sidney, much tanner than before she left, with a tall brunette girl with the longest legs I've ever seen.

"Baaaby!" she coos, rushing forward to hug me. "LJ, this is my friend Ruby; she's the baddest bitch you'll ever meet. You two are going to be best friends. I just know it!"

We chat for a little bit—Ruby throws me off with her southern accent and her exotic looks; she looks like she should be from Brazil but speaks like she should be baling hay—and then I show them my new room.

"Love it!" Sid proclaims, clapping her hands together. "Okay, okay, let's go upstairs and chill. I saved a fatty J for you, LJ, and I got you some ranch corn nuts and a dark chocolate Milky Way! Am I the best or what?"

Having Sidney back brings energy flooding into the house, and I take the stairs two at a time behind the girls and flop onto Sid's futon, just like old times.

"Here," Sidney says, passing me the joint. "This weed that we got from Ruby's friend in Austin is soooo good."

I take a few puffs and tell the girls about my week while Ruby pokes around in Sidney's closet and I roll another joint.

Ruby presses a red dress to her thin frame and turns for our opinions.

"So you just broke up with your boyfriend, right?" Ruby drawls.

Sidney shoots her a look and cuts her off. "LJ doesn't want to talk about that. She's on to bigger and better things, right, baby?"

I smile at her appreciatively. I can keep it together as long as I keep Brody out of my mind, and there's no one better to do that than Sidney. She changes the subject to everything they did in Austin, from the wild nights with some hot guys in the bars to doing shots with Matthew McConaughey and his wife at some laid-back bar.

"Okay, ladies, what are we doing tonight?" Sidney asks, blowing a stream of smoke up at the ceiling. "This totally hot guy just left me a Snapchat to meet him and some friends over at this salsa place to dance. They have a live band. Then, we can do after hours somewhere, maybe 1 OAK; they have a sick house DJ tonight."

"Guys, I have that shoot tomorrow. I might have to skip the after hours," I warn them.

"Whatever, lame-o," Sid says, rising from the bed and stripping naked to get dressed.

I don't want to look like crap at the shoot, so I make a silent promise to myself not to drink too much tonight. We have a blast running around the house, getting ready, chatting with the other roommates, and taking breaks in the kitchen to take shots. I feel so lucky that there was a room open in the house at just the right time for me; it's only been a week, but I already feel right at home here. Party on.

An hour later, we're ready to go, so we call an Uber and take the club by storm. Three tall girls in very short skirts and heels make a big impact on getting past the line at the door, especially at a place where a lot of the guys are professional dancers. One guy grabs me and spins me around the second I walk in the door, and by the end of the night, I'm keeping up with the pros. I try to call it a night at one in the morning, but the girls insist that I go listen to some electronic music with them at another club, and we are having way too much fun for me to say no.

The next thing I know, it's 6:00 a.m., and my phone's alarm rises me from my passed-out state on the bed. Oh my god. I feel awful. I can still smell the booze and cigarettes on me. I take a quick shower and manage to make it over to Hollywood to meet Naomi at my call time.

"Hey, LJ!" she says brightly, but then she recoils when she sees me dragging myself in the door. "Girl! Uh-uh. What is wrong with you?"

"Oh my god...I need coffee," I tell her. We walk over to the table that has the provisions, and she gives me some intense side eye. "Dude, please don't be mad at me. I can totally pull it together."

She puts her hand on her hip and looks me up and down, but before she turns to get in the first shot, she shoots me a smile. A woman with an iPad walks up to me.

"Hi. You're Lillian James Vol-pac-elli, right?"

I smile and hold out my hand to greet her. "Yes, it's so nice to meet you. Thank you for having me on today's shoot."

"Well, we just adored your beautiful pictures and thought you would be perfect. And Naomi said she was a friend of yours, so thank you for coming in today. It's $1400 for today, and we can call your agency about contracts, but I know Naomi already called them and told them that you might be shooting with us today. And we'll get you all together with a voucher for them too. And free jeans, of course."

"Sounds great! Thank you," I say.

This job is awesome; thank goodness Naomi Nicole got me in!

"Okay, great, we'll just get you right over to hair and makeup then."

I quickly make an espresso and a bagel and head over to hair and makeup. I know it's not very model-y to eat at your shoot, but it's either that or die on the spot. I let the makeup artist do her thing while I watch Naomi model the jeans. I have to admire her; she's a really great model, listening to the photographer and just flying with his suggestions. She doesn't even flinch when he asks her to take her top off. She turns her back to the camera and twists around to pout at the camera behind her. I close my eyes while the makeup artist does my eye shadow, and I start to drift off, but, all of a sudden, I hear the photographer say, "That's great, Naomi. Now can you lose the jeans?" My eyes flash open to see her stripping off her jeans and twisting her back to the camera again. Am I going to have to do that too?

"Is Lillian ready?" the photographer calls out.

"Yes, she is!" the makeup artist calls back across the studio. Am I though? I'm in a pair of jeans and a big comfy robe that I'm not quite ready to lose. I've never modeled nude before.

I walk over to Naomi, and she smiles at me as we switch places. An assistant hands her a robe and holds her hand out for mine. Well, here goes. Might as well be free. It's too late to turn back now. Plus, I'm not about to make a scene and embarrass Naomi after she got me the job and all.

"Okay. Right here's your space to work in, sweetheart. Just stand on this apple box for the first few shots," the photographer tells me. I start to pose, imitating Naomi for the first few shots and then getting more comfortable the more we shoot.

"Beautiful, honey! Just beautiful," the photographer shouts, crouching to get different angles. After about an hour, he calls Naomi over to join me.

"Okay, I want them one behind the other, and we'll shoot from the waist down. Then we'll overlap their asses over and over and so on," he tells the photo director. Sweet Jesus. I feel so mortified. My bare butt is being photographed. But Naomi doesn't even flinch. In fact, she's having fun.

She shakes me a little and says, "Have fun, girl!" What she's really telling me is that this is harmless—it's art. And it's just an innocent paycheck. With her up here shooting with me, I start to relax more. And have fun too. The end of the afternoon passes by in a blur of clicks, flashes, and asses.

CHAPTER SIX

The house stays quiet for the beginning of the next week, which I welcome, because it allows me to sleep and recover from my long workdays on the film. Sid and Ruby stay on opposite schedules from me, sleeping during the day and partying all night, but not before texting me long, rambling messages—along with some supercrazy Snapchats—about me being an old lady for staying in instead of partying on yachts in Marina Del Rey with them. I manage to push the girls off until Wednesday night, when driven weak by Sidney's nagging, I finally agree to go out with them.

I go upstairs and collapse on Sid's bed after work, and instantly she's on top of me, tickling me with her bony fingers.

"You're finally coming out with us! Yahoo!" she yells. "You're coming; you're coming!"

I can't stop laughing. "Yes, yes, I'm coming. I'm coming!" I yell back at her.

She rolls off of me onto her bed and rearranges her face in mock seriousness.

"You, young lady, are in for it tonight. Cole has literally been calling me nonstop to see where you are. He's got a major boner for you, sexy lady."

I roll my eyes. "Oh please, Sid, he's so cocky. I can practically smell the stench of his ego from here. Not hot at all." I don't mention that I am slightly more intrigued by this night than I let on.

"Oh, whatever, I'm calling to tell him you're going to Soho House with us for a drink tonight, or there's that Little Red Bar next door too. And then let's go to dinner at Katana. I love the robata with the bacon-wrapped tomatoes and the scallops. Holy shit, it's so yummy! Okay. I'm calling." She starts dialing his number, and I throw a pillow at her, giggling. I realize that I miss this—this anticipation of a good night out with the possibility of a cute guy at the end of it.

She covers the microphone in her phone and whispers, "I'm leaving a message," to me and then rises from the bed, flips her hair, and struts across the room in an exaggerated cat walk, her long legs bending and straightening in a liquid rhythm.

"Cole, my darling, it's Sidney. I'm dragging your beloved LJ to Soho House and Katana tonight. Or The Nice Guy, or somewhere on Sunset. She's just totally dying to see your sexy body. She can't stop talking my ear off about how she wants to fuck you. Ciao!"

"Sid!" I screech and then dissolve into a pile of giggles. "My god!"

"You're totally blushing. I knew you thought he was sexy!"

We're both laughing with tears running down our faces when Ruby walks in, eating a granola bar. "What?" she asks, mid bite, and Sid and I lose it again.

We primp for a couple hours and smoke a little hash that the girls got from the boat party, and I fill the girls in on my naked photo shoot.

"I'm just a little nervous about where the photos are going to end up," I tell them.

"Don't worry," Sid says, brandishing an eye shadow brush. "If they use the ass pictures, which they should because your ass is totally phenomenal, your head will be cut off anyway. It's waist down from the back, right?"

"And you got paid, and you might be in magazine ads too. That's seriously cool!" Ruby adds.

"Yeah, it's too awesome, baby," Sid says. "Okay, ladies, are we ready to roll? We can take my new car. LJ, you haven't even been in it yet!"

We jump in the Jetta, and I make sure to tell Sid how adorable it is, which makes her smile and turn up the music even louder. We make it to Soho House in no time, and we flick our cigarettes down on the pavement as we give the car to the valet. I love this bar. It reminds me of when I was eighteen and the girls on my floor in the dorm at Cal State, Long Beach would pile in one tiny, old, and rusted Toyota and drive up to Hollywood, thinking that we were so cool for trying to get into a club underage. I remember once, in an effort to avoid getting carded at the front door here, a random hottie reached down from the open-air picture window and lifted me into the packed bar. Even now, whenever I come here, my heart races when I hand my license over to the bouncer—even though I'm twenty-one. I'm always surprised when I'm allowed in.

Once inside, Ruby and I follow Sid through the place, stopping occasionally while she says hello to people she knows. Her phone never stops buzzing; she always has a party to go to, people to greet, and selfies to pose for. I don't mind following her through venues like this while she does her princess wave. After a long week, thinking about where to go next is the last thing I want to do.

We play pool for a bit with some people Sidney knows, then go upstairs to VIP and get some drinks from some other guys. We're a great team of girls. We manage to get the royal treatment wherever we go. I love it! And it's always great fun because none of us have the same taste in guys, either. We all find different guys to flirt with, even if it's only for a few minutes before we're whisked away somewhere else, going with the flow of the night.

We're at Soho House for all of an hour when I see Sid press her phone to her ear and wildly motion us toward the door. We run across Sunset Boulevard and into the House of Blues where we're immediately taken to VIP to meet up with some hot guys who invited us over for a drink. Their balcony overlooks the stage, and I can see the band finishing up the show. We settle in the big, cozy sofas and put our heels up on dark leather ottomans above thick Persian rugs, enjoying our drinks and taking Snapchats and selfies in front of a giant fireplace. This is one of my favorite spots in town. It's so moody and different from all the other places we go. It's not completely removed from Hollywood though; I see Benicio del Toro, Nick Jonas, Ryan Gosling, and Drake sitting at the table next to ours. I still can't get over the fact that I can go out at night and see celebrities, and my bed is still not far away when I need to go crash after the bars.

After some time, I manage to convince the girls to go to Katana with me for some food. I can't drink all night without putting some food in my stomach as well, especially since I have to work tomorrow. Plus, I can't pass up the chance for good food—my dad raised me to appreciate food as an art form, and there's no better place to appreciate it than Katana. Paired with the trendy and boisterous crowd, it's the perfect place to grab a bite on a night out.

We arrive and sit down for oysters on the half shell with black caviar and gold flakes, which the girls scowl at, but I absolutely devour. Sid and Ruby think they're too slimy, but I've been eating oysters since I was three years old. Instead of eating, the girls observe everyone around us and impatiently jiggle their feet, waiting to mingle. They're eager to get out to the patio and see who all is here tonight.

I slurp the last oyster, and Sidney jumps to her feet. "Great! Okay, let's go."

"Wait, Sid, we still have to pay," I tell her, looking for our waitress.

"No, we don't," she tells me. She nods at a guy sitting at a table nearby, and he nods back and gestures to the waitress. Some guy that I've seen her around town with, but she's never spoken to me about. Oh well, free food, so I don't really mind what the story is. One less thing to pay for tonight, right?

We grab our drinks and head out to the patio, which is absolutely bustling with foxy people. "Hey, LJ, there's Cole!" Sidney loudly exclaims.

"Good god, Sid, please don't—"

"Hey, Cole!" she screams across the patio.

"Sid, everyone is looking at us!" I say, hiding behind her.

She turns to me, hand on her hip. "Okay, LJ, I'm seriously getting tired of this whole shy-good-girl thing you're doing. You need to move on. You've been single for a few weeks now, and you haven't even had sex with anyone else yet. There's a reason they always say the best way to get over someone is to get under someone else, you know. And here's your chance to fuck a perfectly hot guy that everyone else wants to fuck. Now go, flirt with him. You are the ultimate sex on a stick. A goddess. Think sex. Feel it! Now go work it."

She pushes me forward to him, which doesn't take much since he's already crossed the patio and heard the last part of Sidney's speech. I can feel my face redden, but I remind myself of what Sid said and take a deep breath. She's right. I really need to get myself back out there. I hold my hand out for him to shake, but instead of taking it, he grabs my waist and brings me in close to him. Body to body. He goes straight for my neck. "You smell amazing, baby," he whispers, moving my hair off my neck and kissing me gently several times behind the ear. His sexy cologne envelops me, and I can feel his warm hands circling my waist and moving down over my skirt. I'm putty in his hands, and it's getting harder and harder to resist him.

I can see Sid and Ruby moving away from us, both of them giving me the thumbs-up and making lewd movements with their hips, laughing the whole time. I shake my head at them, but I have to smile. I feel like Cole is a test, and if I give in, I fail. I have to be strong and hold my ground and resist his powers. I guess that's just a residual of being in a relationship though. Trying to be a good girl, loyal to myself. He's just so damn sexy and rough, and I love that he just takes what he wants. He kisses my neck and his stubble tickles me, giving me goose bumps. And I instantly get wet. I know it's only a matter of time before I give in.

I know one thing though, and that's that I won't give in tonight. I can't. I have to work tomorrow, and I'm not willing to give up my dreams for some guy. I pull away from Cole with a smile, and he cocks an eyebrow at me and smiles.

"Maybe another time," I tell him. Before I try to back away, he holds my upper arms tightly. But I push off his chest and back up. And I can't resist sending a wink his way. Best to keep my options open. He gives me a shrug, as if to say, your loss. I smile back and turn to go find my girls.

"Hey, Sid, what do you think? Time to head out? I've got to work tomorrow," I ask Sidney, finding her chatting with a group of people at the corner table around the fire pit.

"Oh, excuse me, everyone, have you met LJ?" she asks the group. "She's a prudish little old lady. And she just *loves* ruining everyone's fun night to go home early."

The group laughs, and I do too, sarcastically. "I mean, I can get an Uber; it's not a problem," I tell her.

"No, no it's fine. Are you sure you don't want your man to give you a good ride? I can go find him for you."

"He is *not* my man!" I tell her.

"Okay, okay, let's go find Ruby."

We find her cuddled up on a couch with a handsome older man who looks like he's in fifties. I never did understand why some girls date men as old as their dads; it just seems creepy to me. But, hey, to each their own, I guess.

We tell Ruby that we're leaving, and she asks us to give her a minute, so we agree to meet her down on the sidewalk. Sid and I head downstairs and light up cigarettes, hips out to the side and eyes slanted toward Sunset Boulevard. The street is jam-packed with cars at one thirty in the morning, and people stream past us on the sidewalk, showing off their hot dates. The energy of Hollywood is intoxicating, and I can feel the claws digging in. Gorgeous girls and handsome guys are checking me out as they pass, and I wink and give high fives back. I can feel their approval, their expectance, their lust. I've never felt cooler, and I've never loved Hollywood more. I've come into my own here.

Ruby arrives, and we walk back down Sunset Boulevard to Soho House to pick up the car. Even on the sidewalk, we're bathed in headlights, cars honking and people yelling, and it reminds me of a wild spring break or Mardi Gras. We're all smiling; the city has a magic spell over us. I strut down the sidewalk, feeling invincible, like I could do anything and it would be okay. Here in LA, there's no line between what's right and what's wrong. The moral boundaries are blurred, and I like it. Something new is definitely brewing inside me; I can feel it hovering near my edges, beckoning me forward into my new self. It took heartbreak to get here, but if pain is necessary for freedom, so be it. I'm ready to loosen the reins of my life. What I don't know is if it will lead me somewhere right...or somewhere very, very wrong. But I'm excited to find out.

CHAPTER SEVEN

I wake the next morning with a headache and smeared eyeliner.
Then I get ready to head out.

On the way to work, I stop by M Café on Melrose for a tea
and some blueberry multigrain pancakes, but I have no cash
and have to charge the eighteen dollars. I seem to spend all my
money going out and buying clothes for going out, even though
half the time we get drinks for free. I don't understand what I
spend it all on. The fabulous life is expensive, and even though
I'm making good money as a stand-in and part-time model, it's
not really cutting it. I want more. I leave M Café pondering
how to make more money, and in the parking lot, I walk past a
shiny-red Bentley convertible with tan-leather seats and the
license plate *nvr-setl.* Okay. I won't.

The workday passes in a hungover blur, and I'm relieved
when it's time to leave. It's strange how the extraordinary turns
so quickly into the ordinary when you get used to it. Keira and
I chat regularly between takes, like old coworkers in the break

room. Even though we're shooting a movie, it's become just another day in the office.

On my drive home, my phone flashes on the seat next to me. It's my mother calling, and I know if I don't answer, she'll just keep calling and texting until I do. I hit speakerphone and take the call.

"Hey, Mom," I sigh.

"Hi, sweetheart. How is everything going up there? Are you in the car?" she asks. I can hear ice rattling in a glass on her end. Great. When she's drinking, she's more forthcoming with her criticism.

"Yeah, I'm just heading home from work now."

She pauses. I can hear her taking a sip. "And just what is it that you're doing now, Lillian? What are you doing to support yourself? The last I heard from you, you were still modeling, is that right?"

"Yes, Mom. I've done a few modeling jobs, but my main job is working as a stand-in for Keira Knightley on her latest film." I half expect her to be impressed—I'm working with a movie star after all. But, then I remember that it's my mother, and I prepare for the worst.

"Kei-ra Knight-ley?" she asks, sounding out each syllable as if it's a foreign language. "Well, that's a big compliment?"

"Oh, thanks a lot," I tell her. "But it's a really great job, Mom. I've joined the Screen Actors Guild now, so I'm making good money, and—"

"So you're just standing there? That's a job?" she says to me. And so it starts.

"Well, it's more than that; sometimes I have to say her lines, learn her blocking...the hours are really long...and..." There's silence on the other end of the line as I scramble to find ways to defend my job. Seen through the eyes of my mother, the illustrious professor and honored Ivy League academic who worked herself through school with four kids, I'm nothing more than a brainless mannequin.

"Now, whatever happened to that internship with Professor Lessig? She was expecting your call, but yesterday she told me that she had never heard from you. Were you just planning on squandering away your education, sullying my good standing with my academic peer, or both?"

"I told you, Mom, I'm not really interested in an internship right now. I've got a good job. Why do I need to work for free?"

"Because why else would you have studied so hard if not to use it, Lillian? Why else would you have spent four years in an institution if you were just going to play footsie with celebrities? I raised you better than that, sweetheart. I raised you to be a *smart girl.*"

"Well, maybe I don't want to work a desk job, *Mom.*" She's riling me up, but I can't stop myself. "Maybe I want to go out and experience the world while I can! And actually, you guys didn't pay for my college, not really. I still have student loans, and I don't see you helping me pay for those. If you wanted me to have an education so bad, why didn't you pay for the whole thing? I know you could afford it."

"So bad-*ly,*" she corrects me. "And we didn't because we wanted to teach you responsibility, Lillian. Speaking of, are you even making payments toward your student loans? I've gotten a few letters saying that you haven't."

"Well, I plan to get to it at some point," I tell her. "Some of us have to pay to live the life we're living as we're living it! And I'm really happy, Mom. I'm doing exactly what I want right now! I'm only twenty-one years old, and I don't want to be sitting around *learning* anymore. I want to be *living on my own terms!*"

A heavy sigh makes its way up the line from San Diego. I imagine her looking out of the window into the backyard, gazing at the plants that she and my stepfather hired an expensive landscaper to put in. They'd look beautiful this time of the evening, the sunset catching the orange and lemon trees and setting the fruits alight.

"Well, I won't keep you from your night. And you don't have to get so upset. I just wanted to check in on you and make sure you are all right. I'd like to come and visit you soon."

"I know, Mom. Sorry. But don't worry about coming up to LA to see me. I'll come down to you. Soon, I promise." I don't want her coming up and seeing the way I'm living now. Better to visit her on her own turf.

"Okay then. Good night, sweetheart."

"Good night, Mom."

The call ends, and I toss the phone onto the passenger seat. I try to get along with my mom, I really do. She makes it so difficult though when she criticizes every choice I make. I didn't lie when I said I wanted to live my life the way I want to live it. Not always doing what I'm supposed to do like my good little sisters and brother. I know it's hard for my mom and stepdad to understand, both of them being magna cum laude and all, but my idea of a good time isn't to spend it learning about how other people live their lives. I'd rather live and learn about my own life, and have an uninhibited good time while doing it. Period.

*

The next few days, I only see the girls at night on their way out the door, looking stunning as always. Going out in the middle of the week really knocked me out last week, and by the time Friday night rolls around, the girls find me in bed after work, trying to get a nap in before they make me go out with them.

"Get up, lazy bones!" Sidney yells, jumping on me in bed. "Ruby has to leave tomorrow, and she needs to go out with a bang!"

I laugh and try to roll her off of me. "I will. I just got home. I'm just sitting down for a second, I promise. Some of us have to work during the day, asshole. Okay? I have bills to pay. And where are we going anyway?"

"Bills shmills. Awesome! That's my girl! First we're going to Koi, and Bob will give us free sushi if we sit and flirt with him at the bar. Then I told some people that we'd meet them at the hottest fucking club in Hollywood. It's a surprise! They put us on the list. It's a private party tonight, and it's going to be so fabulous! No bridge-and-tunnel crowd tonight. And maybe Skybar after too. Or some other rooftop bar."

"That sounds amazing. I have the perfect little black-lace dress I can wear."

I love Koi; it's always a scene. And Bob, one of the sushi chefs there, is such a sweetheart and always hooks us up with amazing sushi. Plus, Koi is always full of celebrities. You can hardly drive up La Cienega Boulevard to valet your car with all of the traffic that the restaurant causes, and with the crush of paparazzi outside. All the chaos is annoyingly incredible.

We get ready, the girls upstairs and me downstairs in my bathroom.

"Okay, let's rock out with our cocks out!" Sid screams as she and Ruby loudly clomp down the stairs in their heels to find me.

"You don't have a cock!" Collin rebuts, muffled through his closed bedroom door.

"Yes, I do!" Sidney yells. "A big fucking cock!" She sidles into my bathroom and starts grinding into me, which makes it difficult to put on my eyeliner.

"Okay, classy-sassy girl, I'm ready! What are you doing for so long in here?" Sid asks, pushing her ass into me.

I laugh. "I'm ready. I just need some perfume, and we're out."

Sidney grabs a bottle of Chanel Chance from my counter and sprays it above all of our heads, spinning around on her toes to disperse it.

"Okay, you're done; you're gorgeous and fabulous and ready to go!" she says, grabbing my hand. I barely have time to grab my purse before we're out the door and in her car, on the way to Koi.

In the back seat, I gaze out at the glittering lights of Hollywood and think about how different my life is from just a few months ago. I used to stay in most nights with Brody and some takeout. And now my friends are completely different too; they used to be surfers, tattoo artists, dreaded-up skateboarders whose idea of a good time was sitting around a beach bonfire with a joint and a guitar. That was my life just three months ago. And I do miss it. But the tempo of my life has definitely amped up; I feel like I'm living life on overdrive, careening through the fast lane in a sports car, passing the VW bus in the slow lane, and watching it disappear in the rearview mirror. The freedom and fun in Hollywood is consuming me in a different way, and there are no rules other than the ones I try to make for myself. And even those are up for reevaluation on nights like this one.

We pull up to Koi's valet, dodging groups of girls screaming as they run arm in arm across a very busy La Cienega Boulevard to the restaurant. A man in a bow tie steps forward to open Sidney's door, and she dramatically extends a long, tanned leg into the air, slowly lowering it to place her stilettoed foot on the pavement. Girls in line give her the stink eye, and guys look at her like they want to devour her. She struts ahead to the doorman. Ruby and I toddle behind her on our heels, trying to keep up.

"We're on Bob's list," Sidney instructs the stone-faced doorman, telling him her name. He glances down at his clipboard.

"Sorry, you're not here," he says rudely, already looking toward the girls behind us.

"Okay! I'll just run in and tell *Bob*, the guy that happens to be the head sushi chef, that we are here then!" she says brightly, trying to edge past the doorman. He looks like he's about to say no, which I'm hoping does not happen. Sid will unleash hell if he denies her entry. He seems to understand this too. "Okay, you can go in. But come right back out!"

Ruby and I stand awkwardly near the doorman until he makes us back up next to the line while we wait for Sid to come back. It's embarrassing standing here, so Ruby and I turn toward each other and make small talk. Minutes pass, and there's still no sign of Sidney. Finally, a group of guys takes pity on us and tells the doorman that we're with them, and we slip right inside. She must have found Bob and sat down at the sushi bar for a drink with him. Oh well.

One of the guys in the group turns to me. "All right, so now you have to have a drink with me," he says, tilting his head to the side as we walk in.

"Um, sure," I say, glancing at Ruby. She's already walking away, and I call after her.

"I'm going to tell Sid that we're in; have your drink! Then find us," she calls back to me.

I stand at the bar and order a Jack and Coke with the guy who I learn is named Matt. We make polite conversation, but I'm not interested. He's very tall and good looking, but he's the kind of guy you could take home to Mom. Not what I'm looking for right now, if I'm even looking. Which really, I'm not.

I drink my Jack and Coke in two gulps. "Thanks for letting us walk in with you guys, Matt, so sweet of you," I say.

"Anytime. Have fun tonight. Here's my number if you want to meet up later. We're on the list at some cool clubs tonight. My brother lives here and seems to be dialed in everywhere."

I put his number in my phone to be polite and then hug him good-bye. There's nothing really wrong with him. He's sweet, just not my type. I walk away, thinking about how so many people like him come to visit their friends or siblings and are convinced they're going to move to LA too. Of course, if they do, they never make it over the two-year hump, and they wind up moving back home. Now I know why Ruby left me right away; she can sniff out the "BPs" as she calls them. Boring and Poor.

I find the girls at the end of the sushi bar, with a seat at the very end saved for me.

"Hey, slow poke, where've you been?" Sid asks, chopsticks paused on the way to delivering a piece of sushi to her mouth.

"Just trying to be polite," I tell her.

Bob nods at me from behind the counter, and I take a seat, glancing over the menu.

"Hey, cutie!" he calls out to me. "What can I get for you tonight?"

"Whatever you want to make for me is awesome! You know I'll eat anything." I know that it's easiest to let him choose, especially since we're getting it for free. Better to let him be the sushi master chef that he is.

"Okay. Just give me a minute, will ya? We're slammed."

"I'm fine; take your time, Bob-O. Thank you."

Just then, the lead singer of Maroon 5 walks up right next to me and smiles and says hello. I nod back. He's obviously waiting to tell Bob something.

"Hey, Bob!" he calls.

"Yeah…what's up, man?" Bob runs around like a chicken with its head cut off, trying to fill all the orders on the counter.

I can see about twenty tickets from where I'm siting, and the restaurant is only getting louder and crazier.

"You remember my situation, right?" he yells to Bob.

"Yeah, man. I've got it."

"Cool, man, thanks!" He turns and heads back to his table after confirming something with Bob.

"Is that about what he can and can't eat?" I ask Bob.

"Yeah, he's allergic to some fish—I mean, deathly allergic," Bob tells me.

"Geez. That sucks," I say.

I turn back to the girls to find them occupied with some guys who are on the other side of us at the sushi bar. They apparently bought the girls a bottle of Nigori sake, and when I sit down, one of the guys pours some for me and passes it down.

"LJ!" Sidney exclaims, turning to me and introducing me to the guys. They're from Europe, and after we're acquainted, they return to their conversation about partying in Ibiza. When the guys start debating the best club on the island, and who has the bigger yacht, the girls turn back to me.

"So these guys are going to 1 OAK too. I told them we should go with them," Sid tells me.

"Totally! Let's do it," I say, taking the spicy-tuna hand roll in soy paper that Bob hands me and thanking him. These guys seem fun. I wouldn't mind hanging out with them some more.

"Who were those losers at the bar you were talking to?" Sidney asks.

"Sid, they got us in. I just wanted to be nice."

"You're too nice, LJ. I don't know what you're doing sometimes."

"I don't know. I guess I'm old fashioned."

"You're twenty-fucking-one. Chill out! There's plenty of time for that old-fart shit when you're old."

"Being nice to someone is old-fart shit?"

Sidney gives me a look that could melt glass. "You know what I mean, LJ." She turns to Ruby and changes the subject. Whatever. I grab my chopsticks and start in on my sushi. It looks incredible: fresh assorted sashimi, another spicy-tuna hand roll in soy paper, and three kumamoto oysters with uni with black caviar and gold flecks on top. My favorite. I catch Bob's eye and mouth *thank you* and bow my hands in prayer. This is incredible, and I'll be eating it all by myself, unless the girls steal a bite.

I eat slowly and check everyone out in the restaurant while the girls, tossing their hair around, gossip and flirt with the guys.

They are picking at their roll Bob gave them to share but barely eating it. Apparently, they ordered spicy tuna on crispy rice. Everyone eats that here. It's definitely a fan favorite on the menu. The girls didn't come to be impressed by the food anyway.

We finish eating, and Sid gets a text from Sebastian, the guy she's dating, telling her that he's in the back room at Koi and that we should stop by and say hi. We tell the Europeans that we'll be back and head toward the back of the restaurant to find him. Sebastian's there with a bunch of his friends, seated around a large circular table. We chat with everyone for about five minutes when, all of a sudden, a girl at one of the nearby booths stands up and grabs her neck with both hands and starts coughing and clutching her throat harder. She then turns blue and, with tears streaming down her face, looks around frantically for help. A guy that is sitting next to her, who must be her boyfriend, bends her over and starts smacking her back as hard as he can, and everyone in the back room freezes, watching him try to save her. I'm at a loss for what to do; I remember learning the Heimlich maneuver in gym class, but that was ages ago. The music is so loud that the rest of the restaurant doesn't know what is happening. She's going to

75

choke to death right in front of us, and I almost turn away so I don't have to watch, but I'm still frozen.

I feel a rustle behind me as Sidney rushes past and walks straight over to the girl. She shoves her huge football-player boyfriend out of the way, grabs her from behind, and gives her three big Heimlich jolts. A piece of steak goes flying across the room, and the color returns to the girl's face immediately. There's a pause, and then the whole room goes wild. Everyone stands and starts cheering and clapping uncontrollably for Sid, and the girl's boyfriend gives her a hug before tending to his girlfriend, who is now sitting in the booth quietly coughing. Sidney walks back over to us, smiling, but we're all still in shock. Sidney literally just saved someone's life right in front of us.

"Okay! Let's go to 1 OAK!" she says, grinning and slinging her purse over her shoulder, as if nothing happened.

"Sid! That was incredible! You were amazing!" I tell her.

"You just saved that girl's life!" Ruby exclaims

"Yeah, well, no one else was going to do it," she says.

By now, the whole restaurant has taken notice, and someone has started chanting Sidney's name. Soon, the entire restaurant is chanting her name and cheering, but she just motions for them to stop as we make our way to the front door. We wave good-bye to Sebastian, who sits there shocked at his table but slowly waves back. We head back to the sushi bar, and Sid asks Bob how much we owe him, but he waves her away, congratulating her instead on a job well done. We tell the Europeans to meet us at the club, and we walk away as they stumble to tell Sidney what a hero she is. They throw wads of cash on the counter and follow us out, rushing to keep up. Sid grabs my hand and drags me through the crowd, all of them still on their feet and cheering. Everyone watches us leave, wondering where we had to go that could've been so important to leave in such a hurry. The unspoken theme of LA is that if you didn't know, it meant you weren't cool enough to be invited. And Sidney got in everywhere.

We dart out of the restaurant into the cool evening air. It's eleven o'clock. Prime time. The night has taken on a new energy, infused with a sense of meaningfulness. It makes me very thankful to be alive.

After I see the line outside, we realize it'll take another twenty minutes for the valet to get the car. There's a special event at the club. Everyone's going to be there tonight, and we need to be there *now*.

Suddenly, a valet ticket is pressed into my hand, and Sid's running off screaming into the street.

"I'm going with Hanas! Take my car! See you over there!"

A brand-new silver Ferrari pulls up to the curb, and Sid and one of the Euro guys from the bar jump in.

"Meet you there! Ciao, bella," Sidney calls as the valet slams her door—but not before everyone gets a crotch shot of my gone-commando girlfriend—and the car screeches away. Sid screams in ecstasy as the car fishtails up La Cienega, and like that, she's gone.

"She's fucking crazy!" I say to Ruby, but she's not listening. She's working one of the other Euro guys who's standing behind me.

"Um, no way, Ruby. You're riding with me over there. Come on. You can't be serious?"

To her credit, Ruby agrees and bids her guy adieu by blowing him a kiss, and the guys leave to get their car from the valet at Spanish Kitchen down the block.

We get over to the club, and the parking is nuts. The fact that parking is this hard makes me more pissed at Sid, but when we finally manage to find a spot and walk to the front, Sidney's already there waiting with her guy.

"Let's go, gorgeous! Come on," she says, putting her arm through mine and kissing my cheek as she leads us inside. We walk in, and the club is madness, beautiful people everywhere and dim lighting making it hard to see where we're going.

"Let's hit the ladies' room. I have a present," Sid tells Ruby and me. There is that grin again, the grin that means Sidney's about to do something bad. We leave Hanas at the bar and make our way to the bathroom, all three of us filing into a stall. Sid reaches into her purse and pulls out a bag of cocaine.

"It's Hanas's. Isn't he so sweet?" Sid asks, taking a key bump and handing the bag to Ruby.

"Well, he's totally hot—that's for sure," Ruby says, taking her key bump, looking up at the ceiling, and putting a finger over one nostril to sniff, making sure it all gets in. "I love tall, skinny men, and he's got that whole hot European thing going for him."

"And you want to know the best part?" Sid asks, taking the keys and bag from Ruby and making a bump for me. "He's superfucking rich!"

"That's great, Sid, hot and rich, the best combo," Ruby tells her, wiping her nose.

"LJ, you've really got to get over that whole poor-man syndrome you have going on. You can just as well love a rich guy and be spoiled at the same time. And you'd better get it together soon, or you'll end up somewhere in the Midwest with some less-than-average guy with a big beer belly, living in the burbs, and buying a new water heater or knitting socks on your weekends!" I hold one nostril and take the bump that Sidney holds out to me. "You'll figure it out someday. I have faith in you."

"Umm…okay. Thanks, Sid. I'm glad you have hope for me that I'll figure it out. I just want to be in love again someday. Ya know? Real love. And if he happens to be rich or poor, I don't care. But I guess you really do! I get that part. Loud and clear," I say sarcastically, wiping my nose to make sure no white powder remains.

"Oh, I do, LJ. I just love you, honey, and I just want the best for you," Sid says, missing the point.

"Wait, so what happened to Sebastian? I thought you two were soooo in love?" I ask. Ruby snorts another bump and laughs and coughs, her eyes turning red.

"We're just dating!" Sidney snaps, glancing at Ruby and sharing a smirk. "All right then, let's take a few more bumps. Then I'm going to need a Jack to go with my coke," Sid says.

We leave the stall, giddy and ready to burn up the dance floor. The girls take a few lollipops from the bathroom lady while they reapply lip gloss, so I leave her a five-dollar bill for a tip, and then we're out.

We dance all night. The European guys have the VIP table next to Rihanna and her posse, super cool, and it's great to have a place to sit and mingle for a minute. Plus, free drinks all night long. Gift bags from the event are everywhere, so I grab three and hide them under the table for us while Sid and Ruby make out with their foreign guys. I don't mind being the one without a guy tonight; I'm in my own world, smoking it up with a group of cool guys and dancing and mingling with everyone in the place. I love being around tons of people. This is an awesome night!

I end up leaving the girls there and driving the Jetta home by myself. I don't want to watch the sun rise with those guys, partying all night. The third European guy kept trying to make something happen with me, and I just wasn't feeling it, especially after all of the coke. I just wanted to sleep in my own bed, if I could really sleep after tonight's festivities. But after a superlong week at work and this long night and a few joints by the time I got home, I peeled off my dress and jumped right into bed, snuggling under the covers. I fell right to sleep.

*

The next morning, I'm woken up by the ear-piercing ringtone version of "I'm Sexy and I Know It" programmed in my phone by my roomie, which does nothing to help the raging headache pulsing in my temples. I grope the nightstand for my phone and accept the call to make it stop.

"LJ!" I hear yelling and laughter in the background. "LJ, it's Sid. Listen, you've *got* to come up here! You're totally missing out, baby! We're having a hella good time at the beach!"

I check the nightstand; it's only eight in the morning. "Dude, you're crazy. Why are you up so early?"

"Oh, we never went to bed, you silly head! We're in Malibu. You've got to see this house; it's incredible! We watched the sun come up, and now you need to come and meet us because we're going to Geoffrey's for oysters and champagne, and I know Geoffrey's oysters are your favorite, so you've got to just jump in that cute little Jeep of yours and get up here now!"

I've only been asleep for a few hours, and I know it's not enough. I need coconut water, Aleve, and more sleep, and maybe an In-N-Out Double-Double Animal Style burger with fries and a chocolate milk shake to cure me. But it's my day off, and I can't resist the crazed pull of a good time. Or Geoffrey's. Yumm-O.

"Okay, okay, I'll come. Should I just meet you at Geoffrey's? Or what?"

"Yes! Okay, awesome, get your ass out here ASAP. And would you bring Ruby's suitcase? Because she has to go to the airport later. And some new clothes for me too? Thanks, baby!"

She hangs up, and I spring into action. I splash cold water on my face, throw my hair in a top knot, and put on a nice, long, flowing maxi dress, most appropriate for the daytime at the infamous Malibu restaurant. I run up the stairs, and my heart beats quickly, so I catch my breath at the top, but I know it's just because I had too much fun partying last night. I'll get some coffee at Starbucks on the way for an extra boost; that should do the trick.

Rifling through Sidney's closet, I grab an outfit for her and throw it into one of the countless bags hanging from the back of the door. Ruby's clothes are spilling out of her suitcase all over the floor, so I shove them back in, sit on it, and zip the whole thing shut; then I drag the it down the staircase and get yelled at by Collin, who's in his bedroom, that I'm making too much fucking noise. Oops.

I'm out of the door at 8:35; if I hustle, I can make it there by 9:40, and they won't have been waiting for me too long. I drive down Santa Monica Boulevard, stopping at a Starbucks drive-through for a double iced white-chocolate mocha before I jump onto Pacific Coast Highway. If I could, I'd take the streets so I could have more of a scenic view, but I need to get there quickly so that I don't make them wait for me.

I'm on the PCH for twenty minutes, listening to my playlist, when I start to see smoke coming up from under the hood. I check the temperature on my dashboard; the car is overheating. The smoke starts to pick up speed, pluming out, so I pull over onto a patch of dirt and pop the hood.

The smoke billows out, and I have to take a step back to catch my breath. There's a puddle of green liquid under the engine. Coolant. Oh my god, this is not happening. I look around helplessly; I don't know anything about engines, and I don't want to have to call AAA and wait for them to get out here. No one pulls over to help though; they only honk and wave as they drive right by. A car full of guys flies by, yelling and giving me a thumbs-up and laughing. I give them the finger back. "Great, that's nice! Thank you!" I holler.

I grab my phone from the cup holder in the car and call Sidney. They're already at the restaurant, but one of the guys suggests I call the Malibu Union 76 station. I have AAA, so I can ask for a tow to the station and then figure it out from there.

I don't have to wait long for the tow truck, and luckily it's within my free tow mileage. Thank goodness my dad kept me on his AAA account. I could've really been screwed.

When we get to the 76 station, Sid and Hanas are there waiting for me in the Ferrari. I sit on her lap in the front seat and head back to the restaurant with them. I'll handle the car later. All I can think to do now is go to the restaurant and try to enjoy myself. Ugh.

"Oh my god, Sidney, what am I going to do about my car?" I say as we walk into the restaurant.

"Don't worry, LJ. We'll figure it out. Everything will be fine." Sidney squeezes my hand reassuringly and smiles, as if the world's problems can be solved with positive thinking and a smile.

"What about work though? I have work all next week on the movie!" I start to sweat as I think about having to cancel work or renting a car, which I don't have money for.

"It's fine, LJ. Just relax. You can have my car for the next two weeks until you wrap up the film." We sit down, and I try to take a calming breath. "You're here now," she says. "Just chill out and have a drink. And enjoy the breathtaking view that is Geoffrey's Malibu! Indulge in some oysters and champagne, and just live a little, would you!"

She giggles at Hanas, and he smiles back at her. Everyone else is walking in from the parking lot with us as we arrive. They're all glowing as if they're in some commercial for supervitamins. How is it possible that they haven't even slept? They pour me champagne and look at me expectantly as I sip it. It's good, crisp and light, really hitting the spot. And she's not lying about the view: the ocean stretches on as far as the eye can see, the sun glinting off of it and nearly blinding me with its brilliance. I can't help but crack a smile, and they all smile back at me even harder.

"Okay, you're right," I tell Sid. "Thanks for the ride, Hanas; that was really nice of you. And thanks for making me come out here even though things got messed up with my car."

"Babe, your happiness is our happiness! But you screwed up by not coming back here with us last night. Great party," Hanas says, laying his hand over mine. I see Sidney eye it, so I move my hand out from under his to reach for the Gucci bag next to me with her clothes in it.

"Sid, I brought you a sundress, and Ruby, your huge suitcase is barely in Hanas's trunk. He almost left it on the side of the road."

"Thanks, doll!" the girls call over their shoulders, sprinting away to the bathroom to get changed. They leave me alone with the guys, which is slightly awkward since I don't really know them at all. Certainly not as well as the girls got to know them last night, at least. They make small talk with me, but I can tell that they're still buzzing on something. I can tell by their big dark shades and their body language that they're still feeling very sexy too. I know how Sidney parties, and they probably all had sex last night. Well, at least someone got some last night! The boys are definitely beaming with that high pro glow.

After we finish our oysters and caviar, we go back to Hanas's rental, a huge house in an ultraexclusive gated community in Malibu. About ten people are still lingering around from the night before, so we join them on the deck to smoke a few joints and chat for a bit. I have a light beer and walk in the ocean with the girls, where they tell me all about their night. They both hooked up with their guys, and of course, Sidney is in love.

"LJ, you don't understand; Hanas is just so wonderful and rich and his cock is amazingly perfect and fucking *huge!*" Sidney yells over the waves. The wind picks up and blows all of our hair around; I take the hair tie off my wrist to tame it, and Sid lets hers blow free.

Ruby laughs and hooks her arm over her old friend's shoulders. "Yep, that's Sidney for ya. Been like that since high school."

"What about you, Ruby?" I ask. "Are you in love too?"

"Ahhh…no. I'm on vacation!" she yells, throwing her hands up into the sunlight. "Woo-hoooooo!"

We cheer for her, for us, for the heady times we know we have ahead. The girls are positively ecstatic, and I wish I had stayed with them for the whole night. While I slept, they had adventures that they'll remember forever. It's been hard getting over Brody, but I have to learn to take fun opportunities when they're presented to me. Sidney's right; I'm acting like an old lady when I stay in. From now on, I'll follow her lead and leave not even one adventure untaken.

"Yo, girls! Girls!" We look up, and Hanas is waving us over. "Your car is here! Out front."

Sidney turns to us. "Time to make our departure, ladies!"

We jog up the beach to him, and he brings us to the car that he's ordered for us. We say good-bye to everyone while Ruby grabs her suitcase from the Ferrari, and Hanas goes out front to the town car and hands the driver a wad of cash. I thank Hanas for everything and jump into the car, Ruby following me, but Sidney jumps up and wraps her legs around him and plants an intense kiss on him, and they nuzzle noses. Finally, she gets in the car, and he shuts the door for her, and Ruby and I sing, "Awww!" at her.

"I love him!" she squeals.

"We know, honey, we know."

CHAPTER EIGHT

"LAX, ladies! Time to wake up!"

We all wake slowly, disentangling ourselves from the pile we collapsed into on the back seat and rubbing the sleep from our eyes. Apparently, we slept the entire way to the airport from Malibu, and we slept hard. It takes a second to get our bearings, and finally Ruby shakes herself awake enough to grab her purse and meet the driver outside to get her suitcase.

"Bye, Ruby. It was great meeting you! Happy travels home!" I tell her as she stumbles on the sidewalk, trying to balance her purse on her suitcase.

"It was great meeting you too. I had a blast! You girls take care of each other, talk to you soon! Bye!"

She ruffles her dark hair and tugs her suitcase behind her, turning once to wave good-bye to us. The only sleep she's gotten is what we were able to get in the car, yet she still manages to catch the eye of everyone she passes before she goes inside.

"Bye, sexy lady!" Sidney calls out of the open window and then gives me a big squeeze and falls back down on my lap.

"Onward, driver!" she says in delirium, throwing her pointed finger in the air.

He catches my eye with his in the rearview mirror. "Thank you," I tell him, hoping he's not offended.

We get home, and Sidney goes upstairs right away to crash. I go to my room, change into sweats, and call my mom. We didn't end things on the best of terms the last time we spoke; she hurt my feelings, but I'm putting that aside. Luckily, she's more understanding than I would've expected; she tells me not to worry about my car, that my stepfather was planning on getting a new car anyway, and that I can have his old work car for five thousand dollars, a loan I would have to pay back. Ugh. More debt.

*

The next day, Sid and I head out for manicures.

"Gorgeous, where did you get that watch?" she asks as we approach a stoplight.

Sidney takes her eyes off of the road to inspect my wrist. I had gone through the gift bags I grabbed from 1 OAK last night; we actually got some pretty good stuff in there. I tell Sid as much, and her eyes widen.

"What? Where's mine?" she asks, brows furrowed.

"Down in my room. And Ruby's too. I forgot to bring it up yesterday morning. We'll have to ship hers to her or something."

She relaxes. "Oh, that's so seriously dope of you. What else did we get?"

"Some good makeup, Too Faced blush and NARS lip pencils and stuff like that, some Dior perfume, some other skin stuff. Kiehl's, I think. Oh, and a Kylie lipstick kit! There was a granola bar and some energy powders, aviators, and then some cool silver dog tags and some nice gold crescent-moon earrings. I didn't really look too closely at anything. I stopped at the big black box when I saw it said 'Toy Watch' on it."

"Well, I like it. I hope mine is the same. If not, you have to give me yours. I invited you to the party, so technically it's mine anyway."

"What? No way!" I tell her, instinctively pulling my wrist close. "You can have Ruby's bag; maybe there's another one like this in there."

"Oh relax, hot stuff, I'm only joking," Sidney says, swatting me. I know she is, but on another level, I wouldn't put it past her to steal it. Sid always takes what she wants. Even from me.

We spend the rest of the day getting our nails done and stopping at the Coffee Bean to grab a drink and sit outside. It's not my favorite place for coffee; all the drinks taste grainy because they use powders to flavor them, but Sidney wants to sit and be seen on the patio. She tosses her hair and scopes out the guys, texting incessantly and taking a few selfies on her phone as she follows me to a table. I honestly don't know how she does it; it's just so much effort to keep up with that many people.

She glances up once to let me know that her friend Sawyer is going to join us and then goes right back to posting pics on her phone.

"Isn't that the guy who dated Jessica Biel?"

"Was. You remember that we used to fuck too, right?"

"Right, right, but you left him for—"

"That one rich guy with the boat. Donovan. But Sawyer's become a really big star since dating Jess. I think that's why he did it. Dated her, I mean. Now he's getting all these big roles and stuff."

I couldn't imagine dating someone just for the fame, but I guess I shouldn't be surprised. In this town, anything goes. And people will do seriously anything or anyone to get ahead in the industry. Sidney texts up a storm while I sip my coffee, staring at my new pedicure. I chose the cutest red pink; it looks like I have cute little strawberry toes.

Sidney continues to type madly even when Sawyer arrives. Then she sticks her phone down her shirt because Sebastian's always asking her to "send him some nudes." We stand and give hugs and kisses, but he doesn't stay long after he gets his coffee since he has some casting to go to for some superhero part or something.

Part of me wonders why he even bothered to stop by at all, but then I remember how making an appearance can be just as important as having a true conversation. Everything is about getting on people's radar to stay relevant, to keep an agent, and to keep fresh friends. And staying in the know on the who's who and the what's what—if you're not at the forefront of everyone's minds, you might as well be dead. You never want to be telling people that you "can't even get arrested in this town."

Sidney, true to her word, lets me borrow her car for work the next week. She's gone to Hanas's beach house to party and work on her tan for the week anyway, so she hardly notices its absence. Either way, it's cool of her to let me borrow it.

My mom calls me halfway through the week to let me know that my stepdad did end up getting a new car, so I can come down whenever to pick up his old one. I know Sid won't want to give up her weekend to drive me to San Diego, so I go through my mental catalog of friends who might be down to road trip this weekend. Ever since breaking up with Brody, I haven't kept up with any of the friends we shared, even though I know that they'd love to see me. And I'd love to see them too, but it still hurts too much. So I haven't reached out.

I guess it's that I sort of want a clean break from my old life. It's refreshing to have only a few things that remind me of Brody instead of memories flooding my daily life, and I want to keep it that way. So instead of calling an old friend from Long

Beach, I shoot Naomi a text, telling her that I miss her and asking her if she'd like to come down to San Diego with me for the weekend for some fun in the sun. She agrees right away; that's one of the reasons she's so great—she's always down for an adventure.

Naomi knocks on the door Friday night just after I get home from work, as planned. Sidney answers our front door in her red bra and thong, as always.

"LJ, it's for you!" she calls, giving Naomi a tight smile.

"Thanks! Send her back here!" I call from my room. I poke my head out of my room to motion Naomi over, but she doesn't come right away.

"Hey, I actually think we've met on a modeling job before. You're with Elite, right?" Naomi asks Sidney.

"Yes…I am," Sid answers, cocking her head to the side.

"Oh yeah, I remember. That John Varvatos shoot with that other guy, right? Or was it Prada?"

"Yep, Prada. That's the one. Good to see you again."

"Yeah, you too. Listen, I need to finish getting ready, you good?"

"Yeah, girl! I'm good. I'll head back to LJ's room."

Sidney looks confused about the conversation and then turns to head upstairs.

"Hey, girl!" Naomi says, giving me a hug.

"I'm so excited for our trip!" I tell her. "Thank you so much for driving me to my mom's down south last minute!"

"C'mon, LJ, you know I'm always ready. You know how I roll!" Naomi snaps her fingers and dances a little, and I laugh. "Okay, but I have to ask," she says. "Why are you living with old red nose?"

"Who? Sidney? Why do you call her that?" I go back to looking for jeans to pack, but I'm intrigued and still listening.

Naomi laughs. "Uh, because that girl has a reputation. And it's not a good one! You had better not let it rub off on you."

I sit on my bed and give Naomi a look. I'm slightly offended that she's insulting my best friend, but I also don't think Naomi would say something if she wasn't trying to protect me.

"Naomi, tell me exactly what you've heard," I tell her.

"I'm talking about men, women, money, sex, drugs. And a whole lot of crazy! Seriously, she's *known* around town. If you're hanging out with her all the time, you might start to get the same reputation. I'd really watch it if I were you."

"It's okay. I know her really well. She just likes having a good time. It's harmless."

Naomi sighs. "Girl. Please. I know you know how to take care of yourself. But, I've lived here my whole life. You've got a light inside you that most people out here don't have. You've got a bright, honest energy, girl. And a good heart! And don't you let anyone take that away from you, because if you let them, they will. They see it too, and they'll hold you down and keep trying to take it for themselves. These people, LJ, they're vampires. They'll suck out all your goodness until all that's left is an empty shell. I'm for real! And all the drinking and drugs just brings you down more!"

I take all of this in, but I also can't forget that Naomi doesn't know Sidney the way I know her. She doesn't know how Sidney took me under her wing after the breakup, how she let me use her car when I was desperate. How she adds excitement to my life when otherwise I would be alone. She's my family, and I can't just discount that because someone tells me otherwise.

"I get what you're saying, Naomi, I really do, and thank you for thinking enough of me to put all of that out there. I can see the bad stuff too. I really can. But I can make good judgments for myself, and I know where to draw the line. I know Sidney is wild, but I need that right now. It feels so good to go a little nuts!"

"See? That's how they get you!" Naomi laughs. "They make you feel so good that you can't tell that you're dancing with the devil!" She shakes her head. "Okay, girl. I warned you. We'll see if you can cut through the crazy and keep pushin' past them while they're sucking you bone dry. We. Will. See?"

"That's why you're here," I tell her, giving her a big squeeze. "You're my angel here to protect me from all the bad people. So, see? I'm not worried. So don't you worry about me, okay. It's all good, darling! I got this."

"Okay, girl. Okay. We will see."

I finally find a good pair of jeans in my closet and throw them into my duffel, and we hit the road and put Hollywood in our rearview mirror.

CHAPTER NINE

It's almost eleven in the evening when we get to my mom's house in Carlsbad, northern San Diego. My mom and stepdad aren't home; they went to dinner in Del Mar and said that they would meet us after. I jump out of the car to punch in the code for the gate so that we can drive in, and once the gate opens, Naomi drives her car into the circle path to the front of the house.

"Wow, this place is really nice," Naomi says, craning her neck to look up through the windshield.

"Yeah, it's cool, thanks. I didn't grow up here, unfortunately. Isn't it stupid when your parents save the cool houses for after you move out?"

Naomi laughs. "Girl, you told me you grew up with horses in your backyard. I think you've always had the cool house. Okay!"

She's got me there, having horses is pretty cool, I guess. When my parents got divorced, I mostly lived with my mom and siblings in her parents' basement. Granted, it was a very nice basement in a gorgeous house, but it wasn't an ideal living situation. My mom yelled a lot, mostly about my dad being a bastard, which was to be expected since she was twenty-five years old and left with little kids, no child support, and grad school expenses. What wasn't expected was when she would direct that anger toward me and my siblings and tell us she wished she'd never had us. Then, the belt would come out. On me only. I still feel like a burden.

I shake my head and try to push those memories out of my head. It doesn't do anyone any good to bring them up now. I use my spare key to get into the place and show Naomi to her room, and we both change into pajamas to chill. By the time my mom and my stepdad get home, Naomi and I are in front of the TV in the living room with glasses of white wine, happy to relax after our road trip. My mom comes in and kisses the top of my head and introduces herself to Naomi. She gets a glass of wine and joins us in the living room while my stepdad goes upstairs to get ready for bed.

"That's so sweet of you to bring Lillian down to see us, Naomi. I'm so glad she's got some real girlfriends up there."

"Oh, no worries at all, Mrs. Adams. It's nice to get away from LA every now and then. And LJ and I have become really good friends. It's great to have her in my life. She's real, and it's so rare to be around real honest, good people that want you to do well too."

"Oh, so you're from LA originally then." My mom laughs.

Naomi laughs too. "Yes. It's my hometown. My parents live in Silver Lake. But yeah, LA."

I'm thankful for Naomi. She's keeping my mom on her best behavior. If not for her, my mom would definitely be continuing our last conversation about my "lack of intellectual ambition."

"So are you girls celebrating something?" My mother motions to Naomi's wine glass, which is bubbling.

"No, just life!" Naomi laughs again. "I like to add a splash of Sprite or 7Up to my white wine. I know it's not the best wine manners, but it makes it just sweet enough."

"Oh that's...different. You've adapted your own etiquette. It's quite inventive." Great. My mom is getting judgmental again. I knew it was only a matter of time.

"Yeah, well I don't actually drink that much. I guess I'm just not that used to the bitter taste. I need it to be sweet."

My mother's face instantly relaxes. "You know, that's such a relief to hear, Naomi. Here I was thinking that everyone in LA was a hedonistic party person!"

"Most of them are. But no, not me. I mostly just hang out with my feisty boyfriend when I'm not working. I'm definitely not into the club scene."

"Well, that's really the right choice. I'm so glad Lillian's got you to keep her on track."

"Okay, guys, I'm right here you know," I say, laughing. "I can take care of myself. Give me some credit, will ya?"

"I know, I know," my mom says, getting up from the couch. "Okay, you two have fun. I'm off to bed. I've got to get up early tomorrow to get some research done. Naomi, please make yourself at home. I'll see you girls in the morning."

When she leaves, Naomi turns to me. "I like your mom a lot, LJ. What is she researching?"

"She's a nuclear engineer, specializing in energy and radiation systems used to derive benefits for other systems around the world. Her IQ is off the charts. She's basically a genius."

Naomi nods and takes a sip of her sparkling wine. "Wow. That's impressive. You know, I don't think she liked what I did to her good white wine."

"Oh, she loves you; don't worry about it. She is kind of snooty though. You're not wrong about that. She's actually kind of pissed at me for not doing something intellectually stimulating. Everyone on this side of the family has their masters degree or PhD. I'm the black sheep with a BA that I don't use. She's pissed that I'm choosing to figure shit out for myself, but I've always moved to the beat of my own drum. It's more fun that way. People are too damn politically correct and follow too many rules these days, and it drives me crazy. I like to make jokes! I hate having rules! I just have to do my own thing. You know!"

"Hey, don't be so hard on yourself, LJ. You're a great person, and that's all that should matter. And she can't be all that bad, girl; they're giving you a car, right! Okay. My family's never given me anything. Actually, my mom makes me give her my paychecks from modeling to pay her rent for her and my two sisters and brother."

"What?! Why do you do that? I could never imagine giving money to my mom. It's supposed to be the other way around. And I have to pay them back for the car!"

"Awww, girl, she can't help it that she has health issues, and she's my family. And if she needs the money, I'll give it to her."

"Yeah, but you still shouldn't let her take advantage of you like that. It's your life, and you should be able to use your money the way you want."

"I do. Don't you worry about me. That's my job. Remember?"

We laugh, and I can tell that we just understand each other. My mom may drive me crazy, but she is right about one thing: I'm lucky to have a friend like Naomi.

*

The next day, Naomi and I just relax around the house. My mom woke up early and got us ham-and-cheese croissants and bear claws from down the street, which we pick at by the pool in the backyard. Around three, Naomi tells me that she has to get it together for a shoot she has with Adriano Goldschmied jeans tomorrow and that she should head out soon. After she gets showered and packed up, I walk her out to her car and thank her again for driving me down. We hug and I send her off; I'll stay another day and drive my new car back tomorrow.

My mom invites me to go shopping with her at the Carlsbad Outlets before I leave the next day. We head out early on Sunday and pick over the clothes at Barneys and the cashmere outlet, coffees in hand.

"So…have you seen Brody since you moved out?" she asks, holding a turquoise cashmere turtleneck up to me.

"No, not at all," I tell her. "And really it's better this way. I'm doing really well now; it's just going to take some time to get myself completely back to were I need to be emotionally. But I'm getting there, and my friends are helping."

"Sure, sure. It's such a shame what happened. I am so sorry you had to go through that, honey." She puts her hand on my shoulder, and I welcome the touch. It almost makes me want to cry, but I manage to barely hold it together.

"Thanks, Mom. I know you liked him a lot. I'm still so brokenhearted." And I let a few tears fall.

"Well, not as much as I like you." She smiles at me and then buys me the cashmere sweater that I know I won't be able to wear anytime soon in LA with the Santa Ana winds kicking up.

Mom and Ron walk me out to the Ford Taurus that afternoon and send me off after I thank them for saving me with the car. They stand in front of the house and wave to me until I can't see them anymore, and at once, I feel happy and at peace, especially knowing my new payments for the car kick in a month from now. Thanks for the one free month, Mom. Geez.

*

I race back up the highway toward Hollywood with a newfound sense of freedom. I love this feeling, this escape from the suburbs, a mad dash toward the life I want to live instead of the one that's comfortable. It was great to be home, but I can't wait to get back to the craziness that is my real life.

I pull up to a dark house at 11:30 p.m. While I was driving, Sidney called and asked me to meet her at Skybar on Sunset, and although I'm still stuffed from dinner at my mom's, I drop my bags inside my room and rush to get changed into an outfit that will hide my awesome dinner belly. A little black dress will do the trick.

I pull the silver Ford Taurus up to the valet and get some strange looks from the assholes waiting outside for their hot cars. I get out, put my head up and shoulders back, and act like I've got the hottest car in the place. I'm so absolutely happy to have a car at all that nothing is getting me down tonight.

Sidney's waiting for me at the bar at Asia de Cuba, surrounded by men as usual. On the phone, she said that she met some hot young media executives that I just have to meet. As I walk up, I have to say she was right.

"Hey, sexy lady! Guys, this is LJ. The most gorgeous girl in town. Isn't she fucking beautiful?" She plants a big smooch right on my cheek.

The guys check me out and give me their approval as I smile and wipe pink lipstick off my face. She introduces me to the guys, Zane and Cooper, and tells me that they were waiting for me before going next door to Skybar to dance. The guys turn to pay for the drinks, and Sid whispers in my ear that Zane is my guy for the night. I laugh and nod my head. She treats guys like such possessions; it's hilarious. But I guess that guys do the same to us girls all the time—might as well do it to them, right?

We arrive at Skybar and make our way through the crowd to find a spot by the pool. I love the view of Hollywood from this deck; it's so serene. The boys leave to get us drinks, and I chat with Sidney while we wait for them.

"So your weekend was good?" I ask her. She seems distracted, glancing around the pool and assessing who's there.

"Yeah, good," she says. "Crazy. I did so much coke; I think I'm going to be up for three weeks. You got the new car okay?"

"Yep, it's great. I'm so glad to have a good car that won't break down on me. And home was fine, quiet of course, but good to see my mom and stepdad."

"Oh, I'm sure it was quiet, especially since you brought that one girl with you."

It takes me a second to realize that she's technically insulting Naomi, but before I can say anything, she's turning to a group of guys and taking a hit off their joint.

"Thanks, guys!" she says, batting her lashes. "Mind if my friend here takes a hit too?"

They nod, their eyes glued to Sidney's body. She gives them a coy smile and hands the joint off to me. I breathe in deeply, filling my lungs. This is some high-quality shit. I breathe out, coughing a few times, and then hand them the joint.

Sid turns back to me. "So I'm going to New York next weekend. And you're coming with me."

"I am?" I ask her. My head is already swimming from the giant hit I just took, and I start to sway with the beat of the music.

"Yeah. I already bought you a ticket on JetBlue with me. You're coming! I've got it all planned out. We'll have Jona or someone from the house drive us Friday night to the airport, and we'll come home Sunday late. Have you ever been to New York City?"

I'm shocked, but in a way, I shouldn't be. Of everyone I know, Sidney is the person who *would* buy me a plane ticket and whisk me away at the last minute. She may be crazy, but you can't say she's not fun.

"Um, I went once with my dad when I was a teenager. And that's so nice of you to buy me a ticket. I'm totally in. Is this just a spur-of-the-moment thing, or are you going for a reason?"

She gives me a look out of the corner of her eye. "You know why I'm going, LJ."

I flash back to a girl in a pink jumpsuit with a monkey, telling us about the high-class prostitution position that's ready to be filled.

"You're not seriously considering that, are you, Sid?"

She looks at me, her eyes as serious as I've seen them.

"What do you think?"

CHAPTER TEN

I can't believe Sid is going to be an escort. I knew she was fearless, but this just throws me.

"I thought you said you wouldn't."

"I said I'd *wait*. I'm tired of these credit card bills. I'm swimming in debt. I'm totally doing it…if Alexandra likes me. And you should too!"

Me? I want to snort a laugh. I couldn't do that!

"Sidney, I—"

"Good god, LJ! Spare me your good-girl drama bullshit, please! Listen. If you're too chickenshit, that's fine with me. We'll just explore New York together; it'll be fun! It's beautiful around the holidays. We can go see the big Christmas tree and ice-skate at Rockefeller Center and get some warm Nuts4Nuts."

"But, Sid…" A million thoughts swirl in my mind. She could get arrested for doing that. She could get hurt. She'd be…a hooker? I mean, was she really considering it? "It could be dangerous. It could be…" Bad for you, I want to say, but don't.

"LJ." Sid turns to me, voice low. "I *need* to do this. I need the money, and I think…I mean, I think it could be fun too"— she squeezes my shoulder—"don't be scared. I know what I'm doing. It's just me, your best friend. I love you. Go dance! We can talk more about this at home later. And come back over to the boys with me in a bit at the table, or Zane will be very, very sad that you left."

"Okay, will do, Sid." I smile and give her a hug. She really is a good person, and I know no one can stop her once she's made up her mind about something. Even me. I pause. Does anyone ever listen to the advice they are given? Hmm.

I wander around the deck, looking at the crowd standing in the twinkling lights. Could they resist the pull? Or was everyone here okay with selling themselves, for movie parts, for relationships, or for Birkin bags and a house in the hills? Why do I feel like the only one second-guessing it? No one else seems to even bat an eyelash.

I rest my hands on the edge of the deck, light a smoke, and stare out at Hollywood. I feel weird, like I don't belong. Or is this where I do belong, with all the artists and misfits? I've felt like I don't belong for most of my life. Even growing up in St. Louis, I just wanted to see the world, to experience everything I could. I never wanted to settle like my friends back home, who all have serious boyfriends and are thinking about marriage at twenty-two. They're going to live and die on the same street, the thought of which suffocates me. Someone back home once told me that our state had the most cradle-to-grave population than any other state. I was blown away.

Was I supposed to be proud of that statistic?

At least I got out of there when I did, but I'm not sure I'm really exploring the world like I want to. I've been in California for a while now. And I've seen all of the SoCal life. Sidney really brings me out of my shell and encourages the adventurous life that I've always wanted. And it just feels right.

*

I spend Friday morning packing for New York. I don't think I can talk Sid out of it, and she's completely backed off from trying to convince me to do it too. I keep hoping she'll just change her mind.

Part of me thinks she might not go through with it when we get there.

Before I know it, Sidney and I are riding with our roommate Collin to the airport, backpacks filled with gloves, wool socks, and warm jackets that are usually in the back of our California closets. We make it to our plane by the skin of our teeth, and the second we sit down, we ask for champagne from the passing flight attendant. Sidney got us first-class tickets, so the flight attendant promptly brings us the champs, and we order a second round, followed by a third.

Shortly after the plane takes off, Sid pulls out a Kiehl's face mask, and we tipsily smear the gooey blue masks on each other's faces, giggling and singing a Taylor Swift song loudly the entire time. We certainly have no fans in our section. After ten drinks, about an hour goes by, and we take turns washing them off our faces in the small airplane bathroom. Sidney spread blue droplets all over the counter, so I wiped up her mess before going back to my spacious leather seat and passing out.

Flying over New York City, I'm struck by the sheer amount of light emanating from Manhattan. The night is filled with the glowing spires of colossal buildings and skyscrapers, all of them competing for space on one tiny island. The city looks full of life and intoxicating. I feel like, if I were to open my little plane window, the sound of jazz trumpets, the smell of amazing food, the extraordinary art and fashion, fast taxi cabs, and lively debates on the street would fill the plane up with an East Coast vibe.

We land at JFK and take a cab into Manhattan. We're staying with a friend of Sidney's who lives downtown. He's a very well-known graffiti pop artist named Jonny Church. He not only has countless paintings in museums around the world, and displayed on many collectors' walls, but he apparently also did a famous painting on the Berlin Wall. I feel lucky that we're staying with such a fascinating artist and that my reintroduction to New York City as an adult is one filled with culture and hip downtown energy.

We arrive at his building and take the elevator up to the top. The doors open to a giant loft; twenty-foot-high ceilings give way to at least two dozen enormous windows in a basketball-court-sized living room. A large easel stands near the windows, and from behind it comes a man to greet us.

"Sidney! You're looking amazing, as always, sweetheart. It's been too long, my dear. Way too long. And this must be your friend?"

Sidney and Jonny embrace, and she introduces me. Jonny is the consummate host, offering us espresso and cookies after our long flight. He brings us to the guest room, explaining that he's just repainted it a light-violet color named songbird, and we drop our bags with relief. Sidney immediately goes into the adjoining bathroom, strips down, and begins to fill the Jacuzzi tub with warm water. I follow Jonny back into the living room, not keen on watching Sid bathe. I perch on the arm of a sofa with my espresso. It's nice to be staying in a private home, and I tell Jonny as much.

"Oh, of course, LJ, it's my pleasure to have you girls. I'm always here painting. I love having friends over to keep me company. Especially ones as magnificent as you and Sidney."

I walk over to his easel. "Do you mind if I peek?"

"Be my guest."

His painting is heart stopping, a mix of bright, happy colors, swirling and abstract. It's pleasant at first glance, but there's something dark beneath its layers. Faces. Very thought provoking. I tell Jonny this, and he smiles.

"You've got a good eye, LJ. Very insightful."

"Well, you're the artist here, Jonny. It's just my interpretation. I'd say you are the one with the eye."

He looks me in the face, and I feel the artist's gaze searching deeper than the surface.

"No, you're an artist too. I can see it in your eyes. Figuring out a way to express your pain," he says. "Just an artist of a different medium. You see things differently. You can look past where other humans stop. Seeking simple beauty and love. Or is it self-destruction and chaos? Or both? Don't tell me you don't know this about yourself."

"I guess you're right. I guess that's why I'm here in New York." I sip my coffee, at a loss for what to say. "Well, I guess I'll go get settled in our room and leave you to your painting. Thanks again, Jonny."

"No problem at all, LJ. Help yourself to anything. Or come back out to talk. I'm always here."

"Okay! Thanks."

I walk into the bathroom where Sidney is relaxing in the tub, hair knotted at the top of her head and eyes closed.

"Hey, Sid, I kind of think Jonny was just hitting on me."

She lets out a short simple laugh. "No way, silly. Jonny Church loves having beautiful women around, but he never touches. Well, hardly ever. I think he has a girlfriend or a boyfriend, or two of each that he really likes? I can never keep up with that man's sexcapades. If you live in New York for as long as he has, I think you just turn into a freak. Freak nasty, I mean."

I laugh too. It makes staying here a lot less complicated and awkward.

A delicate gray cat with a sweet, little meow and tiny white paws prowls her way into the bathroom, and I reach down to scratch her between her ears. "All right, Sid, so we're here; now what's the plan?"

She finally opens her eyes, excitement gleaming in them. "Let's just walk around the city and see where we end up. It's early still; nothing's going to get started until at least eleven tonight."

I wince at the idea at going out so late after a long flight. I can barely keep up with her. We primp and change into our dancing gear and then head into the living room for our coats. Jonny's at his easel again, a line of concentration furrowed between his brows. He's a machine.

"Okay, handsome, we're out," Sidney tells him with a flourish.

"Us intrepid city explorers are venturing out and seeing where the night takes us," I add.

"Sounds very exciting, ladies!" he says. "If you're hungry, go down Prince all the way to Elizabeth Street. There's this great little place called Café Habana. Get the grilled corn and the Cuban sandwich; you won't regret it. See you later, girls. The door's always open. I'll be up late."

Walking down the crowded streets of downtown Manhattan on a Friday night is something magical. The twists and turns of the streets keeps me glancing around corners for the next surprise, be it a cool store or a couple kissing against a wall or a woman getting out of her town car dressed head to toe in fur for her night out. Los Angeles is still such a new town; it's surprising to see a city laid out not by city planners but by fur traders and Native Americans. I do remember a few fun facts from my history class.

It's surprisingly cold out for November, so we take refuge in Café Habana and sit at the bar to enjoy our orange Hornitos sodas and an order of grilled corn each. Jonny's right; it's the best damn corn on the cob I've ever had, grilled and spread with mayo, cilantro, cayenne pepper, lime wedges, and Cotija cheese. The warm corn bursts in our mouths, gets stuck in our teeth, and brings smiles and some life to our cold, wintered lips.

Walking back outside, we're met with a burst of cold wind that flaps our jacket hoods and makes us cling to each other for warmth. We've been California girls for a while now and are in no way prepared for this nor'easter. Deciding we've had enough freezing weather for one night, we head back to Jonny's at midnight, and we are stopped on the street by an unassuming actress on a random corner and asked if we are interested in keeping her brother company that night. She said she would pay us too. I shouted *no* while Sidney shouted *yes* at the same time. And I just started walking away toward Jonny's house by myself. Sidney ran after me, of course, and swore it was no big deal. And I did find it kind of funny, and a little flattering, that an actress from a show I loved asked us such a direct question. Random. Do we look like call girls? Maybe it was a sign I was supposed to do it? When we walked in the door at Jonny's, we found him still awake and painting, just as we left him, but working on a new piece, having finished the one he was working on when we left.

Sidney makes us fruity vodka drinks while I make my way around the apartment, looking at all of his unbelievable works of art. I ask about his paintings, and he tells me that many of them will be shipped off to Europe. He makes more of a commission by selling them there, he tells me. He's been living in this apartment for over thirty years, and he goes on about how much the city's changed, some for the better, some for the worse. I scratch his playful purring cat, Mr. Hamilton, behind the ears while I listen, and he continues to paint broad brushstrokes against the canvas, transforming it into a wonder of fantastically bright colors and precisely trippy faces.

Even though we're still on West Coast time, and it's only nine o'clock our time, Sidney and I are exhausted from our flight. We bid Jonny good night and snuggle in the queen-sized bed together, cozy and warm in our New York City abode.

CHAPTER ELEVEN

The new-morning sun streams through the room at 7:00 a.m., highlighting the violet walls, the white dresser, and the brunette girl rifling through our suitcases.

I sit up straight in bed. "Um, excuse me, who are you?"

"Oh hi," she says, barely tearing her eyes away from my suitcase to glance up at me. "I can't find my dress." She throws my clothes all over the room, and a pair of my underwear hooks itself on the footboard.

"Can you please not go through my stuff?!" She seems strung out on something; her movement is sporadic, and she can't make eye contact with me because she's twitching so badly. She is wearing a tight bandage dress and probably hasn't gone to bed after her night out.

"Sid!" I give her a hard push to wake her.

"What..." she says, rolling over.

"Wake up, there's someone in here!" Sidney sits up just as the girl walks out the bedroom door.

"Who was that?" she asks.

"I don't know. I just woke up, and she was going through our stuff! She said she was looking for her dress or something."

"That's too weird. Okay, let's go back to sleep now; she's gone." Sid drops back down onto her pillow and starts snoring right away. I'm awake though, so I check my clothes to make sure nothing's gone. Everything seems to be in place; even our makeup and jewelry in the bathroom looks fine, so I grab a white robe hanging on a hook and go into the living room. I immediately smell espresso, and the scent alone makes me more awake.

"Good morning, LJ! How'd you sleep?" Jonny calls from behind his easel. He's still painting and smoking in the same spot. I wonder how long he slept, or if he even slept at all. "There's cappuccino or espresso, or you can make regular coffee or tea if you'd like. It's all there."

"Thank you!" I head to the kitchen and make a cappuccino with some bodacious foam and then walk over to see his new painting. "Wow, I love this one! It's insane. Hey, can I bum a cigarette?"

"Sure, I think I left the lighter in the kitchen though."

"Thanks, I'll grab it. Hey, who in the world was that girl who came in our room this morning?"

Jonny's face clouds over. "That was Harley. She's a mess. Doing hard drugs, not sleeping or eating. She's lost it. I just can't do it anymore."

"Did the two of you date or something?"

"No, she just stayed here for a while in your room. I told her she could come up one last time to find her dress, but I'm done with it. I like to have young models come stay with me. I get to keep the great company of beautiful girls all the time—what guy wouldn't like that? But sometimes you girls get into so much trouble. And I can't be responsible for that. And that's when you're no longer welcome in my home. I tried to help, but there's only so much I can do. She's stolen from me and ruined a few of my paintings."

"Oh, god! Sure, Jonny, I understand completely. No need to explain. That's got to be hard if she was initially your friend. She scared the hell out of me though! She was all erratic and shaky, throwing clothes everywhere, and she never once looked at me. She's scary. I completely understand why you wouldn't want someone like that staying with you."

"Hey, everyone's got demons to deal with. And I tried to help her as long as I could. And, yeah, sorry if she scared you. I did tell her to be quiet and not to wake you girls. I shouldn't have even let her up."

"It's okay. I just hope she'll be all right."

Jonny pick up his paintbrush and shrugs. "Yeah, me too," he says as he exhales a stream of smoke.

I sit and watch him paint and then watch a little TV and read a few art magazines before waking Sidney around ten. She finally gets up and has coffee, and we lounge around the apartment for a few hours. I know New York is famous for its small apartments; it's funny that my first experience staying in one is essentially like the top floor a warehouse. Huge.

Jonny announces that he's taking us to lunch at Balthazar, so we all go to our rooms to get showered and changed. We walk to the restaurant—it's lovely that New Yorkers don't have to deal with cars, parking, or traffic. How nice it must be to just walk everywhere and know that infinite possibilities are just outside your front door.

Before we arrive, Jonny tells us that he's invited a few friends to join us, and walking in, we're greeted by five girls waiting in a corner booth near a window. They're all stunningly gorgeous and in their early twenties, as I'm learning is typical for Jonny's friends. Sidney gives hugs and introduces me to each of them, as she's met a few of them on her previous trips to New York.

We all chat and drink bottles of champagne and eat from an enormous three-tiered seafood tower. What starts as a simple lunch turns into an amazing five-hour extravaganza of booze and food, after which we give hugs good-bye and stumble out into the weak winter sunshine. Sidney tells everyone that we have to leave for an appointment, and I know exactly where this appointment is taking us.

Sid says we have time to kill, so we take the subway and then walk for a bit. I buy sunglasses on the street and a cute winter hat. We stick out like sore thumbs walking in the city; in a city where everyone wears chic black, we're both wearing bright puffer coats. She glances at her watch and pulls me onto a street of swanky brownstones. It's time.

As we walk down the tree-lined street, I notice that each set of steps in front of the buildings has a pair of girls sitting on each perch, about twenty girls in all, lining the whole street, as if they all had appointments and were waiting for their turn. We walk down the street, and the girls' eyes follow us. I can feel their eyes on my body, and I suddenly feel even more self-conscious in my out-of-place coat. Sidney finally turns to walk up a set of stairs, and I follow behind her. She presses the intercom and gives her name, and we're buzzed in.

Walking in, I can barely see the apartment; it's so blacked out and smoky. The blinds are drawn, and the air feels heavy and stale, perfumed in an ill-conceived attempt to mask the smell of stagnate cigarette smoke. Once my eyes adjust, I see three older women with frizzy hair, working on thin laptops and answering phones but speaking so quietly that I can't make out the conversations. It looks like an illegal call center, and with a jolt, I realize that that's exactly what it is. I nod and smile when the lady by the window makes eye contact with me and then looks me over.

A woman comes from a back room, dressed in a tight purple velvet dress with her hair piled on top of her head. She's wearing a few layers of makeup and fake lashes, and when she draws near, the perfume from the room gets stronger. It's her perfume that permeates the room, and with that I grasp that this is her call center, her organization. She is the madame.

Kissing Sidney on both cheeks and then turning for me, she introduces herself as Alexandra. She's clearly not American; her accent tilts and sways as much as she does on her stilettos. Russian, perhaps.

"Sidney, I'm so, so glad you were able to make the journey here to New York City. You're just as beautiful as your photographs—so beautiful in fact that I already have a call lined up for you tonight."

Her long, red dagger-like nails dig into Sidney's shoulder as she gives her a pink slip of paper with the information. "Everything after this will be handled via text, as we discussed. No specifics of course—anonymity is quite imperative to me. Just attend your date, be your beautiful self, and mail me my allowances afterward. Money order preferred. Three hundred dollars for an hour. You keep the rest. And have fun! We're all in this for the good time, aren't we?"

She winks at me over her shoulder. Sidney grasps the piece of paper and just nods at Alexandra, looking as if she were a spy receiving a secret mission.

"And what about you, honey? Would you like to go on a VIP date while you're here visiting our city? You're just lovely. I could set something up right now. I have just the man for you."

I'm conscious that she's talking to me, and for once, I'm at a loss for words. This is my moment of truth—do I take the plunge or do I play it safe?

"I…I'm not sure just yet," I tell her.

She smiles and nods understandingly. "Of course, you take your time, honey. Here's my card. When you're ready, you give me a call. I'll work with you in New York, LA, or anywhere else in the world you'd like to go. And I mean *anywhere*, honey—you want to go on a vacation, you just call me, and I'll set it up for you. You will make lots of money with my help." She pats me on the shoulder. "You think about it, honey, and you give me a call."

We leave the apartment, and the girls on the street glare at us. They see the pink slip of paper in Sidney's hand; they know that they've got more competition. We head to the subway, and Sid nearly bounces down the street, she's so excited. She chats about how much money she's going to bankroll and what she's going to do with it, like buy a fantastic condo in Hollywood, and how much of a rush it all is. I stay quiet, thoughts swirling through my head. Thinking about the money. But, did I really almost consider becoming an escort?

It just seems so very, very wrong but rebellious and exciting at the same time. But why now is it in front of my face? Is it another test? The offer is here in front of me and there's no one that's going to stop me, so why don't I stop myself? I tell myself that my parents would kill me, Naomi would kill me, my friends back home would kill me...but then again, am I really the kind of person who lets what other people think dictate my life? And what's the purpose of having such rigid moral boundaries if all they get me is more responsibility and debt like everyone else?

Sidney is to arrive at the Soho Grand Hotel at midnight, according to her pink slip of paper, so as soon as we get back to Jonny's, she jumps in the shower and starts getting ready. It is understood that she is not to take me along; since I had declined Alexandra's offer, I am not a part of the business, and I cannot attend calls. Besides, it is a double date, and the guys specifically requested two leggy blondes, Sidney told me.

As the time gets closer, Sid starts to get more excited than nervous. She makes a cocktail and drains it, reapplying her lip gloss afterward.

"LJ? What if you just came with me? I'm a little nervous. I don't know what to expect. You could just hang out in the living room or whatever. Would you come with me? Please."

"What about Alexandra?" She seems nice enough in person, but Alexandra certainly isn't the kind of person I want to be on the wrong side of.

"I don't care, LJ. Please, come with me?" Sidney looks so scared. I've never seen her like this before.

"You don't have to do this. You really don't."

Sid shakes her head and bites her lip. I hope for a minute that she'll reconsider.

"No," she says, shaking her head. "No, I have to do this, LJ. I mean…if I don't…" She trails off. "I might have to move home. To Texas."

I stare at her, shocked. "Is it that bad?"

She nods. "I want to stay in LA. Please, LJ!"

At once, I knew I couldn't let her go alone.

Our cab pulls up to the hotel, and we get out, dressed in delicate dresses underneath our puffy coats. The second we walk into the lobby, we take our coats off, eager to look as in the right place as possible. I'm conscious of other people knowing what we're there for, but there's no need; the only person who glances in our direction is the man at the front desk, but he merely nods once and gets back to his work when we stride past him. Maybe he knows, and maybe he doesn't, but at a hotel this nice, it's his job to show discretion more than anything else. I feel like everyone knows what we are up to. Are they watching?

We punch the elevator button for the penthouse suite, and as we rise, I can feel Sidney's excitement plagued with anxiety fill the elevator. I have to admit that I'm glad that I don't have to go through that; all I have to do tonight is hang out on a couch and keep myself occupied while Sidney does her job. It's surreal for sure, but then again, this isn't really any different from what Sidney does on a regular basis back in LA for free. What's the harm in getting paid for what you'd be doing anyway?

We arrive on the top floor and knock on the ornate wooden door. A stunningly handsome and impeccably dressed young, blond Australian man answers the door and smiles at us, crinkling the corners of his eyes. "Come right in, ladies," he says, motioning us in. We walk into the living room area and see another incredible-looking blond guy doing rails off the coffee table. "Oh, hey girls, want some?" he asks. I don't know what I was expecting to see, but it certainly wasn't two extremely hot guys. These are the guys who are paying for sex? I'd have sex with them for free!

Another knock sounds at the door, and a girl who looks just like that new blond supermodel walks in. We all exchange greetings, and then the guy sitting down points to me. "So I said two blondes—what the fuck is she doing here?"

Sidney jumps in right away with a coy smile. "She's my friend. I asked her to keep me company. She'll just hang out, if that's okay?"

"Yeah, sure, fine, I guess," he says, laying out lines for each of us.

We all do a few lines and have a few drinks, just listening to Led Zeppelin's "Stairway to Heaven" on blast. It feels like just another normal night, hanging out with new people and chilling. Then one of the guys stands up, turns the music up really loud, and grabs Sidney's hand to lead her to his bedroom. She turns and gives me a quick smile before they disappear inside; she looks super happy and excited, all nervousness erased by the familiarity of the situation, and the drugs. A few minutes later, the other guy grabs the other girl's hand and leads her into the same room.

Alone, I light up a cigarette, crack the window, and jam out to Led Zeppelin, watching the first snow of the season drift down through the streetlights outside. I drag a large, comfy oversized chair right up to the giant windows and just enjoy the view, lost in my own world, when suddenly I feel a tap on my shoulder.

"Hey." I turn around, startled to see the first hot guy standing there in a white towel with a bottle of water. "Are you thinking about doing this?"

"I'm...not sure," I answer truthfully.

"I don't think it suits you. You can do better." He gives me a wink, hands me a huge joint, and walks back to the bedroom. The music's still super loud and has switched to Coldplay on the playlist; I'm thankful I can't hear the wild orgy that's playing out in the bedroom behind me. I sink into my big leather chair, light the joint, take in the view, and think about what he said.

CHAPTER TWELVE

At three in the morning, Sidney and the other girl emerge from the master bedroom. The other girl leaves, and Sid walks right up to me with a huge giddy smile on her face and wild hair.

"We can go home now," she says, positively bubbling with energy. She sits on the arm of my chair and helps me finish my Scotch.

"How did it go?" I ask.

"Here," she says, handing me back my empty glass. "Let's just go, and I'll tell you in the hall."

The guys are nowhere to be seen, so we leave the suite and wait for the elevator. Before it arrives, Sidney reaches into her purse and pulls out a wad of cash.

"What the fuck, Sid?!" I scream.

"It's five thousand dollars."

"*What*?!"

"Yep, it's two grand an hour," she says, glowing. "Plus tip because it was more than one person."

I'm shocked; I've never even seen that much money in cash before. Sidney grins ear to ear as we walk into the empty elevator. She touches my arm and leans in to put her head on my shoulder and purrs.

"You know what, LJ? It felt *really* good. They were all so hot and that chick was incredible! I had so many fucking amazing, super orgasms. It was so much fun!"

I can't believe she made five thousand dollars for having *orgasms* while I sat in the living room watching the snow like an idiot. Of course, she'll have to give some of it to Alexandra, but she'll get to keep most of it for herself.

The doorman hails us a cab downstairs, and once we're inside, Sidney turns to me in the back seat.

"Tell me the truth; what are you thinking, LJ?"

"Well...now I guess I'm really scared."

"Why? Because you're thinking you want to do it?"

"Honestly, yes. I'm considering it. After I just saw how hot those guys were. And that huge wad of cash in your purse. Holy shit, Sid! I'm pretty fucked in my thinking of what's right or wrong at this point!"

She holds my hand and leans her head back against the seat. "Don't worry, doll face, you'll figure it out. Me and my five thousand dollars will be here for you either way."

As soon as we walk into the loft, Sidney walks right over and shows Jonny how much money she made. I'm in shock; will her loud mouth get us kicked out? He very explicitly told me that he doesn't tolerate crazy behavior from the girls who stay with him. The next thing you know, he's giving her a hug and congratulating her and asking me when I'm going to make some money. He can see I'm confused, and he laughs.

"You girls have to make it while you've got it! As long as you're young and having fun! Why not?"

I have to interject. "But isn't it wrong?"

"Why? It's been happening that way since the dawn of time. You're going to sleep with guys while you date around anyway, right? So it costs your chosen guy three dinners if you want to tease him and make him wait to get into bed with you…what's that, a few hundred dollars he's paid? Or if it's a one-night stand, a few drinks? Lucky guy. If either way you're going to sleep with him, better to make some money that you can actually use."

I was stunned.

"Not what you were expecting me to say, kid?" he asks, amused.

"Um, actually no…Jonny, I was thinking you'd give us a lecture on ethics and religion and rational thinking or something stating why this is very bad behavior for young women…or maybe something about selling ourselves short? Or some other deep insight on focusing on the good and positive things in life. Not lying and working hard!"

"God, no. Sweetheart, you're just conditioned to think it's wrong, because all those sad housewives sitting at home are scared that their husbands are going to pay you to have sex with them. You see, if their husbands are going to do that, it's them to blame, not the girls making the money and being smart about life. Not just sitting around pondering it. And as for selling yourself, isn't that what we're all doing?" He motions to his easel. "Am I not selling my talent, my work, my name, my soul? People buy my art because it captivates them, really moves them, and they want to appreciate that intricate beauty in an intimate setting. And how is what Sidney's doing any different? She's selling herself the same as I am."

"Ha! You're funny, Jonny. Totally hilarious!"

I never thought about it that way. It's all certainly a lot to think about, but it's late, and I can't think anymore; my brain hurts. I say good night to the both of them and head to bed, and not long after, Sid joins me for what ends up being one of the deepest sleeps we've both had in quite a while.

*

The next morning, we have coffee with Jonny and pack up our things for the flight home to LA. I'll miss hanging out with Jonny Church and his playful cat, smoking and talking about art, and life in the big city and his incredible loft. We spend the morning watching him paint while munching on fresh macaroons, and before long, it's time to head for the airport.

"You're welcome here anytime, girls. I'm always here. Oh, and the next time you come in, my mother would love to cook you dinner," he says, giving us big hugs.

"Okay. Wow. Sounds great! Thanks so much, Jonny!" I say.

"Thanks, man. You rock, dude!" Sidney calls as we step out the door. Down on the curb, the driver loads our bags into the town car, and we're on our way. Sid holds her head high as she steps into the car; I can tell she's proud of herself for being able to afford a nice car for us—her first little splurge. Once we're inside, she turns to me with a grin. "Next time, I'm packing a black coat!"

*

Sidney passes out on the plane ride home, leaving me with my book and my thoughts. I can't help but think about my sex life, or rather, the lack thereof. I've only been with two guys in my whole life: Mercer, the twenty-five-year-old from Malibu I lost my virginity to when I moved out to California for college, and then Brody, of course. I wasn't like Sidney, just listening to what my body wanted to do and living in the moment, sexually. Which isn't to say that I don't have those desires—I've just never let myself act on them before. I never really thought it was an option, and when I was in a relationship, it wasn't. But now I'm single and free...the only thing stopping me is myself. Is that enough?

We land in California fairly late that evening, and when we get home, Sidney heads straight upstairs for bed. I see that Naomi left me a voice mail while I was in the air. I'm nervous as I hit play; surely she saw my pic on Instagram in front of the Scoop store in New York City and has something to say about it. As soon as I start listening though, I feel guilty for doubting her. She says that she gave my comp card to the makeup-company people, and they want to use me in two weeks, and then they'll need me four days a week for model shoots for the next three weeks. I breathe a sigh of relief. This means I won't have to scramble around for work as much. I'll still need something to supplement, but at least I won't be totally broke. She also got me in a runway show this Saturday night, and she said she's excited to see me and hear all about New York.

Well, I'll give her some details but certainly not all. Even if she has an inkling of what went down, I doubt she'll push me to talk about it. She's smart; she knows when to back off. But I'm sure I'll still get the evil eye. I go to bed that night with a smile on my face; it feels great to have such a great friend in Naomi, who clearly went above and beyond to get me work when she knew I didn't have anything else lined up. She's the best!

I barely see Sidney all week; she texts me occasionally to keep me updated on her comings and goings, but I don't see her in person until Friday. I know that she went on a few dates for Alexandra and was busy going to all the newest club and restaurant openings in Hollywood, but I was hesitant to join her, even though, strictly speaking, I really was available. Ever since I got back from New York, I haven't been feeling the best, so I spent the week resting from the trip and going on a few go-sees.

Friday evening, she knocks on my bedroom door and flops on my bed.

"LJ, what's up with you, baby?" she asks, shaking my leg. "You've been in bed a lot and have been absolute zero fun since we got back."

"I'm just tired, Sid. I'm okay," I tell her.

"Well, I just had the best week. I'm making money faster than I can spend it, I swear to god. I'm saving up for a condo on La Cienega. I saw that there was one up for sale—I can't wait." She gets a wistful look in her eyes, imagining her new life in a sun-filled condo, right in the heart of Hollywood. "Okay, gorgeous, are you all rested up now or what? Are you coming out tonight with me, or what? Come on."

"I don't know, Sid..." I say, eyeing my open laptop. I've been binge-watching concerts on Palladia, and I really feel like doing that instead of dealing with people tonight. Plus, I'm waiting on my second absent period, and I know I'll get all bloated and be miserable the moment it hits.

"Oh my god, you can't just stay inside by yourself all the time. I'm dragging you out. Here, you don't even need to dress yourself. I'll do it for you." She opens my closet and pulls out a royal-blue dress.

"That's backless," I tell her.

"No shit. It's also come-fuck-me hot on you! Now, where are your come-fuck-me pumps at? And I know you have that black pashmina thing you always carry with you around here somewhere; you can wear that because I know you like to look classy sassy, bitch. See? I do pay attention."

I smile and take the dress she tosses at me. It feels good for her to get me going. I probably do need to get out of the house.

"Okay, you have twenty minutes to get ready, and then I'll be back down for you. Let's go to Boa Steakhouse for dinner or Ago for that awesome homemade truffle pasta you like. But I think Boa. We could go to the one in Santa Monica? What are you feeling? On me, baby!"

"Sid, you're the best. Um…a rare bone-in filet and a glass of really good Pinot Noir sounds absolutely amazing right now. Yumm-O! But that beet salad with burrata at Ago they always make for me sounds pretty heavenly too."

"Okay, whatever you want. I'm taking my baby out tonight! Be back down in a few!"

I drag myself to the bathroom and straighten my hair and do the best gray smoky eye I can do. Nude lips, a spritz of Chance, and I'm ready. Sidney bounces down the stairs, and we take off in her car for the evening. Boa Steakhouse hits the spot, and we spend dinner catching up and indulging in great food and wine. I'm glad she took me out. I guess I did need this.

"Let's go down to the club and dance this off, LJ," she says.

"Okay, I'm ready to dance!" I tell her. After a bottle of wine and a dirty martini with blue cheese–stuffed olives at the bar, I'm starting to melt into the magic of the night quite nicely. We drive past the club on Fairfax; it's packed, with a line pouring into the street; there's no way we're going to get valet parking there. Sid does a U-turn and somehow gets the valet to park her car in the full lot next door.

She knows all the tricks.

"Stay close to me, LJ!" she says, grabbing my dress as she works her way to the front of the line. I put my hands on her shoulders and try not to get lost in the bustle of people vying for prime placement inside the club. Just then, my phone starts vibrating.

"Girl!" Naomi yells through the phone. "I saw you from the street! I'm coming up there to meet up with my friend Teá. I'll see you in there! If you can't get in right away, tell the doorman you're on Ox's list."

"Thanks, Naomi, you're the best! I'll see you in there!"

Just then, Sidney yanks my arm and drags me inside.

"Wow, it's crazy out there!" I tell her. "Naomi's coming in too; we'll see her in a bit."

Sidney narrows her eyes. "I don't know if I can get her in," she warns me.

"Oh, no worries, she can get in on her own," I tell her.

If the place was crazy outside, it's insane inside. People swarm the dance floor, and the music has reached a fever pitch. I can feel it thumping in my bones and the energy lifting me up and making me move—I have to get on that dance floor now!

"Sid, I'm going to go dance, okay? Look for me texting on your phone every once in a while. I'll meet up with you later," I tell her, knowing that she'll want to meet up with other people as well.

"Okay, have fun, chicky; find me later!" she says, kissing my cheek. I start to head toward the floor when I hear her call me back.

"Here, I almost forgot," she says, pressing something into my hand. "You'll love this."

I open my hand to find a small white pill. "What is it?"

She laughs, shaking her head. "You're so cute. I forget how innocent you are sometimes. It's Molly! MDMA! Ecstasy. Just take it. You'll totally be into it. Just don't drink too much water, okay?"

"Okay..." I tell her before she takes off into the crowd. I'm always hesitant to take new drugs, but if Sidney's taking it too, it can't be that bad. Here goes. I dry swallow the pill and head to the bar for a drink. I'm glad we made it in; this is the club's opening so it's the place to be tonight. Otherwise, we wouldn't be here on a Friday—Sid always scolds me not to go out in Hollywood on the weekends since those are bridge-and-tunnel nights, or when outside people come in to party like tourists. Local people and celebrities party Mondays through Thursdays, she informed me. I always thought it was funny that she called the weekends bridge-and-tunnel nights, since bridges and tunnels aren't really a thing in LA. The saying comes from New York City, when people would come in on the bridges from Jersey to party on the weekends, and true New Yorkers would avoid the clubs in order to steer clear of the "tourists."

I'm still waiting for my drink when I hear my name and see Naomi waving over the crowd.

"Hey, girl!" she says, pulling me in for a hug.

"Hey, I missed you!" I tell her. "Listen, thank you so much for getting me those jobs; you're really helping me out so much. Let me get you a drink!"

"No worries. We've got a table over here! Come meet my friend Teá and her man, Jamie. Have a drink with us. Come on!"

She leads me over to a table with a few other models seated around it and introduces me to all of them. When she gets to the man sitting in the middle of them, my jaw drops: it's none other than Jamie Foxx. I try to keep it cool and act as if it's not a big deal, but she gave me no warning, and I end up nervously shaking his hand across the table.

"You didn't tell me Jamie Foxx was here!" I whisper to her as she pours me a vodka cranberry.

"Oh yeah, he's dating one of my friends. He's really cool."

I hang with Naomi and her girlfriends for a while, even moving to the dance floor so that we have room to really shake our asses. The girls are a ton of fun; I'm the only white girl in the group, but they totally love me and even throw me into the middle of their circle and cheer me on as I dance. I'm moving harder and faster, blending my motions with the music and when a wave of euphoria rolls over me, I start feeling happier than I've ever felt in my life. I'm grinning from ear to ear, and I feel like I could just float away. Everything is perfect and in its right place, and the music is so excellent that I feel like I can sense it deep in my soul. I'm experiencing everything to its fullest extent, and I'm vibrating with the crowd, sharing their energy as we're all pressed together and moving as one. The Molly is feeling oh-so good now. Holy shit!

The music shifts to a slower beat, and I need water, so I say good-bye to Naomi and her friends. One girl even hugs me and screams that I'm her "favorite white girl!"

It's because I made her laugh trying all her dance moves on the floor and I'm sure, all the while, looking like the village idiot doing them. So much fun! I blow kisses and make my way out of the crowd. I check my phone and read a text from Sidney telling me she's upstairs at a table, so I head upstairs and take a lap around, searching for her blond head. Of course, I find her sipping champagne and making out with some cute boy. She'll tell you she likes tall men, but she really digs the petite metrosexual guys, which works for me because I don't. I like men who actually look like real men. She sees me and waves me over, pouring me a glass of champagne. She's got her legs on the guy's lap, and he strokes her thighs suggestively as he watches her pour the champagne. It makes me cringe because he's sorta creepy looking, and I want to take her away, but she's clearly into him, so I don't say anything.

"LJ, this is Andy," she says, handing me the glass.

"Hi, nice to meet you," I say, reaching out to shake his hand.

"Nice to meet *you*," he says, missing my hand and grabbing my crotch under my dress.

"What the fuck?!" I yell, stepping backward away from him. I'm tempted to throw my champagne glass in his face, but then I recognize him. I was just groped by a famous comedian.

"Andy, you're such a dick!" Sidney squeals, going right back in to kiss him again.

Repulsed, I leave the table and head for the patio. I need air and a cigarette.

I find a quiet corner and manage to bum a cigarette from a nice guy nearby. The night really is beautiful, the lights twinkling and the crisp air licking my sweaty skin. Wearing a backless dress was a godsend.

I can feel someone's eyes on me through the crowd, so I turn and instantly make eye contact with Cole. I haven't seen him in a while, but there's no time lost. He doesn't move from his spot in his group, but he holds my gaze and slowly smiles, as if we're sharing a secret across the club. Tingles race up and down my body. I take a deep breath…and turn and run into the sea of people. This is all too much to deal with right now—I'm so fucked up. I work myself into the middle of the crowd and start moving with them. I'm not sure why I ran away, but I do know that I feel better in the middle of people, protected in some way. Maybe it's just the drugs? Maybe I really do like him?

I've been dancing for about ten minutes when I relax and assume he's off with his friends. I start to really get into the music again and throw my hands up into the air, swirling them in the brilliant vitality floating about the heads of the dancers and following the tracers. I move my hips in figure eights and throw my head back, and then I feel hands tightly circle my waist. I don't pull away. It's him.

"Hello, love…" he whispers into my ear and quickly turns me around to face him. He found me after all. He looks incredible and smells the same, and his eyes penetrating mine are making me weak in the knees. He has his arm around me and is caressing my bare back, moving his body in response to mine. We're liquid together. He leans down to put his forehead on mine and starts to kiss me softly all over my face and then pulls my hair a little so that he can kiss my neck. He kisses me everywhere but my lips, and the anticipation drives me wild. We're dancing so close that I can feel his bulge through my dress, and I move closer to him. I've never felt such a strong sexual attraction to someone in my life; he's got me so heated and wet that I'm ready to fuck him right here on the dance floor. Unable to stand it any longer, I put my hand on his neck to bring his face to mine and hungrily bring my lips to his, wrapping my arms around him. We're explosive; we kiss so hard that the rest of the club detonates, and all that remains is the two of us in a musical dreamland. He slips his hands down the back of my dress and grabs my ass with both hands, and I push myself even closer to him.

I can't stand it anymore. "Let's get out of here," I tell him, grabbing his hand and leading him toward the door. I see Sidney on the way and tell her I'm heading out. She eyes Cole and mouths *finally!* and pats my back wildly with a big smile. Pulling me next to her, she opens her purse and pulls out a huge wad of cash and about ten condoms and shoves them into my purse.

"Have way too much fun!" she calls after us teasingly.

"I will!" And with a double air kiss, I'm gone.

CHAPTER THIRTEEN

I get into Cole's shiny black BMW, and we zoom right over to his place. When we arrive at his gorgeous three-thousand-square-foot apartment in Beverly Hills, we barely make it through the door before I'm slammed up against the dining room wall with my hands pinned up above my head, the front door still wide open. I wrap my legs around his waist, and he kicks the door closed and carries me to the dining room table, kissing me the whole time.

We have the kind of sex where you lose track of time, where your limbs go numb from the pure ecstasy of it all, where you light the room on fire. We're left panting on the floor after fucking on the table and in dire need of refreshment, so I slip back into my dress, and we raid the freezer for some fancy Russian vodka on the rocks. As I gain my bearings and actually look around the apartment, I can tell that he was probably not the one who decorated it, with its big white columns, parquet floors, and chocolate velvet tufted sofas with matching tasseled pillows. Either he's got a wife, which I highly doubt since he's always out without anyone, or he lives with his parents.

I decide to take a gamble. "So…where are your parents?"

He smiles and gives me the side eye while he rolls a joint. We're sitting on the balcony floor with our drinks, resting on the cold concrete with our legs tangled and leaning on each other.

"My mother is on a yacht eating cheese cubes in St. Tropez. Or off the coast of Italy, or probably shopping somewhere. She's working on billionaire husband number four. I don't see her that much."

"What about your dad?"

"Oh, he's long gone." He stands up and offers his hand to help me up after we take a few puffs. "Come on, LJ. Let's put the devil back to hell."

I grin and let him help me stand. "Isn't that Shakespeare? Something about the monster with two backs? Referring to sex, right?"

"It's so fucking hot that you're smart," he says. "No one has ever got that before," he says, tearing my dress off with no hesitation. We have sex on the huge fancy dining room table again. Then sex on the extravagant Persian rug on the living room floor. We move to his room and have sex standing up, against the wall, on the nightstand, rolling on his floor and breaking the floor lamp in the process and laughing about it. We crawl into bed and pass out naked together, his arms wrapped around me. It's a deep, comfortable sleep, nestled against his chest in his perfect king-sized bed.

I wake the next morning with Cole sensually kissing my back, making me feel like I'm still dreaming. The air is warm and still heavy with sex. I can't keep the smile off my face. We laugh. Then he puts my heels back on me, and we get right back into the swing of things, using my last three condoms. We take a shower together, getting all fresh and soapy and washing each other down, then putting good use to the built in bench on the wall. After our shower, I put on my wrinkly, torn dress, and Cole lets me borrow a sweatshirt to throw over it and gets on his phone.

"My friend's going to pick me up for the gym. We can take you home on the way. Does that work?" he asks me.

"Sure, that's fine. Thanks," I tell him. We get down to the parking garage where his friend is waiting for us, and as we're getting in, Cole realizes he's left something upstairs and says that he'll be right back.

"Thanks for giving me a ride home," I tell his friend.

"No problem," he says, turning around to look at me in the back seat. "He really likes you, you know?"

"What?"

"Yeah, he called me while you were still in the shower and was acting all weird and told me about you."

I'm at a loss for what to say. "Really?" I offer lamely.

"Listen, I've known the guy for over ten years. He's never let a girl spend the night with him. He always throws them out."

Luckily, the car door opens then, and Cole gets in close beside me. His friend winks at me in the rearview mirror and puts the Porsche into gear.

"What's up guys? Why so quiet?" Cole asks, putting his arm around me in the small back seat.

"Nothing, man, but dude I'm not your chauffeur. Get the fuck up here," his friend says. I can see him smile and shake his head in the mirror, like *whatever.*

They drop me off at the house, and after waving them good-bye, I run upstairs and knock on Sidney's door. I hear a groggy noise from inside, so I take that as a go ahead and run inside and start jumping on her bed.

"No, LJ, nooo, stop." She groans, pulling a pillow over her head.

"I just got home!" I tell her. "Sid, that was the best sex I've ever had! The best! Hands down the best. Holy shit, it was awesome! You were right. I needed that soooo bad!" I start playfully poking her.

"Oh my god, stop. I just got home too. I'm so sleepy. Come sleep...come here and lay with me." She pulls back the covers, and I get in bed with her. She turns to me and grins.

"Okay, so tell me. I bet it was so hot."

"Sid, it was seriously so hot. I've never had sex like that before. We literally had sex all night! We used all ten of those condoms you gave me. It was soooo crazy. Totally insane! I feel so good!"

"I'm sure! He's so hot. Everyone wants to fuck him, but he's so picky with who he fucks. He's been hunting you for a while now. I bet you're only saying it's so good because you've only had sex with two guys though...well, wait, now three. Ha! You whore!"

"Hey!" I say, bashing her head with a pillow.

"Ow! Okay, stop. I'm going to puke. Ugh. So, what, do you like him now?"

"I don't know about that, Sid. I'm just getting started! I'm just gettin' warmed up! I mean, I'd see him again, but I'm not trying to get serious with anyone just yet. I think I'll play the field for a while."

"That's my girl, just young and wild," she says, patting my leg. She tells me about her night, about the party she ended up at in the Hollywood Hills—some guy's place with his own club on the third floor of his glass house—the celebrities she saw, and the hookups that the gossip rags would cover tomorrow. I nod off while she tells me all the tales of Hollywood debauchery, and when I wake up, I see she's sleeping too. I check my phone for the first time and nearly jump out of my skin.

"Holy shit! I have to be at my fitting for the fashion show in five minutes!" I yell, startling Sidney from her slumber.

"Run, Forrest! Run! Call me later, sexy," she calls after me as I stumble down the stairs. I fall down the last few stairs and twist my ankle a little, but there's no time to check.

"You okay?" Elliott asks from the kitchen.

"Ow! Fuck! I'm fine. I'll live!" I tell him, running into my room. I change and wash my face. I have no time for a real shower, so I douse myself in perfume and run out the door.

By some kind of Hollywood miracle, I make it over the hill from the valley in less than twenty minutes. No one notices me coming in late because they're all busy dressing the other girls. A woman with a clipboard comes up to me, and I check in with her. She sends me into a fitting room with my two changes, telling me to come out when I'm ready. I don't see Naomi anywhere, so I just go into the dressing room and try them on.

The outfits look great, very punk Euro chic. I walk back and forth in them for the woman with the clipboard, and she nods and makes notes, and before I know it, I'm done with the fitting. I never did see Naomi, so I leave her a Snapchat as I'm walking out of the store. I'm just finishing up the message when a figure on the street lunges out at me.

"Boo!"

Naomi grabs me around the waist and laughs as I get my breath back.

"Holy shit, Naomi! You scared the crap out of me! I kind of needed that though. Hey, where were you? I never saw you in there?"

"Sorry, girl. I couldn't resist scaring you. I got fitted earlier. I had to go meet this photographer real quick. I was just walking by, and I saw your car on the street and wanted to come in and give you a big hug. How was the fitting?"

"It was great. Thanks again for getting me in."

Naomi cocks her head to the side and looks me up and down. "LJ, what's going on with you? You look like you're all drugged out. Is everything all right?"

"Yeah, dude. I'm great! Actually I just had sex with someone last night, all night, and it was amazing. He's so super hot. It's weird having sex with someone other than Brody after all those years, but I had a great time, and I feel like a new me. And yes, I'm hungover. I did do some crazy pills with Sid."

"Oh, girl, no, no, no. That sounds crazy! You're crazy! With one of those club boys you met with old red nose? Uh huh. Don't be getting on no crazy drug wagon on me now—"

"Naomi, I feel great! Just because you're all work and no play...come on now. Listen, I'm fine. I'll see you tonight, right?"

Naomi laughs and shakes her head.

"Yeah, yeah, I'll see your crazy behind later. Love you, girl."

"Love you too. See you then. Thank you so much!"

On the drive up Highland Avenue, I go over the details of my wild night in my head and smile the whole way home. I feel so good. I really let myself go, and I really had the time of my life. I consider calling Cole but decide against it; I don't want a boyfriend right now. I just want to have fun being single. I get home and take a long, hot shower and use every body wash I have in there to unwind and relax, and then I watch some TV before it's time to go back to the rag & bone store for the runway show.

When I arrive back at the store, it's quite a different scene than it had been that morning. They have a red carpet stretching from the front to the street, and people are already beginning to arrive and set up cameras on either side of it. I skip the carpet and go in through the back entrance, and as soon as I walk in, I find Naomi in a hair-and-makeup chair. As busy as she is, she always seems to make it to jobs earlier than I do.

"Hey, LJ," she says, kissing me on both cheeks.

"Hey, doll, you're lookin' superfly," I tell her.

The woman with the clipboard comes up to me and leads me to a chair for hair and makeup, and soon enough, we're all beautified and ready to walk. The show goes perfectly; all the models look stunning, and we walk the store in front of a celebrity crowd. After the show, they even make an announcement backstage that we could each pick a pair of shoes to take home. That's easy for me to do; I'm in love with the baby-blue pumps that I wore in the show. Naomi snags a cool yellow retro pair with pastel-blue and white circles on them.

Shoes in tow, I finally say good night to Naomi and head home. I'm absolutely exhausted; going from a crazy sex night straight to a runway show is a killer. I don't know how Sidney does it all the time with all of her modeling jobs.

A few days go by where all I do is sleep and rest after my wild weekend. I get a text from my friend John to join him for dinner with a few of his director friends. I almost say yes but end up declining; the last time I went out with them I had a great time at first, but then all of these famous directors and screenwriters ended up talking about fucking their supermodel girlfriends with different farm-fresh vegetables. It was totally weird; what was originally a wildly sophisticated Hollywood night out quickly became a dinner with someone's gross little brothers. I can't say I was surprised though. I just nodded and smiled and drank tons more fabulous Cabernet, pondering what sex really would be like with a zucchini. Or a bumpy gourd.

Cole calls, but I send him to voice mail. I'm not ready to talk to him just yet. Yes, our night was amazing, but, I know if I pick up that phone, I'll see him again, and I just don't know if I'm ready.

I'm busy anyway, since Thanksgiving is later this week, and I'll have to pack and get ready to drive down to San Diego to spend it with my mother, stepfather, and two younger sisters. (My little brother, Torre, won't have enough time to make it home due to his busy pro-hockey schedule.) They're both bringing their boyfriends, and I realize that this will be my first Thanksgiving without Brody there with me. The night before I leave, I chug some NyQuil and go to bed early so that I won't stay up late thinking about him.

I wake up early the day before Thanksgiving to an empty house. Sidney and all of my roommates have already gone home to their families, and it's spooky being in such a big house by myself. I shower, throw on some yoga pants, and jump in the car with my bag of clothes and makeup for the long weekend. If I leave early enough, I'll beat the Thanksgiving rush, and I'll be able to get there without spending hours in traffic.

I speed down the freeway and blast music. I miss the open air of my Jeep, but the speakers are better in my new car. Besides, it's not like I'm at the beach all the time anymore; it's not like I really need a car that can fit surfboards in it. It's strange how quickly your life can change if you let it. You can go from waking up early to spend your day at the beach, swimming and surfing, to sleeping through your day so you can spend your nights dancing and doing drugs. I'm not sure which one is better, truth be told—they're both pretty great.

My phone pings with a text from my youngest sister, Jule, asking when I'm going to get there. It's been a while since I've seen her, since she lives in San Francisco with her boyfriend and all. She and her man, Jet, are so hippie chic and adorable. They'll probably get married. They both also probably have new tattoos since the last time I saw them. I shoot her a silly Snapchat telling her I'll be there soon. I can only imagine her getting super excited hearing that I'm on the way down and jumping on our middle sister, Harper, begging her to get the margaritas flowing. Harper will be there with her boyfriend, Todd, both of them flying in from our hometown, St. Louis, Missouri. I glance at the sun rising over the horizon, setting the ocean alight, and speed up a little on my drive down the 5 freeway, watching the seagulls soar, eager to see my family after what's been a whirlwind few months.

At last, I park in the driveway behind Ron's new car and pop out to stretch my legs. I lucked out on traffic and made it by nine in the morning, so it's likely that everyone's still getting ready for the day. I find my mom in the kitchen, making breakfast for everyone, and ask her if the girls have gotten into the margaritas yet.

"Oh...Lillian! Don't be silly. So glad you made it, honey," she says, kissing my cheek. She goes back to chopping vegetables for omelets, and I plop down on one of the barstools at the island.

She does a side hair flip and tucks one of her blond strands behind her ear, a move I know I've done many times when concentrating on something myself. "So what's going on with you? How's the new car treating you?"

"It's great, Mom. Thanks again for coming through on that. Greatly appreciated. You totally saved me. I will try to have you guys all paid off in a year. At least that's my goal. Everything's going well though. I'm actually starting a new job that'll last for a few weeks. It's for a new makeup line." I decide to leave out my trip to New York; there are too many questions she could ask that I'd rather not create lies for.

"Oh fine, dear, that sounds interesting," she says, focusing on her vegetables. I know she'll never be impressed by what I do, but sometimes I wish she'd at least pretend to care.

"So has anyone been down to help you?"

"No, I think everyone's still getting ready. I hear them moving around upstairs. Someone's in the shower I think. They'll be down soon. Hey, what about your writing? You've always had such a gift for writing, with all the plays and stories you wrote in school. You really should do that, honey. I'd hate to see your brilliant imagination go to waste."

"I know, Mom, but who's going to take me seriously about that? I have no real work experience, but I do have a funny new screenplay I'm working on. But it's really more of a hobby."

I think about the file of the story on my laptop, the one I've been kicking around in my head. Sid features prominently in the pages as one of my characters because she's so larger than life.

"Honey, I really do think you have the ability to write something for Broadway even! You should never take that off the table. This modeling thing is not going to last forever," she scolds.

"Okay," I say tightly, wondering how even her compliments feel like insults. "Sure, Mom. Thanks."

I get up and pour a cup of coffee and glance in the oven to see what's cooking. She's got a wide variety of pastries warming there and bacon frying on the stove. She's even got tofu and Fakin' Bacon ready for Jule, and the waffle maker's out and ready to go. My mom and I might not be on the best terms most of the time, but she certainly knows how to throw a good breakfast.

"LJ!"

Jule bounds down the stairs, looking freshly washed and dressed in her typical maxi skirt, tank, and Birkenstocks.

"George!" I say, evoking the old nickname I'd given her as a child. It's still unclear how she'd made it from Jule to George, but the name stuck. I embrace her, breathing in her familiar patchouli scent. She's as opposite of LA as you can get, and right now, that's what I need. She just love, *love*, loves San Francisco.

She holds me out at arm's length. "You're too skinny, LJ. You're going to have to eat a lot this Thanksgiving to make up for it."

I laugh, blushing.

"Well, you know that model life," Ron teases, on the way down the stairs. "We'll have to force-feed her if she's going to eat anything!"

"Hey! Not true. Come on! I eat," I say as Ron gives me a hug. Everyone else follows him, and suddenly the kitchen is filled with hugging and teasing, everyone filling coffee mugs and helping Mom make the omelets. It's such a relief to be home, to not have to worry about how I look or being "on" all the time.

We relax over breakfast, catching up and making playful jabs at each other, and then lace up our gym shoes for a long hike through the dirt trails around Mom and Ron's neighborhood. They've always been athletic, each of them working out every day for as long as I can remember. I've never really gotten on that train; I always swam and rode horses growing up, but I could never get used to the labor of going to a gym.

After our long walk, we settle in for dinner. Ron puts filets on the grill, and my sister and I do side dishes while guzzling margaritas. It's just like when we were younger, all of us coming together to make a meal for the whole family. There's such a warmth to it, especially when compared to my usual dinner of hummus and veggies.

I make a salad and brussels sprouts with bacon while Jule makes something with tofu for her vegan self. Harper and Mom dig around in the wine closet for the perfect bottles for the occasion and are gone for longer than necessary; Mom and Ron are on every mailing list in Napa Valley and have quite the collection. They eventually reemerge with a few magnum bottles that they open to breathe a little and then set out some cheeses, olives, and bread with infused garlic and rosemary oils for dipping.

It's tough watching my sisters so in love, their mates chasing them around the kitchen and pinching their waists when they think no one's looking.

I'm happy for them, of course; they're both with sweet, smart, adoring guys who love them just as much as the girls love them. At least I can be thankful for that this year.

I think of Brody, suddenly, and feel a pang of longing. I'd gone weeks without really thinking about him at all, but now, here with family and seeing all the love in the room, I miss him.

This is the first Thanksgiving in years, I realize, that he hasn't been here. It really hurts.

We sit down to dinner and dig into the amazing meal we've all prepared. Everyone shares stories about their work and funny little things that happen in their lives, and as the night wears on, I know that I'm getting quieter and quieter.

What can I share from my life that they'll possibly understand? *Oh, hey, Mom, guess what? I went to New York and watched my friend bang some dude for money! Oh, what did I do last weekend? I banged some hot guy, but don't worry—it was for free!*

Instead, I offer innocuous stories about moving into the new house. I talk about the time Smalls got into my box of Cheerios and made a mess all over the kitchen floor. I'm trying to avoid our usual flair up of sibling rivalry.

Then, I talk about what it was like to have Keira Knightley as a coworker. I wonder if my sisters are holding back their own wild stories, but somehow I doubt it. They look so wholesome and happy, glancing at their boyfriends with loving admiration.

I want that. Real love, I mean.

After dinner, we take our wine to the couch and put on a movie, only getting up to refill our glasses and indulge in more pie. I sit on the floor and give the couples the couches. When the movie ends, we all head up to bed, slightly tipsy and with Thanksgiving on our minds. I fall asleep quickly, my empty wine glass stained red on the bedside table.

I wake the next morning to pots and pans clanging downstairs. It's barely eight, and Thanksgiving is already in full swing. I'm clearly the last one up; I can hear everyone chatting downstairs, so I brush my teeth and head down for coffee.

"Hey! LJ's up!" Harper says, pouring herself a mug of coffee. "Happy Thanksgiving, sister!"

"Happy Thanksgiving to you too, doll!" I tell her, joining her at the coffeemaker. "Has anyone put the parade on yet?"

"I got it!" Ron calls from the living room, switching the TV on NBC.

"Bird's already in the oven. We should be ready to eat by two or three," Mom tells me, kissing the side of my head as she hustles by with a dish full of yams. Everyone else gathers in the living room with their coffee, not keen to spoil their appetites before the big meal, and I follow close behind. This is what I love; ever since I was a kid, whether or not it was at my mom or dad's house, mornings were spent hanging out in our PJs and socks, just rolling out of bed from a good night's sleep and drinking a big mug of coffee over the paper or the newest fashion magazine, just being together. It's awesome.

"Here, LJ," Harper says, tossing me the latest issue of PORTER magazine. "I brought this one for you, and I've got a few gossip magazines too; they're on the kitchen counter."

"Aw, thanks, my sweetest pea," I tell her, rustling her hair. She may be an adult, but I will always see her as my sweet little sister.

We spend the morning lounging and helping with the cooking and then go up in shifts to get ready for our Thanksgiving feast. Mom always likes to take a ton of pictures, so we have to get dressed up and look presentable. I go upstairs to change into the dress I brought for the occasion, and when I check my phone, I see that Brody texted, wishing my family and me a happy Thanksgiving. He even says to tell them hello from him and that he misses being here with everyone. A tear drops onto my phone before I start subconsciously twirling the silver ring on my finger with ocean waves engraved on it that Brody gave me four years ago.

I don't even know why I'm still wearing it. I should've gotten rid of it weeks ago, but it had been such an ingrained habit to wear it.

Brody has been with me for so many family holidays over the years, it's so painful not to have him here.

It's strange missing him so much while still knowing in my heart that I've already moved on. I could never go back, even though I feel a big void without him. It really sucks to be heartbroken. Nothing worse. I spend half an hour contemplating what to write back before simply writing, "I will. You too."

I take off the ring and set it on the nightstand.

Then, I get a text from Cole. He wants to know if I'm in town.

I hesitate, feeling a little thrilled that he's messaging me but worried about whether I'm willing to see him again.

Plus, my emotions are still churning about Brody. I decide to wait to respond.

I put on my dress and head downstairs.

When I make it downstairs, Ron hands me a glass of champagne, and we toast the day. I get the feeling that they've been waiting for me to eat, but no one says anything, more than likely because my face is still puffy from crying.

"Do you miss him?" Jule asks me in a low whisper, as if reading my mind. She's always had this ability to just *know* what's wrong. It's one reason I love her so much.

The rest of the family starts chatting among themselves, careful to give us space in the little breakfast nook.

I nod.

"You'll be okay," she says and gives my hand a squeeze. "You made the right decision leaving him."

"I know. But why is it so hard?"

Jule shrugs and gives me a big bear hug.

The rest of the family is gathering around the table, and we join them.

The meal is incredible, as always. I eat until I can't anymore and then top it all off with as much wine as I can handle. We take turns going around the table saying what we're thankful for, and I end up rambling on about family and friends and my adventures in Hollywood for a while. Even while I'm talking, I'm aware of how unhinged I sound, but I keep going. It's strange being home; it's like I've uncorked all the emotions I've been bottling up, and they have come bubbling out. It's the booze talking.

My mom's face looks pinched and tight at each new story. I can feel the judgment coming off her in waves. I even see a bit of uncertainty in my sisters' faces, as if they're not sure whether to laugh along with me or to possibly stage an intervention.

Is my life so out of control?

Suddenly, I feel like the dining room is closing in on me.

I'm already ready to go back to Hollywood. I feel like I'm missing something.

CHAPTER FOURTEEN

I do stay for the rest of the weekend to appease my family and then jump into my Ford early on Sunday to beat the traffic and get home as quickly as possible. Tearing back up the 5 freeway, I feel myself getting stronger with each mile I put behind me. Some might call it denial, but all I know is that in LA, I don't feel judged by my intellectual family, and people don't look at me like they pity me because I party too much and have random jobs.

In fact, they look at me with a mutual respect because they all have the same gypsy lifestyle. I shoot Sidney a text to let her know I'm coming home, and she responds with a million emojis and tells me to hurry up so we can go to lunch and catch up. I smile and speed up; I've really missed that girl. And right now, I feel like she's one of the few people who actually gets me.

"LJ!" she screams, throwing her arms around me. "I've missed you so much! Okay. Yeah! I'm so glad you're here; let's go to lunch in a few minutes. Then I want to go shopping on

Rodeo Drive or on Robertson. I've decided I need a new bag. A new *it* bag. Like a Chanel, or a Gucci, or maybe a new Louis! But what I really want is a Fendi baguette." She winks at me, tossing her hair over her shoulder like a Valley Girl.

I laugh. "Okay! Let me just change. I've been in the same clothes for two days just chillin'. I'm so excited to be back!"

"Gorgeous, you know it wasn't boring in Texas. I partied with all my old school homies. And I did get a killer tan while I was there too."

I run down to my room and change and then jump into her car. Sidney's more energetic than usual; I guess the visit home recharged her too.

Sid zips down the streets, talking a mile a minute about her visit home. When we finally get to the restaurant and order matcha green teas and small Tuscan kale salads with a light peanut dressing, she continues to tell me that she's got a job later that night. Then we get moving on to her shopping spree.

"Baby, you have really got to get in on this thing. I've got almost twenty thousand dollars in cash in a shoebox under my bed. I'm going to get that condo so soon. And it feels amazing! It's been so much fun meeting all these guys. It's been awesome! You're crazy not to do it."

I look at her cockeyed and think for a minute. I can't even imagine what I'd do if I had that much money stashed away. I could pay off most of my student loans and my car; that's for sure. And get a start on my credit card debt too. I wouldn't have to wince every time I check my bank account, and I'd know that I could pay my bills as soon as they came in. I could go shopping! And I would be completely independent, not having to worry about needing anyone for anything. And I could dress exactly how I wanted without having to hope for new clothes from the few fashion shows that I've walked in.

We get to Barneys and valet the car. Our first stop is the shoe department on the first floor since Sidney is absolutely smitten with designer shoes. She tries on every pair that catches her eye, eventually deciding on a pair of Stuart Weitzman nudist stilettos. I check the price tag out of curiosity; they're close to five hundred dollars. Luckily, I'm not as obsessed with shoes as she is, probably because I'm already five foot nine, and I hate towering over people. My addictions are beautiful handbags, winter coats, and bikinis. I can't indulge in the winter coats as much now that I live in Southern California, but bikinis come in handy plenty, as do the handbags. Women in Hollywood and Beverly Hills don't cut any corners when it comes to carrying an incredible bag. I go look at the bags while Sidney checks out at the register, but there's no way I can afford any of them. To console myself, I walk through the makeup counters to see what's in. Out of the corner of my eye, I see a big, gorgeous black-and-white mastiff go up the stairs to the second floor. I love Barneys so much more because they allow you to bring your dog in to shop with you.

Sidney finds me drooling over a pair of sparkly diamond earrings near the makeup counters.

"I saw you with that new Chloé Drew bag; were you going to get it?" she asks.

"I wish," I tell her. "It's three thousand dollars!"

"Well, you know how you can afford it," she says with a wink. "Hey, listen, want to head home? I'm meeting about five guys at the Havana Room for dinner with two other girls tonight, and I want to have time to relax and get ready. Do you want to come? They're so fucking cool, LJ; you should come party."

"Are they...I mean, paying you...to...?" I suddenly find it hard to get at what I mean, but I really don't feel like going out with her if she's just going to have sex for money. I mean, I don't want to judge, but at the same time, I don't want to feel pressure to join if I don't want to.

Sidney goes still for a moment, her eyes narrowing.

"LJ," she says, voice careful. "They're just friends. Not clients."

I feel like I've insulted her, though I didn't mean to. How am I supposed to know the difference? Now I feel I have to go, even though I'd rather spend a night in.

"Oh, okay. Sounds fun."

"Yeah, baby!" Sidney says, "That's my girl."

We go outside and walk down Rodeo Drive to pick up the car from the restaurant valet. It's a perfect sunny day—one of those days in LA when the smog isn't too bad and the sun bathes everything in a warm, crisp golden light and makes everything shiny and perfect just like the movies. Sidney eyes some men in a passing silver Range Rover, and they slow the car and roll down their windows to gawk at her in her short shorts and sky-high heels. She blows them a kiss and almost does a bend and shake at the waist to show off her assets too. They honk. I don't care. I'm always happy to be without makeup and in my flip-flops and spotted second. If spotted at all.

I watch Sidney carrying her designer bags and wonder about the choices she's making. Am I the one being dumb for not doing it too?

"Okay, babe, I'm going upstairs to try on clothes," Sidney says, trotting up the stairs as soon as we get home. "Why don't you wear that tight black bandage dress I gave you the other day and those cool blue rag & bone heels you got from the show? Or I'll let you borrow my Stuart Weitzman thigh-high boots if you want."

"Yeah, maybe, thanks Sid," I tell her. I'm already dreading going through my closet, as nothing's been feeling right lately.

I know I'm also nervous to go to the bar with Sidney to meet these guys. For some reason, I can't shake the feeling that she wasn't telling me the whole truth. What if they're not friends? What if they are clients?

I realize, deep down, that I'm not worried I'll be pressured into doing something I don't want to do. I'm worried that I'll *want* to do it.

I think Sidney knows this.

Finally, I'm showered and squeezed into my tiny black dress and light-blue heels, as Sid suggested. I wander upstairs to see what she decided to wear and find her posing in front of her mirror in a high-wasted miniskirt and a modernist white cropped shirt with stacked necklaces and a few more bracelets than usual.

"Hey, chicky, that looks awesome," I tell her.

"Does it?" she asks, furrowing her brow in the mirror and sucking in her stomach.

"Totally. Hey, should I wear tights with this dress?"

"No way...who wears tights in LA? If we were going out in New York, then yes. Hey, listen, are you sure this looks hot? I mean, really fucking hot?" She hikes the skirt up a little more and I catch a glimpse of her underwear.

"You're on fire, Sid, seriously. Stop it. You're crazy. And I'm impressed you are actually wearing panties tonight. I know it's a big step for you, so good job!" I don't mention that I'm not wearing any.

"Okay, okay. Haha. Whatever, bitch. Hey, want to smoke before we go out? I borrowed Jona's bong. I only have a little-bitty nug left though, so maybe you hit it and blow it in my mouth because you can always take bigger hits than me."

"Yeah, that'd be awesome, sure. Here, I'll pack it. And would you mind doing a cool smoky eye on me again, Sid? I just can't do it like you do."

"Sure, babe, no prob."

I sit on her futon and pack the bowl, taking my hit and leaving the rest for Sid because she ran out of the room. I'm blowing smoke at the flat screen when I see our faces flash across the TV. I sputter and cough; it's the music video she and

I did for an up-and-coming boy band a while ago, and it looks like its getting traction.

"Sid! Sid, it's us; we're on TV!" I tell her, and she comes over and laughs as they show clips from our video on the E talk show we're watching.

"That's too funny. I've never seen it. Hey, did you grab my boots?" she asks. She shakes her head and goes back to finish curling her hair. I can't pull my eyes away from the screen. We look great! Sweet boost.

*

We get to Beverly Hills and valet Sid's car, and suddenly we're left standing outside of a building with no clear entrance.

"I don't get it; the directions said that it would be right here..." Sidney says, scrolling through her phone. She texts one of the guys, and he writes back immediately that he'll be down in five minutes. We exchange a curious glance; this is either something really awesome or really sketchy.

Suddenly a gorgeous tall, dark, and handsome man comes around the corner with a smile. "Hi, girls, follow me." We follow him around the side of the building to a locked door, which he uses a key to open, and then into a dark elevator. Just as I'm starting to get a little nervous, the doors slide open to a beautiful bar four stories up, filled to the brim with absolutely gorgeous businessmen smoking cigars. So this is where the real men in LA have been hiding all this time.

I smile and sit down next to a man named Dalton, and when the waitress comes over to get our drink order, he suggests I get a Manhattan. So I do. When it arrives, he asks me to go to the cigar room with him to choose a cigar. So I do. The room is large and quiet, all sound dampened by the personalized wooden lockers and the humidifiers meant to keep the cigars fresh. He pulls two cigars from his box. "Will you smoke one with me after dinner? These are the best Cubans."

"Of course," I say slyly, as if I smoke cigars regularly. When we get back to the table, we discover everyone diving into an enormous amount of sushi. I notice the other girls picking around with their chopsticks, only putting little bits in their mouths. The food's too good to pick at—this is not the time for dieting. I pile my plate with colorful sushi and listen in on the conversation around me. After a few minutes, I realize that they're talking about international arms deals and billions of dollars changing hands between countries. I look down at my plate; should I be hearing this? This is the kind of conversation that people kill nosy bystanders over. The guys don't seem to care though, and the other girls aren't even listening. They're too busy taking selfies and talking about makeup, hair, and the next cool club. I lean in to the guys' conversation. After some time, I can tell that they know I'm intrigued, but they don't seem to want to include me in the conversation. But, who would I tell anyway? I do know there's power in guys underestimating you.

The waitress comes by with fresh drinks, and the girls excuse themselves to go chat at the bar and hit the powder room. I exchange a glance with Dalton, and he nods—I'll stay with the guys. He hands me my drink and the cigar, and I lean in to the guys, thrilled that they're bringing me into their inner circle. The conversation gets more intense—talk of micro chips inserted into generals' eyelids that allow them to see where the enemy is positioned at war, drones that civilians don't know about, the whole gambit of military intelligence. I chomp my cigar between my teeth and puff on it like they do, relaxing in the haze of smoke and privileged information. I love the intense power around me. It feels safe. Powerful men are so extremely sexy.

"Well that's enough business for one night," one of the guys says, winking at me. "Now, where did your girlfriends go?"

"They're still at the bar. I'll go get them," I say, getting ready to leave.

"Wait! You need a picture with that cigar first," Dalton says, pulling out his phone. I pose with the cigar in my mouth, biting it between my teeth and bending my neck back seductively.

Dalton looks at his phone and shakes his head. "God, this should be an ad for this place. You could crush a man's soul with those looks, honey."

I blush and stand to get the girls at the bar. "Yo, girls! You're wanted at the table. Move those tushies!"

"Okay, we're coming, LJ," Sidney says, pulling me in for a kiss and a hug. "We're coming. Don't get your panties in a bunch, doll face."

The ladies make it back over to their dates slightly more tipsy than when they left.

"Let's go over to Whiskey Bar," one of the guys suggests, and everyone agrees.

"Shall we?" Dalton asks, standing and holding out his arm to me.

I smile and take his arm. "We shall."

When the doors open on the ground floor, two huge men in suits and dark glasses are standing waiting for Netté, one of the guys we are with. He's obviously a man involved in something big, to need two huge linebackers for bodyguards. He was also the rudest at the table; you could tell he was from a country where they treat women like dirt. I get the feeling that if you were his girl, you wouldn't be allowed to speak.

We all stand on the corner waiting for the valet to come around with the cars when suddenly a limo pulls right in front of us with tinted windows and something like a shield layered around it.

"Excuse me?" I hear behind me. I turn to see Netté standing there, towering over me. "Would you like to be my guest this evening and ride with me over to the hotel?"

"Oh...well I told Dalton I'd ride with him, I think?" I fumble.

"He won't mind," Netté says, taking my hand and leading me to the limo.

"Okay..." I say, my consent clearly not needed. I turn to the rest of the group on the sidewalk, dumbstruck as to why he didn't take his own date with him. "See you guys over there, I guess?" They nod and wave good-bye to me, Sidney enthusiastically and Dalton confusedly.

As the car door closes and the bodyguards go up to the front seat, Netté raises the divider and opens a bottle of champagne.

"You like champagne?" he asks, pouring me a glass.

"Yes, very much so, thank you," I say, taking it from him. I'm very aware of sitting up straight and not slouching. I'm not exactly used to riding around in limos and sipping champagne with international arms dealers. So I try to exude certainty.

"Well, LJ. This is a very special bottle we are going to drink tonight. I wanted to be in good company for one moment to relax and breath and enjoy this remarkable bottle in peace."

Ah, so I'm a pawn in a power play between him and his date. I get it now.

"What...kind of champagne is it?" I ask, unsure of what to talk about.

"It's a Cristal Brut from 1990. Her name is Methuselah. Have you heard of this?"

"No. But it sounds like there's an amazing history behind it. Please enlighten me," I reply.

"I just bought a case of them at auction, at Sotheby's when I was in New York City last week. I was told I was the only one to purchase the gold label. They are quite rare."

"Oh...very nice, Netté. Thank you so much for sharing this with me," I say. I try to swirl the crisp liquid in my mouth and appreciate the rarity. It's likely I'll never taste champagne this good ever again.

"I'd like to make a toast...to the tenacious girl who loves the art of war," he announces, raising his glass.

"Oh, well, thank you," I say. "And thank you for letting me listen in; it was fascinating."

"I noticed that you listen very intently. Especially to the international arms deals and military conversation between men at the table. It's intriguing to me that a woman would find our conversation interesting."

"Well...I have always been interested in world travel and other cultures and in the way the world really works. I hope I wasn't prying too much. I was just very captivated with what you had to say."

"No, no, dear. Not at all. It's just, most young women your age don't care about how the world really works, only trivial pursuits."

"I'm not most young women."

"Yes...and I can see that it separates you from the rest of the girls. Do you know why being fluid is so important in life and in business, LJ?"

"Well...if you are constantly changing, like a chameleon, then know one will know you're coming. Not even your enemies," I reply with a smile.

He looks me up and down, appraising me. "I'm impressed. Very smart, LJ. Yes, you must assume formlessness, because in taking a shape, you open yourself to attack."

"Like water. Fluidity. You should go with the flow and be on the move, to retain power."

"Yes. You have a very keen sense about this. Everything changes. It's always changing. The scenery is always changing. And you never want to be perceived as a relic."

The conversation pauses, during which we quietly sip our champagne. I purse my lips. I know I should be offended that he assumed so little of me that he was impressed by any amount of intelligence I had, but I can't deny that I'm flattered. I'm very excited that I've impressed this worldly man. It feels good to be appreciated for my wit.

"So where in the world are you off to next?" I ask.

"I have business in Moscow. I'll be leaving Los Angles the day after tomorrow. Would you like to join me? I have my plane on standby. It's just been completely renovated on its interior."

I can't say I'm not tempted, but the voice in the back of my head tells me that he could be potentially dangerous. It's usually not the best idea to jet off to Russia with a man who has two armed bodyguards on deck at all times. I have to deflect his question with another and flatter him at the same time, otherwise he'll be offended. Talking to this man is like a game of chess, and I know if I lose, I could be in trouble.

"Wow! That is a tremendous offer, Netté," I say, widening my eyes innocently. "And I would love to see Moscow…but won't your girlfriend be upset?"

"Oh, LJ," he tisks. "I thought you knew how the world really worked."

Just then, we roll to a stop in front of the hotel, and his bodyguards get out and open the doors for us. Before getting out, I turn to him and put my hand on his.

"Thank you. I've had a brilliant time talking with you, Netté."

"The pleasure was all mine, LJ." He raises my hand to his lips and plants a gentle kiss on it, and just like that, my ride with a James Bond villain is over. We walk into the bar together where the rest of the group is already waiting for us; I notice that the driver must have circled the hotel a few times to give us time to talk since we left before they did and should have arrived first. Sidney takes my hand right away and pulls me to the bathroom to get the scoop.

"What happened?!" she asks as soon as we're inside.

"Nothing! We just talked and had an amazing bottle of champagne."

"Liar!"

"No, seriously, Sid. We just had a nice chat...and I'm feeling a bit tipsy at the moment. Shouldn't have had so many Manhattan's at the bar earlier; they were so strong. Woo! Well...he's a really smart guy; we actually had a great conversation. I just love to talk to wise, worldly people!"

"Oh my god! Please! You would say that. Wouldn't you. Well, Skylar's pissed that you left with her man."

"Well...he pulled me into the car! What was I supposed to do? I thought I would get a ride with you or Dalton over here."

Sid rolls her eyes at me. "She's a serious up-and-coming actress. And I need to stay friends with her if I'm going to get into all the award show after parties this season! Now, how am I going to get in? She was *our* way in, I mean. Ugh. Why are you such a problem sometimes?"

"You'll find some other way to get in, Sid. I'm sure! You always do. Defriend me then. I don't have to go."

"Stop. I'm always on your side, LJ. Fuck that actress! I can't stand her constant resting bitch face anyway. Let's go."

"Hey, wait. Thanks, but which guy is your 'john' for tonight?"

"Oh no, these are just friends of friends that invited us for dinner tonight, sillyhead. I told you. This has nothing to do with that. I'm meeting the other guy at one thirty at his condo in Bel-Air for an hour for my job."

"Okay, then can you bring me home before you go over there?"

"Try to ask Dalton, and if not, I'll take you. Now let's go get another drink; shake that ass baby. Work it!"

We glide right up to our party, and they greet us like old friends. Dalton seems to forgive me for leaving him on the curb and insists on buying all my drinks for the rest of the night, sending glares in Netté's direction every so often, but the party takes on the same lighthearted ambience from the cigar bar. Skylar, the up and comer, even seems to forgive me once Netté puts his arm around her, though I doubt we'll be best friends anytime soon. We party right up until 1:00 a.m. when Sidney comes over and gives me a kiss on the head, waving bye to everyone else.

"Dalton, I'm getting a bit tired. Do you think you could take me home?" I ask before Sidney leaves.

"Of course," he says, motioning for the bartender to cash out his black card. We head across the street to retrieve his car, and when he punches in a code to open the gate, I realize that this is his apartment building. He's a perfect gentleman though and takes me right to his car in his garage, only mentioning that he's got this place as well as one in New York City, where he primarily lives. That's real, real fancy bicoastal living—by Hollywood standards, it is the crème de la crème. Super chic.

We get into his car, a fabulous hybrid supercar BMW i8 that I know enough about to compliment on. It's pretty sick with its wing doors that scissor open to the sky. And he's so very "green." Impressive. I've always been a Rolls Royce kind of girl, but I'll just keep that to myself. Besides, at this moment in my life, I'm a blown-up-Jeep, inherited-silver-Ford Taurus kind of girl. And that's just my reality.

After a quick drive over the hill, he parks in front of my house and turns on the dome light. "Here, LJ," he says, pulling out his business card. "I'm putting my cell number on the back.

I'd love to take you to dinner sometime next week when I'm back from New York."

He hands me the card, and when I move to take it, he leans in for a kiss. I quickly give him the cheek.

"Oh…which is it? Just friends, or are you a tease?" he asks playfully.

"You'll just have to wait and see, darling," I say with a wink, opening the door. "Thank you for the fine, fine ride."

I sprint up to the house and heave a sigh of relief. I look at my phone; I've had four missed, cute Snapchats from Cole, but I have no desire to call him back. I do like him. But to be honest, I'm so worried about getting played. And I know I will. The wounds from Brody are still fresh. So maybe I'll just be a tease and have fun for a while. Good idea—thanks, Dalton.

CHAPTER FIFTEEN

Now that I'm waiting for my makeup-modeling job to start, the weeks become longer since the film has wrapped, and I'm just waiting around for my agent to call with any other job availability. On Wednesday, she does call with another stand-in offer, which I do for a few days before the TV show wraps for the season, and then it's back to waiting. I certainly didn't move to LA to sit around. By the time the weekend comes around, I'm chomping at the bit to see what Sidney has planned for us, and she doesn't disappoint. We're meeting at the famed Chateau Marmont for drinks with some of her friends, so I change into a stylish dress I bought on sale at Curve on Robertson and head out with a very low neckline and very high expectations. It's the Chateau, after all.

When I arrive at the famed hotel, Sidney's waiting for me in the driveway so there's no confusion with the doormen over whose list I'm on. We are ushered right in, and she takes me over to two handsome guys in the lounge area.

"This is Miles," she says, motioning to one of the guys. "And this is his good friend, Eric. Guys, this is my stunningly gorgeous good girl of a best friend, LJ. She is everything!"

"Ha ha, thanks, Sid. Very nice to meet you guys," I say, sitting on the couch next to Sidney in the lounge. The guys immediately order a bottle of outstanding French Bordeaux, and we fall into easy conversation. I can tell that Sidney's really into Eric from the way she delicately places her hand on his forearm when she wants his attention. He must be the one with the money. She can smell money; it's her ultimate aphrodisiac.

Miles and I find a way to end up at the bar together, leaving Sidney alone with her date. We've discussed everything from our life philosophies to our favorite places to go out in LA. I can feel our connection building; there's definitely something there. He's a supercool guy. And I don't hate the way his baby-blue-gray eyes pierce mine either.

"Where do you want to go, LJ?" Miles asks, leaning in and drawing circles on my knee.

"You mean in life, on vacation, or tonight?" I ask.

"All of the above." He laughs seriously.

"Well," I say, sipping my drink to stall time. "In life, I guess I want what everyone wants, to be happy. But, I also want more than that. I want love, real love, the fairy tale, you know…and excitement and adventure, to meet everyone and see everything in this world, to lead a life that isn't like anyone else's. I think that's what makes me want to be a playwright, or a novelist maybe. So that I can record everything I see and create my own reality. However dark or beautiful I want it to be. I want to be in charge. And it would be the icing on the cake if I could really entertain people and bring them on a ride with me. You know? Make them laugh and make them cry, have them truly enjoy themselves! Like how *Saturday Night Live* makes you feel, the brilliant puns and insane energy of it, or help make some incredible film that really moves people."

"Wow, that's all?" he says, leaning back to take me in. "You're such a good model though! And after that, then you should settle down around twenty-six and start a family. You'd be a damn good wife and mom. I can tell."

"Well, thanks," I say. I'm a little miffed that he just skimped over my dreams and went straight to motherhood. As if we're all meant to be barefoot and pregnant in the kitchen. I can't pretend this isn't the first time this has happened though. It's like guys can't seriously comprehend the idea of someone besides them having goals. Symptoms of an alpha dog, I guess. But, I want to be the alpha. I will always dream big and enjoy being different. And I remember it's our first drink together and to keep my knee-jerk reaction to myself. I am having a good time chatting with him.

He motions for the bartender to bring us another round and then turns back to me. "Okay, so vacation. Have you ever been to Napa Valley up in northern California?"

"No. I haven't. My mom and stepdad go all the time, and it looks absolutely beautiful, but I haven't been there yet."

"It is," he says, eyebrow cocked. Is he hinting at something?

"Okay, and for tonight. I think first we should go and get them in the lounge, and then you and I should get out of here. Yes, yes?"

I hesitate for only a brief second before nodding my head. He cracks a smile and grabs my hand. Its warm strength envelops mine, and my pulse quickens. And I'm sure I blushed. We take our drinks back to the lounge and find Eric and Sidney practically in each other's laps.

"Hey, let's go, bro," Miles says to Eric.

"I'll go get the car," Eric says, standing up.

"Hey, LJ, come with me. Let's go hit the ladies room," Sidney says, grabbing my hand and pulling me away from Miles.

"Okay, we'll meet you guys outside," I tell Miles.

Sid talks to me through the bathroom stalls, telling me how rich Eric is from some app he created and sold for millions. And that he now lives in some ginormous home in Palo Alto up north.

"That's awesome, Sid." I cut her short. "Hey, should one of us drive too, just in case?"

"In case what?" she asks. "Nah, let's just go with them. We'll get a ride back later. And you'd better be on the lookout for a rich husband here in LA sooner than later. Or God forbid, if you let yourself get too old, you'll end up with some bald, fat guy that wears khakis, living in the burbs in some subdivision where all the houses look the same in the Midwest." She shakes her head.

"Yikes, Sid. But, I'm from the Midwest, so it might not be too bad. And thanks for the vote of confidence. I always knew I'd be a failure. And you can kiss my ass, Sid! I will never marry a guy that wears khakis—that's for damn sure!"

"Okay, LJ. Whatever. You lovestruck, hopeless romantic. Seriously, the fairy tale you seek is just a fantasy. So get it together. We'll see who of us ends up where. Now, let's go!"

We walk outside and climb into the totally blacked-out Range Rover with the guys and start up into the Hollywood Hills. I just know we're going somewhere nice, more than likely with a great view. I'm a sucker for a great view.

When we arrive at the house, I know I was right. Eric disappears quickly while Miles gives me and Sidney a tour of his home, stopping in the kitchen to make us drinks and admire the view from his floor-to-ceiling sliding-glass living room doors. Eric comes back with a bag and starts to cut lines for us on the table.

"Anyone?" he asks, and Sid hops right over to him.

"I'll have one! And so will she."

"Well, thanks for answering for me, Sid," I tease, and she rolls her eyes at me. We do a few lines and then sit and talk for a bit, and after some time Miles, pulls out a special Mondavi vintage.

"This is from my family reserve," he says, pouring glasses for all of us.

Sidney's ears instantly perk up. "You're a Mondavi?"

"Yeah," Eric answers for him. "Miles Mondavi."

"So you have a vineyard, Miles?"

"Yeah. Well, my family has vineyards in Napa, and we've just acquired land in Tuscany," he answers.

Just like that, everyone's positions around the table change. I suddenly find myself next to Eric, and somehow Sidney gets on Miles's lap. Right then, I know it's over. I knew she'd try to sleep with him that night, and I wasn't going to have a chance. I can tell that Eric is confused as well, and when he and I excuse ourselves out on the deck for a cigarette, we see Sidney and Miles leave the living room and head upstairs. My stomach sinks, which surprises me in a way. It's not like I'm looking for a relationship with anyone, but if he had asked me out, I definitely would have said yes. He was handsome and sweet, and we got along really well. Sidney knew that we'd been talking all night, but she didn't care. She just stepped right over me to get what she wanted. In a way, that was even more crushing than the fact that he went with her. He only knew me for a night, but Sidney's my best friend. If she's not looking out for me, who is?

The one thing I know for sure is that I can't just sit here while she fucks the guy I liked upstairs.

"Eric, could you take me home?" I ask.

"Yeah, sure, let me just grab the keys from Miles," he says.

I can't stand to be in the house another minute, so I go out to the driveway to wait for him. It's scary outside; the driveway is long, dark, and very steep. I can hear the coyotes howling back and forth through the canyons to each other. I'd still rather risk being eaten by wild animals than be inside.

At least the coyotes are upfront about the fact that they'd devour you in a heartbeat.

Eric bumps the music as we cruise down Mulholland Drive at four in the morning. I open my window and chain smoke the entire way, leaning my seat back and hanging my bare feet out of the window, shaking them with the beat. I've gone past the point of caring anymore, and Eric doesn't seem to care either. No. We're both actually pissed, and when I offer him a cigarette, he takes it and smokes it angrily. When we arrive at my house, he gives me a hug and tells me not to worry about Sidney and Miles.

"Thanks, Eric, I appreciate it. Good luck with everything," I tell him.

I walk inside and try not to feel too bad for myself, but it's hard when all I want to do is rip Sidney's head off. Survival of the fittest comes to mind; I could've had him if I wanted, but Sid just weaseled her way in there first. I tell myself that guys who fall that easily for sex aren't worth it, and though I know it's true, it's somehow less reassuring when you're tucking yourself into bed alone.

CHAPTER SIXTEEN

I wake the next morning to the sun shining and my cell phone vibrating the whole nightstand.

"Hello?" I ask groggily.

"LJ, my love! I'm so sad you left last night; we missed you! I just wanted to let you know that I won't be around today. Miles and I are heading up to Napa for the weekend. We're actually getting on his private jet right now, so I can't really talk, but I'll catch you up on everything when I get back, okay?"

"You know what, Sid? Fuck you!" I tell her, seething. "You're a shitty person, and I can't believe it took me this long to figure it out. Have a nice flight, asshole."

I jam the end button on my phone, robbed of the satisfaction of slamming a phone on the receiver five times. I throw my phone across the room anyway. Fucking great. So, he's taking her to Napa instead of me. We even talked about Napa last night, and he totally hinted that he'd like to take me out there. She's stealing my life, and she had the nerve to call me and brag about it, acting like she just wanted to let me know where she was going so that I wouldn't be worried. I really did like him, and I liked him before I knew he was the heir to an enormous fortune. How is it that someone so fake beat me? Isn't it supposed to be that good always wins over evil? If being nice and doing the right thing and really being genuine didn't get me what I wanted, maybe it's time to be bad. Fuck it.

I spend the rest of the day licking my wounds and planning my revenge, mostly centered on me sleeping with any guy Sidney shows interest in. When my good friend, Damiano, suddenly Snapchats me, inviting me up to his house for dinner, I can't respond yes fast enough. He's like a brother to me, and I could really use some of his authentic Italian pasta, vino, and good advice. He's having a few people over, he told me, so I throw on a comfy black sleeveless cashmere dress with low biker boots, pull my hair up into a ponytail, use my new fuchsia lip pencil, and head straight for the hills.

Driving up to his house automatically feels cathartic. Damiano always brings me back down to Earth. I wind through the Hollywood Hills and finally make my way up to his house, parking at the space at the top of his driveway. He always leaves the space open for me; all of this other guests usually brave the steep hill down to his house, but I'd rather park and walk down the outdoor garden stairs to his house. One time, when I was bored, I actually counted the stairs: 101 red-brick steps down to his patio. His house is such a beautiful oddity—a huge green yard with two big oak trees and a hammock between them, all overlooking Sunset Boulevard. As I walk down the steps, the view of our town stretches as far as the eye can see, the lights starting to twinkle on as the sun dips below the horizon. It's the perfect place to be at twilight. I can see that a lot of the people have already arrived and are talking loudly and dancing around Damiano's house, but I want to stay outside and enjoy this moment a little longer. I lie on the hammock to rock and relax before I go inside, gazing out at

Los Angeles and thinking about my life. It's funny how insignificant the town looks from up above, how much less significant our problems are once we get some perspective. I guess this is why people always go seek higher ground in a flood.

"I knew I'd find you here, man," a deep voice says from behind the hammock.

"Right on time, brah," I say in my best California surfer voice. Damiano crouches down beside me and gives me a small kiss before handing me a glass of wine.

He's always so full of love and good energy. Whenever I'm around him, I can see the beauty that he sees in the world through his eyes. I pat the hammock, and he slides in next to me, putting his arm under my head for a pillow.

"How's it going in there?" I ask. "Do you need help cooking?"

"Nah, let's let them heathens inside just handle it for a minute. Let's swing," he says as he puts his arm around me.

We sit in silence for a moment, just enjoying the fading colors in the sky as the dusk settles around us. He's one of those great people that you can just sit with and relax, and he doesn't assume anything or judge anything, and no matter what, you always pick up where you left off. It's like a breath of fresh air being with him. I value our friendship more than most any other relationship I have.

"What's going on with you, LJ? You've got something on your mind. I can hear your brain on overdrive."

"Everything's great..." I start, before catching his eye and knowing he'll see right through me. I sigh. "Dam, I don't know? It's like everything I thought was good and right isn't actually true. And I'm considering this thing, and it could either be really good or really bad for me. The problem is that I can't tell which."

"Will it change who you are?" he asks.

"I think so. Well, I dunno? Not the core of who I am. But I think I'm just drawn to it because it's something that's forbidden. And I'm curious to see what it's like."

"Is that a bad thing?"

"That's the problem. It might not be? I can't see clearly. I need you to yank me out of this fog I'm in."

"I guess then…just try it and tread lightly. You're too curious of a person not to try everything once. Just be careful. And don't get killed like the cat does. You're my favorite person, LJ. I need you around for a while. And you know, I don't care what you do. I'll always love you, brah."

I have to laugh at that. "Right back at you, Dam! Love you too. You're the craziest speed demon I know with all of those fast motorcycles in your garage. Scares the hell out of me! Between the both of us, we've probably blown through eight of our nine lives already, so one of us is living on the edge."

"I know, I know." He laughs. "I guess I have to take my own advice too. But, LJ, I've known you for so long, even when you were a sweet little surfer chick, and the thing I've always known about you is that you're a grateful person—you would never hurt anyone…except yourself. You're a survivor, and you'll always do what you need to do to make it through in this life. And you can't pass up an adrenaline rush. I know you too well. Especially if it's something no one else will do. You live to be different! Push yourself past the limits. It's exciting and sexy. Come on. You know it."

"I know, but that doesn't help! Tell me what to do!"

"Nope. Can't. But I'd rather you not do it. And I do know what you're talking about." I nod. "You have to figure that out for yourself, LJ. The one thing I do know for sure is that you'll choose the sickest thrill ride."

"Well, thanks for *nothing*!" I laugh.

He laughs and knuckles my head like an older brother.

167

"My hair!" I shriek as he hops out of the hammock and sprints away from me. "Oh my god, you're the worst!"

"Come inside!" he calls behind. I have to smile; Damiano is truly the big brother I never had.

The night is everything I could have wanted. Twenty-some people came over for Damiano's phenomenal lobster saffron risotto—artists, hipsters, and people in fashion breaking bread, telling stories, and laughing around the enormous dinner table together. It feels like being home with my family, but even better because these people really understand trying to figure yourself out in Hollywood. Soon enough, I realize that I'm the last guest, lingering over the wine and doing the dishes. Damiano comes up to me at the sink and asks if I want to crash a neighbor's party with him; we fill our wineglasses to the brim and walk up the street to a house bumping with music. We get past the doorman by pretending to be angry neighbors pissed about the noise, and we end up talking with everyone and dancing until three in the morning. When I head out, Dam gives me a big hug and tells me he loves me and that he's always here to talk. I know how lucky I am to have him in my life, and I drive home feeling so much better than I did on my drive up.

I spend Sunday with a pillow over my head, trying to block out the sound coming through the wall of Elliot randomly strumming his guitar. I'm tempted to ask him to lay off so I can sleep in, but I know it's his passion, so I just curse him silently. Besides, the rest of the house already teases him for always carrying his guitar around the house with him; we can't all gang up on him. I finally find some spongy yellow earplugs in the bottom of my junk drawer that will do the trick, and I pass out with my mind reeling of Damiano toasting "the good life" at his dinner and Sidney and her new boyfriend fucking on a private jet. What does it all mean?

*

Monday arrives bright and early with me cruising down the highway en route to shoot the new makeup line with Naomi. I'm glad to be working again; my bank account has been getting dangerously low, and I'll get a full three weeks of work with this job. After that, I don't know. I like to think of myself as a free spirit, going where the wind blows me, but working job to job like this kinda freaks me out. I guess I'm missing a strong foundation, as my mom would say. But I know that. I'm just finding my own way to build it.

I shoot with Naomi for twelve hours and catch up with her when I can. I'm tempted to tell her about what Sidney did, but I don't want her to hate her even more than she already does. After a long day, I jump straight in the car to go home, without washing my face, crazy feather eyelashes and all. The makeup artists were too good, and I don't want to sweep away all their hard work just yet.

When I walk into my room, I see that Sidney left a note and a red rose, a joint and a lighter on my pillow, apologizing for everything. I sigh a little and decide to take a shower after all; I need to be refreshed if I'm going to deal with her crap.

As soon as I'm done towel drying my hair, I head upstairs and knock lightly on Sidney's door. My stomach is up in knots. I really hate confrontations, and I'm honestly just eager for this to be over with.

"Come in!" Sid calls from inside. I push open the door and find her lying on her bed watching TV. She sits up a little straighter when I walk in.

"Hey," she says. She punches the mute button on her remote to silence the TV.

"Hey." I stand awkwardly in the doorway, not wanting to leave but not wanting to make things comfortable for her either.

She takes a deep breath and lets it out slowly. "Listen, LJ, I'm really sorry. I didn't know you liked him that much."

"Yeah, well, you didn't exactly ask me," I tell her.

"I know, I know. Like I said, I'm sorry. Look, can we just get past this? I'm going to watch *Trainwreck*. I know it's one of your favorites. Are you still mad?"

"Well…I was. But not so much anymore. You did practically steal a guy from me." There's a silence during which Smalls ambles into the room and nudges my hand for a pet. I indulge him. "So what, do you have any pot?"

Sidney grins. "Yes, ma'am. You know I do! But where's the joint I gave you?"

"It's downstairs. I'm saving it for a rainy day."

"Well, it was a gift. Okay, fine. No worries. I have more all rolled up for you on my shelf behind the red candle. There should be two joints back there. Hey, how's the new makeup thing going?"

I tell her about my new job as I light the joint and then pass it over to her. I can tell she's happy that we're friends again, and if I'm being honest, I'm glad too. Even when I was angry with her, I missed her company. She's too much fun to be angry with for long. But three strikes and you're out in my mind. She's on thin ice.

"Naomi hooked you up with that job, right?" she asks.

"Yeah, she's been great. She's really awesome! I couldn't love her more. She's one of the only girls I know out here that is truly happy for you when something goes your way. Like you book a commercial or have a great boyfriend or something. Most girls just want to throw you under the bus. Seriously. Run over. Dead. Flat. Road pizza like."

"Yeah, I know. She's super sweet to you. Totally dotes on you. Anyway, guess what?" she asks, her eyes growing bright. "I've got almost all the money I need to pay for my condo!"

"No way!" I say, shocked. She would have had to save thousands and thousands of dollars to do that. She reaches under her bed and pulls out a tan shoebox bursting with cash.

"Holy shit, Sid, oh my god! I don't think I've ever seen that much cash in person before. How much is that?"

"Thirty thousand," she says, clearly proud.

"Shut the fuck up," I say. I'm truly speechless. Seeing that much money stashed under her bed throws all of my qualms with what she does right out the window. In a world where it pays to play the game, she's really winning.

"I know Naomi doesn't like me," she says, gazing at her shoebox.

"Oh, Sid, I wouldn't say that…can I hold some of it?"

"Here. It's fine. I know she thinks I'm going to get you into trouble. But you're a big girl. You can decide for yourself what you want. I don't care what she thinks of me. I just want us to be good. Are we good, LJ?"

"Yeah, we're good. Wow. Thirty grand feels amazing! This is a whoooole lotta cheddar."

"For real?" she asks, meeting my eyes.

"Yeah, for real, we are good," I say, smiling.

"Good! Love ya, hot stuff. Hey, before we watch the movie, let's go get takeout salads or a burger! I know you love the garlic mashed potatoes at Moe's. What do you think? On me!"

How could I ever stay angry at her when she offers mashed potatoes? We spend the evening grabbing food and planting ourselves on her bed in front of the TV. It's so cozy and fun, and I'm glad that we're back to normal. She even invites me to a Bad Santa party later in the week, but I'm hesitant to go since I have a 5:00 a.m. call time the next day. I tell her I'll play it by ear, but when she says okay, she gives me a look like she knows I'll end up going, anyway.

"Hey, why haven't you called Cole back?" Sidney asks, tossing a piece of spinach into her mouth.

"I don't know. I guess I don't want to start anything with him."

"Well, gorgeous, you have him majorly bugging out like I've never seen! I think you're the first girl in history that hasn't called him back!"

"I didn't mean to do that. I just didn't really think about it."

"Yeah, dude, well, you're really pushing his buttons. His ego has really taken a blow. He really likes you, you know? Throw him a bone, or a boner, will ya." She giggles.

"Come on. He only likes me because I haven't called him back! Listen, it's not like we didn't have an amazing evening, 'cause we really did. It was totally insane. Best sex ever. I told you that. Maybe I'll see him around, and we can do it again sometime. But I'm not really worried about it. If it happens, it happens. But I'm not going to call him. Lay off me!"

"Okay. All right. I really like this new LJ! You're a player! Take no prisoners. You can't have me! Look out, boys, we've got a fucking man-eater on our hands."

"Oh, god, stop it! I'm not trying to hurt his feelings. Not like they're really hurt anyway," I tell her, throwing a balled-up napkin in her direction.

I'm not being totally honest when I say I haven't been thinking about Cole a lot. His incredible lower stomach muscles that frame his nether regions like sculpture keep running through my mind like someone hit repeat. But more than anything, as we start watching *Trainwreck*, what I can't stop thinking about is how if I had thirty thousand dollars stashed under my bed, I wouldn't have to be so worried about getting up on time for work the next day and paying my bills.

I model the new makeup line every day with Naomi and go out to the clubs every night with Sidney for the rest of the week. We end up at wild house parties with infinity pools, glowing dance floors, DJs, oversized purple-velvet lounge chairs, and popular pop princesses. We even go to a casino party where we witness a few hot celebrity guys playing a super-high-stakes poker game where the buy-in is fifteen thousand dollars. The Bad Santa party at the end of the week is super sick too, and afterward, we hit up a party in a private home with a full-service bar, drop-dead gorgeous burlesque girls performing an amazingly choreographed show, and a laser-light show. We even end up at the most expensive mansion in Los Angles, and somehow Sidney's sweet talking gets us permission at the gate to "drive on in" in her little Jetta. Together, we are invincible.

We dance all night, doing blow in the bathroom with a few movie stars. I find myself flirting with actors from some of my favorite shows while women wearing only body paint flit through the festive bash. While waiting for Sidney's car outside, a major actor walks up to her and starts chatting with her, and they end up going home together. I thought I read in *Us Weekly* the other day that he was engaged to some gorgeous brunette? But I guess in Hollywood, it's all a show. And nothing's real. I drive Sidney's car home, listening to *Afternoon Acoustic*, and scroll through the host of new numbers in my phone from famous actors; it's so freeing to have no obligation to anyone but myself. I absolutely love it! When I get home, I fall asleep with a smile, dreaming of the countless great times to come.

*

By the end of the weekend, I check out my calendar and notice that I've missed my period for sure for the second time. I break out into an instant sweat and run upstairs to tell Sidney.

"Okay, yeah, dude, it's totally okay. Don't worry about it. This shit happens. I wouldn't worry about it too much. It could be anything. I'm sure it's nothing," she says. "Do you want me to run out to CVS and get a pregnancy test for you?"

"No, oh my god. No!" I say. In a weird way, not knowing is easier than knowing. Ignorance is bliss. She ignores me and leaves for CVS anyway, coming back with three different tests.

"I don't want to know. I'm scared, Sidney," I tell her, tears filling my eyes as I pace the hallway.

"Ah. Well, LJ, you're going to know sooner or later whether you want to or not. So just do it!"

"Yeah, I get it. I get it! I'm just really fucking scared!" I look down at my stomach. How many times had I been careful? I rack my brain, trying to think about my recent sexcapade, but we used ten condoms. "Oh my god, Sidney," I tell her, tears streaming down my face. "I know I am! I just know it's Brody's. Oh my god! This sucks. What do I do?"

She puts her hand on my shoulder and directs me to the bathroom across the hall from her room. "Go in there, and take the test. I'll be right outside the door."

I go in and then come back out and sit on the hall floor with Sid. She sets the timer on her new watch and holds my hand while we wait, letting me rest my head on her shoulder crying as we watch the numbers click down to zero.

"It's time," she says, and my stomach clinches even tighter.

"Will you go check?" I ask her. "Please."

She gets up, and I find it hard to hold myself up without her support. She comes back and crouches down next to me. "Every one of them, all positive," she whispers.

I rush downstairs in a blur and lie down on my bed, sobbing. My mind is racing; things are happening too quickly. Sidney comes into the room and sits down on my chair, waiting for me to quiet down.

"What am I going to do?" I ask her.

"Call Brody, I guess. It's his, right?"

I think back and realize that the timing does mean that it's for sure his. At least it's not Cole's. That's a relief I guess.

"Hey, listen, this is exciting, right?" she says. "You're going to have a baby!"

I pause, looking at her incredulously. "You're kidding right now, right?"

"Well, you wouldn't think of the alternative, would you?"

I sit up on the bed. "Sidney, I'm twenty-one years old. I just broke up with my longtime boyfriend who cheated on me, probably more than once, whose baby I'm now pregnant with. I would have to move back in with him in our apartment in Long Beach, where I would sit around with a screaming baby, waiting for him to come home from work only to tell me that we don't have enough money for diapers!"

She stares at me, uncomprehending. Thinking of this future brings fresh tears to my eyes, but I get angrier as I think about my life with a child.

"Or, let's think of the alternative. I'd move in with my parents, being a burden again, living in one of their guest rooms, with my child growing up thinking that his grandmother is his mother, and I'm just an older sister who can't provide for him. That's not how the fairy tale goes in my head! No, thank you. I can't do this! I'm just not ready for this, Sid!"

"I can't believe you, LJ. You'd actually consider abortion?"

"Why can't you? What, are you suddenly a Christian fundamentalist or something? You're supposed to be my supportive friend. Why are you making me feel morally guilty for this? What the fuck, Sidney? How many of those men you fuck on a daily basis are married with babies, wives, and families of their own at home?"

Sidney gets up and storms out of the room, slamming my door behind her.

"Hey, are you okay?" Jona pushes my door open a bit a few minutes later, nudging his head inside.

"Yeah, I'm fine. Sorry for the screaming. I'm sure you heard everything."

"It's okay. Do you want to talk about it?" He looks like that's the absolute last thing he'd want, but he's so sweet for asking.

"Thanks, Jona. I'd rather be alone for now. Thank you. I'll figure it out."

"Okay. Can I bring you some tea or something? Do you want Smalls in here?"

"No, thanks. I'm fine, Jona. Thank you. I'll be fine."

"Okay. Good night then."

It's four in the afternoon, but Jona knows I won't be leaving my room until tomorrow. Alone with my thoughts, I start to do what I do in any crisis: plan.

I start by calling Naomi and telling her I won't be in tomorrow since I have to fly home a week early for Christmas vacation because my grandmother had a stroke. I hate lying to her, and lying about something so horrible, but it's something that needs to be done. She asks if I need her to come over and to talk about it, but I just say no. She says that she'll take care of everything at work for me, and that I should still have a bit of work after the New Year to come home to.

Well, that's taken care of. Now for the hard part. I dial Brody and wait for him to pick up. I don't even know if he will answer, but just as I'm losing hope, he picks up. I tell him that I took a pregnancy test and it was positive, and that I've got to go to Planned Parenthood tomorrow morning to make sure that I really am pregnant. He's clearly rattled and needs a minute to absorb the information, but then he tells me that he'll stand by me and do whatever I need, and that he'd be all right with whatever decision I make. His support makes me feel a little bit better, and it makes me miss him. We set up an appointment, and then I curl into a ball and cry myself to sleep. So scared. What is the right thing to do?

The next morning, I drive to Planned Parenthood and wait for four hours in the waiting room. When they finally call my name, I pee in a cup and am sent to a private Pepto-Bismol-pink room with mint-green plastic chairs, and all those pamphlets just stare at me while I wait for the nurse to come in; my heart's beating so loudly that I can practically hear it in my chest. I crack the door. Finally, I see her coming down the hall smiling at me. Oh my god. Does that mean good news, or bad news? I feel like sinking into the floor.

"Hi, Lillian. Okay, well the pregnancy test did come back positive today," she says, with a giant grin. She looks like a mannequin to me, frozen there at her desk with a plastic smile plastered on her face. I'm catatonic. I feel as though the wind has been knocked out of me. Why can't I get happy? I'm supposed to be happy, right?

"Lillian...Lillian! Are you all right? I'll be right back. Let me go get you some water."

As soon as she leaves the room, I get my cell phone out of my purse and call my mom. "Mom...I'm pregnant," I say as soon as she picks up. Then, I lose it entirely, sobbing uncontrollably into the phone. She stays silent for a while, letting me take comfort in her presence and calm down.

"Lillian, shhhhh," she says. "Listen, where are you now?"

I tell her where I am, and she clucks her tongue. I know she wishes I had gone to a private doctor, but I don't have insurance right now. This is my only option. It seems, lately, I'm getting forced into lots of things.

"Okay. Well, honey, all I have to say is this is a tragedy either way you go about it. The only thing that can be changed is how you let it affect you. I know you can't see yourself raising a family with Brody, but you should know that I had you when I was twenty years old. And, I was making my way through school after just marrying your father. I know that I could have never made the choice to get rid of a child. Never! But, honey, I guess the decision is up to you."

She doesn't really make me feel any better, worse in fact, but I know she's right. The only thing I can control here is my decision. The nurse comes back with a plastic cup of water with orange flowers on it, so I get off the phone with my mom and tell her I'll call her back.

"So, Lillian. Do you want to talk about your options?"

"Yes. Can you do the procedure tomorrow? I know you do them on Tuesdays. Can I schedule something for tomorrow?" I say, trying to control my breathing while crying.

"I think you should think long and hard about a decision like this. You're upset right now and not thinking clearly. There is also the possibility of adoption."

"I know all that. But I want to make an appointment for tomorrow. Let's get it made. Okay!"

"Okay, Lillian. I'll be right back." She leaves the room and returns with a green slip of paper. "I have an eleven o'clock opening tomorrow morning. Does that work for you?"

"Yeah. Great. Thank you…I'll be here." I stand up, still trembling, and grab my purse and paperwork.

"Lillian?" she says, looking concerned.

"No. It's okay. I'll be fine. It's fine. Thank you for your time." I walk out, through the waiting room, where all the other girls see me leaving shakily, with my red, puffy face. I try to look as calm as possible, remembering how I was once one of them, searching the girls' faces for hope and comfort. They're all there with their own worries. I try to pull it together, walking out, not wanting to add to that.

I get to the car and call Brody. He tells me that he'll come over tonight and then take me to the clinic in the morning. It breaks my heart, living through this nightmare. Having a baby is supposed to be a happy time, being married to the man of my dreams and enjoying decorating a nursery, not this. I don't want to make this decision, but I know for me, it's the only decision. I can't raise a child now, not when I'm just starting to really live my life. I can't live with having my choices taken away from me. I have to take them back for myself. The bottom line is that I'm just completely unprepared to be someone's mom. And I'm terrified to turn into my mother, treating my child as a burden.

Brody comes over that night with a case of Gatorade. Apparently, he Googled pregnancy terminations and saw that I'd need electrolytes for after the procedure. When I see how sweet he's being, I dissolve into his arms. We spend the night cuddling in bed, taking turns crying. We say that we don't know what the right thing to do is, but it's a lie. We do know that this is the right decision for us at this time. But it's extremely hard to swallow. I don't want to do this.

The next morning, Brody takes me to the clinic and waits in that same waiting room with me. This time, I don't worry about holding it together in front of the other girls. I just sit, heavy hearted, with Brody and let him hold me. When they call my name, he squeezes my hand and reminds me that it's okay to change my mind if I want to. And he'll be out here waiting for me when I'm done.

I walk back and get undressed and wait for my exam. I'm so afraid. Two beautiful, blond female doctors walk in and ask if I want an ultrasound and start to tell me details of how far along I am, but I stop them. I don't want to know the details. They exchange a glance but then nod. I can't help but wonder all the things they see every day. Tough job. They smile at me sympathetically and give me a speech designed to give me a final moment to think about the many other options I have—a way out of my final decision if I want to take it. A moment to really stop and think of the future. That's the right thing to do on their part. And I understand that. But I'm doing it.

I'm sent to a dim back waiting room in my white-paper gown with my rolling IV attached to my arm. There are five other women in there, all of them different ages. It doesn't matter what age you are though. We all feel the same. Horrible. They all look up at me as though I'm bringing some sort of hope into the room, but as I sit in the dark room to join them, we all fall right back into the nightmare. Never speaking. Just knowing we are all in misery. The doctors come in, calling names, and one by one, each of us are called from the room. When it is my turn, I walk with a very nice doctor, who makes me feel a little more at ease...and that's all I remember. I wake up at home in my bed, with Brody asleep in my big white armchair.

"Bro...Brody. Hey. Wake up," I whisper.

"Hi," he says, rubbing his eyes. "How do you feel?"

"I'm so sorry. I'm so sorry..." I say as I start to cry. "I feel empty, and so sad to have done this...but, I think it was the right thing to do for us. Did we do the right thing? This is horrible. I feel horrible."

"Hey. Hey, hey..." he says, getting up to sit next to me on the bed, brushing the tears from my eyes. "I told you that I would support you, no matter what. Now stop. Here's a Gatorade."

"Thank you," I say, taking the blue bottle from him.

"And I got you some chicken-noodle soup from Moe's. It's in the fridge, and there's mashed potatoes, spinach salad, and a big burger in there when you get hungry. And I put your name on the bag so none of these hungry dudes around here eat it."

"Thanks."

"And here's your case of Gatorade by your bed, and I put a few in the fridge too."

"Thank you."

"Do you want me to stay?"

"No. I think it's time we should be alone now. Don't you? I'm so drained. My brain hurts. My heart hurts. My everything hurts. I don't think I could be more brokenhearted."

"I know. Me too. Whatever you want, LJ. Just call me later, and I'll be here in a second if you need me."

"Thank you. Was I too much trouble to get in the car? I don't remember anything."

"You were definitely out of it. I just carried you."

"Thank you for being here and taking care of me. Thank you so much. I was so lucky to have you here. I can't say it enough. This has been a lot to go through. I'll call you later. Safe drive home, Bro."

For some reason, I can't stop thanking him. I just want to do anything to draw attention away from myself. He kisses me on the forehead and leaves me nestled in my covers, and I feel relief when I hear him close the door. I was lucky to have Brody come and take care of me, but it was more painful for us to look at each other rather than just be alone. It's time for us to move on. I realize that now. And after this, so does he.

For the next few days, I stay in bed and lounge in my robe and pajamas, eating my fridge full of takeout and recovering. My belly feels empty. And my heart is in pain. My stomach feels so sore, as if my insides were scraped out by Freddy Krueger. I am uncomfortable and having hot-and-cold spells and sharp, stabbing cramps. I think I have a fever for the whole following week. The house is quiet, like everyone's gone. They know I need some rest and avoid the house. Very sweet of them. I'm disappointed in Sidney though; she never once comes home or texts me to see how I'm doing. She really turns her back on me, and although I shouldn't be surprised at this point, it still hurts.

Well, I'm not going to have a baby just to make her happy. That's what this is all really about. She just wants to play with a baby and cuddle it, all cute like, and doesn't care if it affects the rest of my life. My mom does call a few times during the week to check on me; she only tells my stepdad, since we agree that it's best not to tell my siblings. And I never tell my father. There are just certain things that you don't tell your father. Plus, I'm going to see him when I fly home for Christmas tomorrow, and I don't want that to color our holiday.

The next morning, I feel back to myself physically but a total mess mentally. I gather the bags I packed earlier in the week and drive to LAX, parking my car in the long-term parking lot and waiting for the shuttle to take me to the terminal. I'm nervous to go home and see my family after such an emotional ordeal, and I'm scared that they'll be able to tell that something's wrong. I have my two best friends picking me up at the airport though, so I try to look forward to that as the shuttle driver loads my suitcase in along with everyone else's.

CHAPTER SEVENTEEN

As the plane lands in St. Louis, a sense of relief washes over me. Getting out of Los Angeles and spending time with family is the perfect way to recover. As soon as I turn my phone off of airplane mode, I get a ton of Snapchats from Izzy and Slone, all talking about how excited they are to see me. I text them back that we've landed and that I'll let them know when I've got my bag, and suddenly I find a smile on my face for the first time in a week. These girls will get me happy again, I think, as I retrieve my bag from the carousel. They've been my best friends since high school, when I met the twins freshman year. We got even closer when their parents died during our junior year in a horrific plane crash over Long Island. We'd driven them out to the airport that day in St. Louis; they were taking a second honeymoon in Paris, but the plane never even made it out of New York for the second flight of the trip. We were barely seventeen. Their lives changed forever that day. The girls stayed at my house a lot after that, and I became almost like a third sister to them. We've seen each other through more than you could imagine over the years, and I know I can always lean on them no matter what.

When I see them waiting for me at the curb, I already feel uplifted. They squeal and jump and hug me tight, and I can't stop smiling.

"LJ! My girl, it has been way too long! How are you doing?" Izzy asks, taking my suitcase and dropping it into the back of the SUV.

"Ah, better now that I'm home and with you guys. It's soooo good to see you two; you don't even know, ugh," I say, hugging them again.

"Has it really been a whole year?" Slone asks, getting into the car.

"Yeah, I think so," I tell her. "We need to do better. You guys have to come out and see me in LA. Seriously. You should just move there!"

"Oh, we will visit for sure!" Izzy says.

"Okay, so where are we going?" I ask them. They always have some sort of plan in place, which is why we were always up to no good in high school. I grin as I remember the mischief we caused in our old school days.

"I told some people we'd meet them at Ice & Fuel for a few drinks. Are you cool with that?" Slone says, looking over her shoulder at me as we get on the highway toward Kirkwood, the suburb of St. Louis where we all grew up.

"That's perfect," I tell them. It'll be great to catch up with old friends from high school. I could use some good nostalgic laughs while everyone's home for Christmas. "Let me just call my dad and tell him I'm here and that I'll be home late."

When I get my dad on the phone, he sounds excited that I'm home but slightly disappointed that I won't be home right away. He tells me that my sister, Jule, will be at the bar with some of her friends too, since she flew in from San Francisco earlier that day.

We spend the night sitting in the back of the bar by the dart board, our old spot that tempted fate as people got drunker and the darts began missing the bull's-eye more and more. The twins keep the drinks flowing; I always scold them for paying for everyone's drinks, as they always have a huge tab by the end of the night. I hate that other people take advantage of their generosity. They never mind though, as long as everyone's having a good time. I've always tried to be sneaky and pay for my own drinks, but there's no escaping them after we'd had a few. We start to get really rowdy, and they start ordering shots for everyone in the bar. They love supporting a good time!

It's great hanging out with people I have real memories with, as LJ, the sporty girl, who always had people over at her dad's house for bonfires and pool parties. The dive bar certainly doesn't measure up to the glamorous bars I'm used to in LA, but it's an incomparable soup for my soul to be here.

"Okay, these are just for us ladies," Slone says, handing out seven shots to me, her sister, and a few of our girlfriends from high school. We slush them around the high-top table and raise the shot glasses in the air. "Okay! Okay!" Slone says, getting everyone's attention. "Here's the toast...I have it! Okay...here's to the men that we love!" The single girls start booing, and Slone shushes them. "Stop! Let me finish! Okay, here's to the men that we love! Here's to the men that love us! But the men that we love aren't the men that love us. So fuck the men! And here's to *us*!"

We all cheer, our rebel yells attracting way too much attention across the bar. Soon enough, we have a crowd around us, and our rowdiness gets really out of hand. Rory, the owner, stands on the bar just as she always does when her bar is packed at closing.

"Everyone, we're closed! Pay your tabs, and get the fuck out of here. Now!" she yells, stomping her feet. It makes me laugh, watching her kick people out. We've all known her since she was ten years old, and she used to stomp her feet just like that when she was frustrated at losing in kickball. Some guys yell back at her, and she lets the profanities rip right back at them. Nothing's changed at this bar; all of the alumni from Kirkwood High School mix in when everyone's home for the holidays, and the partying always gets way out of control.

As the crowd gets chaotic, Rory motions us over and hands us a few twelve-packs from behind the bar. We pass her some cash and a nice tip; the after party is on.

"You ever drive a hybrid before?" Slone asks me as we head out to her car. I shake my head, and she hands me the keys. We load the beer in the back and head to our friend Squint's house, blasting music with her new five-thousand-dollar sound system so loudly that I don't hear when she tells me to turn left into Squint's neighborhood. She taps me and tells me to turn around, so I quickly flip a bitch in the middle of the street, the girls laughing their heads off. I turn, and red-and-blue lights start flashing in my rearview mirror.

"Oh, shit!" I say, turning down the music. I'm definitely not sober. I'm going to go to jail before I've even been home to see my family!

"Pull over!" Izzy yells.

"Hang on just a minute. I'm thinking…shh!"

I'm in Warson Woods, a neighborhood where the cops are notoriously strict. I know that if I'm going to get out of this, I've got to get my story straight. The lights continue to flash behind me, setting a timer to my decision. Suddenly, up ahead, I see a bunch of kids walking into a house party. I pull into the driveway and turn off the car.

"Wait, do you know them?" Slone asks.

"Nope."

The cop comes to the window and asks for my license and registration, telling me that I made an illegal U-turn. I smile and try not to let him see me shaking as I hand the materials over.

"I'm so sorry, officer. I just flew in for Christmas from California. I'm just so used to making U-turns out there that I forgot they were illegal in St. Louis. I truly apologize for my actions, sir."

He gives me a tight smile and goes back to his car to run my license. The kids continue walking into the party, giving us sarcastic thumbs-ups and laughing.

"You know, that cop looks really familiar," Izzy says. "He looks like this guy I used to go to Catholic school with."

"Maybe it is, but don't make a bigger scene than it needs to be, please, Iz. I don't want to go to jail," I tell her. "I'm just trying to get out of here without handcuffs on."

The cop comes back up to the car and hands me my license. He looks me in the eye. "Ms. Volpicelli, would you please step out of the vehicle?"

My heart starts really pounding; he can smell the alcohol on my breath for sure. He asks me to touch my finger to my nose and asks why I'm driving my friend's car.

"I'm the designated driver for the night, sir."

He stares at me through slitted eyes.

"Oh my god! Billy! Little Billy Emerson! Now I know!" screams Izzy from the back seat. That's it; we're all going to jail two days before Christmas. Izzy rolls down the back seat window and sticks her head out.

"It's Izzy and Slone Anchormen, from Carmelite Catholic School. Remember? You have to remember."

The officer squints. "Izzy? Is that you? Oh my gosh!" His face softens and a friendly smile spreads across it. He walks over to the window, and he and the girls immediately start reminiscing about school pranks, old teachers, and skipping class. I stand by myself on the street in shock.

The cop turns back and points a finger at me. "No more U-turns, California. You girls just get to where you're goin' now." And just like that, he gets back into his car and leaves after high-fiving the girls and promising he'll call.

I breathe a sigh of relief and walk around to the passenger seat. "Shotgun," I tell Slone, shaking my head. "I'm done driving tonight."

Izzy laughs and shakes my shoulders from the back seat once I sit down. "Relax, girl! He's so cool. Shake it off, sister! No one's going to jail. Yahoooo! Let's party!"

"Thanks, Iz. You saved my life."

By the time we make it to the party, we're riding the adrenaline of a near miss and are ready to celebrate. It's just like old times, playing beer pong just like we used to in high school. By four in the morning, we're ready to head home, so we all go back to my dad's house for a late-night snack. Whenever his kids are home, Dad always makes a big vat of angel-hair pasta and marinara sauce that we can microwave when we stumble in after a night out. He knows very well that we'll be raiding the fridge with our friends in the middle of the night. We're all eating at the kitchen island when Jule and Harper walk in with their friends and ask if there's enough for them too. It's good to be home, all of us eating and reminiscing. We tell them about the incident with the cop, and I make her promise not to tell Dad, at least not until after Christmas.

As the sun starts to rise over the Missouri hills, we retreat upstairs to pass out. Dad's passed out on the couch, TV blaring, and we all try not to laugh as we tiptoe through the living room, getting a full view of his plumber's crack hanging out of his pants. It's nothing new; I've done this walk past dad with friends a hundred times. It's still as embarrassing as it was in high school, but it's always good for a laugh.

The next day I wake up, and my friends are gone, probably doing last-minute Christmas shopping. I look around the room and notice the horseback riding ribbons I've won. When was the last time I went riding? Inspired, I throw on my old riding pants and run over to Jule's room, where she and her friends are still snoozing.

"I smell breakfast. Get up, you lazy asses!" I yell, throwing a pillow at her head.

"Get out! Diablo!" she screams, just like she used to when we were kids.

"Fine! See you dudes later…but I'm going to ride, so if you feel like joining the living, just come out to the barn. Or I'll be out in the big field, riding."

I bounce down the stairs, energetic from my sleep and all the love from seeing my buddies last night.

"Hi, Daddy-O!" I chirp, giving him a hug and a kiss on the cheek.

"Well, hello, jelly bean! You do exist! How are you feeling? I saw you girls got into the pasta last night."

"Surprisingly better than usual! You outdid yourself. Did you see the twins leave this morning?"

"Oh, yes, I did, and they looked a lot worse off than you. How much did you guys drink last night?"

"More than we should've." I laugh, pouring myself some coffee.

"I can tell! There was marinara sauce and Parmesan all over the counter and pasta stuck to the wall behind the toaster."

"What?! That was Jule and Harper and their friends. They came in after us. We had already cleaned our mess up."

"Uh huh," he says, not believing me. I grin. He scoops scrambled eggs with asparagus and bacon on a plate for me and sets it on the island.

"Thank you, Dad! I miss this so much."

"Well, I really miss having you kids home. It's too quiet here without you."

"Okay, I'll start coming to visit more," I tell him. "Hey, is it cool if I ride?"

"Sure, Georgia should be here soon. She'll saddle up whoever wants to ride."

We catch up over breakfast, me telling him that I'm doing well in Hollywood. He reminds me to keep writing my plays and screenplays too and tells me that I can always come home if I need to, and I give him a hug.

"Thanks, Dad. I'll figure it out. Hey, have you talked to Torre?" I ask.

"Yeah, he's coming in later tonight."

I hear Georgia pull up outside, so I put my plate in the sink and head out. I find her with a huge trailer of hay hooked up behind her rusty, red truck, so I greet her and offer to help her unload. She's been renting space in my dad's barn for about ten years now, and she's the one who taught me how to ride dressage and jump horses. She throws me some gloves, and as I walk up the stairs into the dusty hayloft, all my little-girl memories wash over me. I remember making mazes out of the hay bales and jumping off the huge stacks into fluffy hay piles, and the smell of the hundred-year-old barn is just as amazing as I remembered. The sun's rays filter through the cracks in the old wood walls. As I swing open the large second-story loft doors out into the driveway, Georgia's two cowboy friends drive up in a big white dually to help us unload. I'm very happy to have that extra help; as they back up the flatbed trailer and the guys begin to toss up the large bales to me, I'm already sweating.

After sixty-five bales of hay have been stacked in the loft, I go downstairs and drink cold water from the hose and saddle up Georgia's beautiful palomino, strap on my black helmet, which matches my boots, and mount up. Of course, Georgia makes me do a posting trot for forty-five minutes straight before she lets me jump even once. Nothing changes. She's still a drill sergeant. But, she's the boss while riding. I learned so much about dressage from her; she's really a great teacher. Plus, the rush feels amazing while jumping the horse. My mind empties of all of my worries and stress, and all that's left is just me, the power of this amazing animal, and the breeze.

After my ride, Georgia makes me walk and wash the mare, and pick out her feet, and all of the other stalls in the barn had to be cleaned too. It was a ton of work. She's tough, but in a way, this is what I've been craving. This is my chance for my feet to touch solid ground for an instant before flying back to La-La Land.

*

The next day, I wake to a light snow. I change into jeans and boots and wander to the barn, where I find Jule riding Susie, a gorgeous quarter horse with a creamy-gray coat and pink nose. I feed the other horses carrots while she rides, and then I jump on one while Jule gets ready for dinner. Riding in the peaceful snow, when all you can here is the crunch beneath their feet, is phenomenal. I feel my mind empty again, and I can't keep the smile off my face. I've not been this at peace in a year.

The evening is spent at my favorite Italian restaurant on The Hill with the whole family, even my little brother, which only furthers my happiness. All of my troubles in LA seem galaxies away, as if they were lived by some other person in a different life. As I sit next to my nana, and she pats my hand and tells me how proud of me she is. I can't help but wonder if she'd say the same thing if she knew what I was considering, and what I had done. I feel so ashamed and take a deep breath to hold back my tears when I look at her. But, maybe she did some crazy things in her day too.

Winter settles into St. Louis the next day with a snowstorm that blankets the streets in a foot of clean-white powder. Jule, Harper, Torre, and I make hot chocolate with milk and have friends over to sled down our hill in the small pasture. When the boys complain that the hill's too small for them, we load up the trucks and drive over to the country club to hit the steepest and fastest hill in town. When we were kids, we used to dare each other to go down it, but now that we're adults, we're even more fearless, and after a few beers and a joint, sledding down on our stomachs and breaking a few plastic sleds in the process is some serious fun. A few hours later, we're all bruised and beaten up but laughing our asses off after sledding our infamous Greenbriar hill. We all say good-bye to our friends, knowing that we won't see each other for a while; tomorrow's Christmas Day, and we'll all be celebrating with our families.

The next day, my whole family comes over, and we feast on so much food that I'm ready to pop. We celebrate all day, opening presents around the massive stone fireplace, admiring the twelve-foot Christmas tree, and catching up with each other. It's wonderful. The best thing is seeing my little brother, Torre, for once. He is my heart. The traveling life of a pro-hockey player is unforgiving in its demands. It's so good to see him.

CHAPTER EIGHTEEN

The second my plane hits the tarmac in LA, I feel a dose of adrenaline and can't wait to get back to the house. Any sad thoughts from before the holidays have evaporated and left me with an airy lightness. I feel as though I've escaped from the prison in my mind and have a whole second try ahead of me now. No one can hold me down. Look out, world.

Even though Sidney was horrible before I left for Christmas, on the drive home, I reason that she only behaved that way because of her conservative Texas upbringing. It's not her fault that she was so against my decision, and I shouldn't hold it against her. Besides, there's no room for anger or sadness in my life right now. Only fun and adventure are allowed, and nothing says fun and adventure like Sidney Steele.

As soon as I walk in the front door, I hear music blasting upstairs and smell weed; Sidney's home, and clearly ready to go out. Despite my long flight, I'm antsy and ready to go out too. I drop my bags in my room and charge up the stairs, throwing open Sidney's door with a bang.

"Honey, I'm home!"

"LJ!" Sid calls from a pile of skirts and dresses on the floor. She's completely naked and looking tan and fabulous from her trip down south. "I was hoping you'd be home tonight, hot stuff! You're coming out with me, right?"

"Yes, of course! I'm totally in, babycakes," I tell her. Clearly, she's just as keen to ignore our fight as I am. I see her glance at my stomach briefly, but that's the only acknowledgment I know I'll get from her. She knows she'll risk losing her permanent wingwoman if she brings it back up. Besides, it's clear to her that I will never feel good about what I'd done.

"Can I wear this?" I ask, holding up her favorite black dress. If she lets me borrow it, I'll know that we're fine. I see her wince slightly and then self correct and smile with a nod.

"Hurry, and get ready. I need champagne and cocaine!" she says, slapping my ass as she squeezes past me to do her makeup in the bathroom.

"All right, all right!" I laugh, darting down the stairs. I throw open my suitcase and grab my makeup case, rinse my face in the sink, throw on Sidney's favorite dress, and run back upstairs to do my makeup with her.

"Here, I just lit it," she says, handing me a smoking joint. "Hurry up, and get ready, grandma!"

"Geez, okay," I say, taking a few hits. "Let me just do my makeup, and I'll be ready. Take a chill pill."

"Okay, but then move your ass! I'll be in the car."

I know that when she's in this much of a hurry, it only means one thing. She knows where Sebastian will be, and that's exactly where we'll be going too.

We pull into Skybar's valet and charge through the lobby. There's a big crowd trying to get into Asia de Cuba, and true to form, Sid pushes her way to the front of the line, dragging me by the wrist and demanding that we're on the list of the hot new club. We are, and the doorman lets us right in, to the groans of the people behind us that are still waiting in line. Sure enough, I see Sebastian and his buddies off in the distance, lounging in a cabana by the pool with bottle service. I laugh, imagining my hole-in-the-wall Midwestern bars (that I truly love) compared to this magnificent, shiny place. I wish all my friends would come visit and see it someday. After my pause, I find myself strutting next to Sidney as we beeline it to the table. Hollywood has deeply changed me. I can't resist any longer.

"Hey, boys," Sidney purrs, settling next to Sebastian. "Long time no see."

"You're sure right about that," Sebastian says. But he doesn't look at Sidney. He stares at me, eyes wide and mouth drooling too obviously. I start to smile back at him but then remember Sid and glance over at her. Her entire face has closed off as she notices the interaction.

"You ladies want a drink?" one of the guys asks. He makes us vodka cranberries, and Sidney takes hers reluctantly.

"Fuck it," I hear her mutter. She throws back her entire drink and jumps on the table, grinding and throwing her arms over her head with the rhythm. The guys start cheering, and she leans over, flashing them the hot-pink lace thong beneath her tiny skirt.

The guys yell louder, and she blows them kisses. She catches my eye and gives me a big sinister smile, flashing me her perfect ass. I laugh and raise my glass. She's so carefree and does exactly what she wants in each and every moment, and for that, I admire her. No rules apply to her; she's simply untouchable.

"Hey, babe! Why are you over here all by yourself staring off into never-never land?" Sebastian asks, nuzzling up against me. He leans in and puts his arm around me and kisses my cheek, almost hitting my lips.

"I'm great! I'm having a blast!" I say brightly. I see Sidney jump off the table and disappear into the crowd. I'm sure she saw what Sebastian just did and is pissed off. It's not my intention to piss her off; they just always play these little games to make each other jealous. I'm tonight's pawn, I guess.

"Hey, I've actually got to go get Diana in at the door," I say, making an excuse and edging away from his body.

"Yeah. Okay, I'll spark this blunt in about ten minutes when my boys get here. Bring her back to the table with you."

"Okay, I will!"

Instead, I head to the bar where I know I'll find Sidney, and sure enough, I see her leaning into a cute guy, her hand on his chest.

"Sid! Sidney!" I call, working my way through the crowd. She looks over her shoulder at me and tosses her hair, rolls her eyes, and turns back around on her barstool. Now I know I'm in trouble. I make my way over to her through the crowd regardless and see her talking to a couple of guys. I know one of them, Storm, from parties like this one, and when he sees me walking over, he reaches through all the people to grab my hand and pull me toward him, his eyes glassy. He nuzzles my cheek and points to his closed mouth and then puts his arm around my neck and brings my lips to his, and when I open my mouth, he fills it with blunt smoke.

"Really? What's up with this bullshit, LJ?" Sid narrows her eyes. "Is it because you've never worn a tampon, is that why all the guys love you and your tight little vagina?"

The guys look away, embarrassed. "What? No! Sid. Why would you say that?" I ask, hurt. "You know, I came over here to make sure you were okay and not mad at me, but I guess clearly you are."

"Fuck that, LJ. I don't care!"

"Really? Because it looks like you do! You were the one who stormed away from the table."

"Whoa, whoa, whoa," Storm says, putting his hands up between us. "What's going on here, ladies? It's time to chill this shit out! The blunts are coming back around. Let's everyone just calm the fuck down." He tries to pull me down into his lap, but I stay standing.

"Sid! I was just sitting there. He was the one who came over to me. You can't seriously be angry at *me* for this. You saw the whole thing! He's just trying to make you jealous or make us get in a fight. Or both."

She holds her hand to her ear and points to the speaker above her. *I can't hear you* she mouths at me.

"Ugh, Sid, really?" I grab her hands and look her in the eyes. "You know I'd never try to mess with you and Sebastian. I'd never do that to you! Or to anyone else, for that matter. This is bullshit. Let's stop fighting!"

She rolls her eyes and then shakes her head. "Fine! Whatever. Here, go do a key bump. Let's just party and shake it off, okay. It's fine. Whatever. I don't care."

She hands me a small vial filled with cocaine and sends me to the bathroom, and when I ask for her to come with me, she refuses. Fine, if she needs time to save face and cool off, so be it. I wait in line for the bathroom for ten minutes to take my bump, and once I do, I forget about my worries and twirl and dance back to the table. I find everyone still at the bar; I can't believe Sidney would stay away from Sebastian for so long—she must really be pissed at him. But she does seem to be having a really great time with Storm and his friends. When I arrive, they're all laughing and smiling.

"Here, I got this for you, gorgeous." Sidney hands me a drink with a wink. "Double shot of Jack, baby!"

"Thanks so much, Sid. That was really sweet of you. So we're all good tonight, right?"

"Oh, you know I love you, LJ. We're all good, sister. Drink up! Every drop."

I sip my drink and wince at the bite and then take the hand she offers me and follow her onto the dance floor. We start dancing with the crowd, and a big smile grows across her face as she blows me kisses and does some slick dance moves.

*

I wake up with a start. Where the fuck am I? I don't recognize the navy-blue walls around me or the cluster of music pictures on the walls. My head is pounding, and when I bring my hand up to steady it, I see that I'm in a bed with maroon sheets. I look to my left and see a guy sleeping naked, bare buns up. And blond. Oh my god, what the hell happened? I lean over the guy and see that it's Storm. Well, at least I know him, but I have no memory of coming home with him at all. In fact...I rack my brain for memories from the night. The last thing I remember is Sidney bringing me out to the dance floor. I must have had too much to drink.

I get out of bed and start to put my clothes on, and Storm wakes up from the noise.

"Hey. Where do you think you're going, pretty lady," he says, still groggy.

"Hey," I say, awkward. "Um, home. I really don't know how this happened. Sorry, I have to go."

"Oh yeah, well, we were doing shots last night."

I nod. That still doesn't explain why I would go home with him.

He shrugs. "Sidney sort of pushed you on me. But you couldn't resist me either."

"She did what?"

"Just playin'. Don't be mad. I had a great time with you, LJ. I really like you."

"Yeah, I'm sure you do, Storm. You like me after one night together? Look, I've really got to go. This is too fucking crazy. See you around."

I walk outside into the sunlight, which burns my retinas and makes me sweat. I feel miserable, and all I want is to go home and pass out. I call an Uber and wait for it on the corner, using a streetlight to prop myself up. I can't stop the thoughts swirling through my pounding brain, even though I try.

Why did Sidney push me on Storm? She was already complaining that guys liked me too much, so why would she ensure that one of them did? As the cab pulls up, I realize that the key here is Sebastian.

She wanted to show Sebastian that I didn't like him and make sure that he didn't have a chance with me. She got me drunk on purpose, so I'd leave with Storm.

Still, I know my drinking limits, so how could this have happened?

And, anyway, who does shit like that? As soon as this thought enters my mind, I know it's true. It has to be. It feels like it's true. She just used me for her own benefit. I feel empty, like nothing more than a receptacle. I don't understand why she was so angry anyway; she is currently fucking three guys a day for cash or otherwise and then coming home and sobbing to me that she loves Sebastian. What a load of bullshit!

I slump in the back seat of the Uber and will myself to stay alive long enough to get home. I try calling Sidney; I want to yell at her, get some explanations, something, but she doesn't answer and instead texts me back that she's at the airport, hopping a plane to New York City "to see some people." I want to be angry at her for the level of bullshit that is her wild life, but all I feel is relief that I won't have to deal with her until she comes back to LA. All I want now is my bed and to stop feeling like I need to throw up.

When I wake up the next morning, I feel better, but I can't shake the nagging feeling that something else happened that night besides what Storm told me. I'm not the girl who gets blackout drunk and does split-second crazy things. Well, I guess not until recently.

I try to put those thoughts out of my mind as I shower and get ready for my audition. I'm auditioning for a national Banana Boat commercial; it would be great money if I get the part I want, which I really do need at this point. My bank account is dwindling lower and lower by the day.

When I arrive at the audition, I can't help but feel disheartened. I'm directed to a folding chair in a cold, fluorescent-lit room with about forty other girls, all of us sitting uncomfortably with our head shots in one hand and our scripts in the other, muttering our five lines to ourselves repeatedly. I keep rubbing my arms to smooth out the goose bumps and warm up until finally they call my name, and I walk into the room with the casting directors. They direct me to stand on a tiny strip of orange tape in front of a camera. I recognize Debbie, one of the casting directors, and offer her a small smile, and she returns it and tells me that they're ready when I am. They're all business, and I know they have to be since they have to see about a thousand other people today. I try not to let the odds affect me. I take a deep breath, hold my head up high under the bright lights, and deliver the lines in the best, most cheerful way I can for the character.

"Great job, Lillian, really great," Debbie says. I'm shocked. Not only did she give me a compliment, but she knew my name.

"Thank you, ladies. Have a great day!" I say, smiling. That really makes my day. Debbie does casting for great commercials and tons of big films. Even if I don't get booked for the job, I feel great that she knows who I am. I'm not even a classically trained actress, so any kind of recognition I will take as a compliment.

While driving home, I get a call from Jean Paul; he had a model cancel on him and would love for me to be in a fashion show tonight at a loft downtown with an up-and-coming designer named Bobby Augustine. I say yes right away.

Bobby Augustine is amazing! He's from Germany but works with amazing Italian leather designers, creating simple yet sexy, soft leather dresses and jumpers, in a sort of classy uptown girl meets downtown laid-back rocker chic look. I've got to race though. I've got to get ready and be down there as soon as possible in case there's an issue with the way the clothes fit. I leave the car running in the driveway and dash into the house, grabbing a few evening essentials, and then book it down to the show. Sidney calls a few times on my way down there, but I don't pick up the phone. I'm having a great time. I don't need her ruining it with her drivel. She sends me a text saying that she misses me and wishes that I were there in New York with her, of course acting like nothing at all is weird between us. I put my phone on vibrate and throw it in my bag. She can freeze her butt off in New York for all I care.

I'm walking in a bomb-ass show tonight.

I turn down a dark, vacant-looking street in downtown LA, following Jean Paul's directions. I'm relieved as soon as I see a few dozen cars in line at the valet, and as I get closer, I hear heavy bass vibrating through the walls of the giant warehouse. About a hundred people are in line, and the show doesn't even start for a few hours! This is going to be epic.

I throw the valet my keys and tell the doorman that I'm modeling in the show tonight, and the people at the front of the line change from irritated, because they thought I was cutting in, to impressed and handing out high fives. He unhooks the rope for me, and I stroll through the space, looking for the set of stairs that'll bring me downstairs, below the stage, to the hair-and-makeup area. The large space is filling quickly with people; tonight isn't just about fashion, it's about music too, since three world-famous DJs will be spinning all night. I can't wait to walk down the runway to music that people pay hundreds of dollars to see. So sweet.

I finally make it backstage and find Jean Paul across the room. The second he spots me, he puts his hand over his heart in exaggerated relief that I made it and comes right over.

"Girlfriend, you are doing me a solid tonight. I won't forget this," he says, quickly spinning me around and directing me to a hair chair.

"No worries at all. Thanks for thinking of me! I'm so excited!" I tell him. "Do you know the DJs here tonight? They're crazy famous, right? This is so awesome!"

"Sure, sure," he says, distracted. He waves a stylist over and starts playing with my hair. "We need long, flowing hair with tons of volume on this one. I want fierce!" he tells her. Before she can respond, he's off into the sea of people, barking orders, and waving his hands in the air.

Before long, I've got the waves of a Greek goddess and the sexy makeup of a valentine vixen, and I'm feeling pretty great after downing three Jack and Cokes too. A wardrobe person already fitted me for my soft-leather dress and I can't stop running my hands over the buttery material. I could live in this dress. We are all ready with not a second to spare. I find my spot in line and wait with the other girls to walk, the caffeine and alcohol working its way through my system and building my anticipation. The music is thumping as the curtain parts, and the first few girls walk out, and the roar of the crowd makes my whole body tingle. When it's my turn, Jean Paul sweeps back the curtain and the bright-white strobe lights hit me like a shotgun. I turn on my best supermodel walk and prance down the runway, but I can only manage to keep my serious face on until I'm halfway down the runway. It's just way too orgasmic.

I walk the rest of the way down with an ear-to-ear smile. The music pulses through my body, and I feed off the energy of the crowd screaming and dancing and having a blast out there. It's such an intoxicating feeling, and it keeps me moving up and down the catwalk through two more complete changes and the bombshell last walk of all the girls that completes the killer show. #badass.

After the last walk, the models gather backstage and circle around the designer, applauding him for an excellent show. When someone sprays him with champagne, I hold my breath; who knows how he'll react? He's not too happy sometimes. He laughs uncontrollably though, and in a fit of generosity, shouts out to the models that we could keep whichever dress we wanted from the show. I can't believe it. These dresses are worth thousands! I run over to the racks with the rest of the girls and snatch my favorite dress, a sexy navy-ombré suede dress I wore for my first outfit change. As soon as I have my dress, I back out of the chaos; I was lucky to be close to the racks, because now the girls are fighting over dresses like bridezillas. I take off the dress I came in and ball it into a little ball in my bag. I just have to wear this new dress tonight, with its gorgeous deep V-neck and softness that hugs me in all the right places.

As soon as I make it out into the crowd, I stash my bag under a nearby couch and jump onto the dance floor with gusto, throwing my arms up and spinning around. Nothing's going to hold me back tonight, not my bag, not my roommate, nothing.

Just as I really start to let go, a hand grabs my arm and tugs me forward. With a sinking heart, I realize it's Storm.

"Can I talk to you?" he screams over the music. He makes a cigarette motion with his hands, and I nod. Fine, if he wants to be weird and talk about last night, I'll endure it for a few minutes. I'm trying to forget it even happened. But after he says his piece, I'm coming back out to the dance floor, and he's not allowed to mess up my night anymore.

He brings me out to a back patio and drags me through the crowd to a corner, where we have a little bit more space. He lights a cigarette and hands it to me and then glances nervously at me while he lights his own.

"I have to tell you something pretty fucked up," he says. "You're not going to like it."

Oh god. This guy is seriously so sappy. Is he trying to say he loves me?

"What, Storm? Just tell me. What the fuck is going on, are you okay?"

"It's not me. It's something about you," he says, averting his eyes. "Um...so I don't know if Sidney wanted me to tell you in her own fucked up way, but she called me this morning, and asked if I loved our wild night of hot sex..."

"Yeah, so?" I ask, annoyed. This is all so juvenile.

"Well, she also said I should be thanking her since I've had a crush on you for so long..."

"That doesn't mean anything! Oh my god, Storm—just spit it out! What? What is it?"

He takes a deep breath. "She said she put two crushed-up Vicodin in your drink when you were in the bathroom last night," he says quickly.

"Wait, what did you say?" I yell, not comprehending.

"I had no idea. I swear I didn't know! I'm not that kind of guy! Ever since she told me, I've been feeling so guilty, and as soon as I saw you tonight, I knew I had to tell you. I'm so sorry; that was really fucked up of her. I think she wants to kill you or something for flirting with that guy she likes."

"So basically you're telling me that Sid roofied me?"

"Yeah. I guess so...I'm sorry."

"My best friend roofied me? Great. I'm leaving. This is so fucked up," I tell him.

"Wait, are you okay?" he says, grabbing my arm again. I shake it out of his grasp, turning away before he can see my eyes welling up with tears. I push through the crowd, trying to get back to my bag I stashed under the couch. I've almost reached the VIP area when someone grabs both of my ass cheeks with one big hand.

"Where are you going with that sexy ass of mine?" Cole whispers in my ear, sweeping my hair to one side and biting the back of my neck. Goosebumps run over my entire body; he's the only one who has ever gotten me that hot that quickly.

I don't turn fully around, choosing instead to tilt my head so that he has to lean forward to hear me.

"I'm leaving," I tell him coyly. My anger at Sidney has relegated itself to a small part of my mind, this moment taking over everything else in my head.

"Well, then, leave with me. I miss you."

He pulls my hair, forcing my chin up and allowing him to kiss my neck a few times. He turns me around to face him and presses himself against me. He lowers his forehead to touch mine, and when our eyes meet, I smile.

"So you want to get out of here?" he asks.

"I can't. Not tonight. Shit's too crazy right now," I tell him. I kiss him on the cheek and glide my hand down his arm until our fingers come apart in midair, and when I meet his eyes one last time, I see genuine hurt there, and for a minute, it throws me.

Am I making the right call?

Does he really care about me?

*

I regret my decision a bit on the ride home, picturing him naked and the both of us lost in endless hours of passionate sex, but it's a good idea to clear my head from boys. Even if it is just for one evening.

But, I can't stop thinking about Sidney's betrayal.

This time, I fear, she's gone too far. I'm over her.

CHAPTER NINETEEN

I don't have time to dwell on Sidney.

The next morning, I get a call from my agent that I was chosen for the Banana Boat commercial I auditioned for. I'm ecstatic; my friend may roofie me, but one thing she doesn't do is book national bikini commercials. They want me at the shoot at five in the morning the next day, so I spend the day drinking tons of water and going to a yoga class, and then I go to bed early that night so that I'm in tip-top shape. I arrive at Zuma Beach that next morning and lie around in a white bikini on a big Banana Boat beach blanket with three other girls, surrounded by a beach full of hundreds of extras all day. It's the easiest job I've done so far, although we all ironically get sunburns while shooting an ad for sunscreen. I guess that's what happens when you lie out for twelve hours straight.

By the end of the day, I'm exhausted and have sand in every orifice of my body from the last shot, when they had a helicopter hover over the beach to get some overhead close-ups. I'm ready to head home to shower and get a few more z's, but as I pull up in the driveway and see Sidney's car parked there, my stomach clenches. I don't want to talk to her. When I walk in the door, I walk straight to my room and lock the door, ignoring her hurried footsteps down the stairs.

"Hey!" Sidney calls out, knocking on the door.

"Can you just leave me alone, Sid? I need to shower."

"Why? Can't you just let me in? I need to talk to you."

"No! You roofied me!"

"What? What are you talking about? Just open the fucking door, LJ?"

"Whatever. Go away! Please. I'm exhausted."

"I'm not leaving until you talk to me, so just open the door."

I sigh and unlock the door. She walks in and sits on my bed cross-legged, raising her eyebrows at me.

"What's wrong with you?"

"What's wrong with *me*? What's wrong with you? Okay. Well, for starters, Storm told me that you crunched up two Vicodin and put it in my drink the other night so that I'd blackout and go home with him."

"What? Oh my god. That's such bullshit! He really said that to you?"

"Yes, he did."

"And you believed him?"

"Well, yeah. I kinda do believe him. Because I don't remember shit from that night. Why would anyone make that shit up, Sidney?"

"LJ. Seriously. Would you listen to yourself? I would never do anything like that. What, do you think I'm psychotic or something? That's really crazy talk. He's such an asshole!"

"Well, Sid, actually you were really pissed off at me because you thought I was flirting with Sebastian, or he was flirting with me, or whatever the hell you thought! And by the way, gross! He seriously sucks. I would never ever in a million years come on to that guy!"

"I did not think that at all, LJ. Come on! Seriously now?" Her eyes are big and round and innocent looking. I feel doubt wiggle into my brain. I force it back.

Sidney's done too much already. I know what she's capable of, and I know the cold, selfish streak that runs through her heart. I think about how she stole Miles from me, how she's generous only when it suits her syllabus.

"Yes, seriously! You did! You were livid and trying to punish me, and him. You would've pushed me in front of a bus that night, for all I know! Thankfully, we weren't out on the street. Don't fuck with me! I'm so incredibly pissed at you, Sid."

"I would never do that. You're my best friend, LJ. Listen, Storm was probably just feeling guilty that he hooked up with you when you were so fucked up, so he made up some story to make himself feel better. I would never do something like that. I love you. I couldn't see my life without you. Come on. Stop it. This is crazy." She starts to tear up, and she hurries to wipe the tears away.

"I don't know what to believe. But I do know that I can't remember shit! Can I just take a shower now? I'm so spent from the day I've had. I seriously can't deal with your ridiculous bullshit right now!"

"Will you come up to my room after your shower, and we can watch movies tonight? I'm staying home."

"Nah, I'd rather rip my fingernails out of their nail beds one by one. Or stick forks in my eyes. But thank you. I'm done. I'm just going to turn in early. Okay. Sorry, Sid, I'm just so confused by all this crap! But I do know that something does feel a little phony with this whole story."

"Okay, LJ. Take all the time you need. I'm going to call Storm and have him call you."

"Fine. Whatever. Later, Sid."

I don't know what to believe, but I do know that I need time to think about it. It's all so fucked up.

*

After another day at the beach working on the commercial, I get a call from my old friend, Romin, who says that he and his friend, Josh, are heading to LAX and want to know if I'd like to go to Hawaii with them.

"There's no better wingwoman than you," he says. "Come on, pack your bags, and meet us at the airport. We'll pay for everything! Let's do this! Come on, LJ!"

With an impossible-to-pass-up offer in hand, I race home and pack a bag and then take a cab straight to LAX. It's a perfect time to get out of town, and I know we'll have a fun trip. I skid around the terminal corner in my flip-flops as the airline makes the last call for the flight, and I finally breathe a sigh of relief as I plop down next to Romin in first class.

"Awesome, doll. You made it!" he says, handing me a glass of champagne. "Now, you can relax and enjoy."

He pats my knee as the plane takes off, and I jet away from Los Angeles, leaving all of its craziness behind me.

The flight is a quick five hours, made even faster by the delicious food and champagne that Hawaiian Airlines provides with such a gracious smile. We get off the plane in Oahu and get covered in orchid leis, and we're just a little bit tipsy to boot, ready to start the weekend off right. The air is super clean and fragranced like heaven, absent of the perpetual smog that hangs over LA like a shroud.

The boys and I skip through the airport with our carry-on luggage, delighted to be out of the city for the weekend, and find the car service that will take us to their friend Binky's parents' vacation house on the other side of the island. She gave Romin the key. We zip through the island with the windows open and find the house in no time, claiming our rooms and running right back out again to hit the bars. Once we find a pool hall, we know we've hit the jackpot; Romin has seen me play the dumb-girl routine and take tough guys on the pool table for all they've got, and when we meet up with some of his surfer friends, he winks at me and keeps my secret. I end up making over a hundred dollars by sipping my umbrellaed drinks, doe-eyed, while absolutely owning the pool table; the sound of waves crashing on the beach outside is the soundtrack of my triumph.

I spend my winnings buying everyone beers and loading up the jukebox with great music to dance to, returning home with the guys at the end of the night drunk, broke, and happy. Leaving LA was exactly what the doctor ordered, as well as just hanging out with cool guys, who don't care if you're a model or a celebrity or how much money you have, who are happy just hanging out and playing pool all night.

A bunch of people follow us home, so we order five pizzas and turn up the music, continuing the party into the early hours of the morning. We're dancing hard in the living room when I spill almost an entire dark beer on my dress. I go to my room to change clothes, and it isn't until I'm rifling through my suitcase that I realize I'm not alone.

"Hey, Romin, I just need to change right quick, and I'll be back out," I tell him. He doesn't say anything; he just stands in the doorway and smiles. Reaching out, he turns off the light. Suddenly, he's pushed me on the bed and starts to kiss me.

"Hey, stop! We're just friends; get off of me!" I tell him, pushing away from his face with both hands.

"Oh come on, LJ, you know you've been wanting this to happen. Why did you come here with me?" He starts to fumble with his jeans, and I push against him harder.

"What? No, I really haven't. Please, just get off. This is too much. Now, Romin!"

He pushes off of me. "Just hold on a minute."

He sits on the edge of the bed and looks down. I think he feels bad for pushing himself on me until I hear the strangest sound coming from his lap, a crinkling sound like a noisemaker party favor. I feel like I'm hearing things until it continues, the air blowing though something. Inflating.

"What the hell is that sound? Romin, seriously, what the fuck is that?"

"Shhhh...just wait."

"Just wait?! You are too drunk and really freaking me out right now! Move!"

I push him off the bed, and he hits the floor with a thud.

"I'm staying in your room tonight," I tell him. "And I'm locking the door. You can sleep in here."

"Aw, fuck me. Sorry, LJ! Can we still be friends?"

But I don't answer him as I slam the door behind me.

*

The next morning, I wake up confused and annoyed, less so with Romin and more so with the fact that drama seems to follow me wherever I go. I let my guard down with Sid, and she drugged me, and now Romin thought he owned me because I came on this trip.

I'm not a suspicious person by nature, but I realize I need to stop assuming people around me have the best intentions.

The thought is hard and cold and makes me feel suddenly worn out and grown up. I realize I've been following fun without thinking about consequences, and now, suddenly, being carefree doesn't seem like such a good idea anymore. I can't seem to figure out what, or who, is good for me.

Things with Romin could've turned out way worse than they had. What if Romin hadn't let me leave the room? What if he'd…forced me?

Now, I suddenly feel vulnerable and alone. The world looks bleak and full of people trying to take advantage of me.

I walk into the kitchen and find Josh bedheaded and sitting on the kitchen counter in his boxers, sipping coffee, eating Lucky Charms out of the box, and looking exhausted.

"Hey, girl, morning," he says.

"Hey, Josh. Morning. How did your night end up? Did the hot blond girl you were making out with at the bar ever come over?"

"Yep. And we kicked it. Hard. She just left," he says, nodding his head with a smile and taking a sip of coffee. I smile back and pour a cup for myself and refill his as well.

"Well, I'm glad that at least you had a fun ending to your evening."

"Yeah, dude. Romin came in my room this morning and told me how embarrassed he is. I told him he shouldn't have done that to you, but he's had a crush on you for so long, and now he's hoping that he didn't ruin a good friendship."

"Yeah, well, let me tell you. Some weird shit happened last night."

"I know. The penis pump thing," he says, nodding his head again.

"What? Is that what that fucking thing was!"

"Yeah. I told him that it scares all the babes away."

"Wow. Why does he have that thing? And what is it exactly?"

He laughs and shakes his head. "It's exactly what it sounds like. It just pumps him up when it's time to get down. He can't help that he needs a little help in that department. It's a personal problem."

"Oh…god. I never knew."

"Well, why would you? It's not like he brings it up all the time."

In spite of myself, I start to giggle. "Wait, but I'm still confused. He always has the hottest girls hanging around. I thought that…"

"That he would be lucky in the love and ladies department? No. Almost every girl gets scared by that thing and quickly beelines it to the nearest exit."

"That's exactly what I did too." I start to really laugh, and it feels good to break the tension from last night. "Why doesn't he just go natural? That thing makes crazy noises; he should really give girls a heads-up on that one."

"Yeah, well, he can't get it up at all, so it's the pump or flaccid city for the chump."

I really start to lose it then, tearing up, and Josh grins and shakes his head at me. It'll be fine between me and Romin now. He and his penis pump don't seem so threatening anymore.

"Aw shit, here's the man himself," Josh says, hopping off the counter and giving Romin a fist bump as he leaves the kitchen. Romin pours himself a cup of coffee and avoids my eyes.

"Listen, about last night—"

"Hey, it's okay," I tell him. "Let's just go back to normal. No need to get all weird. It's no big deal. I'm fine. You're fine. It's fine."

"Okay, thanks, LJ. But I'm still embarrassed as fuck!"

"Yeah, well, it was super weird, but it's fine. Really. I'm already over it."

He relaxes his shoulders and finally makes eye contact with me. He looks like he's barely slept, poor guy, and probably stayed up worrying about how I'd react in the morning. Which, part of me is glad he did. Maybe he *isn't* the bad guy I thought he was last night. What he did was out of line, but clearly, he hadn't meant to hurt me.

"Well, hey, listen, do you want to hit the North Shore today? I think some of the other guys are already there surfing. Binky said we could drive her mom's green Explorer as long as we fill the tank back up before we leave."

"Totally! I'm in. Yeah, let's do it!" I say, overly exuberant to demonstrate how over the weirdness I am. "Give me ten minutes to put my suit on?"

"Right on!" he says, perky as a puppy.

"Sweet! Let's fucking do this!" Josh says from the living room, clearly listening to the whole conversation.

"God dammit, Josh! Really?" Romin says, laughing.

We dig our toes into the warm, smooshy sand on the North Shore of Oahu and all heave a collective sigh. The sun is hot and bright, highlighting the water in the most brilliant, fantasy-like shades of blue that seem almost contradictory to the bone-crushing waves that shake the ground. Surfers glide effortlessly on them, seemingly unafraid of the twenty-foot drops. Winter for us land dwellers living on the mainland is the most perfect time of year for surfing here in Hawaii, especially on the North Shore, where all of the biggest surfing competitions are held. I lay out my towel to tan while the guys jump in, and I spend the day being thoroughly entertained by watching some of the world's best surfers do what they do best.

We head home as the sun begins to set, most of us sunburned and all of us ready to go out. I keep the shower on cool and find a flowing, white dress to drape over my sensitive skin. I love how easy it is to get ready here; keeping my hair in beachy waves is nothing compared to the time I usually spend on my hair, and a little mascara and peachy gloss are the only makeup I need. I find myself alone in the kitchen, waiting for the boys to finish getting ready.

Bored, I look at my phone for the first time in a day and find tons of Snaps and texts from Sidney, saying how much she loves me and that she hopes I'm having fun. I don't respond.

Coming to Hawaii is my break. I'm not willing to get involved again just yet. If ever. Part of me feels like I need to say good-bye to Sidney for good.

The idea of trying to find a new place to live, and the endless drama surrounding a friend breakup, stops me though. I'm not ready yet to fully walk away.

I do respond however to a few texts from Naomi, who has an audition with La Perla tomorrow. I'm dying; she'd be perfect for that company. They're so effortlessly flawless, delicate, and feminine, just like Naomi.

Finally, the guys are ready, so we head to their friend JJ's house to pick up some weed and smoke a bit before going back to the pool hall from last night. JJ hooks us up with some great kind bud before we leave; he and his girlfriend are both sponsored pro surfers, so we clean up with some DaKine, Quicksilver, Roxy, and Rip Curl backpacks, stickers, and tons of other swag.

I even get some cute cropped shirts and a bikini. Not a bad start for a night where I plan on winning more money from unsuspecting island boys. It looks like I'm going to leave this minivacation with more booty than I came with.

We walk into the pool hall and take over the back table, and once again, I absolutely run the house. I even get an audience after schooling this huge Hawaiian guy, who is supposedly the best pool player on Oahu. He insists that we keep playing, even after I take over two hundred dollars from him and make him buy my friends a few rounds of drinks. Each time I land another ball, he gets angrier, and I have to admit that it's fun to see this so-called pool champ squirm.

After another game, I take a break from the pool table to spend my earnings on some music at the jukebox, and as my buzz starts to really kick in, I begin whirling through the breezy bar. I see people laughing at me and become aware of the fact that I probably look drunk, but I couldn't care less. I'm in Hawaii, and the night has been good to me.

I don't remember getting home, but I do remember doing shots of tequila at the kitchen counter with about ten people and loudly rapping some song together. The party is getting bigger than I'm conscious of, with more people pouring in the front door. I squeeze past the surge and hug the hallway wall, trying to get back to my room before I pass out in the corner of the formal living room.

"Here, I can help you to your room."

I look up and see the seven-foot-tall Hawaiian dude I played pool with.

"Thanks, bra," I slur. He walks me down the hall and steadies me with a tight grip on my arm, and when we get to my room, he gently takes my cross-body purse and shoes off of me and lies me on the bed, covering me with a thin, yellow blanket. As I start to pass out, I fuzzily see him sit down in the big floral armchair next to me, putting his head back to rest and letting out a big sigh.

The next thing I know, he has my legs pinned behind my head with one hand, his other hand clamped over my mouth. My dress is completely ripped and with rising panic, I realize that he is completely inside me. I try to scream, but his massive body weight and large hand blocks the noise from coming out. I feel my eyes pop out of my head, trying to comprehend what's happening. He looks away from me, turning my head to the side, refusing to make eye contact, just thrusting harder and harder. He's so heavy that I can feel my hip bones cracking and popping while they try to support the weight of his violent movements. He grabs a pillow to cover my face as I keep trying to scream, and suddenly I can't breathe either. He pulls out and flips me over, and when I try to squirm away, he slams me facedown into the bed by the neck and pulls away the remnants of my dress while scooping up my legs in one hand. I'm completely hog-tied, and there's nothing I can do to stop what he's doing to me. I turn my head to the side and gasp for air.

"What would you do to the bastard who did this to your sister?" I scream, trying to get him to see me as a human. He stops and then backs off the bed slowly. I flip over and scoot backward to the top of the bed, and he finally makes eye contact with me. Shaking his head quickly, he pulls on his shorts and runs out of the room, slamming the door behind him.

I burst into tears, the pain coursing through my body nothing compared to the realization that I've just been raped. I look down through my hair at my torn clothes hanging like rags over my used body, and I know that I'll have huge hand and finger-print bruises on my wrists and ankles, and probably my hips, thighs, and neck too. I think about getting pregnant again. I think about getting AIDS. I think about how I've just been savagely violated by a man the size of a bull. The dim room looks hazy through my tears, and when I start hiccuping tequila, I run to the bathroom to puke. When I come back, I see my purse dumped out on the floral armchair. He took back the two hundred dollars I had won from him earlier that evening in the pool game. Monster.

I gather myself up as best as I can and then go to find Romin and Josh. I don't hear any music anymore as I wander through the long ranch-style house. I wonder how long I've been in that bedroom.

"What the fuck happened to you? Oh god…" Romin says when he sees me. He and a few other guys are hanging in the kitchen, but most of the crowd has gone.

"Um…it was that huge guy from the pool hall," I tell him, whispering and dissolving into tears again. I feel like I'm dying.

"Holy fuck! Are you okay? Do you want to call the cops? Or should we go? Go to the cops. We'll take you right now!

Where's that fucking coward now? Is he in your bedroom? Shit!"

Josh starts pacing around the kitchen and waving his hands in the air. "He did this while we were right here? *Fuck!*"

Romin comes over and places his hand gingerly on my shoulder. He looks tortured. "I'm so sorry, LJ. Let's go to the cops right now!"

At that moment, I realize I don't have the strength for it. I'd always thought I'd be one of those girls who would adamantly prosecute any attacker, that I wouldn't be one of the shy, silent ones who did nothing. I'd always been so smug about that, feeling that I could do the right thing.

But now, realizing how much I had to drink, how I'd let him take me to my room…the shame of it, of waking up with him inside me. It's all too much.

God.

Telling a stranger? Telling a cop? Getting an exam at the hospital? Telling the doctors and nurses too? I see a whole parade of people judging me, inwardly thinking it was my fault.

Dumb party girl. What did I think would happen?

Nausea rises again in my throat.

"I don't know if I want to relive it all over again. Or do an exam or anything and be violated all over again either. I'm so scared I'm going to be pregnant from this. He didn't use a condom. I just don't think I can go to the police station right now, Romin. I can't go through all the poking and prodding or hours of questioning. I just can't! I have no energy. I just want to sleep it all away."

I can still smell the stench of his BO on me, feel his sweat snaking down my torso. Images of his gold cross and chain clanking and hitting me in the face. I feel like my soul's been sucked out of me. Everything means nothing to me anymore. I'm a hollow shell of the woman I once was.

"This is fucking crazy! Look at you. You look like a dog attacked you!" Josh says, still freaking out. "What the fuck? How did you get him off of you? Why didn't you scream for us?"

"He covered my mouth. Then had a pillow over my head. And the music was too loud anyway," I offer meekly.

"*Fuck!*" Romin screams, punching a hole through the kitchen wall. "I'm going to kill that piece of shit. Josh, come on, let's go."

"Please don't go!" I plead. "You'll get arrested. Just don't leave me. Just promise me you'll stay here! I can't take anything else bad happening. I just can't take it tonight, guys. Please stay here! I just need to sleep. Rest. Be quiet. I feel like all the wind has been knocked out of me. I'm so deflated. It will only make it worse. Please."

Romin and Josh look at each other. They look livid. Roman takes a deep breath to relieve his red face. "Fine. If that's what you want."

"I do! Thank you. Yes, that's what I want. The sun's coming up now, and I'm going to go to sleep in the other guest room. What time do we go home tomorrow?"

"Not until late. We're on the red-eye back to LAX," Romin says.

"Can you guys leave me the car for tomorrow?" I ask. "I'd like to have a day alone, maybe drive to Sunset Beach, try to process what just happened."

"Sure, LJ, of course. Whatever you want."

"Thanks, guys. Really. Thank you for wanting to help. But, I might go just sleep until we need to leave."

"Of course," Romin says, hugging me tightly. "You're my girl. I'll still go kill that guy right now if you'll let me."

"I know you will," I say with an anemic grin. "Thanks again. You guys are too good to me. Good night."

Shakily, I make my way back to my room. I don't know if I'm making the right decision, but I know it's the only one I can make right now.

CHAPTER TWENTY

As the plane touches down in LA, I say my good-byes to the boys. We don't mention what happened, and I'm pretty sure they won't mention it to anyone. I know I don't want to tell anyone myself, not even Naomi. As I walk off the plane, I decide that I've moved on. I take a deep breath and push it under the rug and then black it out of my memory, just forget it ever happened. Move on. Move forward. It's over. As much as I try to deny it, something has definitely changed in me though.

I'm harder after this. I feel soulless, spiritless. Like a dead man walking. I don't care what happens to me. I feel more reckless than I ever have, like I want to escape myself, cut myself out of my own skin and escape. I want to prove that I'm alive and tough. That I don't give a fuck, and I don't take shit from anyone. I'm an emotional gangster. I want to challenge myself to do the *bad job*. I feel self destructive. This is the straw that broke the camel's back.

In the cab home, I call Sidney and tell her that I want to go to New York City next weekend. She's thrilled; she knows exactly what I mean by that. She says that she'll arrange everything. I hang up, exhilarated and looking forward to disappearing in my own extreme secret life of pleasure and pain. Fuck it. Fuck it all.

I pack my black backpack and meet Sidney at our front door the following Friday. She flings her arms around me and kisses me all over my face when she sees me, leaving hot-pink-gloss kiss prints everywhere her lips touch.

"I missed you, baby! Can't help myself. I want to smother you with all my affection! How have you been?" she asks, putting my bag in her car for me.

"Swell, Sid, just swell," I say. I'd been avoiding her all week, dodging her invitations to parties with some new boy she was "totally in love with." She'd sent me a massively long text about how she'd had a wild night at some guy's parents' mansion and had sex outside under the full moon in their elaborate rose garden, running naked through their shrub-lined labyrinth with him, only stopping to fuck underneath a marble statue of David as the sun rose. I had to admit it was a little impressive, and that I was maybe a little bit jealous. Sounded like a castle in the air. A good dream. Who wouldn't want to have sex in a romantic rose garden just east of Eden? Well, she wouldn't be the only one having fantastic adventures from now on.

"Well this is going to be a totally superduper, swell week-end in New York, hot stuff. So hold on to your sweet little ass tightly." She laughs, driving to the airport, and when I roll my eyes, she sticks her tongue out and scrunches her nose jokingly. When I still don't laugh, she reaches over and gives me a wet willy.

"Stop it, asshole!" I say, slapping her arm down.

"For fuck's sake, LJ, chill the fuck out! God. Have a little fun!"

I try to hold back a smile, biting my lip, but I can't help it, and she catches me. She holds up her hand for a high five and finally, I meet it. I know that we're going to have fun. Smiling, I light up a smoke and lean back and exhale, letting the badness wash over me.

We valet at The Parking Spot, hitch a ride on their squeaky bus, speed through the security line, and run *Home Alone* style to our gate, just making it in time.

*

Flying to New York this time is different. Where before we were silly girls on a spontaneous trip, now I'm a woman on a mission. I spend the flight lost in my headphones, only chatting with Sidney when she insists on it. As soon as we touch down, we head straight to Jonny's to drop off our bags so that we can make it in time to Alexandra's. I only have this interview to get through, and then I'll have the freedom to do whatever I want.

The energy of New York City infuses my blood with its reckless spirit, and with each step toward the townhouse, I feel more daring and more independent.

We pass street vendors selling earrings, copper twists, and baubles displayed on black-velvet-covered tables. I hesitate at a Jamaican man's table and lift a pair of long, rectangular copper earrings off the display.

"When you're done, you'll be able to buy huge diamond earrings at Bergdorf's if you want," Sidney whispers in my ear. I smile and hand the guy twenty dollars, ten more than his sign asks for. Maybe the extra ten will help him keep making his art for the world. Or at least by him some lunch today. As we walk away, I stab my new earrings into my ears.

When we arrive at the address, I start to walk up the brownstone's crumbly stairs until Sid quickly yanks my arm down and pulls me back onto the sidewalk.

"What the fuck, LJ, keep moving. We haven't gotten the text from her yet," she says. We wait on another brownstone's steps for the text that tells us to come in for my appointment, and as I fumble in my bag for my violet-mirrored aviators, I notice that there are two sets of girls sitting on every stoop all the way up and down the street. Girls just like us, waiting on their appointments. I instantly feel a little competitive with these girls. But, mostly it's just plain, simple girl insecurities at work in my mind. God, they are all so pretty.

I pull out my iPhone to idle away the time as I wait; I also can't help but think about these girls' lives in comparison to mine. They're all clearly models who aren't making ends meet, just like me. Are they also looking for adventure, or escape from their mad worlds, or is it just the money talking? The girls on the steps next to us look very normal, respectable even. One looks European, and the other looks sweet, like she was raised on a farm in Kansas. They probably don't want to go home to live with their parents either, admit that their dreams aren't allowing them to pay their rent. I'm sure only the people closest to them know what they do, just like Sidney. And I guess, like me.

When we get the text to go in, Sid and I gather our things and head into the brownstone. Before I follow behind her though, I turn to the girls on the steps next to us and offer them a smile. The girl with high cheekbones and long, dirty-blond hair turns away from me, but the other girl gives me a dimpled smile and a little wave. As I turn to go in, I laugh. I used to be just like her, optimistic and full of smiles and softness. This business is going to crush her heart. Or maybe it's already been crushed like mine, and we only have our soft, sensitive grins to offer some warmth to one another in this cruel, cruel world.

*

I pull up to my first *bad job*, apartments in Beverly Hills, one day after we get back from New York City, and sit with my car idling. The palm trees lining the front walkway sway slightly in the evening breeze, lit up by tiny, glowing outdoor lights. I shoot Alexandra a text to let her know that I've arrived at the location and then turn my phone on vibrate. Well, no time like the present.

I step out of the car, the heels of my strappy sandals clicking delicately on the walk up the driveway. Pulling my skirt down, I stare at the tiny outdoor lights. They remind me of being a teenager in St. Louis, when I would go to this girl Mallory's parties on Friday nights with my friend, Zeke, blasting some gangster rap in his old burgundy hoopty. He'd always kick the tops off of her walkway lights because he hated her sister, Coco; he called her "farty," after the cops, chasing them for a noise disturbance at a party one time, found their hiding spot in the bushes because Coco farted so loudly. He was such an asshole, but all the girls still swooned over him, and I had to love him anyway since we'd been friends since we were fourteen. Before I ring the doorbell, I knock the top off one of the little lights with my blue-suede sandal, for nostalgia.

The door opens, revealing a man dressed in half a suit, clearly relaxing after a long day at work. His white shirt is untucked, and his rolled-up sleeves reveal a gold Rolex. He's not old, I realize with relief. He's probably in his late forties. Not a bad start.

"Angelina, I presume?" he asks. "Come in."

I follow him inside the small apartment, reminding myself to answer to my fake name while I'm on the job. Sidney laughed at me when I told her I would change my name while I was with these guys, because she never did, but I wanted to make sure my alter ego doesn't follow me into my separate, real life. She told me I should use the code name Bunny, because soon I'd be fucking all the time like a cute little bunny rabbit. She's so funny sometimes that I forget to laugh.

The apartment may be small, but everything in it is very expensive. I've seen his couch at the Pacific Design Center on Melrose. I know it's not something I could afford. Or, maybe I'll be able to afford nice things someday.

"How are you doing?" he asks me. He turns the TV down, which I just notice is blaring loud EDM music. "I hope you like this? I'm streaming the Ultra Music Festival live from Miami. Do you want a drink? I'm making martinis. Dirty, or..."

"Uh, dirty is fine. Or, actually, neat is better. Neat, please. Just vodka. Thank you."

I need to calm down and be better at this. He's looking for a confident girl, not someone who is fidgety and doesn't know how she likes her martinis. I sit on the couch and coax my shoulder blades down my back, trying to convey a sense of confidence that I don't totally have right now.

"Here you are, Angelina. Hey, listen, don't be nervous. Let's just talk for a while. Drink your drink, enjoy. Unwind. I don't bite."

He sits on the couch with me and smiles, and I smile back at him. Either he can tell how nervous I am, or he just wants me to be nervous. Every guy wants a good girl that knows when to be bad. They always want to be the one who corrupted them, the one who sullied them, the exception to their rules. Fine, I'll play his game. I put my hand on his knee and look up at him with wide eyes.

"Thank you. You are so kind. This is my first time doing this, you know."

He smiles even wider. "I do know, actually. I always ask Alexandra for the new girls. I like to be the first to have her new girls, and I pay extra to her for that privilege. Because it *is* a privilege, Angelina. And I will give you a little something extra when you leave to prove that to you."

"Oh…well, thank you very much," I say, downing my drink. So much for surprising him with the innocent act—it's exactly what he's looking for.

"Here, I'll make you another," he says, taking my glass.

"You know, I don't actually live here," he says from the kitchen, pouring our drinks. "I just use this apartment for when I need space from my wife and five kids."

Holy shit. *Five kids?* This is going to be harder than I thought.

"Well…I guess five kids is a lot to handle? It makes sense that you would need this space." I hate myself for even saying these words as they pass across my lips, but what am I supposed to say?

"Oh, I love my kids. And I love my wife. She just can't give me what I need anymore, so I make sure that I'm taking care of myself so that when I come home, I can be a good husband and father for them."

"So you do this a lot then?"

"Well, I wouldn't say a lot, but I guess whenever Alexandra has a new girl in LA for me…" He thinks for a moment. "Well, actually, I guess lately it has been a lot. Lots of new faces out there, just like you!" He pokes me in the thigh to make it clear that I'm the new kid, not him. I chug the drink he hands me and stand up. If we're going to do this, we need to do it now before I have time to really listen to what he's saying and talk myself out of this.

"Oh, an eager one! Okay then, Angelina, let's get to it shall we?"

He leads me to the bedroom and lies down on the bed.

"Why don't you make yourself comfortable?"

I wince at the cliché but undress anyway. I get down to my black-lace bra and panties and stand there frozen next to the bed. I don't know what else to do. It's so strange being this intimate with someone I don't know, or when it's not after a night out drinking. A legit one-night stand. Really though, it's strange that there's not really a choice. This is my job. I have to do it now. I'm here.

"Angelina, are you ready for this? I know it's your first time. If you do this, you'll have a hard time stopping. The money is very good, but not every man has your best interests in mind. You have to be careful. It's a risky business. I have daughters. I know what's out there. I want you to know that you can leave right now if you want to."

I take a deep breath. He really is being nice, even if it's weird that he requests this. Maybe he sees himself as some kind of Good Samaritan, a gentle introduction to the land of sexual industry. What I don't like is that he thinks I'm just a weak, naïve girl, someone who needs to be gently introduced. *I* chose this. *I* want to do this. I don't need him to help me. This is my choice, my situation. *I'm* in charge.

I lean over and crawl toward him on the bed until I'm right over him. He holds my gaze, fascinated.

"I'm not leaving," I whisper, breathing softly in his ear.

He glides his hands down my back and loops his fingers through my panties, almost ripping them off. I take off my bra and flash him my breasts, and he instantly gets hard. Taking his boxers off, he twists me around until I'm on top of him in reverse, but not before telling me that I have the most perfect breasts he's ever seen. I hear the rip of a condom wrapper and watch as he slides one on. He's surprisingly well endowed. "What kind of condom is that?" I ask.

"Sheepskin, love. Ever tried it?"

"Ah...no. Is it safe? You know, like a Trojan?"

"Yes, it is. Don't you worry your pretty little head about it. Now shh…"

He reaches forward and touches me between the legs. "Ah, Angelina, you're ready," he says. He eases himself into me, filling me up completely. It feels incredibly good. He caresses my back again and moves my hips up and down against him. I bend over his legs and reach down to his feet as he thrusts harder. Before I know it, he cums and lets out a loud groan. It's over. He gets up naked and walks back into the kitchen.

"Do you want another vodka?" he calls out to me.

"Yes, thank you!"

That was surprisingly quick, and easy. Once we got going, I felt like he could've been anybody. I take inventory of myself; I feel like I'm Alice falling down the rabbit hole into an incomplete wonderland. I feel like less of a person than I did a few minutes ago, like I left a piece of myself with him. I feel like I deserve to feel this way. Guilt washes over me. Guilt for the bad things I've done, guilt for the bad things I let happen to me. Oddly, I feel empowered at the same time, like I can do anything I want. And no one cares anyway. I get up and walk back out to the living room, where the music festival is still playing, and turn up the Bang & Olufsen stereo until he turns around from the kitchen and raises an eyebrow. I lie down naked on the living room floor, like a snow angel, with my head against the speaker. The music sounds so good and feels even better vibrating through my body, the vibrations traveling from the top of my head down to my toes. In spite of myself, I feel tears traveling down the sides of my face, and when I open my eyes, I see him sitting on the sofa with both of our drinks. My crying suddenly turns into laughing hysteria, and I feel like I'm losing my mind. Who am I? Is this my metamorphosis? Have I gone completely mad? I stare at the ceiling without blinking.

"Are you okay?" he yells over the music. I don't answer, closing my eyes again and letting more tears fall as the music takes me into a trance. When I come to, fifteen minutes later, I realize that I need to go home now. I sit up and look at him, and he nods at me with a smile, sipping his dirty martini. I go to the bedroom and put my clothes back on, and when I come back, he's standing by the door in a fluffy black robe. I guess that's my cue.

"Here you are, Angelina. Thank you. And good luck to you." He hands me an envelope and pats me on the shoulder and then closes the door behind me. I turn and walk down the path in slow motion, the little black lights winking at me on my trip back to the car. I stop and fix the light that I broke at the end of his walkway. When I open the car door, I check my phone before I get in and see that I've got a missed call from Alexandra. I was supposed to be done thirty minutes ago. I'd like to think she's just looking out for my safety, but I'm sure she just wants her cut. Before pulling out of the driveway, I open the envelope and count the money. Two thousand dollars cash. I'm stunned—I was only supposed to get one thousand and give the New York office three hundred. I smile, text Alexandra that I'm finished and that I'll send her her cut, put on my aviators, and pull away from the curb with the glowing-pink California sunset and palm trees encompassing the horizon.

When I open my eyes the next morning, I take an inventory of my body again and find that I feel different than I did the previous morning. I glance at my nightstand that has a stack of hundreds on it. It's heady, knowing that I can command that much money for just an hour or two of my company.

I swing my legs off the bed, twist my long hair into a low side knot, and throw on my worn skinny jeans and a soft white T-shirt. Today's agenda is simple: I'm going to have some "me time" and marinate in my new virtual reality. A quick sweep of translucent powder over my face, a gargle of mouthwash, and I'm ready to head to Fred's café at Barneys to treat myself to fancy coffee while I wait for the store to open so that I can do some very necessary shopping. On second thought, I throw my computer in my bag; maybe I'll even work on the screenplay I haven't touched since college and make my day extra productive.

By ten in the morning, I'm finished with a whole new scene as well as my second cinnamon latte and plum tart. I'm ready to go shopping. Rummaging in my old purse, I pull out my torn wallet and leave a 100 percent tip on the table, pop a mint into my mouth, and walk to the elevator. I wish I could always tip 100 percent on everything; it feels amazing. I try to resist looking back at the table while I wait for the elevator, but I can't help myself, and I turn in time to see the waitress's shock when she cleans my table. I was a waitress all through high school and through most of college; I know how hard it is to deal with people every day. I'm glad I'm able to make her day a little brighter.

When the elevator doors opens on the first floor, I'm momentarily blinded by the brilliance of everything, from the white floors to the sparkling jewelry. I'm buzzing with caffeine and the knowledge that I have so much money at my disposal, and as I float past the counters lined with glittering jewels and stop for a spritz of Chanel perfume, I find myself heading straight for the shiny-black Chloé Drew bag with the gold chain that I was coveting the day I came here with Sidney. I see it at last, glowing with perfection, and when I pick it up, I can feel the softness molding into my hands. It's beautiful. It's classic. It's almost two thousand dollars.

I get a pang of anxiety thinking about blowing all of that money in one shot. My great aunt's voice rings in my ears, the old reminder she used to give us whenever she came over for dinner to always "live within our means" or else spend the rest of our lives like so many other Americans, in debt. But what the hell. This cash is burning a hole in my pocket. I shoo Aunt Verna's voice away, throw the bag over my shoulder, and do a little dance in front of the mirror. My aunt isn't here right now, and I can't deny the bag when it beckons me.

Keeping the bag tucked snugly under my arm, I walk over to the women's shoe department and immediately eye up an amazing pair of red alligator heels by René Caovilla. A sales associate rushes to my side, clearly understanding that if I can afford to buy the Chloé bag, I can afford to buy the shoes as well. He asks me my size, and as he starts to leave to retrieve the correct pair for me, I call him back and ask to try on two pairs of Louboutins and a pair of suede kelly-green Saint Laurent pumps as well.

I've been bitten by the Barneys bug, and I can't stop this train. I try all of the shoes on with a newfound pep in my step, and I'm not sure if it's the intoxicating smell of leather or the freedom to buy exquisite things paired with my live-life-like-there's-no-tomorrow-and-have-a-blast-doing-it mantra, but I can't stop from handing the clerk my card and asking him to check me out right then and there. I'll have to do another job or two until I can pay for all of it, but I just can't walk away from such beauty. When he presents my purchases to me meticulously wrapped and compliments my taste with a wink and a smile, I realize that I've defined my own rules. I feel so alive and stimulated doing something forbidden, something I was afraid to do, and I have to admit that it feels incredible to be bad.

I push down the misgivings that pop into my head just then. What if my mother found out? My dad? My siblings?

No.

I can't think of them right now.

It's going to be hard to keep my secret, but easy lives make boring people, right? Striding out of the store with my shiny Barneys bag filled with thousands of dollars worth of elegance,

I feel powerful. I don't care if society sees how I can afford everything as negative. I just want to be able to spoil myself forever.

As I drive home while glancing at the shopping bags nestled in the back seat, my phone pings with a text from Alexandra asking if I'm free this evening to work. At a stoplight, I tell her I am, and she writes back right away, saying that she'll get back to me with details but to keep the eight o'clock hour open for the call. If I'm going to have these kinds of shopping habits, I certainly can't say no to jobs, at least not for a while.

I remember what the man said about it being hard to stop. I feel a slick, oily feeling in my stomach for an instant.

Then, I'm over it. I can stop whenever I want, I tell myself. No problem.

It won't be hard.

I'll go home and take a nap to energize for tonight. I can't be looking tired, because these guys expect me at my very best.

The alarm on my phone goes off at six o'clock, raising me from my cozy nest of blankets. Time to get ready. I shower and straighten my hair and then smooth on foundation, followed by a light-cream blush Sidney gave me that she found on NET-A-PORTER. By the time I get to eye makeup, I notice that I'm putting it on with more force than usual, as if it's war paint, and I'm preparing for battle.

My eyes look back at me in the mirror, tough and jaded, and it's as if an entirely different girl is using my bathroom instead of the purely natural girl who moved in just a few months ago from the beach. I'm not upset though. I look good. I *feel* good. And I'm still a good person who would never hurt anyone else. A tiny voice in the back of my head reminds me that I'm actually hurting myself, but I shush it with a swipe of red lipstick that matches my new shoes. It's not self-destructive behavior, I tell myself. It's just plain fun to push my own limits.

As I pull on my black-lace dress, reaching to pull it down over the tops of my thighs, I get a text from Alexandra telling me to go to a private house up in the Hollywood Hills for my call this evening. A whole house...it must not be a guy like the one last time, who has to have a separate apartment for his "dates." Or maybe it is, and he can just afford a whole house this time.

I debate adding black fishnets for a pretty-punk sort of look but end up deciding against it, not wanting to go all *Pretty Woman* in my new job. I pull on my new red heels instead and look at myself in the mirror. The high neck of the dress makes the short hemline seem proper instead of trashy, and the red lipstick matches perfectly with the heels. If I were some guy up in the Hills waiting for a girl, I'd be happy to open the door to this, I decide, as I grab my shawl and new *it* bag.

"Sidney?" I call upstairs, wanting to say good-bye to her. When I don't hear anything back, I borrow four cigarettes from her pack on the kitchen counter and stuff them into my purse so that I can chain smoke as I wind through the Hills to my call.

I arrive at the address reeking of cigarettes, so I douse myself in perfume while peering up at the hedges surrounding the house. The only thing I can see is a large metal door flanked by two huge glass gas lanterns; the house beyond the gate is obscured by shrubbery and trees. I leave my car on the street and press the button to be let in. A red light blinks once, and suddenly the wide metal door slowly swings open to reveal a black-brick walkway leading up to a white front door. As I walk up, the front door opens.

"Angelina?"

Framed in the doorway stands a man so unbelievably hot that I'm instantly embarrassed to be entering his home under these circumstances. His loosely worn charcoal-gray shirt doesn't hide his lightly muscled arms lined with tattoos, and his dark slim jeans hang perfectly from his hips and are just begging to be pulled off. I finally make eye contact with him and am shocked by the resemblance to a young David Beckham. *This* is the guy paying me to have sex with him? I feel like I should be paying *him*!

He offers me his hand and introduces himself as Blaine, and I take it, hoping that my hand isn't clammy.

"Hi, um, it's nice to meet you."

He smiles generously. "It's nice to meet you too. How are you doing on this fine California evening?"

"Oh, I'm really good," I tell him, blushing. "And you?"

"Outstanding, Angelina. I'm just outstanding." He nods toward my shoes. "Spending some of your extra income, I see?"

"Ah, yes, well I needed a new pair..." I falter.

He laughs and shakes his head. "Well, come on inside. What would you like to drink?"

I follow his perfectly muscular back into the home. I'm surprised; the house was colonial from the outside, but it's very contemporary on the inside; it must have had a complete overhaul at some point.

"I'll have a Jack and Coke if you have it," I say. "Just a splash of Coke, please."

He walks over to the largest Sub-Zero refrigerator I've ever seen, and I catch myself staring at his ass. I need to get it together. I'm supposed to be cool here.

He brings the drink over to the counter and places it on a coaster in front of me. I smile and try not to blush when he smiles back.

"Where is that barking coming from? Is it from your neighbor?" I ask, nodding outside at the incessant barking that I only just then notice.

"Oh. That's my dog, Stella. She can go a little psycho when I put her out in the courtyard when anyone comes over."

"Stella and Blaine. That sounds like a sweet love story," I say, smiling.

"Ha! Yeah, it would be, except she just ate through my twenty thousand dollar leather sofa, and her little black hairs are stuck to everything I own."

"Well, I'm sure she's a very sweet girl."

"Yes, well, I'll let you know," he says, winking. "Hey…can I ask why you drink?"

That's a new one. Usually people in LA do everything without hesitation. I've never had anyone ask me a question like that.

"Um…because I always have I guess. I dunno. Don't you drink?"

"No. Not for six years now. And you shouldn't either. It will really age you as a woman."

Well, damn, this guy is presumptuous. I start to fire back something fiery but then realize that he's paying me to be here.

"I guess I'll consider it. It'll be hard to stop cold turkey…but for now, can I have another Jack and Coke?"

"Sure, Angelina. You'll quit tomorrow, right?"

"That's the plan!" I giggle, toasting him.

He hands me my drink and walks out of the kitchen, motioning for me to follow him. I slide off of my stool and trot around the corner into the dark hall after him when all of a sudden he grabs my arm and spins me around, pinning me to the wall. His big hands slide up my thighs, gripping my lace thong and pulling down.

"Whoa! Hey!" I say, holding my drink out of the way. "Careful, I don't want to break your glass."

"Fuck my glass," he says, taking my drink and putting it hastily on the edge of a hallway table. It falls to the floor and shatters with a loud crash. He doesn't flinch, going right back to pulling my panties to the side and spinning me back around over the hall table. I hear his belt unbuckle and his pants drop, and I'm instantly wet. I arch my back and open myself up for him, and when he enters me, I let out a soft moan and reach back to him. We fuck as he pulls my hair with a sharp tug. He's large, and it feels insane! He drops my hair and moves both hands down my back, caressing my curves, and puts his fingers around front making me cum harder than I ever have before. I'm a rag doll in his arms, and it enters my mind that part of the appeal of this to him is that he can just have me whenever he chooses. I feel a tenderness in his touch though. He's hard but gentle, and honestly, he can do whatever he wants to me.

He spins me around again, lifting me high against the wall. I wrap my legs around him, and we start to kiss. Hard and lustful. He sits me on the table, and we continue to fuck. He's so hard, and it feels so amazing—I never want it to end! He pulls out and takes me into his bedroom. When he throws me on the bed, one of my shoes goes flying, hits the sliding glass door, and bounces to the floor. He immediately picks it up and puts it back on me. He slides me almost over the edge of the bed with each of my legs on his shoulders, and I can see Stella staring at me through the glass door. She starts racing back and forth along the glass wall, barking like a maniac. I close my eyes, trying to ignore her, and relax as the euphoria rushes over me like an erotic wave, and I cum again.

Afterward, we cuddle up into his big feathery pillows. They are Bordeaux silk and probably very expensive. My dress is unzipped down my back, and my heels are still on, and I can tell that my hair and makeup are a mess, but I don't care. We lie there, still vibrating from the incredible sex. He stares at the ceiling for a moment and then rolls over to kiss me.

"Your hair is a mess."

"Thanks," I say with a smile. "Yours looks great too."

We both smirk and roll off the bed in opposite directions.

"I'll meet you in the kitchen. You can use my bathroom to get yourself together."

"Okay. Thanks." No time wasted with this guy. I go into his blindingly white bathroom and fix myself up, twisting my now dreaded up locks into a side bun, and reapplying powder and red lipstick and cleaning up my smeared mascara. I may be a mess, but damn if I don't feel like a hot mess right now. In a good way.

"Hey, Blaine?" I call as I walk out of the bedroom.

"Hey, Angelina. I'm in the living room."

As soon as I walk in, he looks me up and down and smiles. "How do you feel? You all right?"

"Yeah. I feel totally awesome! I really had fun here with you tonight."

"Well, let me walk you to the door."

"Okay. Sure." As he places his hand lightly on the small of my back and walks me over to the front door, I can't help but feel a little disappointed. I guess I wanted him to want me more, which is outrageous. He paid for me; this was always the arrangement.

"This is for you," he says as he hands me a thick stack of cash.

"This is way too much, Blaine."

"You earned it. Well deserved," he whispers as he pins my hand holding the cash behind my back and plants an intense kiss on me, totally ruining my red lipstick again. He clearly wants to leave his mark.

"Nighty night," I say, blowing him another kiss as I turn to walk to my car.

"Later," he says with a wave and closes the door behind me.

CHAPTER TWENTY-ONE

The next morning, I wake up with what feels like déjà vu but can only be reality since I can touch the stack of cash on my bedside table. He gave me three thousand dollars. Not only did I pay for all of yesterday's extravagances with one hour of mind-blowing sex, I now have even more to spend. I can hear my roommates getting ready for work, and I have to smile a little; I have nothing to do today but send Snapchats and have amazing sex with hot guys for more than my roommates make in a month. The thought makes me giggle at how unhinged I've become. I now understand why Sidney was so adamant that I try this for myself.

As I get out of the shower, I hear someone rustling in the kitchen, and when I pass by in my towel, I see that it's Sidney.

"Hey!" I call out.

"Hey, baby. What do gay horses eat?" she asks, leaning against the counter.

I smile at our old joke. "Haaaaaay!" I say, snapping my fingers. We both crack up laughing.

"I'm making some green tea; do you want some?" she asks.

"Sure, let me just go throw some clothes on," I tell her.

I go to my room and slide on a pair of boy shorts, throwing on my huge, cozy college sweatshirt over them. It's big enough to cover my butt, so I forgo pants and head back out to the kitchen.

"So how's everything with you?" Sidney asks, handing me a cup of tea.

"Everything's just great," I tell her. "It's weird but surprisingly very good."

"Really? Like how?"

I blow on my tea a bit to cool it and take a sip. "Well, the first guy was a little older but wasn't bad at all. He was actually sweet. And the guy I had last night, holy shit, Sid! You would have lost your mind! He was *hot*, and I mean David Beckham– *Thelma & Louise*–Brad Pitt *hot!* It. Was. Insane. I could marry that man! Seriously insane."

"Really? That's cool," Sidney says, her eyes drifting toward the kitchen window. "Hey, did that first guy live in some condos over in Beverly Hills?"

"Um…yeah, he did."

"Yeah, and he said that it was his secret apartment and doing this makes him a better father and husband and a bunch more crap like that?"

My eyes grow wide with realization. "Shit, Sid. You're not saying—"

"Yeah, girl. I fucked him too."

"Oh my god, gross! So I fucked him after you?"

"Yep."

"Yuck-O! Oh my god!" I shiver, imagining Sidney in that same living room. Did he play music for her too? Did he entice her with martinis too? I suddenly feel like I'm just a numbered Ping-Pong ball bouncing around in a giant wind machine of chaos. Nothing is special; nothing is sacred. But then again, if what we're doing is prostitution, how can I expect anything to be sacred?

"Hey, chill out, it's no big deal! Wipe that face off your head," Sid says, rolling her eyes. "Everyone has fucked every dude before you if you really think about it. And their not always hot."

"I know, Sidney, but not like this. It's different. It's just not right. It's fucking weird and fucked up. I feel all icky."

"Oh, please! Get over it. Don't be so dramatic."

I shake my head and try to clear the image of Sidney fucking that man out of my mind. I wish she wouldn't be so cavalier about it. It would be nice to have someone to commiserate about this with, but I guess she always likes having the upper hand.

Sid walks over to the sink and rinses out her mug, leaving it on the counter. "So, I saw some Barneys bags in the trash can, and I'm just assuming they're yours since I bet none of these boys have ever stepped foot inside a Barneys before."

"Yeah, I went shopping," I say, the glow from yesterday's trip instantly returning. "It was great! I got some amazing red shoes and a new bag—want to see?"

"No. But that's nice. Just don't blow it all before you have it all, doll face."

"I know," I say, deflated. I was expecting her to get excited with me. "It just felt so good to go out and spend money on myself, you know, not to have to worry about being smart for once. And I just had to update my look a little. I'm trying to keep up with you and your awesome closet!"

"Sure, baby. And that's totally cool. I get you. I really do. But you should save for a condo, like I'm doing, or a house or something substantial."

"Well, I'm not really a saver, but I'll try. And you know, it's hard to save ninety thousand dollars without fucking three guys a day."

"Hey. I don't fuck three guys a day!" she says, throwing a *Glamour* magazine at me.

"Okay, two guys, same difference."

"Oh stop. You're just jealous."

"Yeah, you know what, I am jealous," I tell her. "You've got ninety thousand dollars in cash under your bed now, so you bet your ass I'm jealous. Jealous of your bank account. That's a shit ton of money, Sid! Most people on this planet won't even see that amount of money in their whole lifetime!"

Sidney laughs and shakes her head. "Well, you can get there too if you just learn how to save, babycakes. So, you're really okay keeping this secret? *Our* secret?"

I think for a moment. Other than Sidney and Naomi, and Damiano, I don't really have many friends left over in LA after my breakup with Brody. I don't talk to my parents enough to make it awkward lying to them. In all honesty, I don't really have many close people in my life at all. And my hometown friends live way out of touch from my life here.

"Are you kidding? I don't want anyone to know either. I like being able to do whatever the hell I want. Plus, it's not really lying anyway. It's just not telling people our own business. And! It's no one's business, anyway! I'm figuring my own life out for myself. At the end of the day, it's our own lives and decisions. My lips are totally sealed, dude!"

Sid smiles and squeezes my knee. "That's my girl. Mine are too. Okay, I have just one more question for you," she says, nodding to the TV screen. "Why do they call it a typhoon instead of a hurricane?"

"Because it's in the South Pacific," I answer. "I think hurricanes, cyclones, and typhoons are really all the same weather phenomenon, but they just get a different name based on where they are in the world."

"You're so fucking smart, LJ. I wish I went to college so I knew some real brilliant shit like you do."

"Aw, Sid, you know plenty! Like dieting and makeup tips, and demonstrating how to give the world's most amazing deep-throat blow job on a banana," I say, teasing her.

"Oh, shut up, asshole. You know the only reason you can't lose that extra five pounds is because you can't give up cheese and crackers and all those fatty salad dressings."

"See? Right there, that's what I mean. Diet tips," I say, patting my belly. I'm out of tea, so I get up and go to the kitchen to refill it.

"Hey!" Sidney calls from the living room. "I'm running over to Diana's house in Venice in about an hour, and then I have a job, but later I'm going out to dance. Text me if you want to party!"

"Will do, chicky," I tell her, heading back to my room to get fully dressed. I shut my door and check my phone. I have a text from Alexandra. My next job.

CHAPTER TWENTY-TWO

I park on Sunset Boulevard and touch up my lip gloss in the rearview mirror to kill time until my favorite song stops playing, and I belt out the last few lyrics before turning my car off. One last glance in the mirror reveals perfectly lined eyes, pouty pink lips, and flawless, glowing skin. It's show time.

The street in front of the address Alexandra gave me is filled with cars, so I have to walk up the hill for two blocks from where I park my car to this man's house, pulling down my black jean skirt and trying to walk carefully in my red heels all the way. By the time I arrive, I use the back of my hand to blot the shine from my face while ringing the buzzer at the gate. I wait for a few seconds and…nothing. I ring it again, wait, and then ring it again. Where the hell is this guy? Every light in the house is on; he's got to be there. I'm tempted to sit on the curb and rest my aching feet, but it wouldn't do for him to see his high-class call girl in the gutter. A few minutes pass though, and I can't stand it anymore, so I sit and rub my left ankle and sigh. Rummaging in my new bag, I pull out one of the smokes I bummed from Sidney. I wish they sold them in smaller packs; sometimes you just want a few cigarettes instead of a whole pack, and they'd make so much more money that way. I light my cigarette and have to laugh at myself; if anyone were to see me now, they'd never guess that I commanded such a high hourly rate for my company.

I text Alexandra and tell her that there's no answer at the door, and she immediately texts back to try again. Sighing, I leave my shoes at the curb and buzz again, and this time I see a man in a robe abruptly appear in an upstairs window. My heart sinks a little as the door buzzes, and as I scramble to gather my shoes and bag, I can't help but think about how disheveled he looks. I wonder if I can come up with a good enough excuse to get out of this if I have to.

I brush my feet off and put my shoes on and walk up the gray-flagstone driveway to the enormous house. I pass the large white columns, and when I reach out to knock on the door, it eerily creaks open and an arm shoots out from behind the door, frantically waving me inside.

"Come inside! Quick, quick, quick!" a man's voice says, muffled from behind the door. I walk into the grand black-and-white marble foyer and turn around to see a small man closing the door behind me. When he turns around and offers a shaky smile, I smile back.

"Hi, I'm Angelina," I say tentatively.

"Hi. I know who you are," he replies.

"Oh, great," I offer. "And I'm guessing you're Edward?"

"Yes. Edward. That's me, Edward. I'm Edward."

Well, he's definitely strange. He has red, bloodshot eyes like he's been awake for a week, and he looks sweaty, almost clammy. His hair looks damp as well, in a sort of spiky, falling-over Mohawk hairdo. This is certainly a change from my last client, but I guess this is exactly why I get paid the big bucks.

"Are you sure you want me to be here tonight? I could come back some other time if you'd like," I say. Maybe he'll just dismiss me, and I won't have to deal with him at all, even though I'd love the money.

"No. No. Please. Come this way. Upstairs with me. I have champagne for you upstairs."

"Okay, great," I say and then remind myself that I need to sound very enthusiastic about anything he offers me. "Sure! That sounds great, thank you!"

"I just got out of the shower," he tells me as I follow him up a wide staircase. "Okay. Sorry I was late to get to the door."

"Oh, no problem!" The fake grin on my face must look forced, but he doesn't seem to notice or care. We continue down a bright white-carpeted hallway toward two closed double doors, and as we get closer, they open automatically, like doors in the front of a grocery store. Once we walk inside, my jaw drops, and I have to remind myself again to play it cool in front of a client. The room is the size of an ice rink and filled with piles and piles of scripts and manuscripts that are stacked from the floor to the ceiling. There must be ten thousand at least, all shown in bright relief since every single light in the room is on and what looks like every single lamp in the house has been dragged into this room and turned on as well.

"Let me get you a glass of champagne," he offers, walking to the only corner of the room not filled with scripts where a bottle of champagne waits in a standing ice bucket. "It's Veuve Clicquot Rosé. That's all I have," he says apologetically.

"That'll be wonderful, thank you," I say brightly. He pops the champagne and pours a flute for me, and I take it from a shaking hand. Who in the hell is this guy?

"I hope my smoking doesn't bother you. Will it?" he asks. "I need to smoke while I read. It helps me think."

Wait, are we going to be reading today? Sounds good to me.

"No problem! Actually, I'm a smoker too; do you mind if I bum one?"

"Sure, here you are; go ahead," he says, giving me a cigarette from the pocket of his robe. "The lighter's on the coffee table over there."

I walk over to a coffee table by a window and find not only a lighter but a pile of cocaine with rolled-up bills scattered among several old lipstick-stained champagne glasses. He must have had a little party or a couple of other girls over the night before or something?

With both of us smoking and no window open, the room begins to fill with smoke and I imagine a fire starting from one of the eight full ashtrays I can see lying amid the stacks of paper. The room is claustrophobic and mad; I can imagine this man relegating himself to this lone room in the entire house, living here for months in a coked-out search for the right script. He glances at me and, seeing me taking in the state of the coffee table, offers, "I'm getting a divorce."

I nod, understanding that people deal with heartbreak in many different ways. Maybe everything I'm doing now is just my way of dealing with my own heartbreak. Maybe it's just me having an adventure. Or a way of emotionally cutting myself? I don't really know anymore.

"Please, have a seat," he says, walking over to me and motioning to the couch. "Take those shoes off and get comfortable."

He sits on the white-leather sofa, and I choose the floor, preferring to sit lower in this cocoon of scripts. "Bump?" he asks.

"Sure, why not," I say, kneeling over the coffee table and rerolling one of the hundred-dollar bills. "Thanks," I say, wiping my nose.

"Yeah, so I'm going through this separation and really just immersing myself in my work right now," he says. It's clear he wants to spend more time talking to me than he does screwing me. Fine. However he wants to spend his money is his business. I have no problem sitting here and doing blow and talking about his past.

"That must be tough for you," I tell him. I briefly think about telling him the story about my ex but then think better of it. I need to be an illusion, a dream, the girl you can only have if you pay for her time. "It looks like you have a lot of important work to do though. You must really value your career?"

He glows at my deliberate ego stroke. "It's a lot, but I'm the only one to do it. I guess with this separation, it's just something I'm going to need to just figure out. Like a giant screwy puzzle. But I have to tell you…it's like a bullet straight to the heart losing my family."

"I'm so sorry, Edward. That must be extremely hard. And you know, everyone's got something to figure out in their lives. And I'll just say the cliché I hate to say, but I really believe what doesn't kill you does make you stronger."

"Right, sure. Uh huh. I think you're right, Angelina," he says, sadly nodding. "For me, it's not seeing my kids again. She took them to our house in Connecticut, and they've been gone for three months now." He hangs his head. "I haven't seen my own kids in three months."

I reach over and put my hand on his knee. So that explains why he's been holed up in this room like a crazy person. "That's horrible! Could you see them if you wanted to?"

"No, she won't let me see them. That's why I'm working so hard. I just need to keep working. Just keep working. Keep going. Find the right one."

I start to wonder why his wife won't let him see the kids, but I stop myself from going down that path. It's not any of my concern. I'm just here with this man because it's my job. I nod, at a loss for what to say.

"Do you want some more champagne?" he asks.

"Yes, please!" I chirp, eager to brighten the mood.

"Okay! Let me go get another bottle from the fridge." He walks with a bit of a bounce in his step, eager to please. I feel bad for this man who misses his children, who has to throw himself into his work to ignore his pain. In spite of my initial misgivings, I do actually want to help him.

We chain-smoke Parliament Lights and talk about life, death, and the purpose of it all for two hours, doing lines of coke between thoughts to let it make our minds race faster and faster. I can feel myself getting more and more comfortable talking to him, and after a certain point, it just feels like I'm in an old friend's house, having a deep conversation about everything that interests us. Once I start getting a little too existential, he crawls off of the couch and over to me on the floor. We start to kiss, and he slides the straps of my tank top off of my shoulders, feeling the smooth skin on my arms until he gets down to my hands.

He gently pushes me over and gets on top of me; I can feel that he's already hard. Slipping his fingers up my skirt, he pulls my panties off and fingers me; then he goes down on me as I arch my back and gasp my way through an intense orgasm. I hear a rip; then he slips inside me and comes almost instantly. Sighing, he pulls out and falls over on his back next to me.

"Wow, that was..." I start to say.

"I know, I know. Short. It's the coke," he says apologetically.

"No! I was going to say pretty awesome!" I insist.

"Angelina, you can be honest," he says, giving me the side eye.

"I am! I feel great. What a fun night. Thank you, Edward. I really had a nice time."

"Oh sure," he says. He gets up, but I can't tell if he believes me or not. "Let me get you your money."

He walks to the adjoining bathroom, and when I hear a snap, a blue condom goes flying past the door. He returns to the room with a wad of cash clenched in his hand.

"Here you go," he says, handing me the money. "I had fun too. It was nice talking with you. I have work to do now. Can you see yourself out?"

"No problem, Edward. Let me just grab my shoes. I think they're under the coffee table."

I reach under the table for my shoes and when I rise, I see he's already standing at the bedroom door, waiting for me to exit. Just like that, he's back to the awkward man he was before our amazing conversation.

I can't help but wonder if this is one of the reasons his wife left, the fact that he moves so quickly between moods, from fairly positive and engaging to sad and awkward. I stuff the money in my purse, slide my shoes on, and with a nod and a smile from the man in the red robe, the big white grocery store doors close behind me as I walk down the hall.

I feel sadly empty somehow, like maybe his sadness might have been contagious.

CHAPTER TWENTY-THREE

I wake the next morning to an instant headache from Sidney slamming a pillow over my head.

"Ow! Fuck!" I yell, pushing myself up. Sid bounces on my bed and then drops down to her butt, giggling.

"Sorry," she says, exaggerating the word. I glare at her, and she cocks her head to the side. "Okay, fine. I'm sorry! I didn't mean to hit you that hard."

"Uh-huh. Sure you didn't. I'm going to have a headache now for sure." I can still feel last night's drug fest coursing through my body. I need to start saying no. Drugs aren't helping me. They make me feel better for a little while, but in the end, they always make me feel worse.

"I'll get you some Advil," Sidney offers. She darts out of my room, and I hear her rustling through my things in the bathroom. I wince when I hear a shatter; she probably dropped one of my makeup compacts on the floor.

"Bottom right drawer!" I call out to her. "You're paying for that!" She returns with the bottle of Advil, triumphant, and shakes out two pills for me.

"Thanks," I say and swallow the pills. I glance over at my nightstand and see that it's completely clean. I realize with a start that it wasn't that way when I went to sleep.

"Sid, what the fuck? Where's my cash?"

"What cash?" she asks, rifling through the perfume collection on my dresser.

"The stack of hundreds that was on my nightstand! You probably smelled it from your bedroom—that's why you came down this morning."

"Ohhh, *that* cash," she says, winking at me over her shoulder. "I was just keeping it warm for you." She reaches down into her sweatshirt and pulls out my money from inside her bra.

"What the hell? Why did you take that?"

"Oh god, it was just a joke. Lighten the fuck up! You've always been so uptight."

I hold out my hand, and she hesitates but then hands me the money. My heart is pounding so quickly.

Why do I get the feeling that it *wasn't* a joke? That if I hadn't called her on it, she'd have stolen from me?

"You know, you really should be giving me a cut of that," she says. "I was the one who got you into this in the first place."

"Give me a break. I'm too tired to bicker with you right now. Just get out, please!"

"I'm just joking!" she says, hands in the air. Yet, I'm not sure she is.

"I just want to know what happened last night! If these guys are taking my girl away from me, I deserve to at least know what they do to you!" She sits down on my bed and leans forward conspiratorially. "So what happened? Did he fuck you up the ass? Did you give him a blowjob and then toss his salad?"

I feel uneasy for a second. Were those things on the menu? Would I have to do them at some point?

Eventually, I laugh it off and throw a pillow at her. "No, nothing like that. That's just what you do," I tell her.

"Well, then what? That's three thousand dollars there! What did you do for him to give you all that cash?"

"Honestly? We talked for two hours about life, and then he fingered me, I came, and we had sex for about five minutes."

"What? Get the fuck out of here! You talked for two hours about life? Seriously? How boring."

She jiggles her foot, uninterested with my stories already.

"Yeah, well, I actually did enjoy it," I tell her. "Now leave my cash alone and get out of here, so I can sleep a little longer. Please?"

"Well, hang on, I'm actually here because I'm going over to Runyon Canyon to meet Diana for boot camp this morning. I thought you might want to go with us?"

"Um, no," I tell her. "I'm not cool with that jersey chaser anyway. You two are perfect for each other. I think she should be your new best friend! And that hockey player she's dating won't marry her until he's forty. She's just wasting her time."

"Okay, then, fine. And he will marry her if she 'pulls the goalie' like she plans on doing," she says, standing up. "Well, I hope you enjoyed the lovely finger blast last night, baby. We're going to sushi tonight. I already made a resie for us. Rest your pretty little perfect head, take your disco nap, and call me later."

"You two girls are straight evil."

She starts to walk out of the room and then pauses in the doorway. "Maybe we are, but you and I will always be best friends, LJ. It's just the way it was meant to be. Sweet dreams, bitch!"

*

I sleep all day and night in an effort to cleanse myself, and when I wake up the next morning, I feel refreshed. As I pull on my patterned yoga pants and tank top, I check my phone and see that I have about thirty texts from Sidney last night, asking where I am and why I'm not getting sushi with her and Diana. There are even a few hundred Snapchats of the two of them flicking me off in some loud club, some guy's dick, and perfectly glossed, pursed duck lips and cheeks pressed together with confetti raining down like some old prom Polaroid.

In the old days, I'd have felt bad for missing a night out of fun. But, these days, a night out with Sid just doesn't feel so fun anymore. Sucks I have to deal with her as a roommate. I thought about her with my money down her shirt, and I was glad I'd slept through that party. Jerk.

As I finish scrolling through Sidney's crazy texts, one comes in from Naomi asking if I'd like to get a late lunch, and I immediately write back that I'd love to see her beautiful face. We agree to meet in the parking lot at Sunset Plaza at three and to pick a place from there, and I shoot Damiano a text to see if he can meet up with us as well. Then I'm off to yoga to meditate and detox with a few downward dogs.

Later, when I drive into the parking lot, I see Naomi's forest-green Lexus. As I pull up beside her, she waves hello and motions to give her a second; I can see she's on the phone, and she's not happy. I get out of my car and walk around to her side of the car, and immediately she starts motioning wildly and mouthing *I'm going to cut you.*

I'm cracking up and shaking my head when, at last, she gets off the phone and gets out of the car.

"What in the world was that about?" I ask her.

"Some crazy old lady hit me this morning," she tells me while giving me a hug. "Can you believe this? Girl! These people around here are such bad drivers!"

"Naomi. Honey. It's been four little fender benders now. And I'm starting to think the common denominator here might be you?"

"What? Oh, girl, no, no, no." She smiles and winks at me. "You know I'm the best driver there is—don't doubt. Okay!"

"All right, all right. So where do you want to eat? Le Petit Four? Maybe they have something outside?"

"Sure, that works for me. I just have to catch up on some calls, and then we can hang."

"I don't care. All I need is a glass of Pinot Noir, and then I'm good to go. And, hey, would you want to go to Beverly Hills Porsche with me after lunch?"

"Sure, girl, whatever you want."

She pulls me in for a kiss on the cheek, and we walk up the back stairs arm in arm into the restaurant.

We take our favorite table outside in the back corner, and while Naomi makes phone calls, I flip through the new book she's reading about how to build a successful business and sip my glass of wine.

My phone buzzes; Damiano can't make it because he's test driving Ducatis today in celebration of finally signing a huge contract that he and a famous rapper friend had been working on for years, trying to get their headphone design picked up by a mega company. Apparently, it came down to a bidding war, and at last, the design was sold to the highest bidder. Dam's so excited that all of his texts are misspelled, and I don't blame him. His share is fifteen million dollars, and he'll get it all at once.

He tells me to come by for dinner later so that he can tell me all about it. And to celebrate. "No excuses," he writes. "I already called the Turnbull Wine Cellars and ordered you a case of your favorite wine to be shipped to your house, so now you're obligated to come over and drink with me."

I laugh and tell him I'll be there. He's such a great friend. I'm so lucky to have him in my life.

As lunch with Naomi winds down, I pretend to leave to use the restroom, but really I pay the bill. I know that she won't let me pay if I don't do it behind her back, and she's been so generous with me lately that it's the least I can do for her. She finishes up her penne chicken when I return, and once I finish my chilled gazpacho and endive salad, I jump up and push in my chair.

"What's up?" she asks.

"I paid. Let's go," I tell her.

"What? Girl, I will cut you!"

"Cut me later. Let's get over to Beverly Hills Porsche! I'm so excited. I'm thinking of getting a new car!"

"Oh, girl, no. Are you on crazy pills? What are you trying to get now?"

"I really want a black 911. They're so hot but still classy." We get up from the table and start walking back to our cars.

"Yeah, but aren't those super expensive? How can you afford that?"

She pauses at the top of the stairs as I continue down them. I look back up at her, my hand on my hip. "What? I can afford it."

Her mouth is a straight line as she glares at me. "Do I even want to know what's going on with you, LJ?"

Now, it's my turn to pause. "Probably not," I answer.

We're at an impasse; Naomi isn't moving, and I'm just standing there, holding the door open, waiting for her.

"Are you coming?" I ask.

"I'm not sure yet," she answers. "I thought you said you could handle yourself around all of this Hollywood bullshit?"

"I can! I'm fine, Naomi. I promise. I wouldn't do anything that I didn't feel was right. Now come on; shake a tail feather; let's go!"

"That money's just burning a hole in your pocket, huh?"

"Come on. Stop being so silly. It will be fun! Get down here."

She finally walks down the stairs, and I put my arms out for a hug. She breezes by me with a stink eye.

"I just love you, girl…" she says seriously.

"I know, Naomi. I love you too."

I've never appreciated Naomi more than I have in this moment. For her to be able to understand what I'm doing and react with worry but without judgment is huge. Plus, it's such a relief for someone other than Sidney to know my secret and love me anyway. She continues into the parking lot, and I chase after her and tackle her with a hug, both of us laughing. I know our friendship will be fine. I just hope that I'll be fine when this is all said and done too.

CHAPTER TWENTY-FOUR

We take my silver Ford Taurus over to the Beverly Hills Porsche store and find a salesperson to walk us around and give us the rundown on a lease or purchase of one of these babies. The cars gleam and glitter in the sunlight, and my fingers itch to wrap themselves around the tight leather steering wheel of one of those bad boys. Finally, we're given the keys to a black tinted-out 911 with red interior, and suddenly we've got the windows down, sunroof ajar, and the wind whipping through our ponytails. Naomi is in shotgun, and the sales guy's in the back. Even Naomi can't keep the smile off her face as we glide through the California streets in my fantasy car. As we hand the keys back to the handsome salesman after my dream cruise and get back into my car, I ask Naomi what she thinks.

"I think you've completely lost your mind, that's what I think," she says, shaking her head.

"No, silly, about the car. Hot, right?"

"Girl! You're going to get into some serious trouble with this one. Just lost in the sauce and keep on going till the wheels fall off…damn. You really are one hot mess! You know that?"

I laugh nervously. Part of me knows she's right. The other part doesn't care to dwell on it right now.

"No, I'm not. Lighten up. Come on, it's amazing, right?"

"Yeah, the car's amazing. It surpasses the ultimate driving machine! But I just don't think you can afford that kind of amazing right now on a struggling model slash aspiring writer's salary."

"Now you sound like my mom," I tell her. I'm annoyed that she won't just have fun with me. Does she always have to be the voice of reason? Can't she ever just have fun?

"Well, maybe you should listen to your mom!" she says.

"Look. The salesman did say that my trade-in would be worth ten thousand dollars, and if I bought it, then my payments would be nine hundred dollars a month and roughly one hundred for insurance. I could totally swing that. My rent is only seven hundred for my room at the house. And then I have my cell phone and paying my mom back—that's it."

"What about your student loan, genius?"

Okay, I've had enough of this inquisition. I'm an adult after all. I don't have to answer Naomi.

"Naomi, you've got to stop worrying so much. I can defer my loans; I'll be fine. I know you're really buggin' out, and I know you've got my back, and this is all out of love, but honestly, I've got this."

"Oh, okay. You've got this; that's exactly what it looks like," Naomi says, rolling her eyes. "Just don't come running to me when everything comes crashing down and you need a dollar for Jack in the Box two-for-one tacos because you haven't eaten in a week."

"Okay. I won't. I'll just eat yours."

I push her playfully, and she finally cracks a smile.

"Want to order takeout and watch movies tonight?" she asks.

"Can't tonight," I tell her. "I have to do something for a few hours, and then Damiano invited me up to his house for dinner with some of his friends that are in town. Want to come? It'll be fun. And he just loves you to death."

I remember the time the three of us went to dinner; Naomi left satisfied that I had at least one decent friend besides her in LA.

"I love that boy too," she says. "You know, he's the only person I know who would literally give you the shirt off his back."

"I know. There's no one like him."

She cocks an eyebrow at me as I start the engine. "And what exactly is it that you have to do tonight before dinner, LJ?"

Ah, damn. I knew she wasn't going to let that one slide.

"Ahhh, well…" I start, not making eye contact.

"Uh-huh," she says disapprovingly. We drive the rest of the way back to her car in silence. I know it's killing her not to scream and go off on me again, but she's clearly met her quota of motherly advice for the day.

We pull in the Sunset Plaza parking lot next to her car, and she gets out without a word, and I don't bother to chase her down. Honestly, I'm tired of trying to convince her of something I'm going to do either way. She starts to walk to her car and then pauses and turns back, knocking lightly on my passenger window. I roll the window down, and she leans down to make eye contact with me.

"Please. Just be careful," she says. I've never seen her look so serious.

"I will," I tell her, smiling up at her.

"No. I'm serious, girl. Be careful! This is not a game you're playing with these men."

"I promise I will. I'll call you if I'm ever in trouble, okay? And I know that you will come running to save me."

"You better always call me! I love you."

"Love you too."

She walks away and I feel a flood of a relief, like I've gotten permission to do something bad. Which, in a way, is exactly what I've got now that Naomi knows my secret and has my back. I daydream about driving my hot new car around Los Angeles as I do a happy car dance all the way home.

*

As soon as I get home, I hear Sidney's music blasting upstairs.

"Sidney! Is that you?" Collin yells down the stairs.

"No, it's LJ!" I yell back. The music is thumping through the house and making it hard to concentrate.

"Ugh, fuck!" he says, stomping on the floor. "Do you know where she would hide a key to her room? Her fucking door is locked, and her retarded dance music is giving me a fucking headache! I'm trying to work!"

"Okay, hang on; let me look!" I call back to him. I go upstairs and pull a chair out of Collin's room to feel above her doorway. When I come back with nothing but dust, I move over to the window in the hallway. Bingo.

"Found it!" I yell to him. He storms out of his room and grabs the key from me and then uses it to throw open her door and turn off the music.

"Thanks," he says as he stomps back past me and slams his door.

"Your chair's out here!" I remind him.

"Leave it there!" he calls back through the closed door.

"Okay, geez. Angry much?" I mumble and head back downstairs to get ready for my night. I check my phone again, and sure enough, Alexandra has texted me the details of my job for tonight. Sunset Tower Hotel at eight. I slip on my red dress and nudist heeled sandals, and I'm out the door.

*

I pull up and toss my keys to the valet in a hurry so that I can get to the elevator and not be spotted by anyone I know. As soon as I'm up to the tenth floor, I use the hallway mirror to check my hair and makeup one last time and then walk to the end of the corridor to suite 1025. Two deep breaths and then I knock.

"You're not the girl I asked for."

The voice in the doorway is jarring, and I don't know how to respond.

"Are you coming in?" he asks.

"I guess so..." I say, confused.

He sighs. "Never mind what I said; it's too late now. Just come in; you'll be fine."

I walk into the dimly lit room and hesitate near the doorway. It's not a great feeling to not be wanted, and part of me wants to just leave now. He must sense my awkwardness because he motions for me to sit on the bed and offers me a small grin. I sit, trying to appear more comfortable than I feel. It's not his job to make me feel at ease—it's mine.

Although the sheer gold drapes are drawn, I can still make out the fabulous view of the city through the window. He crosses in front of it to sit in a plush chair and picks up a waiting martini from the side table.

"I hope you don't mind that I smoke," he says, lighting a cigarette.

"No, I don't mind; thanks for asking," I say, trying to exude self-confidence. I can't place his accent—British perhaps, but not the kind I'm used to. He looks like Daniel

Craig, so maybe I'm just assuming he's British. He's certainly pulling off the whole James Bond look anyway, sitting there in his slim-fitting slacks, Gucci belt with matching shoes and no socks, and crisp white button-down shirt with the sleeves rolled up just once. His shirt is unbuttoned one too many times to be appropriate, but then again, he doesn't need to be buttoned up in his own hotel room.

We sit in silence for a few minutes, and I get uncomfortable all over again. He hasn't offered me a drink, and I'm too polite to ask for one. After another minute, I can't stand the silence anymore.

"So…are you in town from overseas?" I ask.

"No," he replies, lighting another cigarette. I nod, pretending to mull that over.

"Are we waiting for something?" I prod. I'm not about to just sit here awkwardly, even if that's what he's into.

"My wife," he says. "She's in the bathroom changing."

"Oh, okay," I say, trying not to let my voice shake. What the hell is happening right now? Alexandra didn't tell me anything about a wife.

Just as I start contemplating texting Alexandra, the bathroom door opens, and a magnificent woman walks in, her hair the perfect glowing shade of light brown that bounces and shines as she moves. Her bangs sweep across her porcelain skin that's complemented by a blotted wine pout, and her face is completed with smart black eyeglasses. A classically beautiful woman in a black-velvet knee-length pencil skirt and a fitted white button-down shirt, she looks like a Victoria's Secret model that decided to go back to school to study architecture.

I melt as she appraises me. I've never been instantly seduced by a woman before. If I had any doubts about what was about to happen, they vanished as soon as she walked in the room.

"I'm Angelina," I stammer, standing up from the bed.

She looks me up and down and then turns to her husband.

"Thomas. This is not the girl we ordered."

"I know," he says, waving once toward me and sipping from his martini.

"If you're not happy, I could..." I begin. For some reason, I want nothing more than to please this woman.

"Walk over here," she says. I obey, moving next to her. I'm slightly shorter than she is, and when she leans forward to rub her cheek against mine I get goose bumps. She pulls back and nods approvingly to her husband, and relief instantly washes over me. She turns back and smiles and then caresses both of my arms lightly with her fingertips. Her hands travel down my body until they reach the bottom of my dress, and when she curls her fingers under it and pushes it up and over my head, I'm overtaken by warm, tingling chills. It's just me now, standing there in my baby-pink lace bra and heels. She appraises me once again and then leans in for a kiss, her smooth lips softly touching mine. Her fingers trace my stomach and then slide lower, down inside of me, as we kiss. It feels so sensual, having someone this tantalizing pleasuring me, and our heads tilt and sway together as she drives me as crazy as a wild animal in heat. She stops then, and I immediately ache for her. Walking over to the king-sized bed, she undresses down to her garters, unveiling a beyond-perfect body.

"Do you want to join me?" she whispers.

"Yes," I pant.

"Come over here," she says, motioning me over and lightly patting the bed beside her.

I crawl onto the bed and stand on my knees. We start to kiss again, and I run my hands through her soft hair. She tastes like candy. I've never felt this sensual before; usually when I'm about to have sex, I feel uninhibited and dangerous, but here with her, I feel like I'm on a puffy pink cloud surrounded by a luminous lavender heaven.

When she touches me, I tremble, and in response, she pushes me down and straddles me. She undoes my bra in one swift move and kisses my breasts, her body soft like satin against mine and her perfume intoxicating as she moves down. She pauses a moment and looks me in the eye, and the moment hangs there between us. Then she dips between my legs and slides her tongue into me. I'm moaning in ecstasy, clinging to the pillows behind me. Dear God.

I can finally understand why men love women so much; she's so unbelievably soft and supple that I can't help but hold her against me. She uses all of her fingers and her tongue, kissing my thighs when I let out a euphoric groan and tremble with my second super orgasm in ten minutes. I'm in love.

"Your skin is as soft as silk," she tells me, rising from between my legs.

"Oh my god, this is amazing," I tell her. "You are unbelievably amazing!"

Just then, I hear the chair move back from the table by the windows. Her husband. I completely forgot he was here—I was so consumed by her. He just sat there, watching. I'm instantly nervous again, and I watch him closely as he puts out his cigarette. What does he want?

He unbuckles his pants slowly as he watches his wife kiss my stomach and then drops them to the floor. He's very well endowed and already hard, and I look away despite myself, eager to stay in this erotic space with his wife. He gets on the bed with us, and his wife moves aside for him. I instantly miss her warmth but am now entranced by his sculpted form. His faint cologne and impeccable chest capture my attention first. He pushes me down and gets on top of me and grabs me tightly while his wife kisses his back. Suddenly, he's inside me, slowly pushing deeper. He fucks me while he fingers his wife and then flips me over on all fours and fucks me doggie style, roughly pulling my hair to arch my back. He kisses me then, and his wife crawls underneath me and licks and softly bites my nipples. Then she and I kiss passionately as Thomas releases my hair, and I cum while he puts a hand around my neck and squeezes, the other hand over my mouth to stifle my scream. I cum harder than I ever have in my life, the two sets of hands sweeping all over my weakened body.

I'm suddenly tossed aside like an old dishrag, and I hear the snap of a condom and watch it sail to a nearby trash can. He grabs his wife in the heat of the moment, and I slip off the bed and watch them kiss and fuck from the floor, his hand reaching down to the dimples in the small of her back to thrust her closer. They are so beautifully entwined that they resemble an infamous piece of Italian art. She shudders and moans, and he pulls her even closer, as if she will never be close enough to him.

"Your money's in an envelope in my jacket pocket," he pants, focusing only on his wife. He rolls over to his back and puts his wife in reverse cowgirl on top of him to marvel at her beauty. Just like that, I'm snapped out of my insanely sexy porno dream; I guess that's my prompt to leave. I gather my crumpled dress from the corner of the suite and slip it back on, trying to be as quiet as possible. It's pleasing to see how into each other they are; a freight train could probably run through the room at full steam and they wouldn't notice. I stop by his jacket on the way out and then breeze through the door, quietly shutting it with a click behind me.

I'm still vibrating and trying to catch my breath as I wait for the elevator, and as I watch the numbers click down, I catch sight of myself in the hallway mirror and see that my dress is on inside out, and my hair's an absolute wreck.

Holy shit! I have to get in the elevator, walk through the lobby, and wait at the valet like this. Anyone can tell that I've just been thoroughly fucked. My cheeks flush more with the thought of anyone noticing, and I tug my hemline down in an attempt to make it slightly better. The image of the wife tugging the same hemline up my body flashes through my mind, and I feel hot and bothered all over again.

The elevator doors open with no one inside, and I breathe a sigh of relief. Come on—let's get this elevator down as quickly as possible, I pray. Come on, baby, let's go. The doors ding open at the lobby, and I step out, pretending to have more confidence than I really do. I fluff my hair in an attempt to hide my smeared face and speed walk through to the valet as quickly as possible. All good so far.

I hustle up to the attendant, and he takes my ticket, cocking his head to the side.

"Is that some kind of weird fashion statement I don't know about?" he asks me, snickering.

I give him my bitchiest face. "Ha ha, you must be a comedian? Can you go get my car now, please?"

"Okay, sorry. Sorry," he says, bowing.

"Yeah. Thanks a lot," I reply.

He runs off to fetch my Ford as I take stock of my surroundings. It's odd that it's not so busy on the strip tonight. Usually, valets are running so quickly to get everyone's cars that they don't have time to comment on your appearance. At least I lucked out by not seeing someone I know.

I get in the car and give him ten bucks as he closes the door for me, smiles, and runs off. Before I leave though, I have to see how much is in the envelope. I pull the top flap open, and my jaw drops. Three thousand dollars cash. I place it in the seat next to me as I drive away and start to laugh hysterically, tears falling down my cheeks.

My favorite song comes on, and I turn it all the way up, nearly blowing my speakers out and shouting the lyrics out at the top of my lungs. I can't believe it. I just had an extraordinary threesome with the finest two people you'd ever want to be naked with, and I got paid three grand? I'm blown away. This is too easy.

I get home and pull myself together. Hide my cash, check. Change into jeans and a T-shirt and try to make it look like I didn't just have some of the best sex of my life, check. Then, I'm right back out the door to head to Damiano's for dinner. I can't wait to give him a big hug, but I can't help but think that he'll know right away that something's up when I waltz in with my high pro glow and an ear-to-ear grin.

Dinner at Dam's flies by in a blur of veal scallopini, red wine, and laughter with ten of Damiano's closest Italian friends. Everyone comments on how much I'm glowing, and I have to admit that I haven't been this happy in a very long time.

Damiano sends me home with two bottles of my favorite champagne, and whenever I take a sharp curve on the road, I can hear them clinking against each other in the back seat. My phone buzzes with a Snapchat from Sidney, asking me to come and climb in bed with her when I get home. I text her back a smiley face, and she writes back asking if I'd also pick up some Ben & Jerry's Phish Food ice cream for her. I run by the grocery store to grab it, and when I finally make it to the house, it's completely dark except for the dim flicker of the TV in Sidney's room. I open the front door and am almost blown away by the pungent smell of weed permeating the entire house.

Well, Sid's having a good time then. I run by the kitchen to grab two spoons and a roll of paper towels and then make my way up the dark stairs. It's Friday night so all the boys are out on the town; it's actually surprising that Sidney's not out too; she's probably got some crazy-dramatic reason why she's staying in tonight. Or else she's trying to avoid her dreaded bridge-and-tunnel crowd.

"Hey, Sid," I say, opening her door. "What's up, darlin'? Where are you? Are you sick or something? Why aren't you going out tonight?"

"Hey," she says softly from the pile of blankets on her bed. "I'm right here. Did you get my ice cream?"

"Yeah, dude, I've got spoons and everything."

"Thanks. Let's cuddle." She throws back her covers and waits for me to get in bed with her, and once I do, she lays her head on my chest.

"So...what's up?" I ask. "Is everything okay? Are you just chillin' tonight or what?"

Sidney takes a deep breath and closes her eyes. "I think I might be pregnant. I'm five days late."

"Whoa, are you serious?" I lean back and try to look at her, but she keeps her eyes clamped shut. "What the hell, Sid? Is it Sebastian's? Or...geez, it could be half of Hollywood's for all we know!"

"That's not really funny, LJ."

"Yeah. Well it kind of is...I'm kidding! Sorry. That wasn't cool. Sorry, Sid."

She sits up a little to look at me, wiping her eyes. "I bought a test already. I was waiting for you to come home before I do it. I'll go in a minute. Ugh. If I am, I hope it's Sebastian's. I really think we'd be great parents. And I'd love to marry him."

"Honey, you might be delusional. I don't think he'd marry you if he knew what your *other job* is," I tell her, laying the back of my hand on her forehead.

"Shut up. He wouldn't care about that! You're so mean to me. Just hold me."

"Okay, Sid. Just eat your ice cream, and we'll take the test in a little bit."

"Thanks. Just watch the end of *Pretty Woman* with me?"

"Okay."

"LJ?"

"Yes."

"You're my pretty woman."

"Thanks, Sid. You're mine too." I lean down and kiss her forehead a few times. The irony of two willing escorts watching a fairy tale about a prostitute escaping her life doesn't elude me. It's hopeful at best.

We snuggle tight and dig into most of the pint of ice cream before Sidney finally decides that she's ready to go to the bathroom to see if her life will change. Rolling off the bed, she grabs the purple box from her nightstand and leaves the room, only to pop her head right back in to ask if I'd come in with her.

"Sure, Sid. No problem. I know how it is."

I sit by the sink while she pees, feeling some déjà vu from my own pregnancy a few months ago. I squeeze my eyes closed tightly to try to clear the memory of the heartbreak. Finally Sidney caps the test and places it above us on the counter and then sits on the floor next to me and lays her head in my lap. We sit in silence for ten minutes while I stroke her hair, and when her phone's timer goes off, she asks if I'll look at the test.

"Are you sure?" I ask.

"Yes, I'm sure. You do it."

I reach up and grab the test.

"Well? What does it say?" Sidney asks, her knees pulled up to her chest as she sits next to me.

"You're...not pregnant."

Sidney's shoulders sag, and for a second, I can't tell if she's relieved or disappointed.

"I need a cocktail, and you do too. I'll make you one downstairs. I think we have some CÎROC vodka in the freezer."

"Nah, fuck that, we're going out!" Sidney says, jumping up from the floor. "Let's get our hot asses dressed and go dance!"

"I don't know if I'm down to go out actually; it's been a superlong day."

"Shut the fuck up! I was almost a mom; we need to celebrate that I'm not!"

"You're so fucking cuckoo," I tell her, laughing and shaking my head.

"No, *you're* cuckoo! Seriously, go get dressed. You can even smoke one of those lovely joints you rolled."

"Fiiine," I say, stretching out the word. I beeline it to her nightstand and grab a joint and light it up, passing it to her behind me. She puffs it once and then smacks me on the ass. "Okay! Now go!"

"All right, I'm going, but I'm taking this joint with me."

"Cool beans! I'll be ready in five minutes. Just meet me outside. And make that cocktail to go! I'll drive."

Sidney didn't ask, and I didn't tell her about my wild threesome at the Sunset Tower. She's all wrapped up in her own drama, as always, so I just avoid conversation altogether and just focus on her. It's easier that way. I get ready and mix a cranberry vodka for myself in a to-go coffee mug and run out the door to meet her, and before long, we're blasting music and screaming out the windows as she peels out onto our street. And that's all I remember. I wake the next morning hanging halfway off of Sidney's futon, my makeup and dress still on. I get up and rub my sore neck, wandering over to the bed to see if Sidney's alive under the covers.

"Hey," I say, poking the lump under the blankets.

"Yeah?" she says.

"I'm going downstairs. I'm still fucked up."

"Me too," she says, popping her head out. "Come back up later. Last night was so fun."

"I don't remember," I tell her, shaking my head.

"You were the ultimate dancing queen!" she says.

"That's great." I offer her a weak smile. "My head hurts. I need to go lie down. Good night."

I go downstairs and wash my face, the cool water doing wonders for my swimming head. Once I'm back in my bedroom, I yank my dress over my head and crawl under the covers.

When I wake up again, it's dark outside. I check my phone; I slept for twelve hours, and it's ten at night. I instantly feel like shit for wasting my entire Saturday. No one notices but me. Depressing. I go to the fridge and slam an orange Gatorade and then take a frozen Snickers and a liter of coconut water back to bed with me, and I sleep until 8:00 a.m. I tell myself I'll go to yoga at nine, let the Zen purify me while in lotus position, and then drink a fresh green juice and a wheatgrass shot from the raw juice bar. Completely absolved again. Game on.

It's a lovely Sunday morning when I finish my clarifying routine and head back home for a shower. I daydream on the sunny drive back, thinking of what I'll be doing in ten years, and what I'll even be doing with the rest of my day. Maybe I'll get some writing done or organize my room a bit. I'm totally off kilter, not having a normal job and routine to think about starting on Monday, but the money I'm making doing what I'm doing is too good to pass up. I might as well enjoy it while I have it. Another old saying of Aunt Verna's creeps into my head, and I shudder because it rings true: an idle mind is the devil's playground. And I smile knowing that I'm having fun daring him to come and get me. I can't resist.

As soon as I walk in the door, my phone buzzes with a text from Alexandra asking if I'm available for a job this afternoon. It's an early call, two o'clock, but I'm not doing anything else, so I text her back and jump in the shower to get ready.

When I pull up to the Beverly Wilshire Hotel's valet, I can't help but feel a little out of place in my Ford Taurus. The sooner I can get my Porsche the better. I can't do anything about it today though, so I just put on my big black shades and wrap my shoulders in my lilac pashmina, arranging my face to look like I belong here, my nose slightly in the air. I walk into the elevator with a nice-looking redheaded gentleman and just nod when he says hello to me. I'm not breaking character for anyone.

I'm going to room 1201, a suite on the top floor. The man rides all the way up with me and holds the door when it opens for me. I start down the hall with my head held high, but I notice he's right behind me. Wait…is this the guy I'm supposed to be meeting? I hear him slow down as I come to a halt outside of room 1201, and when I knock, there's no answer. The man walks a few steps down to me and quietly reaches into his pocket and pulls out his key.

"Hi," he says, smirking.

"Oh. Hi. Are you John, I guess?"

"What gave it away?"

"I…ah…well, I'm sorry. I didn't know it was you in the elevator."

"Why would you? Shhh. Come inside."

He holds the door open for me while I walk inside. It looks as though he hasn't even slept there; the bed is still made, and the living room is very neat and clean, but the door leading out onto the balcony is open.

"Will you shower before we get started?" he asks.

"Well, I actually just showered," I tell him.

"I insist," he says, smiling.

"Okay. I'll be right back then. Do you want to join me?"

"No. I have to catch up on a few e-mails. How long will you be? Ten, fifteen minutes?"

"Yeah, probably around that," I tell him, confused. This guy must be some kind of hypochondriac.

The shower is amazing, of course. I use the shower cap to preserve my straightened hair and lather up with the divine-smelling Bvlgari soap. I get out, dry off, and walk into the living room in the hotel's fluffy, white towel. He turns from his computer and frowns.

"You didn't wash your hair. You need to wash your hair."

"Oh, I'm sorry. I didn't know that you…"

"It's all right. I didn't say so. Fix it."

"All right, I'll be right back," I say, smiling sweetly.

Now I'm really weirded out by his snappy requests. I rinse my hair out and run some conditioner through it so that he can smell that it's clean, even though I already washed my hair once today. I don't like that he just demanded something so stupid, and I have to do it, but I guess that's the deal I made.

When I return to the living room, he's out on the balcony with headphones on. I walk over and tap him on the shoulder, careful not to walk outside and be seen. He seems as though he really wants this to be kept a secret. I back up so that he can come back into the room, and he does so and walks right to the bed without even acknowledging me. I guess that's my signal to follow him.

He stands by the bed as still as a statue and points to the floor beside him. Once I've taken my place there, he rips my towel off and, in one quick motion, flips me into the air and onto the bed, landing on top of me and planting an extremely hard kiss on my lips. My face is covered with soaking-wet hair, but that doesn't stop him from turning me over and grabbing a handful of my mop, forcing my knees open, and fucking me so hard that I let out a scream. He quickly covers my mouth and pulls my body close to his from behind, stopping for a moment to bite my neck and back several times before releasing his grip over my lips.

I'm shocked at first, not knowing what's happening, feeling, for a second, the hot, heavy flashback to that night in

Hawaii, the forceful, cold way of the behemoth man on top of me.

Am I making a mistake? Dark, sick feelings rise up inside me, trying to interject.

But then he takes his hand and squeezes my breasts and then moves down to finger me. I don't have a chance to react before he flips me back over again, my head hanging over the side of the bed, legs straight up in the air on either side of his head. He continues to fuck me so hard that I have a hard time differentiating between pleasure and pain.

Screwing him is like roller coaster ride; one moment, I'm looking over the top of a steep hill in fear, and the next, I'm losing my stomach racing down the tracks in orgasm. When I let out my final scream after a full hour of the most acrobatic sex I've ever had, he lightly turns my head to the side while he cums.

"Wow," I say when he collapses next to me. "That was...wow." I can hardly catch my breath.

He doesn't say anything from his side of the bed, only gives me an Elvis half smile and excuses himself to the bathroom. I just shrug it off. My body is vibrating on a level above all other humans right now. I can't be concerned if he's acting weird or not. I can't stop smiling between the sheets; when I woke up this morning, I certainly didn't think this was how I was going to be spending my afternoon. I find a moment to ponder. Is this *bad job* going to be my only future? Am I willing to stop myself? Am I worthy of true love? I don't know.

John reappears from the bathroom, and I immediately perk myself up on the bed, but he avoids eye contact with me and breezes right past me into the living room. Okay, then, it's time to make my departure. I go to the bathroom and gather my clothes, surprised to see them neatly folded on the marble counter to the left of the sink with my hair clip nicely placed on top as if housekeeping came through.

Forget hypochondriac—this guy's straight OCD.

When I come back out fully dressed, he's behind the desk again and on the phone.

"Okay, in ten minutes," he says and then hangs up. "Here you are?" he says to me and hands me a stack of crisp new bills.

"Thank you, John, I had a really great—"

"Never mind," he says, waving me away. "You seem tense. How about a massage?"

"Sure...I guess I could stay for a while?"

"No, down at the spa. With my girl Jessica, she's the best! And your nails too—they're chipped. It's all taken care of. I told them that you'd be down there in ten minutes. You'd better get down there! Go."

"Oh wow. That's too much, John. I don't know what to say!"

"Don't say anything; just don't be late!"

"Okay! Wow, thank you so much!"

He mouths the word *bye* as he starts to do something on his phone, so I walk out and close the door behind me. I can't believe my luck. I'm going to spend the entire day at the spa! Wow.

They welcome me at the spa like I'm the duchess of Beverly Hills and whisk me away to a private room for my afternoon of pampering. He's right about his masseuse Jessica—she's incredible. Throughout the massage, she teaches me relaxation techniques, telling me to visualize a gold ball of light slowly moving through my whole body, radiating health, happiness, light, and love. Then, I move directly into my nail appointment. I float out of the hotel that afternoon smiling from ear to ear with my nails glistening in perfection, feeling like a more-polished version of myself.

I looked my fear in the face today and conquered it.

I tip the valet twenty dollars and feel so good that I drive straight to the Beverly Hills Porsche showroom and buy the

911. It's almost seven at night before I finish all of the paperwork, and I finally get to drive my hot new whip home. I turn up the incredible sound system and cruise down Santa Monica Boulevard, singing along to my acoustic-music playlist and feeling alive, free, and on fire. There's nothing I can't do. I create my fate now.

I go to sleep after finishing a few more scenes of my screenplay, feeling like I'm exactly where I'm supposed to be in my life. Letting destiny lead me.

CHAPTER TWENTY-FIVE

"What the fuck is in our driveway, you crazy bitch?"

Sidney bursts into my room early the next morning and shakes me awake.

"What the fuck is what? Hey, where did you sleep last night?" I ask. I had gone up to her room to say hello, but she wasn't there.

"You know damn straight what the fuck is *what*. And don't change the subject! So what the fuck is it?"

"A Porsche 911," I say, hiding my face under the covers, smiling.

"Stop. Just stop. You're totally nuts, babe. Absolutely. Totally. Fucking. Insane!"

"You told me to buy something!" I say in my defense, throwing a pillow at her.

"I told you to save for a place of your own! To *live* in! Don't get it twisted, baby."

"So does that mean you don't want to take a spin?" I ask her with a sinister grin.

"I thought you'd never ask. Let me go get my black Chanel shades. Meet you outside in five!"

"Okay!" I call after her as she runs upstairs. "But there's no smoking in my new ride!"

"No shit, Sherlock!" Sid yells from upstairs.

*

We cruise around the town for hours, stopping for milkshakes and candy on Melrose and driving out to Venice Beach to shop and have breakfast on the boardwalk, ending our trip by driving the long way home in traffic on Pacific Coast Highway through Malibu. We don't care that we're stuck in traffic; we're exactly where we want to be, car dancing and enjoying the incredible California sunset over the ocean.

"Hey, can you check my phone?" I ask Sidney as we make our way home. "I think I got a text."

"Sure thing, chicky," she says, retrieving my phone from the cup holder.

"Anything?"

"Yeah, one from Alexandra. You have a client tonight. Should I tell her yes? I guess so, right, so you can pay for this G-ride?" She lightly punches me in the arm. "You also have one from your mom, and a Snapchat from Cole, saying 'hi.' Ooooh, he's so cute. He loves you; he loves you," she sings at me.

"Stop it!" I say, laughing. "And tell Alexandra, no, I want to stay home tonight and catch up on my writing."

"Don't be a fucking bore! Honey, please. You just signed your life away on this new car. I'm telling her yes! You can thank me later."

"No! I don't want to...Sid!"

"Too late, you're going. I just hit send. You can't afford to miss any more jobs. Ever."

My stomach sinks a little, the luster of the day fading a bit. Is Sid right?

"You suck, Sid."

"Maybe later. I'm seeing my baby tonight. He does love it when I baptize his perfect dick."

"Oh god, gross! Are you still going to marry him too? And will you do me a favor and not text Cole back or anything? I'm ignoring him."

"Yes, I'm totally marrying Sebastian! He told me that we'd go ring shopping next weekend! I want a flawless six-carat pear-shaped diamond. You and Cole should come with us! And that's really mean, not responding to him. He's the hottest ticket in town, and all he dreams about is you. He told me so."

"He did not! Shut up, Mrs. Wintercorn."

"He did so. But fine, whatever. And I think that has a nice ring to it. Don't you? Mrs. Sidney Annabelle Wintercorn will be boarding her private jet for Staad, Switzerland, to go skiing. And you could go with me, Mrs. Cole Brinkman! But fine. I won't text him if you don't want me too. But there's no reason to be so mean to him."

"Oh god. He'll get over it. He just wants me because I'm not talking to him. His poor ego will probably survive the heartbreak."

"Fine. But you're coming to dinner at Katana tomorrow night with all the girls. Well, it might be Craig's or The Abby or The Nice Guy or MR CHOW, not sure yet; we'll see what all the guys want to do. Ten o'clock-ish."

"Fine, fine, whatever you want, your highness."

When we get home, Sidney goes right back out to meet Diana for drinks and more shopping on Robertson Boulevard. I stay in and dye my hair a rich chocolate brown and then take a shower and throw on a white faux-leather skirt with a cream-colored button down with a pussy bow on the neck, a dainty sterling-silver linked choker with matching earrings, and very ladylike black patent pumps. I'm in the mood for a very feminine but fresh look tonight, and I need something to go with my elegant new car.

I drive over to the L'Ermitage Beverly Hills and feel the coolest I've ever felt handing my keys over to the valet attendant. Driving this car makes me feel super classy and very, very fabulous. I do not miss that Ford Taurus for one second. I check my phone for the room number and zip right over, finding the swing guard holding the door open for me.

"Knock, knock," I call out, opening the door a bit.

"Come in," a low voice says from the blackened room.

I instantly get a chill as I cross the threshold into the dark room. I walk to the center and let my eyes adjust to the dim lighting. After a few seconds, I can see a shorter, round man with beady eyes staring up at me. He has a slicked-over side part, and his skin is reddish and bumpy. Well, this certainly isn't what I was expecting.

He's the last man on Earth I'd want to sleep with.

I instantly get the overwhelming feeling that I shouldn't be here. We keep eye contact as I take off my purse and place it gently on the floor, and finally he breaks the stare with a small smile and takes a seat on the chair barricading the dark, velvety drapes closed.

"Dance for me! Slowly."

"Dance for you?"

"Dance for me! Undress and dance for me."

"Okay…" I say, ignoring the voice in my head warning me of danger.

I take two steps toward him and begin to slowly move my hips and unbutton my blouse.

"Faster," he says.

"But I thought you said slower?"

"Faster!" he insists.

"Sure," I say, moving my hips faster. I have to remind myself that I'm not here to fight him; I'm here to follow directions and be his fantasy. My personality isn't so well suited for this job. It takes discipline to quiet my smart-ass, knee-jerk reaction to him.

"Over here! By me. Stand here," he says, pointing to the floor in front of him. I walk over to him with my shirt off and my skirt unbuttoned in the back.

"Now, turn around," he says, grabbing my hips with little, puffy sausage fingers and spinning me around. His hands are hot and meaty on my boney hips. He unzips my skirt and lets it fall to the floor and then stands up and unbuckles his belt. He slides his belt out of its loops with a slither, and his pants drop to the ground.

"May I put my belt around your neck?"

"Um…sure?" I say. My consent clearly doesn't matter here; as I utter the last word, he's already fastening the belt around my neck.

He walks me over to the bed like an animal and lays me down on my side and then pets my head and walks over to the other side of the bed so that he can get behind me and spoon me. Feeling me from behind, he begins to immediately fuck me and simultaneously tighten the belt around my neck. I can't move; I feel as though a spell has been cast on me. I start to have my first out-of-body experience, feeling as though I'm hovering up in the corner of the room, looking down at myself lying on the bed in a fetal position being screwed by a greasy little round man. I can't help but think that he was one of those kids who was teased for being so strange in high school. No wonder he has to pay for sex. Suddenly I have empathy for him, for the agony he must have endured.

And just like that, I understand that the fantasy I've been telling myself, that this *bad job* is easy and lucrative, as it's only sex with hot, established men in Hollywood, just became very dirty and seedy to me. I know now how lucky I've been, how naïve.

Looking down on myself from this vantage point, I see how much I resemble a sad blow-up doll that this man would have bought at some sleazy sex shop and would be free to have his way with in his lonely, dark hotel room. But I'm not a doll; I'm a real person with parents and friends and thoughts and feelings. I'm here too. Really, we're both hiding in this depressed hotel room, physically and emotionally cutting ourselves. The camouflage we hide ourselves under makes our obscure illusions of life easier to bear. I feel lost. I realize I'm the kid that will be taunted for my stupid decisions. I've hit rock bottom.

"Can you loosen the belt? Please? I can't breathe so well," I plead.

"Yes. I'm done anyway." He continues to spoon me after taking the belt off though, and an odd still pause passes between us.

"Do you ever wonder what it would be like to be stabbed in the heart?" he whispers in my ear. He's still inside me, slowly going limp. He lightly pushes my hair behind my ear. "Stabbed. Right square in the heart," he repeats, as if I hadn't heard him the first time. "When you meet these men. Do you ever think one of them might want to hurt you? Maybe beat you to death?"

"Um…no, I can't say that I have," I answer, pulling away from him and sitting up. I start to move slowly and walk over to my clothes to get dressed.

My hands are shaking a little. I'm suddenly feeling extremely nervous.

"Lovely blouse," he murmurs.

"Oh, thank you."

"Cream pussy bow?"

"Yes, I believe it's an off-white cream-color blouse."

He pauses, considering this.

"Can I call you sometime, Angelina?"

"Well, you can call the office if you'd like to see me again." I'm so grateful for protocol in this moment.

"No," he insists.

"You mean, call me personally?"

"Yes."

"Sure, that's fine, I guess? Let me write my number down for you." I walk over to the desk for a pen and paper.

"You wouldn't give me a fake number, now would you, Angelina?" he asks, taking the paper from me.

"No! Of course I wouldn't."

"That's special. I can see that you are special," he says in his creepy monotone voice.

I finish getting dressed in sixty seconds flat, and when he hands me a billfold of money, he pauses with his hand tightly clasped over mine. His eyes lock on mine, and dark chills overtake my entire body. I fight not to pull away though and give him a forced, uneasy smile.

"I'm going to call you," he informs me.

"Sounds good."

"I'm going to call you tomorrow. We can go to a movie. There's a new horror movie I've been dying to see."

"I don't appreciate scary movies. They're so unrealistic," I say, gaining confidence by returning to a smart-ass remark. I pull away from his hand.

"Okay. You can pick the movie! Just answer my call tomorrow. And, can I cum on your face next time?"

He eyes me trying to step back and leave. "In a hurry?"

"I have a hair appointment," I lie.

"Oh golly! Why didn't you say so? You should have told me. I don't want you to be late for that! You'd better get going then." His more-chipper persona is taking over.

He walks me to the door and doesn't say another word as he gives me a hard push out of the room, letting the door slam loudly behind me. I run down the hall and hit the elevator button about twenty-five times before the blessed doors open up to carry me away to safety. That guy has got to be an ax murderer. I feel lucky just to walk out of there alive. I know Sidney would just think I'm being dramatic, but I know for sure that something wasn't right in there. I'm so grateful that I didn't do anything to make him mad—who knows how that would have ended.

I remember Naomi warning me to be careful, and now I'm beginning to see that maybe she has a valid point.

CHAPTER TWENTY-SIX

The next morning, I meet Naomi for breakfast at Urth Caffé. Sitting outside with her, soaking up some sun under the palm trees and catching up on each other's lives somehow makes the horrors from last night fade away. Still, I can't help but unburden myself on her.

"I can't believe you got that car, girl," she says, eyeing my Porsche parked on the street. "Well, actually, I can. You've totally lost your damn mind."

"Yeah, well, I love it," I tell her. "And what's the big deal. I'm not hurting anyone."

"Yeah, except yourself," she says, looking at me pointedly.

"Okay...well, maybe you're right. I actually did have a bad night last night. I think this guy was an ax murderer."

"What?! Girl. What in the hell are you doing fooling around with these chicken heads?"

I sigh. "I don't know. I was having a good time with the first few guys, and then last night I got a glimpse of what it really could be like...is like. They can't all be hot, perfect guys,

I guess. And now…I just got this really expensive car, and I'm kind of freaking out about what I've gotten myself into."

"I was wondering when you'd see the light," she says, shaking her head. "But I'm glad you didn't go 'into the light' last night." She laughs, and I find myself laughing with her.

"I get it. Ha ha, real funny. And I had a really bad weekend a few weeks ago too. Alexandra called me and asked if I wanted to go to Texas for a job and said that the pay was eight cash for the weekend. She said it was one of her best clients and that he looks like a young Robert Redford. So of course I said sure. I hopped on that plane to Dallas, ready to make eight thousand dollars, and he also flew me first class. So…when I got there, he had this car waiting for me, and it took me up to his ginormous penthouse overlooking the whole city of Dallas. And we had great sex! He did kind of resemble my stepdad though."

"Ooooh, girl, no," Naomi says, looking repulsed while stirring her coffee.

"Yeah, well that was super weird. But he was nice, and he even let me sleep in his room alone because he was out in the living room working at his desk all night. He said he did some sort of international business or something; I can't remember exactly. Anyway, the next morning he brought me breakfast in bed on a silver tray, and he even put a red rose in a small crystal vase!"

"Okay, girl, so what really went down with him? This can't be good."

"So after breakfast, we took a big bubble bath and had sex all day. Oh, and did I tell you that he had his own private chef prepare our meals?"

"No!"

"Yep!"

"Girl! Just finish the damn story!"

"Okay, okay. So sex all day, blah blah blah, then another awesome dinner, sitting at his table overlooking the city, tons of red wine, then—"

"What?"

"He made me...well I don't know if you want to hear all the explicit details."

Naomi sighs. "You know you want to tell me, girl, so go ahead. Spill it."

"Well, he had me...well, we ended up back in the bedroom, and he had me prop myself up with pillows with my butt up in the air on his king-sized bed, and then he asked me to lightly touch myself, and he continued watching me while I fingered myself...for a while. He told me what to do to make myself cum."

"What? That is so messed up—he watched you? What in the hell?"

"Yeah, well, I've never actually masturbated before, and I did finish myself off, so that was kinda cool."

"Oh my god! You are *so* crazy. So then what happened? He gave you twenty thousand dollars?"

"No, worse. Way worse."

"Girl! I can't even keep up with you."

"We have a bunch more sex, and the next morning I'm getting ready to leave, and he hands me an envelope, and it feels a little light for eight thousand dollars, plus tip. So I look inside and pull out eight one-hundred-dollar bills! Can you believe that?"

Naomi starts laughing hysterically and has to prop her sunglasses up on her head to wipe her tears away.

"What kind of business do you think you're involved in? A legitimate business? Your pimp probably knew exactly what was going to happen and just did her 'good client' a favor while screwing you over. Because she doesn't care about you, girl! Only her business. You're lucky these men haven't cut your ass!"

"Hey, I don't have a pimp. You are right though—how'd you know? That's exactly what happened. I argued with him for about fifteen minutes, and he told me Alexandra was clear with him—the call was for eight. And I told him that I assumed it was for eight thousand because I usually make a few thousand for a couple hours' work. He said to bring it up with her office, so I called her in the car on the way to the airport, and she blamed me for saying yes to a job that I didn't really want to do. I told her she tricked me, and she just said she was busy and would talk to me later and hung up. Can you believe that shit?"

"Yeah, girl, I can."

"Well, now I don't know what to do. Between that weekend and last night, I'm thinking I don't want to do this anymore, but I'm completely fucked now with these car payments. And my mom invited both of us to a Sting concert at the Hollywood Bowl this weekend with my stepdad; they're going to drive up, and I'm super scared for her to see that I traded in the Ford she gave me a screamin' deal on for a Porsche. She's going to kill me!"

"Yeah…she is. I'd love to go to the concert though!"

"Naomi!"

"I know, I know," she says, patting my back. "Just quit that bullshit and finish your funny-ass screenplay! One of those hot chick comedians would probably love to play the main character, um…that Amy girl, or that Jennifer girl she's best friends with…? You should make your passion a priority. Plus, it's way too much energy for me to worry about you all the time. It might be tough for a while, but you can handle your car payments. And you know I'll help you with modeling jobs, and I know the makeup line wants you back. At least it's a steady paycheck for a while. Girl, I've got you."

"Thanks, Naomi. I love you."

"I love you too, girl. Now let's order some food. I'm starving!"

I leave breakfast feeling ten times calmer than when I arrived. Naomi was right after all. I need to get out of the game before I get seriously hurt.

*

At home later that evening, I'm busy getting ready for dinner when I notice a text from Alexandra asking if I'm available for an hour-long job at midnight, and another one tomorrow at noon. I hesitate for a moment and then text her back NO.

I've decided I won't do it.

Maybe not ever.

I'm still freaked out from the ax murderer and pissed at her for the whole Texas screw up. I still have my residual checks coming in from the last commercial I did anyway, and a few more checks should be arriving at the agency any day now from the other modeling jobs I've done. I think I'll be fine without doing this *bad job*, especially since I'm not sure this life is truly me anymore.

"Hey, hot stuff! Why are you staring at yourself in the mirror?"

"Oh!" I startle. "I'm not. I'm trying to decide what earrings to wear tonight."

"Sure you are," Sidney says smugly.

"How long have you been standing there?"

"Long enough to hear you mumbling to yourself."

"I wasn't mumbling."

"Whatever. Just shut the voices down in your cute little brain long enough to have some fun at dinner with me okay? There's no room for your soul-searching meditation and life revelations at the dinner table, chicky."

"I know, I know," I say, stepping away from my mirror.

"Hey," Sidney says, catching my eye. "You don't need to be so weird all the time and overthink everything. Just rock out! Oh…and Diana is outside in the new silver Aston Martin her man just bought her. Wanna ride with us?"

"No way. I'm fine meeting you lunatics over there." I really need the time to finish getting ready. Besides, I've learned by now that it's a good idea to have your own ride home when you're going out with Sidney.

"K. Ciao, bella," she says, blowing me a kiss and flipping her hair.

I drive over about forty-five minutes later and pull into the valet garage, taking the elevator upstairs to the restaurant. When the doors open, I immediately hear a loud witch-like cackle coming from the patio in front of me, and I know it's got to be Sid laughing at some guy's dumb joke.

"Hey, guys!" I say, walking over to their table.

Sidney gives an exaggerated scream when she sees me and gets up to throw her arms around my neck.

"Guys! Everyone, this is my best friend, LJ," she says, screaming over the music and the crowded patio of patrons. "Here, baby, let me get you a champagne!"

I greet everyone and give hugs to the girls I know. I don't know any of the guys, but it looks like a fun, attractive bunch, the typical mix of Sidney's superhot girlfriends and the usual suspects from the Hollywood lucky-sperm-club dudes, with a few actor guys sprinkled in too. Not one of them is at all aware of Sid and my alternate lifestyle entertaining men for money. For some reason, thinking of this while looking at all of their gorgeous, laughing faces makes me incredibly self-conscious, and I'm suddenly overwhelmingly embarrassed for anyone to ever know about it. What have I done? These people are clearly able to live their lives without selling themselves—why couldn't I? What's wrong with me?

I feel better after taking a shot of vodka from the bottle on the table, the alcohol warming me up on the inside and loosening me up a bit. It's a perfectly clear California night, brisk in the way that only a California winter can be. Us girls gather near the heaters in our tiny skin-tight dresses, but the guys are perfectly fine in their trendy attire.

At last, the hostess comes to take us to our table. Sidney directs everyone to a chair in her playful, flirty way, but when she tells me to sit at the end across from the empty chair and next to Diana, I'm not pleased. I know she has her reasons for putting people in certain places, but I don't appreciate it. I give Diana a smile, and she returns a tight-lipped grimace that she must think passes for a smile. Oh great.

The guys order endless bottles of sake and two large sushi boats for the table, and when the food arrives, Diana takes a piece and immediately dismantles it, only eating the fish and leaving little domes of rice all over her plate.

"You don't like sushi rice?" I ask her, trying to make conversation.

"I'm gluten free," she responds, not moving her eyes away from her plate.

"Okay. I'm pretty sure rice has no gluten in it."

"But it's carbs!" she snaps.

"So you're doing no carbs or gluten free?"

"Oh shut up, LJ," Diana quips, narrowing her eyes at me. "You don't know everything!"

"Geez, okay," I say, backing off. Then I can't help myself. "But I do know that rice is gluten free."

"Ugh. Whatever. Don't talk to me anymore. This is why I have a thigh gap, and you don't!"

She turns her back to me, and I can't help but laugh. I love ruffling her feathers. She's such a jerk, and she's not really the sharpest tool in the shed either. But she is still one of the most beautiful girls I've ever seen; I will give her that. And she knows it too.

I pour myself some more sake and start to feel a bit lonely down at the end of the table, staring at the empty chair across from me. I pull out my phone and pretend to be immersed in it, and after some time, I get so sick of being by myself that I'm thinking about leaving. Everyone else is deep in conversation with each other; they certainly wouldn't notice my absence.

I'm just about to get Sidney's attention when I see a new guy come in and make his way over to the end of the table.

"This seat taken?"

I smell him before I reply—a crisp, clean scent, intoxicating in its sharpness contrasted with the warmth of the restaurant. Large hands spread on the white tablecloth, his shadow hanging over the sake bottles. He's well dressed in a white button-down shirt and dark blue jeans. A gleaming gold watch catches the light and momentarily blinds me, forcing my eyes up to his face.

My breath catches in my throat. Thick sandy-blond hair offsetting bright-blue eyes, slight stubble caressing his square jaw. He reminds me of Leonardo Dicaprio, if he were to play the perfect secret agent, but he's more than that. He's in a league of his own. He stares right into my eyes, unblinking. I can't tear my eyes away from his. We stay like that a moment, the tension between us palpable. Then he smiles, leans back, and plops in the chair. I'm mystified.

"Hey! Hey, Angelina!"

A loud voice invades the moment, coming from somewhere behind me in the restaurant. I freeze in my chair, eyes widening. Do I turn and acknowledge, or do I pretend to not hear? Shit, is this actually the moment in time when the *bad job* catches up with me?

The calling doesn't cease, so I turn slowly and see Blaine, of all people, walking toward me with an A-list actor in tow.

He's just as hot as I remember, and I can't help but feel a little ego boost that he remembers me so well. Still, to have this moment now, in front of all these people and this new guy...I'm going to have to play this well.

"Hi, sweetheart, how are you?" he asks when he finally arrives, leaning down to kiss me on the cheek. He leaves his hand on my shoulder when he rises.

"Oh, I'm wonderful, just having dinner with some friends," I say, smiling and trying not to let the panic show in my eyes.

"I can see that," he says, glancing down the table. I can see the actor next to him checking out the girls at the table, and to my relief, I see that everyone at the table is too caught up in some wild story Sidney is telling and cracking jokes to really notice the interaction, and I'm very thankful that Diana went to powder her nose. Lord only knows how much she would love to bury me.

"Hey, listen, do you think I can just talk to you later?" I ask in a purr. I give him a wink that I know the others can't see. He smiles, his dimples deepening.

"Of course! No problem. Have a nice dinner," he says, nodding to me and then to the new guy. He steers the actor away, and they return to the waiting hostess, who guides them to their table, thankfully far away.

I sink down in my chair, avoiding the curious stares from the table, and pretend to be interested in pouring myself more sake. Sidney speaks up loudly from the other end of the table, taking the attention back to herself, and for once, I'm grateful she's done so.

"Who was that?"

The guy across from me is looking at me curiously. I take a deep breath.

"Just...a friend," I answer.

"Okay." He nods, and while he doesn't look totally convinced, he doesn't seem to want to press it. "Well I was going to order a diet Coke. Can I get you something when the waitress comes back, Angelina?"

"Ah, no, I'm fine, thank you." I give him a shaky smile.

I don't know what to do. I sit there while he orders a few things from the waitress and continues to make flirty eyes at me, not knowing how mortified I am. How do I explain that my name isn't Angelina? How do I explain it to the others? What if they've already guessed that there's a reason why someone called me another name?

Sidney catches my eye from her end of the table and offers me a smile. My phone buzzes with a text from her. "Don't worry about anything, you handled it like a pro" it says. I write back, "He called me Angelina!!!" and I see her laugh when she reads it.

"Give me a break; no one even caught that, especially with that A-list hottie next to him!"

I shrug and put my phone away and decide to straighten things out with the guy across from me.

"Hey, so my name is actually Lillian James," I tell him. He leans forward to listen. "But everyone calls me LJ."

He wrinkles his brow. "Are you sure?"

I nod.

"That's real cute, but do you mind if I call you Lily?"

"Sure. I don't mind at all!"

"Well, you look very beautiful tonight, Lily."

"Well, thank you," I say, blushing. I can't let it go though. "Don't you want to know why he called me—"

"Nope. I don't. None of my business. And it's Cash, by the way. Or Cassius, but my parents are usually the only ones who call me by my full name. And only when I've done something I shouldn't have."

I laugh, relieved. "Still getting in trouble by the 'rents at thirty years old, huh? Must be up to no good."

"No, not usually. They're pretty cool," he says with a sly smile and a twinkle in his eye. "And I'm thirty-one."

"Oh! We're exactly ten years apart."

"Well, kid, that is the perfect age to get into some trouble. And I'm sure that you have no problem finding some to get into."

"Who, me? Nah, I'm a good girl."

"In my experience, it's usually the baddest girls who say that they're good girls."

"Oh, is that how that works?" I say with an amorous smile.

"Yep. Sure is. At first glance, you could pass yourself off as a good girl. Well-mannered, seemingly conservative, smart, and incredibly sexy. With a touch of the exotic. And I like that. Italian?"

"You do, huh?" I say, teasing back. "And Italian, yes, Volpicelli. Well, half German too. Fifty-fifty."

"Ooh. Very nice. I was right, and I like it so much in fact that I'd like to take you to dinner tomorrow night. I'll pick you up at nine and take you out to Giorgio Baldi. Ever been?"

"Of course I've been," I respond silkily. "And I'll accept your invitation to dinner, but I'm not impressed yet."

"Good! You shouldn't be."

We pause, and the sexual tension builds between us again. I have to convince myself to sit in my chair instead of leaping across the table and letting him take me right then and there. I've never felt this drawn to anyone before—not with Brody, not with any of the guys from the past few months, not anyone. I barely know him, and I already feel like our sex would be ridiculous. But, it's more than that. It's like we've known each other in a past life or something. It's all too familiar to be new. Looking to distract myself, I glance around the table and notice his soda sitting in front of him.

"Did you just order a Coke? Not drinking tonight?"

"I don't drink," he answers, his eyes serious. "I've been sober for two years."

"That's cool," I allow. I suddenly feel exposed for being tipsy, like a silly little schoolgirl when he's such a disciplined man. I want to be on his level. "Isn't it hard to be sober when you're out, and everyone else is drinking and getting so wasted?"

"No. Not really anymore."

"Well, now I'm impressed. I wish I could be that in control."

"You could do it if you wanted to. I can tell that you're a very bright and determined girl."

I nod, happy that he sees me for who I am.

We talk the rest of the night, and when dinner wraps up, he escorts me down to my car. We pass Blaine and his friend at the front bar on our way out, and Blaine winks at me as we walk by. Cash doesn't say anything, but he places his hand on the small of my back and lightly pushes me out the door, signaling to Blaine that I'm his. My back grows hot under his touch.

"See you tomorrow," he says, shutting my car door.

"Looking forward to it," I say, blushing again.

CHAPTER TWENTY-SEVEN

I wake the next morning with butterflies in my stomach from just thinking about my date with Cash later. He's so regal and handsome and sweet, and he's got that hot streak of bad boy that's such an absolute turn on. We really do have an insatiable magnetic pull to each other. So intense.

I roll over in bed to check my phone; no texts from him yet, only one from my mom, asking me to call her about the Sting concert this weekend. I'm so super freaked out to tell her that I sold her car and got a Porsche instead. I still have to figure that confession out, but for now, I just want to focus on my hot date.

I call my salon and schedule a blow out for three in the afternoon and then pop out of bed to search through my closet for a nice dress to lay out for dinner. Something sexy but elegant. A short black-satin fitted dress, maybe? With my new red shoes, or maybe my nude strappy sandals with fringe? And of course my new-investment bag. I throw on wedgie jeans and a red cropped sweater for the day; I head out to run errands

with my iPad tucked into my bag in case I have time to work on my screenplay while waiting at the salon. I can't stop grinning with anticipation the entire day; it's one of those days when everything feels absolutely perfect, like all the stars are aligned and I'm exactly where I'm supposed to be. I can't wait to see what happens next.

When I get back to the house at seven, I have just enough time to get changed and call my mother and little sister to catch up. At 8:55, I'm ready and eagerly waiting by the front kitchen window, Sidney admonishing me for being too eager. I don't care if I look like a dorky prom date though; I'm excited, and I don't think I should hide it.

At nine on the dot, Cash pulls up in a new black Range Rover, and I jump up immediately. He gets out and starts walking to the door, but before he can get there, I open the door and rush out to meet him.

"Hey," I say, smiling. "Right on time. I like that." I give him a cute shrug and a flustered curtsy. I can imagine Sidney watching from her window and shaking her head at my dorkiness.

"You're supposed to let me at least get to the door," he says, wagging a finger at me.

"Oh, well I was too excited to see you. I had to come out."

"Okay, well let me at least get this door for you," he says, helping me into the car.

"Are you always so chivalrous when courting a woman?" I ask playfully when he gets in the driver's seat.

"I like to think that I have good manners, if that's what you're talking about. And I haven't decided if I want to court you yet. Tonight is your test," he says, winking at me.

But I already know that he's putty in my hands, and he knows I'm putty in his. If he's going to compete for who will let on that they're vulnerable first, then game on. I never lose.

Dinner is incredible. We order half the menu, eating and laughing for hours. He really appreciates that I love food as much as he does and that I'm not afraid to try new things. The entire date is effortless and a ton of fun, and I can't shake the feeling I've known him for years. When we're together, the world just disappears around us. When he drops me back off at home, he leans over and gives me the kind of passionate kiss that sends tremors through the earth and makes the whole world seem completely irrelevant. I go to sleep that night with ignited feelings for him and the intuition that I'm starting something that could change my life forever.

*

The feeling hasn't faded by the weekend, and when I go to pick Naomi up from her boyfriend's house for the concert, she can tell that I'm glowing.

"I might be in love, Naomi," I tell her as we drive to my mom and stepdad's hotel.

"What? So soon? With that new guy? That's not love," she shrieks as she changes the radio station.

"It could be! And you've never even been in love before, so how would you know? You say all guys are too feisty."

"Girl! Okay? You just keep on keepin' on with your bad self. I ain't mad at you though."

"Thanks for always being so supportive," I tease. "I love you so much, my darling."

"Well, you're my family now, so you're stuck with me until we're ninety. I got you. But seriously, what are you going to tell your mom about the car? We're going to be at the hotel in ten minutes."

"Um…I told her we'd meet them upstairs at the hotel bar. I just thought I'd valet the car and not tell her tonight."

"You're going to lie then?"

"Not *lie*, just not tell her what's going on. If she asks me, 'Honey, did you trade your car in for a Porsche?' then I will say, 'Actually, yes, Mom, I did!'"

"Just lost in the sauce, mm mm mm," Naomi says, shaking her head.

"I'll tell her the next time I drive down to San Diego, I promise. Let's just hope she's not waiting outside the hotel for us now!"

"Uh huh. Well, turn here. I know a shortcut."

Naomi gets us in to the valet, and we meet my mom and stepdad for a drink at the hotel near the Hollywood Bowl without incident. After a short cab ride, we're ushered into box seats at the beautiful outdoor concert venue, and we have a phenomenal time rocking out and enjoying the wine, cheese, and crackers we brought along to eat in our private box. Annie Lennox even makes a surprise appearance, walking out onstage and singing a few songs with Sting, completely stealing the show in my mind.

My mom and Naomi laugh together all night, and I keep an eye on them just in case she leaks one of my secrets by accident. Naomi doesn't tell her anything though, only teasing that I'm in love. My mom freaks out, of course, telling me it's too soon after Brody for love, but then she asks me to bring him down to see her so that she could give me her approval. I don't feel like I need her approval, but I tell her that I will anyway, just to keep her happy and grooving.

On the drive home after dropping Naomi off, I get butterflies in my stomach again when I check my phone and see a text from Cash, writing that he hopes I had a good time at the concert and to call him when I get home. I hurry home, beaming the whole way.

After I wash my face and put on my blue clay mask, I call Cash and snuggle under the covers. We talk for about three hours, my phone growing so hot that I have to put it on speaker a few times. It's almost four in the morning by the time we hang up, and when we do, we've covered nearly everything there is to know, from family stories to past relationships, dream vacations to existential theories, and of course, how much we like each other. We've given up not trying to look vulnerable; we both know we're lost causes.

I wash the cracked mask off my face and fall asleep with dreamy thoughts of Cash kissing my eyelids.

*

The following weekend, I find myself with Sidney on the long flight to New York City.

She insisted I come along, even though I told her I was done with Alexandra and that crowd.

The further I get away from being an escort, the less I want to do it. Naomi is right. I can make it without sacrificing myself anymore. What was I ever thinking?

Besides, now I have Cash to think about.

He had a family obligation in New York this weekend, which is the only real reason I agreed to go with Sidney.

It's strange how each time I make this trip, I'm in a completely different place in my life. Thank goodness I'm so much happier than the last time we did this; I'm no longer trying to do things out of vengeance. I'm no longer sacrificing myself either, which feels very, very good.

We land and head to the cab line to catch a ride into the city. When we arrive at Jonny's, we're surprised to find his elderly mother there, cooking an elaborate dinner in the kitchen for what looks like a table set for ten in the dining area. It smells incredible, and we barely have time to put our bags down before his mother ushers us to the table.

"Sit, girls, sit, sit!" she says, waving her arms at us.

"Hi, Mrs. Marchetto!" Sidney says, kissing both her cheeks. "It all smells so awesome! I love you! Be right back. I have to pee."

Sidney takes off for the bedroom while I happily greet Mrs. Marchetto. I always love a good home-cooked meal, and I even recognize some of the Italian dishes from ones my own family makes.

"Take a seat, LJ," Mrs. Marchetto says, gesturing to the kitchen island. "Tell me how you are, beauty."

"Oh, I'm just lovely, thank you," I tell her. I'm finding it harder and harder to give people updates on my life when so much of it is kept in the dark. "Do you need me to help bring food to the table?"

"Yes, thank you, sweetheart. You can take the oxtail ragù out, and then come back, if you could, to bring out the caprese and bread too. I'll bring out the other plates myself, *amore*."

"This all looks incredible. Don't tell me there's dessert too?"

"Does this look like my first time entertaining for a dinner party?" she asks with a wink. "I made an olive oil cake with vanilla oranges and tiramisu with a little extra rum."

"My god! That's incredible."

"Don't use the lord's name in vain, sweetheart."

"Goodness, I'm sorry."

"It's all right, dear. Now go join everyone for a negroni or a glass of prosecco when you're finished here. And thank you for helping me."

By this point, the loft has filled with Jonny's model friends, so I pour myself a drink and greet the ones I met on previous trips. When Mrs. Marchetto brings out the last side dish, we all sit around the long dining table, lit with dripping red candles, and dig in. Mrs. Marchetto sits at the head of the table and regales us with stories of a childhood in Italy, moving to New York City in the fifties, becoming a syndicated columnist, and her current life prancercising around the Upper East Side. Jonny glows with admiration as his mother talks, and it's clear that he learned to treat everyone like family from her.

As the night progresses and we've all had a few drinks, a cute blond girl to my right asks Mrs. Marchetto about her secret for happiness. We all lean in, young women desperate for any kind of guidance in our tumultuous lives.

"Well, girls," she says, standing and picking up plates to start clearing the table. "The secret to a happy life is to first marry for money, then to marry for love."

"Really? That's a super bummer," I say. I can tell I'm being a bit more overt than I would otherwise, but the drinks are really getting to me. Plus, I would still like to believe in an honest life, despite the fact that I've manipulated mine a bit recently.

"Don't mind her, Mrs. Marchetto," Sidney chimes in. "She thinks that love is more important than money."

"That's a very sweet thought, LJ. I don't want to derail your fantasy of the perfect fairy tale, but it will all make sense to you someday, *mi amore*."

"But…that seems like so much work to marry first for money. To keep up an act like that. Why? Why can't you have both?"

The girls around the table start laughing at my sense of indignity.

"Girls, that's enough," she chastises them. "Don't be too hard on her."

"I know real love exists!" I call after Mrs. Marchetto as she brings plates into the kitchen. I turn to the girls sitting at the table, who are looking at me with raised eyebrows. "If all you shallow jerks just want to get knocked up by some millionaire so he will take care of you, if that makes you happy, then go for it! Cheers. But, most likely, the dude will be old with hairy, gray nipples and cheesy balls that you will have to tend to in order to get your Birkin bag! He won't be a young, hot guy. That's for sure. Because, lord knows, there's one of those old men around every corner!"

I put my wine glass down hard on the table, and some of it sloshes out onto the tablecloth, staining it red. I'm getting out of control, and I know it.

I feel a pair of hands warm on my shoulders, and I instantly relax.

"LJ, I admire your moxie," Mrs. Marchetto says from behind me. I crane my head up to look at her, a bit embarrassed at my outburst. "We all know that you have a very loyal, sweet heart, but I'm surprised at you. After doing this job, you should be more aware of how the world really works by now."

I'm shocked; she knows what I've done? The other girls nod, looking unfazed. My stomach clenches knowing that this wonderful, wise old woman knows my secret, and maybe she knows a lot more than she's letting on.

She pats my shoulder and returns to the kitchen, and Jonny jumps in. "I'm sure you've been with enough men by now to know that you must stroke the male ego. You'd be better off taking my mother's advice, so that you ensure a comfortable life for you and your future children. We wouldn't steer you wrong, LJ. We're giving you pearls here."

"There's no point, Jonny Church; she's stuck in her bubble," Sidney says, sipping her wine.

Riley, the blonde to my right, chimes in, "It's okay. I get it. We all want the romance, the fairy tale, the true love. But be realistic. It's just not possible."

"Yeah," Sidney says. "You can have that dream of yours if you want to move back to the Midwest somewhere and live in a track house, have bad hair, wear cheap clothes, and drive a beige minivan. And I'm sure you'd even wear your sexy lingerie for some pasty boring guy...and cook for him too. God, he would worship you forever! Maybe that would work for you?

But what a waste of your life!" She leans forward and giggles with the other girls.

"Okay, Sid, I get it. My future won't be full of Louboutins and Gucci, but maybe I don't want to be some rich bicoastal snob the rest of my life, taking first class and black cars everywhere, spending all my time shopping. It's not enough for me."

"Well. Maybe you're a more high-maintenance butthole than we are."

"Ugh. Whatever."

"You're drunk," Sidney says, sneering.

"*You're* drunk, dummy! I'm going to bed."

I stand up, and Sidney stands with me.

"Come on, it's early; don't be silly."

I pour myself another glass of grappa and shoot her a mean look, say good-bye to everyone, and make my way to the kitchen to hug Mrs. Marchetto for an awesome homemade dinner that was truly beyond belief. I help her with some dishes, and we chat for a while until Sidney comes to get me.

"Hey, everyone's gone," she tells me, rubbing my back. "Come on, let's go out."

I've cooled down enough to agree, and before I leave, Mrs. Marchetto pulls me aside.

"LJ, I know you have a world-class future waiting for you. I know it, dear. Everything will be all right."

"Thank you, thank you so m-much," I stammer. For some reason, this was all I needed to hear, and Sidney pulls me away before I can start crying to Jonny's mother.

"Come on, drunkie drunkerton," Sidney says, pulling me through the loft.

*

I'm touching up my makeup in the bathroom mirror when Sid reaches into her purse and pulls out a bag of coke. My eyes grow wide.

"Where'd you get that?" I ask.

"Riley gave it to me. Well, I bought it from her. I knew we'd need something to keep us going for a few days while we're here."

"Fine. Make me one," I say, sulking.

"That's my girl! This will sober you right up. Here you go." She moves the perfume aside and cuts a big line for me on a round mirror.

We each do a few lines, and in no time, I'm seeing clearer and am ready to party. I desperately want my dark thoughts banished beneath a bright coke high.

Sidney has me put on the dress she asked me to bring, a floor-length black-velvet gown that we bought on one of our shopping trips, and I'm buzzing too hard to ask her why or where we're going. It doesn't matter. If all I'm good for is being a pretty girl meant to seduce rich men, I might as well dress the part.

On the way out, we see Jonny at his easel, smoking a cigarette with the window open despite the cold winter air, painting what looks to be the beginnings of another superior work of art, with Mr. Hamilton curled up on his lap.

"Later, Jonny Church!" Sidney calls out to him. I blow him a kiss from my hand.

He leans out from behind the canvas and looks us up and down. "Wow, you girls look heavenly. Those guys don't stand a chance tonight. Have a good time!"

We get down to the street and walk over a block to catch a cab heading uptown, giggling as we hold our gowns up so they don't brush the street. The cab driver is nice enough to let us smoke a few cigarettes on our long ride, although when I remind myself of my newfound knowledge about men, I figure his generosity has more to do with Sidney's full, blond hair and perfect, bulging cleavage than it does his goodwill. I stay mad.

As we pull up to the curb, Sidney rushes out of the cab and throws some cash through the open window at the driver. She reaches for my hand and drags me up the sidewalk, and it isn't until I see the intricate brick facade that I realize we're at Carnegie Hall.

"Where in the hell are we going?" I ask Sid, adjusting my stole and flicking my cigarette into the street. She walks ahead of me past Carnegie Hall to a beautiful glass building nearby.

She gives me a devilish smirk. "We're going to a black-tie birthday party. It's in the penthouse on the ninetieth floor."

I nod, but she's already turned away and is heading into the lobby. Is this really what my life has become, chasing penthouses in the hope of getting one for myself? Am I destined to spend the rest of my life in soulless relationships with wealthy men because it's good for me to be taken care of? And then what? I have to constantly stay flawless because that's all I am to them? Constantly thinking being the thinnest version of myself is my best accessory, even going under the knife to maintain perfection, keeping my hair and makeup precise at all times...the pressure alone would kill me, and it wouldn't even be for anything except financial security. Is that luxury? It sure as hell ain't freedom.

At the center of my being, I know that money can't buy me, but maybe it's a depressing pill I need to swallow for my own good.

Be present, I tell myself. You're in one of the most amazing cities in the world, all dressed up with everywhere to go. Maybe this party will take my mind off of this discouraging crap.

The man at the front desk asks for our IDs, and as we hand them over, Sidney turns toward me, eyes wild.

"This is going to be an outstanding party. My friend, Asher, is a huge world-renowned real estate developer, and they just finished this building. His good friend and client, America Ramirez, bought the penthouse; it is literally the most expensive apartment in the city. I think it was around one hundred and twenty million dollars or something. She's clearly a billionaire, and she's the first woman to sit on the Mexican Stock Exchange. Anyway, Asher was that guy who flew me to the one-and-only Cabo a few months ago; do you remember? That totally hot weekend I had? I told you about him? Asher Townsend...no? Oh well."

The coke has clearly hit Sidney hard; she can't stop talking a mile a minute. Maybe *that's* the key to happiness. Just stay coked up and shop all the time, and you won't notice the emptiness in your life.

"Was that the guy who owns the race horses?" I ask. We enter the elevator and it quickly moves up, floor by floor.

"Yep, that's the one. And did you know, America, that woman, she's got one of those stories you'd find totally fascinating. She's a real rags-to-riches story. Something about being orphaned at eight years old and becoming a housekeeper in Mexico City to stay off the streets...I'm not sure about the rest of the story, but I know you'd find her story literally inspiring."

"Wow, yeah! That is very inspiring," I tell her. Maybe there's more to this party than I originally thought.

Sidney turns to me in the elevator and puts her delicate hand on her hip. "LJ, I told Asher that you are a stunningly beautiful and marvelously polished lady. So shake that big fucking chip off your shoulder, stand up straight, and be the superfun girl I love!"

"Okay, I got this. No problem," I say, shaking out my hair. "But if I'm going to be the lady, then what are you going to be?"

"Oh…I'll be on my best ladylike behavior too," she says, pinning her shoulders back and down.

"But…do *you* even know how a well-mannered lady behaves?" I ask, my finger on my chin in mock confusion.

"Har har. Yes. I can choose to be a lady if I want to," she replies. At last the elevator arrives at PH.

"Really? I can't wait to see this! After you, my lady," I say, gesturing forward. She turns and smiles at me.

"Okay. Let's go."

As soon as the elevator doors open, I'm nearly blasted backward by the force of the bass. The walls vibrate with the music from the DJ, and the energy from the party instantly puts a smile on my face. Hundreds of people, all dressed in black and white, move with the music and are absolutely mesmerizing, all lit up by black lights. It's an unreal sight, like a modern-day ballroom dance on the Titanic.

As we start to mingle with the most powerful and wealthy elite of New York City, I wonder about the unattainable status this woman must have, to own this kind of apartment and be able to bring in a world-famous DJ from the Netherlands to spin her black-tie sixtieth birthday party, filling the penthouse to the max with the who's who of any place around the world. I feel extremely privileged to be here, even if I'm just the guest of a guest of a guest.

Sidney gives me a kiss on the cheek and runs off to find her man. Alone, I make my way through all the people in the packed grand salon to take in the mind-blowing view overlooking Central Park through the-two story glass walls. Searching for the corner where the glass walls meet, I make it my own private piece of heaven and pull out my phone to see if Cash has texted. Nothing. I'm disappointed that I haven't heard from him.

Well, maybe I should just play the field then, if I'm to be so reliant on men anyway. Taking a deep breath, I pluck a glass of champagne from a passing waitress, who is glowing in white, and start to dance to the beats that are accompanied by a string instrument. Just before I decide to dive into endless, gracious chatter with the people around me, the sea of partygoers parts straight through the room, just enough for me to see Yo-Yo Ma, resplendent in white, playing an electric Lucite cello in the opposite corner of the room. My jaw drops, and I'm immediately drawn to the acclaimed cellist. I pick up the small black train of my dress so that I can move unencumbered over to him, taking my second glass of champagne from a silver tray on the way. He plays his instrument fluidly, and I'm entranced by his clearly insatiable appetite and passion for the instrument. The man has skills. His music gives me chills, and I stand there for what seems like an hour, trying to soak in his sheer genius. His cello sounds phenomenal with the DJ, and at some point, I realize that this is hands down the most insane party I've ever been to.

"Hey! Come with us!" Sidney says, popping out of the crowd and taking my hand.

"Did you see this?" I ask, pointing to Yo-Yo Ma.

"Yeah. That's great. Come on!" she says.

After a quick introduction to Asher, Sidney leads me to a private bedroom that Asher has to use a key to get into. We walk into the bathroom and he cuts a few lines for us to do on the marble countertop. After we inhale them, Sid straddles Asher as best she can with her long satin dress, which I take as my cue to leave. I go right back to my place gazing at the famous cellist and have a few more glasses of champagne, and when the coke hits, I feel like I'm on the moon, moving through the crowd of brightly glowing visitors, strobing with the music, and moving in tandem back and forth as if we were all pieces on a giant moving chessboard. I check my phone a few more times to see if Cash texted. No dice. Instead, I mingle and dance around the apartment while I wait for Sidney to finish fucking her man in the bathroom. He's got good coke though—I'll have to give him that much.

Warm arms circle my waist from behind.

"Hey, let's go! We have another party to go to, baby!" Sid says.

"God! You scared me!"

"Come on," she says, taking my hand.

"Do we really have to leave? No way any party can be better than this one."

"Yes. I've already RSVP'd. We have to go."

Sidney disappears in the crowd and moves toward the door, and I have no choice but to follow her. We miraculously get a cab as soon as we walk out of the lobby, a feat I thought impossible since it's almost two in the morning. Sidney lays her head on my lap and yells, "Eighty Columbus Circle!" to the driver, and we both manage to get in a few smokes before we get there, belting out an Adele song on the radio between puffs.

"Hey, LJ, this way! Down here! Come on, slow poke, hurry!" Sid says, skipping down the hallway of the seventy-seventh floor of the Mandarin Oriental.

"Yeah, yeah, I'm coming. Keep your shirt on."

I come around the corner and suddenly, Sidney's there, looking serious. She puts her hands on my shoulders and her forehead against mine. It feels good, and I lean into her embrace.

"Now, LJ. Just follow my lead. I have a huge surprise for you; you're going to love it!"

"What's going on? I thought this was your friend Teddy's party?"

"Trust me. You're going to love it."

She knocks on a door, and a man opens it immediately.

"Good evening, Sidney," he says. "So glad you could make it. Please, come in."

"This is my friend, Angelina. Angelina, this in my friend, Soren." She turns to him. "She's as hot as I promised you, right?"

My jaw tightens. "Would you excuse us a minute, Soren?"

"Be right back, hot stuff!" Sidney shrieks as I spin her around and drag her to the powder room. I shut the door behind us and descend on her.

"Excuse me! What in the fuck is going on?"

"Okay, now. Don't get spooked."

"Spooked! I wouldn't get spooked if you weren't so damn spooky!"

"Keep your voice down! He's very high profile."

"High profile? That's nice for him, but I really don't care what he is! This is not cool! I wanted to relax and have fun tonight. Why are you making me do another job when I told you I didn't want to do it anymore?"

"Come on, baby doll. Calm down. Don't be mad. I know him well. It's worth your time, I promise. He has some of the best coke I've ever done, he's super hot and super sweet, plus he has a huge dick!" She gives me a mischievous smile.

"Sidney, I told you I quit."

"Come on! You can quit *later*. Why not *one last job*. Just one?"

I hesitate.

"How much?"

"There are four more girls coming." Sidney leans in con-spiratorially. "And, LJ...he's paying us ten thousand dollars for the night."

"Ten thousand for six girls?"

"No! That's ten thousand just for us. I don't know what he's paying the other girls, but I negotiated that for us. I thought you'd be happy. It's just a few hours of your precious time. For five thousand dollars?"

I'm tempted. Five thousand dollars means a few payments on the Porsche. It means less worry for the next few weeks. Still, I promised myself not to do this.

"I'm still deciding if I'm happy about this or not. I'm getting really tired of being some rich man's side dish, Sid. Don't you ever think that we're cheating ourselves by doing dumb shit like this?"

"I just told you. It's ten thousand dollars cash! What's wrong with you?"

"Yeah, and I'm sure that doesn't entail anything freaky or weird." I roll my eyes.

"Okay. I'm done with this convo. Pull it together! You're being a real bitch, and we're being totally rude!" She leaves the bathroom.

I take a deep breath and glance at myself in the mirror, and my reflection holds my gaze. There's no getting around it; I'm lustrous in my soft black gown, the very image of a chic woman out on the town. Everything, from my dark hair, twisted loosely at the nape of my neck, to my shimmering skin, is perfect. I'm no longer the girl from the Midwestern suburbs trying to make it in the big city, the girl trying her best to fit in with the ultrafabulous glamour circling around her. That girl is now just a distant memory. I can hardly remember her, the girl who got up early to watch her boyfriend surf, who sat on the sidelines of life and read gossip magazines while tapping her flip-flops against her heels, who sold clothes in a mall store.

Who am I now? It hasn't even been that long since I lived that life, but it feels like a lifetime ago. I lean into my reflection and reapply my cardinal-red lipstick. Perfection.

I find Sidney chatting at the bar with our host, smiling and flipping her shiny hair to the best of her ability in order to work a good tip. She dips her head down to do a line next to the full glass of champagne in front of her, and when her head tilts back up, it's framed by the large red moon filling the wall of windows behind her. She shakes her hair out and smiles slowly, catlike, her smile hanging in the air seemingly independent of the rest of her body.

"Please don't be shy, Angelina. Come join us," Soren says, waving me over. I walk over to them, sashaying my hips in my long dress. I can feel my train rustling over the rug, and the gravity of it pulls my shoulders back and down. I take a seat at the bar as the doorbell rings, and Soren excuses himself to get it.

"Here, have a bump," Sidney says, passing me a bag. "This is so clutch, isn't it? Soren even said his driver would take us home after we party. We just have to give the guy the password, 'Captain Zero's girls can have anything they want.' Oh, shh, here they come."

"Ladies," Soren says, walking up to us with four stunning women trailing him. "This is Vionnet, Johanna, Poppy, and Paulina. They'll be joining us for the evening."

"Nice to meet you," Sidney says, popping her chest out. "I'm Sidney, and this is Angelina."

We nod and smile at each other, and the girls sit and help themselves to champagne and cocaine. They're all so miraculously gorgeous and elegant, and I can't help but be intimidated by the elegance and smoldering sex appeal that these women exude. Vionnet, a striking brunette with big, glowing green eyes is sporting an arm stacked with gold Buccellati and Cartier bracelets, talking quietly with Johanna, a breathtaking blonde with neon-blue eyes and perfect porcelain skin. A diamond-and-sapphire choker circles her neck. Poppy and Paulina cut lines on the bar, and watching them is like gaining entrée into any man's wet dream. They're twins, wearing matching, shimmering Saint Laurent low-cut black pantsuits, like they just stepped out of a fashion ad, their lithe bodies designed for seduction and sin. They're all truly every man's fantasy, and they're all obviously being paid very well for it. I sit up straighter, reminding myself that I'm part of this group too. I have the same sexy elegance, and I'm being paid to be here as well. But I just can't shake the slight intimidation I feel.

Plus, part of me feels this is all wrong. I don't belong here. I'm not sure I even *want* to belong here.

After some time, Soren pulls out a pipe and a torch lighter and a large bag of drugs that I don't recognize. He lights up and then passes it around to the girls. Everyone takes a hit, and when I do the same, I suddenly feel like I can run around the planet ten times in twenty seconds. I juggle the bag and am able to identify weed, Molly, shrooms, but not all the different types of pills. This guy does not mess around.

Soren turns up the music as we all get fucked up beyond recognition, and then he abruptly excuses himself to the far bedroom. We're left talking by ourselves in the bar area for about fifteen minutes, and I'm beginning to wonder if we're expected to go in there too when a team of five men, all dressed alike in dark-gray business suits and black shades, walk in a straight line out of the bedroom and leave the penthouse altogether without saying one word. I look to the girls to see if they're as creeped out as I am, but they're all at the window admiring the view. I'm the only one who saw anything.

"Um, hey..." I say to Sid, an uneasy feeling sinking in the pit of my stomach.

"Not now," she says, walking away.

"Let's go, ladies. I think we're on," Poppy says, heading in the direction of the bedroom. The girls all start going in the direction of the bedroom, but I stay at the bar and slam another glass of champagne and then lean down to do the last line left on the mirror. When I look up, they're all gone. Well, I guess it's time to do my job. Let's go see what's behind door number one.

I slowly push open the door, nervous to see what I'm getting myself into, and for a moment, I feel like the drugs must have messed with my vision. Soren is handcuffed to the bed, clad only in little black latex shorts. He's completely bound and gagged. He's alone though, so I turn to the corner and see the girls changing into outfits laid out for us on the chaise. There's one remaining, waiting for me.

"Angelina! This one's for you, baby. Bring that tight, sexy ass over here!" Sidney says playfully.

I walk over to the lounge and inspect our chosen ensembles. They're nothing more than little black-and-white French-maid outfits made entirely of latex, complete with garters, feather dusters, and headpieces. Under the sofa rest six brand new Christian Louboutin boxes, and when one of the girls opens hers, I see that they contain black patent leather sky-high heels. The girls are already naked and changing into their outfits, and they look absolutely out-of-this-world stunning. I pick mine up and feel the slick material with my fingertips. It feels foreign, cold, and when I hold it up against my body, I immediately pull it away. This is the exact opposite of the elegant night I envisioned.

I realize then that it's all a lie.

A terrible, sad lie.

I don't want this. I don't want any of this.

I hear a moan and see Sidney, already dressed as a sexy French maid, lightly whipping Soren with a studded crop and getting into position to give him fellatio.

"I can't wait to see you in that outfit," Vionnet says to me with a flirty little grin.

"Oh! Thanks, doll…you look incredible in that too," I say awkwardly. "I have to run though…I have to get something…from my purse…in the living room."

I successfully sneak out of the room without anyone noticing; Sidney and the other girls are already deep into character. The cocaine is still lying on the counter, so I cut another line and then look behind the bar for some good whiskey to shoot. Taking a swig, I grab my bag and start to head for the door when I see that the room's safe is open in the wall. About thirty fat stacks of cash lie there in a pile, calling my name. I pick up a stack labeled as ten thousand dollars and fan myself with it. It does smell good…but I put it back down. If I'm ditching, I can't also steal a ton of money. Even though he probably wouldn't notice. I head for the door and then double back for the bottle of whiskey and tuck it under my stole. Then I'm quickly out in the hallway, breathing hard.

I get down to the lobby, feeling conflicted about leaving. Sidney will be mad, but then again, she tricked me into coming here in the first place. Maybe I've changed in many ways, but this was just one step too far. Walking through the upstairs lobby of the hotel, I pass an older Asian gentleman with a leggy blond girl clearly thirty years his junior. It makes my stomach churn. I hate knowing about the secret, slimy lives people lead and being a major part of it. I hate the ugliness that floats just below the pretty surface. I want to live my life in the daylight and not in the darkness laced with lies anymore.

I burst out of the doors feeling liberated and onto the street where I notice a black stretch limousine waiting in front. "Captain Zero's girls can have anything they want!" I yell at the chauffeur as he opens the door for me. He nods and closes the door behind me, and I collapse in the back seat.

"Can we just drive around the city for a while?" I ask him when he gets back into the driver's seat. I know Soren and his harem will be busy for a few hours, so I won't get pinched. Besides, I'm fucked up enough not to care if I do. I kick off my shoes, roll down the back window halfway, and stick my feet out like I'm back in California, cruising carefree down Pacific Coast Highway to the beach. Opening the moonroof, I lie back on the seat and light up a smoke, watching the awe-inspiring skyscrapers of New York City pass by. Then I begin to cry.

After some time, the driver calls back to me. "Miss? Excuse me, miss?"

"Yes! I'm so sorry. I didn't ask. Is it okay that I smoke?" I ask, sitting up on my elbows and wiping my tears away.

"Yes, it's fine for you to have a cigarette. It's my little daughter; she's sick and running a high fever. I must take her some soup. Is it all right with you that I deliver a few things to her?"

"Of course! Yes, please do so. Then can you just drop me off downtown?"

"Yes, miss. Thank you."

I'm such an asshole, feeling sorry for myself when other people have real problems to tend to. I chose this life; I invited these problems. I'm no victim. Now I'm going to have to choose to get myself out of it—and away from Sidney.

I lie there contemplating my next move, only noticing halfway over that we're driving on the Queensboro Bridge, back into the city. I didn't even notice that we'd gone over the river in the first place. The sun is just starting to rise, and it looks like the city is on fire. I stand up on the back seat and pop out of the moonroof, throwing my head back and arms into the air, letting the wind blow my hair wild. I've been acting like I have limited options, but I don't. This world is mine for the taking, and from here on out, I'm going to live my true life. I grip the sides of the moonroof and grin, letting out a celebratory scream. I'm done with self-destruction. I've totally got this.

CHAPTER TWENTY-EIGHT

I wake up with cloudy vision, buried up to my neck in softness. Where am I? The last thing I remember is asking to be taken to Jonny's, and the rest is a blur. Drinking that bottle of whiskey probably had something to do with it, and then I remember all the drugs I consumed within twelve hours: Molly, coke, crack, weed.

I'm cold, can't move, even though I'm surrounded by what seem to be dirty clothes, and I can still feel that I'm wearing my gown. Fear creeps in, along with chills followed by profuse sweating. I'm a weightless shell. A soothing voice tries to comfort me, and even though I know it's only in my head, I pretend like it's my grandmother, and I'm just sick in bed. Think. Where are you? Burning sunlight seeps in from underneath the door in front of me; I must be in a closet. Maybe I'm in my bedroom's closet at Jonny's? I look at some of the clothes surrounding me and recognize a few. Okay, so that's where I am, calm down. I'm at Jonny's. At least I know where I am. Why is the apartment so quiet though? Or maybe

I've lost my hearing? Where's Sidney? Where's Jonny? I start to tremble. Am I overdosing? I can't breathe. I'm going to die. I search frantically on the floor next to me for my phone and do the first thing I think of—I call Cash. He answers, and the comfort of hearing his voice floods through me.

I don't even know what I say, or what he says back to me, but suddenly he's there, kneeling beside me in the closet.

"Hey. I'm here; it's okay," he says, digging me out of the clothes pile.

"I think I'm overdosing, Cash. I can't stop shaking. I'm scared." Something wet drips off my face, and I realize that I'm crying.

"It'll be okay. Let me get you outta here."

He lifts me up and carries me into the bedroom, laying me down on the bed. I lie there on my side and watch his handsome face. He looks so fit, so healthy, so completely the opposite of what I feel writhing inside of me. I want to be clean, happy; I don't ever want to have this feeling ever again. Right then and there I vow never to do something like this again, to make someone so good sink down to this ghastly level. I'll be good too, I promise.

"Okay, what's yours?" he asks, looking into my eyes.

I point to my suitcase in the corner and tell him to get my red makeup bag in the bathroom, and he gathers everything together and zips it up tight.

"Let's go," he says, helping me stand. "Don't worry. I've got you."

We pass Jonny painting in the living room. "Hey, LJ, I'm sorry. I didn't even know that you'd let yourself in."

"It's okay. Thanks, Jonny."

Cash takes me down to his car, and a driver takes us up to Park Avenue. He tells me that we're going to see his family doctor, and as I lie on his chest in the back seat, he strokes my hair. I feel so embarrassed that this is happening, and the tears won't stop streaming down my face. The more I cry though, the better I feel. My thoughts are erratic, jumping from flashbacks of girls in latex and being stuck in a dark closet, to my family and extreme guilt over my life in general. I try to grab a substantial thought to keep my mind from snapping. I feel nauseated again and pray I don't throw up on Cash. He's so wonderful to drop everything and take care of me.

"Thank you for coming to get me," I say, looking up into his steel-blue eyes.

"Sure thing, kid. Let's get you better." He looks up as the car slows, and he starts to sit up more. "Ah, we're here."

We walk into a building and go straight to the back to an exam room where his doctor enters and immediately takes my temperature.

"What did you take?" the old man asks.

"Umm..."

"It's all right. You have to tell him so we can help you," Cash assures me.

"Okay. Umm. Cocaine. Pot. Wine, champagne...hard liquor. Pills?"

"What pills?" the doctor asks, taking notes.

"Molly, I think...? That's ecstasy. And..."

"Anything else?" he prods.

"Yes...I smoked crack." I start to cry again.

"It's okay, Lily. Let's just focus on getting you well now," Cash says, rubbing my back.

"This is so embarrassing. I've never smoked crack before. I'm so sorry."

"Okay, now," the doctor says, bringing our attention back to the situation at hand. "You do have a high fever, so I'm going to prescribe you an antibiotic. I want you to stay with Cash for a few days, until your fever breaks, before you fly back home. You're going to have to sweat out these drugs, and I'm sure you'll vomit quite a bit. He will take care of you."

The doctor makes eye contact with Cash, and an understanding passes between them. "Okay, now, get her home. Call me tomorrow if her fever doesn't break."

"Will do, doctor. Thank you," Cash says. He walks me out to the car, his hand on the small of my back. I'm still in my tattered gown, and I draw quite a few stares when we walk out onto the street, looking affright.

We go back to his apartment, just a short ride away on Park Avenue. I'm completely mortified as he shuffles me into his building and past his doorman. He hits the penthouse button when we enter the elevator, and when the door opens to his apartment, I'm blinded by blaring sunlight and cover my eyes. He takes me into his room and helps me change into sweatpants and a big sweatshirt and then lays me down to rest.

Over the course of the next forty-eight hours, I run to the bathroom to puke about thirty times, sweat through his nice sheets twice, and take one bath. He washes my hair for me, brings me chicken soup, and never sleeps, just catering to my every need in the delirious comedown of my own stupidity.

"Hey," he says, stroking my hair while I lie bundled up in his sheets. I'm starting to feel slightly better, and his hand feels nice. "Sidney has been texting and calling you, and I just told her that I'd get you home to LA. I hope that's all right? You were finally getting some sleep."

"Thank you, that's fine. And thank you so much for taking care of me. I'm quite aware of how ridiculous I look. I feel like such an idiot."

"It's over now. Rest. I have us on a flight back to California tomorrow afternoon," he says, pulling the sheets back over me.

*

Back in Los Angeles, we drive straight to his house and order some late Chinese food and then lie in bed and watch movies until we're almost asleep.

"I want to make you breakfast in the morning," I whisper to him.

"Pancakes?" he says, spooning me.

"Yes. And bacon."

"Oooh. Bad girl."

We make love while the sun rises and sleep until noon.

"Let me take you to breakfast," he says, going through the mail on the kitchen counter. I sit across from him, gazing at his one perfect dimple, and get a warm feeling.

"Don't you want to know what I've been doing for work lately, why I got so fucked up? Where I'm from, all my dark secrets?"

"I already know everything I need to know about you. And I love it all," he says with a bright smile.

"Okay, but I really feel like I need to bare my soul right now."

"Listen. You're from St. Louis; your full name is Lillian James Volpicelli. Sicilian-German smoke show. And your favorite color is red. How am I doing?"

"Great, but I've made a few really big mistakes these last few months and…"

"So you hooked up with some idiot roommate, and she got you into a little trouble. That's done with. It's just you and me now, and that's all I care about. And, everyone royally fucks something up in their twenties. You're normal, kid."

"I just don't want you to think I've totally mastered the art of being a royal fuck up," I say, hanging my head in humiliation.

"You're with me now, kid. Nothing else matters. Now, go get dressed so I can take you to get pancakes," he says, slapping my ass.

I giggle and give him a hug and a kiss. I'm head over heals in love but trying not to let on. It's almost too good to be true. I'm so entranced by him; it's as if we're in a love story together, and the rest of the world is just silently swirling around us.

Over breakfast, he asks me if I've done much traveling and what countries I've been to. I haven't been to too many places, and I tell him this.

"So, would you like to go see a few countries on your list soon?" he asks.

"Where?" I ask, pricking a bit of pancake with the end of my fork.

"How does around the world sound? With me."

"Um, let me think about it for a minute...*yes!*"

"Okay, then. I'll have my travel agent work on something for us. Do you think six months would be enough time? Can you do six months to a year with me, kid?"

"Wow. Well, yeah! I think I could suffer through it," I say with a wink. "It sounds incredible. Are you sure?"

"Of course, I'm sure! You might have to get a few vaccines depending on the countries we visit. Can you stand a few needles?"

"For a world trip with you? I think I can handle it."

The next two weeks pass in a blur of takeout, movies, and sex. I enjoy his quiet-and-quaint two-bedroom home hidden behind a wall of bushes on a small side street in Hollywood. We don't leave his house much, and I don't answer my phone either, just focusing on hibernating with my man. One morning, he wakes me up and tells me that he just received the confirmed full itinerary for our trip and that we will leave tomorrow. I need to go home and pack, and he tells me that he'll be over later that evening to pick me up to stay with him before our early flight the next morning.

I pull into the driveway and notice that Sidney's home, and it looks like everyone else is too. My stomach clenches; I haven't talked to her at all since New York, and I don't know what she's going to say.

I go inside; it's relatively quiet. I can hear Elliott strumming his guitar, a muffled voice that sounds like Jona on a phone call, and some dance music that I'm sure is coming from Sidney's room. Nobody comes out to greet me; either they didn't hear me come in or they're deliberately ignoring me.

I'm relieved, truth be told. I don't want to talk to Sidney.

I open my bedroom door and get my suitcase out from underneath the bed and begin to go through my closet for any *très chic* outfits I should bring with me. I realize then that I don't even know where we're going, so I just start throwing clothes into my bag. He said he wanted to surprise me and that the only rule is that I can only bring one suitcase with me. But believe you me, I'll be lying on this sucker to zip it closed. Just as I finish, the doorbell rings.

"I'll get it!" I hear Sidney scream.

"I came to get Lily. Can I come in?" I hear Cash say from the door, and I instantly flood with that warm feeling.

"Come on in, honey. She's in her room," Sid says. I hear her run back upstairs, and Cash comes in.

"Hi there, handsome," I say, giving Cash a big hug and kiss.

"Hey."

"What's wrong? You look like you just saw a ghost."

"Um...your roommate. Sidney just answered the door one hundred percent buck naked."

"No, she didn't!"

"Yes, she did. Completely naked."

"Excuse me! I'll be right back."

I run upstairs and burst into her room. She's completely dressed, sitting on her bed reading.

"You really think you just sitting there all nonchalant reading your book is going to make it look like you're not guilty?" I say, standing at the end of her bed.

"What's your problem?" she says, arching an eyebrow.

"*My* problem! Are you kidding me? It's over! You and me, it's over! I will never, *ever* be your friend again. From the minute I met you, you've been nothing but a wolf in a fucked-up sheep's clothing! Throwing me under the bus every chance you get. Making me look like a complete idiot. Trying to kill me. Pretending to be my best friend. Now, you answer the door naked! What the fuck is *your* problem?!"

"I never tried to kill you," she says calmly, pulling her covers around her and pretending to read.

"I have never wanted to punch someone in the face as much as I do right now!" I shout.

"Do it!" Collin yells from down the hall.

"Yeah. Do it. I dare you," Sidney says.

"I hate you," I say, clenching my fists. I start to cry.

"No, you don't! You love me." She winks.

"You know, you really think that you're royalty behaving badly, but actually you're just a total fucking train wreck! You know, you should be careful who you hurt. It could ruin your life one day. Good-bye, Sidney."

I storm out of her room, seething, but not before she can get the last word in.

"Don't let that door hit you in that pretty little ass of yours before Mr. Wonderful can finish kissing it. Have fun, bitch! You're dead to me too!"

Her door slams. Cash is standing at the bottom of the stairs with my suitcase, ready to go. He takes my hand and walks me out, but not before I lock my room so that no one can get inside while I'm gone. I look up at Sidney's window as he closes the car door and walks over to his side, and we lock eyes for a moment before she throws her curtains closed. She's not fast enough though, and I can see that she's crying too. I look over at Cash and remember the journey I'm just beginning with him. He wipes my tears and hands me a tissue as we drive up the street, away from the house where I became the person I'm now trying to run away from.

The next morning, I'm up and in the shower at 4:30 a.m. Cash calls out that he's brought me coffee and sets it on the bathroom counter. He's already packed the car, and he gently tells me to hurry since we have a 6:00 a.m. flight out. I'm so excited to find out where we're going that I almost forget to rinse the conditioner out of my hair. I get out and do a quick blow-dry and then apply some pressed powder, mascara, and lip gloss. Good to go in my long comfy dress and shawl.

*

"What in the world is this? Are you serious?" I say as we pull up to the small airport.

"What do you mean? This is the only way to go, kid."

Our car zooms past a gate and up to a gorgeous private jet. The pilot, copilot, and stewardess are standing by the stairs waiting for our arrival. When our car parks, two men retrieve our luggage, and the stewardess ushers me down the red carpet onto the plane.

"Can I take your coat, miss?" she asks.

"No, thank you, I think I'll leave it on for a bit. It's so chilly outside this morning."

"As you wish. Please make yourself at home. My name is Peppa, and I'll be taking care of you both today. Cash has the whole plane stocked with your favorite food and drinks. Is there anything I can get you before we take off? A warm towel? Hot drink perhaps?"

"Oh that sounds good. Do you have green tea? Or maybe something stronger, like a hot toddy?"

"Yes, miss. Right away. Please make yourself comfortable. I'll bring it straight away."

She brings me to a buttery-leather seat. Sitting there is a small Tiffany bag tied with a tight white bow, and a little card that says "open me." I sit and take the bag into my lap and then smile and blush as I see Cash outside on the tarmac, helping load the luggage onto the plane. I slowly pull the white-satin ribbon and open the box to find two-carat diamond stud earrings nestled in the velvet. I immediately lose my breath.

"Hey, babe. Did you order something from Peppa?" Cash asks, walking onto the plane and heading back to me.

"Yes, I did. She's so sweet. Cash, these are amazing! I don't know what to say. You shouldn't have; it's way too much! Thank you."

"Nothing's too much for my girl. I love you. Let me put them on for you," he says, taking the box.

"You do? You love me?"

"Don't you love me too?" he asks, his eyebrow arched.

"Well, yes…but I thought it might be too early to say it?"

"It's never too early if you mean it. Get your mirror out!" He pushes my hair behind my ears so that I can admire my new earrings.

"They are the most insanely beautiful things I've ever seen. I really don't know what to say." The earrings sparkle and glitter in the soft early morning light coming through the window.

"You ain't seen nothing yet, kid. Come here."

He pulls me down on top of him on the sofa and slides both hands up my thighs. As my dress falls away and the plane takes off, I'm freed from one life and soaring into another. I decide to surrender my untethered heart and let the extraordinary adventure wash over my naked body, falling more in love with my fairy tale future with Cash while joining the mile-high club in style.

To be continued…

About the Author

T.C. Collins has been an avid writer and traveler throughout her life before turning her hand to fiction. She lives in the Midwest with her husband, young son, and huge dog. *Hot Toddy* is her first novel.

Made in the USA
Middletown, DE
06 August 2016